Praise for the

A Deadly Grind

"Has all the right ingredients: small-town setting, kitchen antiques, vintage cookery, and a bowlful of mystery. A perfect recipe for a cozy."
——Susan Wittig Albert, national bestselling author of
The Darling Dahlias and the Texas Star

"Victoria Hamilton's charming new series is a delightful find." ——Sheila Connolly, *New York Times* bestselling author

"Hamilton's Jaymie Leighton completely captivated me . . . I'll be awaiting [her] return . . . in the next Vintage Kitchen mystery." ——*Lesa's Book Critiques*

"A great new series for cozy fans." ——*Debbie's Book Bag*

"Smartly written and successfully plotted, the debut of this new cozy series . . . exudes authenticity." ——*Library Journal*

"Fans of vintage kitchenware and those who fondly remember grandma or mother's Pyrex dishes will find a lot to enjoy in this mystery . . . There are several good suspects for the murderer, cleverly hinted at early on, and searching for the identity of the murder victim adds to the well-plotted investigation." ——*The Mystery Reader*

Bran New Death

VICTORIA HAMILTON

BERKLEY PRIME CRIME, NEW YORK

THE BERKLEY PUBLISHING GROUP
Published by the Penguin Group
Penguin Group (USA)
375 Hudson Street, New York, New York 10014, USA

USA | Canada | UK | Ireland | Australia | New Zealand | India | South Africa | China

Penguin Books Ltd., Registered Offices: 80 Strand, London WC2R 0RL, England
For more information about the Penguin Group, visit penguin.com.

BRAN NEW DEATH

A Berkley Prime Crime Book / published by arrangement with the author

Berkley Prime Crime Books are published by The Berkley Publishing Group.
BERKLEY® PRIME CRIME and the PRIME CRIME logo are trademarks of
Penguin Group (USA).

For information, address: The Berkley Publishing Group,
a division of Penguin Group (USA).
375 Hudson Street, New York, New York 10014.

ISBN: 978-0-425-25883-5

PUBLISHING HISTORY
Berkley Prime Crime mass-market edition / September 2013

PRINTED IN THE UNITED STATES OF AMERICA

10 9 8 7 6 5 4 3

Cover illustration by Ben Perini.
Cover design by Lesley Worrell.
Interior text design by Kristin del Rosario.

ALWAYS LEARNING   **PEARSON**

To Jessica and Michelle . . .
how do you thank those who have given you
your lifelong dream?

Words are inadequate to express my gratitude.

ACKNOWLEDGMENTS

In the publishing world there are so many unsung heroes, those who do work readers understandably take for granted, and make us, as authors, look so professional. When you get on the inside, you see what a difference those folks make to the author's work and publishing life. I'd like to take a moment here to give my deepest appreciation to: Erica Horisk, copyeditor of *Bran New Death*, who went above and beyond in editing the book, and Ben Perini, the cover artist, who brought to life a vision for Wynter Castle that I didn't even know was possible. I hope they know how much I appreciate their work and dedication!

Chapter One

AS A METAPHOR for my life, the crossroads rocked. I sat in my rented Chevy, glaring at the GPS screen, then got out of the vehicle and looked around. On one side of me was an evergreen forest, into which one road descended, and on the other was a rocky prominence, the highway cutting through it like a kebab skewer through shish.

I was not reflecting on my *metaphorical* lostness, however, but my literal situation. The GPS told me I was in front of a Denny's on I-90 as it cut through upstate New York. Looking around at the gloomy walls of evergreen and granite, I reflected that a Denny's breakfast would be welcome right about then, but no shiny, happy hostess came melting out of the woods with a coffeepot and a smile.

My odyssey began in a car rental lot in Jersey City before midnight August 31, also known as the night before, and just now the rosy beginnings of dawn were glimmering through the piney treetops. September first, a good date for a fresh start, *if* I could ever find my way out of the woods.

Some of my worldly belongings were piled in the

backseat and trunk of the Chevy rental and the rest were stacked in a locker at a Manhattan Mini Storage near SoHo. Merry Wynter, adventuress, I thought, my mouth twisting in a grimace. But I wasn't just wandering, I was looking for my inheritance. I leaned back into the car and grabbed the plastic tub of carrot muffins, prying off the lid and inhaling the cinnamony aroma. I took out the last one, peeled off the paper liner, and munched away, the melting goodness of my homemade muffins sweet on my tongue.

While I ate, I considered my options.

After a long night of driving all the way from Jersey City to upstate New York, I was exhausted. With a GPS in the rental I thought it would be easy going, but the trouble was, the probate lawyer who gave me instructions on how to get there had assumed I was familiar with Wynter Castle and its environs, and that I have a reasonably good sense of direction. I wasn't, and I don't. I'd only been there once, as a child. I'd like to say my navigational skills have come a long way since then, but my grandmother told me lying is wrong. I may be thirty-nine, and Grandma may be long gone, but I still hear her voice in my head. When the GPS started screwing up, I wasn't aware of it until I was hopelessly lost.

I learned I inherited Wynter Castle many months before and put it up for sale, sight unseen, with a local Autumn Vale real estate agent named Jack McGill. Why would I do something so stupid? It's complicated, and in retrospect not the brightest move I've ever made. Here's the thing . . . that visit as a kid is not a happy memory, and my own life has been in turmoil the last several years.

Long story short: once upon a time (briefly), I was a plus-size model. I quit work when I married a photographer, but then my beloved husband died. I was still young, and I needed something to do, but I didn't want to be a model again, and I was getting too old for that line of work, anyway. So even as I fought my overwhelming grief, I began styling a few model friends, plus- and regular-size, choosing their clothes, helping each define her look. It's like an advanced game of playing dress-up, the same game I played with Barbie dolls when I was a kid, much to my hippie mother's chagrin. In the meantime, though, my darling Miguel left me reasonably well settled; I thought I could do better and began to play the stock market with my savings.

You guessed it; the economy tanked, my investments disappeared into the pockets of the wealthiest investors while those of us foolishly toying with our life savings suffered, and I was left with very little. But it was okay; my career as a stylist was beginning to take off. As I started doing all right, making enough to live on without touching what was left of my savings, an opportunity came up that I could not ignore. When someone offers you a six-figure salary, what do you do? You grab it and hope no one notices you don't deserve it, right?

So this is what happened. A few years back, Leatrice Pugeot, the internationally famous supermodel (born plain old Lynn Pugmire more years ago than she admits), happened to be at New York Fashion Week, and so was I. I came across her in a corner of a show venue weeping her eyes out. Concerned, I asked if I could help, and she asked me to get her some Xanax. Where was her purse, I asked. She said "No, dummy, just score some from a dealer." I refused, gave her a cup of herbal tea instead, and talked to her for an hour.

At the end of that hour she asked me to come work for her as a personal assistant. I demurred, but she was persistent. Over the period of a few days, she steadily sweetened the pot until it was up to six figures. Here's where it gets tricky; I heard, through the grapevine, that Leatrice was difficult to work with—like, Naomi Campbell difficult, but she *seemed* like a sweet, if troubled, soul, to me.

So I took the job, which *seemed* like it was going to be a lot less effort than the constant push to find clients and stay on top of the industry. The hole that Miguel left in my life was not being filled with work, no matter how hard I tried to stay busy, and I was beginning to worry that I wasn't strong enough to build a whole new career while still struggling with grief. Looking back, I think that my state of mind had a lot to do with why I took the job, despite warnings to the contrary. I needed to be needed, and Leatrice needed me terribly. The next couple of years were interesting, to say the least. Ultimately, everyone was right about Leatrice and it didn't go well. I left (was fired/quit . . . depends on who you talk to, me or her) after she accused me of stealing from her.

About that time I learned about my inheritance, a cash-poor family "estate" in the boonies of upstate New York. Wynter Castle; at first I thought that was one of those bougy names developers throw around, like McSnobbin Estates or Uppercrust Acres, which are really just suburban ticky-tacky boxes thrown up on seven feet of land. I let it slide for a long time while I dealt with the fallout from my problems with Leatrice, hiring a local real estate agent to sell the place. He wanted me to come look at it, but I just couldn't handle it. I did begin to remember Wynter Castle at that point, and my one visit to it when I was a child of about five. My memory of that visit did nothing to make me want to go back there.

It wouldn't be an easy sell, I was told by both the real estate agent and my uncle's attorney and executor, and that prediction was on the money. The castle had languished on the real estate list for months without even a hint of interest. Since I had been scrambling to make ends meet for some time—it's the old story, just when I think I've made ends meet, someone moves the ends—I finally took the advice of a dear friend and did something about it. I gave up the sublet on my tiny slice of Manhattan, and set out without telling anyone where I was going. Correcting the mistake I made several months before in not going to evaluate my inheritance seemed a challenge, but doable. Maybe I was finally getting my act together after a long run of personal tragedy compounded by stupid decisions.

So here I stood, in the gloom of predawn, out in the middle of nowhere, lied to by a freakin' computer. It was quiet at my crossroads; *too* quiet, I thought, looking around. A big bird circled overhead, like a vulture waiting for me to collapse into a heap. It was quite the view: nothing but a long, dirt slope downward in one direction, a rocky face upward in another, and a paved side road slicing through the rock face across it. Wind tossed the tops of the trees, and a scent like a pine tree–shaped car freshener drifted down to me, with the rustling sound of movement nearby. I should have felt alone, but I didn't, having the uneasy sensation I was being watched from the shadowy depths of the forested slope. Turning quickly, I caught a movement in the bushes, and jumped back in the car, my heart pounding.

I was just tired and edgy, I reassured myself. I'd return to the last place that the GPS system made any sense and go from there. This wilderness was not how I pictured upstate New York. Where were the quaint, artsy towns and elegant, country houses? Where were the Martha Stewart clones? Shouldn't they be out picking dew-flecked roses from their perfectly trimmed gardens wearing twinsets, pearls, and flowered gardening gloves?

I drove back the way I had come, past lonely farms and isolated houses that looked deserted, out to an open area. Instead of trying to find Wynter Castle, I'd concentrate on the nearby town of Autumn Vale. Anyone who had negotiated the intricacies of the London tube and the Paris Métro should be able to find a town in upstate New York. Laying my actual paper map on the passenger's seat beside me, I followed the highway, coming to a river. The map was being a good Boy Scout and telling me the absolute truth; it certainly seemed more trustworthy than the disembodied voice that kept telling me to turn right in fifty feet, when there was no right turn available. The road I wanted departed from the river and descended steeply to *another* branch of the same river. That was where the GPS had begun to malfunction, confusing me hopelessly. But now the map started to lie to me, just like the GPS had; none of the road names I was seeing on signs appeared on the map. Hmm.

I'd ignore the road names and just drive. Following a hard-packed dirt road overarched by tall poplars that swayed above, I found Butler Lane, which according to the map should have been Wynter Lane. Hoping I was on the right track, I began to descend and wound along a treed road until the vista finally opened out onto a picturesque view of a village below me, which a signpost announced was Autumn Vale.

"Eureka," I shouted and pounded my fist on the steering wheel. I paused and gazed at the village, still sleeping in the dawn mist. It was a unique experience, like looking down at a model-train town; among the leafy green, I could spot the main street, a solid line of Victorian shops and businesses, all gray, stone buildings, it appeared from a distance, and then roads leading away from it, lined with redbrick homes and gleaming, white-clapboard frame houses, punctuated by civic buildings, construction yards, and the occasional massive garden plot. Now that was what I expected from upstate New York! Maybe there would be an occasional bed-and-breakfast, and perhaps even a quaint inn or two. I was hoping at the least for a cutesy café with some decent food.

My stomach grumbled, but I put it down to too many muffins and not enough real food. I should have packed a bologna sandwich, but muffins are my go-to comfort food. That was the last thing I'd done in my little studio apartment in Manhattan: make a dozen muffins to share with my neighbors. Of course, muffins were also responsible for much of my trouble with Leatrice, but that story can wait.

Buck up, Merry, I told myself. First things first, and that was finding someone who could direct me to Wynter Castle: Jack McGill, the real estate agent, or the lawyer, Mr. Andrew Silvio, or *some*one. It was a little early for a realtor or lawyer though, just six forty-five a.m. by my diamond watch, so anyone who could give me the directions to Wynter Castle would be fine.

I pulled into a parking spot in front of a hardware store (closed), and got out, looking up and down Abenaki, the street that appeared to be the main—or only—business section of Autumn Vale. I needed someplace open to ask directions. The streetscape was adorable, with commercial buildings like ones I'd seen in miniature, painted by skillful craftspeople. Stone fronts with big, glass, bow windows, clapboard-sided shops with gingerbread trim dripping from the eaves; but the reality was a little more grim than the picture-perfect image of small town America. What I hadn't seen from a distance were the multitude of boarded-up windows.

All crammed together as they were, the shops seemed like good friends who leaned on each other for support in tough times. I walked past a bank (closed), beauty salon (closed), a clothing store (boarded up), a convenience store (closed) and another clothing store, an antique shop, another antique shop, a café, a nail salon, and a dog groomers: boarded up, closed, boarded up, closed, closed, and on vacation. The opposite side of the street appeared to be much the same story. Wasn't *anything* open? A cool breeze fluttered down the street, chasing a few stray leaves along the sidewalk. I shivered. The early morning air was misty and damp, and my short-sleeved blouse inadequate. What I needed was a Starbucks.

Aha! I perked up when I saw, across the street, a beckoning Open sign in the window of Binny's Bakery; glowing blue and red neon cheered me immeasurably. I crossed the street, climbed the three steps, and opened the door, triggering a chirpy bell to ring. A yeasty smell and moist warmth enveloped me. Fresh bread! And something else familiar . . . olive oil, rosemary, and cheese? Having eaten four carrot muffins since midnight and nothing else, something *not* sweet appealed.

A young woman wiped her floury hands on her floury apron and approached the counter. "Can I help you?" she asked, looking me over like I was an alien life-form.

I glanced around the bakery, and was riveted by the shelves lining one whole wall. Teapots! Hundreds and hundreds of teapots! I truly was home, in one sense. I smiled, as I turned toward her. "How are *you* this morning?"

"Fine. Can I help you?"

The woman didn't *sound* fine. Her mouth had a natural downturn, unfortunate in someone so young and attractive, I thought, noting dark hair pulled back in a ponytail that was confined in a net.

"You have a wonderful place, here. There is no better smell on earth than fresh-baked bread, is there? And teapots; you have an a*maz*ing collection."

The teapots ranged from a marvelous Mount Rushmore— impractical, but very collectible—to a chintz, porcelain beauty that I lusted after. My not-so-secret passion is collecting teapots in a variety of shapes, sizes, and prints. That's what was in at least twenty of the boxes at the Manhattan Mini Storage: 253 teapots, about half of them miniatures. Another ten boxes held teacups, an uncounted number.

I pointed to an elderly beauty. "That ornate one . . . it's Italian, right? Majolica? And the other one, with the roses and cherubs . . . that's Capodimonte."

Sighing, the woman rolled her eyes. "Look, not to be rude, but I have a million things to do. The focaccia is almost ready to come out of the oven." She glanced over her shoulder at a timer, then back to me. "How can I *help* you?"

I scanned the others—there were English and Chinese teapots, art deco shapes, utilitarian designs, and fanciful animal shapes—but I didn't have time to look them over, as the baker was getting impatient. No small talk, then. Too bad. I'm the master of small talk. In the modeling world, it pays to know how to schmooze, no matter what your position. First as a model, then a stylist, and then, finally, as a personal assistant to a model, being nice to hair stylists, makeup artists, set decorators, assistants, gofers, photographers, and everyone in between had paid off.

"I need directions," I said, holding up the printed map, flapping it around. "This seems to be useless, since none of the roads around here have the names listed on the map."

The woman cracked her first smile. "It's a conspiracy," she said with a short laugh. "Town council and the county can't agree. The names get changed every year or so. You'd think they didn't want anyone to find us. What are you looking for?"

Finally, some friendliness! "I'm trying to find Wynter Castle, on Exeter Road."

The woman's smile died swiftly. "You don't want to go out there. All you'll find at Wynter Castle is death." She turned away as the oven timer *bing*ed a warning.

"What do you mean?"

She bustled around in the back, taking a tray out of the oven and banging it down on the counter.

"Hello?" I hollered. "What do you mean by that?" She wouldn't come back, ignoring me completely, so I stalked out of the place, winding up on the sidewalk again, looking up and down the street.

An old fellow in a trapper hat and plaid jacket shambled past, making use of his cane. He eyed me with interest, his smudgy glasses not quite concealing the intelligence in his beady eyes. I'd try again. "Excuse me, sir," I said. I had to bend over to talk to the elderly gnome, but his eyes twinkled with reassuring sharpness. "Could you help me?"

"Mebbe," he said, bushy brows raised. "Whadyawant?"

"I'm trying to figure out the best way to get to Wynter Castle on Exeter road."

He made a choked sound in his throat and bolted away

from me as if I had a communicable disease. Who knew someone using a cane could move so quickly? *Tap-tap, tappity-tap.*

"Charming." As I stood watching the oldster speed down the sidewalk, a police cruiser slowed near my rental car.

I walked toward it, watching the cop lean across the passenger seat and examine my rental's license plate. If he was so interested, he may as well help me out. I walked out onto the street and leaned over the cruiser, gesturing the cop to roll down his window. He did, and I leaned in the open window. "Hi there! Maybe you can help me?"

He looked down at my cleavage and smiled, then looked up into my eyes. "I sure hope I can," he replied.

Never failed. I sighed inwardly, but smiled back, amused, as always, by the male fascination with breasts. The poor dears just can't help themselves. I read his name tag, and said, "Well, Officer Virgil Grace—"

"*Sheriff* Virgil Grace, ma'am," he said with an attractive grin.

"Sheriff, how . . . Western. Anyway, I'm trying to find someplace."

"I'd love to help," he said, a dimple winking in his cheek. "You looking for the way to my heart?"

He was a definite cutie, but too young for me. I wasn't on the lookout for the trail to *any* of his vital organs. "Maybe another day. Right now I just need directions to Wynter Castle, but no one wants to tell me how to get there, not even the friendly voice on my GPS."

Watching my eyes, he frowned and said, "Why do you want to go to Wynter Castle?"

It wasn't any of his business, but maybe it would help if I explained. "I'm Merry Wynter, Melvyn Wynter's niece and heir. Wynter Castle is my property."

He nodded. "Okay. I heard you were trying to sell it."

"I was . . . *am* . . . but no one seems to be in the market for a monstrosity of a castle in the wilderness of upstate

New York," I said, and stood, hand to my back. After no sleep and hours of driving I was cranky, but had to stifle the urge to snap at him. I bent back down and said, in as neutral a tone as I could manage, "So what is the problem with me trying to find Wynter Castle?"

"No problem," he said, his expression serious. "Follow me and I'll lead you there."

"Thanks!"

"You may not thank me when you see the place."

Chapter Two

❈ ❈ ❈

TWENTY MINUTES OR so later, I followed him up a winding lane, emerging from a thick forest that opened out to a long, green slope up to Wynter Castle. I parked in a weed-infested flagstone drive and got out. The sheriff parked, too, and walked over to me. I was numb with fatigue and something else: a weird, bittersweet feeling of coming home. This was one of the few places I had ever gone with my mom, and the only place I knew of where my father had stayed for any length of time.

But holy catfish, no wonder it hadn't sold! First I scanned the land and shook my head. The landscape, a huge open area rimmed with dense forest, was *riddled* with holes dotted around the long grass—*big* holes, all with mounds of dirt beside them. The yawning cavities littered the open landscape, right to the edge of the woods. The sun rose up over the forest and beamed down beneficently on the weird and troubling scene. Turning in a complete circle, I counted about thirty holes, give or take, and there might be more beyond my field of vision or behind the outbuildings that dotted the landscape. The sheriff stood staring, glancing back and forth between my face and the gaping wounds. "This may be one of the problems with selling Wynter Castle," I said. That was probably the understatement of the century.

He didn't say anything, and I turned to finally look at the building itself. My inheritance really was an American castle, old and shrouded in ivy that coated the hewn, stone walls, almost concealing the diamond-pane, Gothic-arched windows. It was big, even bigger than I remembered from my one visit so long ago.

Just then another car pulled up the lane, a tiny Smart car with a sign on the side that read Autumn Vale Realty. It shrieked to a stop, and a tall, gangly man emerged, unfolding himself like a backward origami. "Miss Wynter?" he asked, approaching at a lope, his hand stuck out. "Jack McGill, your realtor."

"Hey, Jack," Virgil said.

"Hey, Virge, what you doing here?" he said, dropping his hand to his side.

"Showing Miss Wynter the way to her property."

"You should have stopped at my office," he chastised, shaking his finger at me. "I would have showed you the way!" He extended his hand again.

I took it and shook. "I couldn't *find* your office. I couldn't find anything." I paused and looked around, then back at him, examining his beaky, honest face topped by a shaggy shock of reddish-brown hair. "I'm beginning to see the problem here, Mr. McGill, why Wynter Castle won't sell. We have giant gophers on the property."

He broke out into astonished laughter and doubled over, folding like a jackknife, slapping his thigh. "That's a good one, Miss Wynter."

"Call me Merry." It wasn't *that* funny.

Sheriff Grace, who had been leaning against his patrol car listening in, cocked his ear at a scratchy call on the radio in his car and said, "I'd better get going. I would seriously suggest, Miss Wynter, that you not stay out here alone."

"Why?"

He let his gaze travel over the hole-riddled property. "Wouldn't want to see you end up in one of these."

I gasped and spluttered, openmouthed.

"You know, like falling in." He got in and drove off, a hail of gravel from the edge of the drive shooting up in a shower from his back tires.

Was that a threat of some sort? Ridiculous man!

"Don't mind him," the realtor said.

"I don't mind him at all. In fact, I doubt if I'll even think of him after this moment."

He cast me a glance, shaggy eyebrows raised. "Now, I suppose you'll be wondering what caused all these holes here?"

"No, not at all."

"Oh." He was silent.

"I was being facetious," I said, stifling a sigh. "Bad habit of mine. So . . . who is digging the holes? And why?"

"Well, that's just it. We don't know."

I looked at him in amazement. "You don't *know*?" He shrugged, and I strolled over to one of the holes, looking into it, then turned back to McGill. "Why didn't you tell me about this? You'd think you could have mentioned it in all the conversations we had."

His face turned red, right up to his ears. "I tried."

"You did not."

"Okay, well, I tried to get you to come here." He sighed and rubbed the back of his neck. "I told you there were things you ought to handle yourself, and that we needed to talk face to face."

He was right about that. "Why did the baker in town say all I'd find out here is death?" I asked.

"You talked to Binny? Last person you should talk to."

"Why?"

"Well, Binny claims that your great-uncle Melvyn killed her daddy, Rusty Turner, and buried him somewhere on the grounds of Wynter Castle. We think the holes have something to do with her, or with her brother, but we can't prove it."

"HONEST, SHILO, THIS PLACE IS CREEPIER THAN I EVEN remember." I paced beside the rental, holding my cell phone to my ear. It kept cutting out on me and blinking back in, so our conversation had the constancy of a distant radio station. "Shilo, you there?"

"I'm here. I can barely hear you!" Her voice was crackly.

"Crappy reception." Every once in a while I looked back at the castle and shuddered. What was I going to do if I couldn't sell it?

"Mer, honey, you should just hire someone to fill in the holes and leave!" Shilo said as the airwaves cleared for a few seconds. "Come back to New York. Surely you can find work?"

"After that trouble with Leatrice? Nobody is going to hire a thief, Shi."

"No one who knows you believes her!" my friend said.

"But the world is not made up of people who know me."

"She doesn't have *that* much influence! I told one jerk who asked about your trouble with Leatrice why he supposed the police hadn't arrested you, if you really did steal her necklace?"

I appreciated her support. Shilo is one in a million, a model with a solid-gold heart. "I'm working on getting the holes filled in this very minute," I said, glancing over at my real estate agent, who was sitting in his car talking on his own cell phone—organizing some help, I hoped, "But honestly, Shi, the trouble with Leatrice is only one of the reasons I came out here to stay. It's time I dealt with this place instead of ignoring it." I stared at the castle for a long moment. "I need to move on from Leatrice and not let her hijack my life for one more minute."

"I miss you already," she said after a long pause, during which my cell reception blinked in and out.

She was going to make me cry if she kept that up. But I was in upstate New York, not the deserts of equatorial Africa, for heaven's sake! "I have to stay, honey. The estate property taxes are paid up in advance, thank God, but the life insurance Melvyn had was just enough to pay for his burial and the estate expenses for a few more months. There doesn't seem to be any cash. The lawyer says it all disappeared in the last few years." I ruminated on that; where *had* Melvyn's money gone?

But back to the matter at hand. "I have *got* to stay and make this place salable, which is going to be easier said than done since the grounds look like giant prospectors have been digging for gold. It's a mess! I clearly can't trust my realtor to sell it alone." I kicked at a tuft of weeds in the driveway. I hadn't told my best friend everything, and had to confess. "I'm broke, or almost, anyway, and I *have* to stay here until I sell. I didn't tell you but . . . I gave up my apartment in the city."

"You gave up your apartment?" she screeched.

Well, *that* certainly came through loud and clear. I held the phone away from my ear. "Yes."

"Honey, you shoulda told me. Why didn't you tell me? And you left without even letting me know. I should be *fur*ious! Come back and move in with me."

"Into your Cracker Jack box? Why don't you move in with me, instead?" I joked.

"Into the castle?"

"Sure," I said. "I've got *lots* of room," I said, waving my hand around. "*Oodles!* We can fill in giant gopher holes together and ignore the morose people of Autumn Vale." I started to laugh, but then heard the dial tone. What the heck? Had my phone dropped the call? Or had I said something to upset her? Impossible, I thought, staring at my phone. You can't offend Shilo Dinnegan.

The realtor unfolded himself from his clown car and came back toward me. "Well, Miss Wynter, I've found someone who will fill in these holes for you at a rock-bottom cost."

"What is rock-bottom cost?"

He named a number I could live with. "Okay. Mr. McGill—"

"Jack!" he said waggling his finger at me. "You're to call me Jack."

I smiled, and put my hand on his shoulder. "I need to sell this monstrosity, and soon. Mr. Silvio said that even just the land is worth a lot. I need to look at all possibilities, even carving up the property to sell lots."

The realtor shrugged. "Mr. Silvio is not an expert on property, but even he should know things aren't that simple in Abenaki County."

Andrew Silvio was the lawyer who had been responsible for drawing up Uncle Melvyn's will, and handled the estate's probate proceedings. He had encouraged me to put the castle and property up for sale as soon as possible. Even if other claimants came forward—unlikely, he said, because Melvyn had died "without issue"—the castle would still have to be sold to satisfy their demands on the estate.

"I need to sell it quickly, to be frank, because I'm broke," I said. "I know people, a few A-listers and a lot more B-listers. I'm not saying any of them will buy Wynter Castle, but even if they don't they may know people who will." I eyed the castle, doubt plaguing me for a moment. "It's magnificent in its own weird way. I guess. *No* one, however, is going to buy a place riddled with holes."

"And I've solved that little problem for you," he said, rocking back on his heels, then onto his toes.

"When can the hole filler start?"

"Later this morning."

"That'll work temporarily, at least, until the next infestation of giant gophers. If this Binny person is behind it, I'll need to figure out how to stop her. Me staying here might help." I took a deep breath. "Now I'd like to go inside."

He nodded and straightened his shoulders. "Okay. I'm ready if you are."

I tried to judge if that was a "I'm ready for you to shriek and fall into a dead faint" look, or a, "It's not as bad as it looks from the outside" kind of expression. Nothing to do but enter. We ascended to a flagged terrace, which ran the length of the building, seventy or eighty feet by my rough estimate. McGill (he just didn't seem like a "Jack" to me, and I already thought of him just as "McGill") had a big key, which he rattled in the lock, finally unlatching it. He pushed, and the oak, Gothic-arched double doors swung open, the resounding creak like a Foley guy's version of a haunted castle sound.

"It's kinda damp and cold, but it's been modernized, thanks to your uncle Melvyn," McGill said as I slipped past him. "We'll have to get the boiler serviced before firing it up. I can get the guy out today to check it for you. It gets kinda cold here at night, even in September."

He nattered on, his voice echoing as we entered, and the door shutting with a thud that reverberated through the whole castle, but I didn't hear anything else as I gaped at the place. The great hall was enormous, with ceilings twenty or thirty feet high—I'm a poor judge of those things—and stone walls covered by tapestries that did little to hush the sound of my high heels on the flagstone flooring. I was faced by a grand, two-directional staircase that split, climbing to galleries that overlooked the great hall on both sides. As I slowly turned, I saw that the double doors were topped by a huge, diamond-paned Gothic window. If it had not been covered in dirt and ivy, it would have flooded the hall with light.

I was taken back nine years to my wedding to Miguel,

held at a lovely small "castle" much like this, only in Connecticut. I had descended stairs like those to the strains of "Clair de Lune," and down the aisle to Miguel, where he stood, handsome and dark, before the reverend. As the pianist lingered gently over the last notes, we joined hands.

Tears filled my eyes, and I was lost in time. Two years later, the same music played as his friends carried his casket from the church, and the mingled joy and sadness I feel when I hear it takes me back to that lovely, perfect wedding, and the hauntingly sad finale of our marriage. So much joy for two short years. I hugged myself, willing the tears to dry. Had this place ever held such beauty? Would anyone ever fondly say "Oh yes, the Wynter Castle! We had our wedding there."

It was possible. Chairs could be set up on either side of the stairway to form an aisle, and the officiant could stand with the beautiful, old, oak double-doors as a backdrop, under an archway of orange blossoms. Or . . . oh! A winter wedding, with a roaring fire in the fireplace that was along one wall, the enormous oak mantel decked in white orchids and crystal candlesticks, and the chairs facing it, instead of the doors. When I came out of my reverie, I had my hands clasped to my bosom, and was staring in rapt joy upward, where I saw, for the first time, the rose window above the winding staircase, as one beam of light blazed scarlet through it.

"You see it, don't you?" McGill said gently. "You see what this place could be."

I cleared my throat and asked, "How many rooms are there?"

"Well, the main floor here has the kitchen in the back, a dining room, parlor, a library—it's in the turret room— along the east side and a long ballroom along the west, with a breakfast room in the other turret room. Upstairs, there are twelve bedchambers, two with attached sitting rooms, and three more rooms that could be converted into bedrooms, including two neat ones in the turret rooms above the breakfast room and library. There are also two big rooms with a bathroom between them. Melvyn had new bathrooms put in the two suites, but that's as far as he got."

"So that's . . . how many?" I did a quick calculation. "Seventeen bedrooms in all?"

"I guess so. Lots of small country inns have less."

I didn't answer his suggestion; I had already thought it would make a lovely country inn, but it would need a lot of work, and it was more than I would or could do myself. "You knew my uncle, right?"

He nodded. "I did. And I liked him. Don't believe what Binny says. Melvyn didn't kill her father. We don't even know if the guy—meaning her pa, Rusty Turner—is dead. No one knows what he was up to."

"Why didn't this place sell? Besides the giant gopher holes?"

"No vision," the realtor promptly said. "No one could see what you just did."

"What do you mean?"

"You're like Melvyn; you see the castle's potential. Actually, probably *more* than him. He muddled along with this place for almost forty years but never got done." He paused, staring at me in an odd, intense way. "I don't know what was going on in your head a few minutes ago, but you saw how this place could be used."

I nodded. "As an inn, an event venue, for weddings, symposiums, retreats . . . so many possibilities!"

"Exactly! There's a place not too far from here, Beardslee Castle. You should see it. That's what they've done—four-star dining, weddings, the whole bit—and it's beautiful!"

I looked up at the rose window, and the light increased as the sun climbed in the sky. Brilliant color played across the floor, a pinwheel of indigo, eggplant, rose and ochre, and tears prickled in my eyes again. I owned this place, *owned* it! But for all that I saw the hidden beauty and potential beneath the drab façade, I couldn't keep it. Alone, just me in this vast behemoth? It was too much. My life was in New York, not in some backwater near the pea-size town of Autumn Vale. I needed to bring it up to scratch with whatever modest repairs I could afford, sell it, and get the heck out. "Is there anything wrong with this place besides neglect?" I asked.

He shook his head, but I wasn't convinced. "Let's see the rest of it. If I stay, it's only going to be to fix it up to sell, McGill."

"Of course," he said. "What else?"

We peeked into the ballroom first, but the place looked haunted, and I shivered. It had to be forty feet long, and a cold breeze shuddered out of it. Something over in the corner was shrouded in white; it looked like a pipe organ from some off-Broadway version of *Phantom of the Opera*. I slammed the door shut. The turret rooms were cool, but dusty and dark.

The castle interior, aside from the flagstone floor and stone walls in the great hall, was warmed by a lot of wood: natural handrails supported by oak balusters winding up the staircase, wood floors in most of the rooms—some were herringbone patterned, others just straight hardwood with a patterned edge—and lots of natural wood paneling in the family rooms, like the dining room and parlor. It was also almost fully furnished with some lovely old pieces and some modern ugliness, especially in the rooms my uncle had used.

Most of the furniture was tented in white sheets, like the ghosts of furnishings past, so what I noted here was only what I saw as I lifted the edges of the covers to peek. As we walked, and McGill talked about room dimensions and other boring details, I reflected on what little I knew of the Wynter side of my family. My father was the only son of Melvyn's late younger brother. When my dad died, we were living in Tarrytown. We stayed there for a year afterward, then came on the infamous trip to Wynter Castle, and moved in with Grandma—my Mom's mother—on the Lower East Side in New York.

After that, I don't remember my mother ever voluntarily mentioning my father's side of the family, and I have never known why. Grandma and Mom died within six months of each other when I was twenty-one, and had already embarked on my short-lived modeling career. There was never any knowledge or sense that I was the heir to anything as amazing as Wynter Castle until Andrew Silvio, my uncle's lawyer, found me and told me of my inheritance.

I suppose that was one of the reasons why I didn't even want to see the place at first. I felt afraid, but also like I would be dishonoring my mother's memory by going to a place she would never talk about. You had to know my mother to understand. She was rock solid on her ideals. A true remnant of the sixties flower-child movement, she belonged to Amnesty International, Women for World Peace, and End Apartheid Now. She burned her bra and marched on Washington. She was there when they tore down the Berlin Wall. If she didn't want to associate with Melvyn, there had to be a reason, and it likely had to do with her passionate idealism. Mom and I weren't alike in many ways—I don't have the guts to be that idealistic—but I admired her, even when her passion took her away from me and left me feeling alone.

So there were many reasons I had just wanted to sell the castle and be done with it. But now that I was here, I was curious. Who was Melvyn Wynter? Why had he left the castle to me? Surely he didn't owe me anything? And why, if he was going to leave me the castle, did he not try to find me earlier so I could ask him about my father's life and their family and maybe find out what had really happened during that last visit with my mother?

The flood of emotion was probably what I was hoping to avoid by not coming to Wynter Castle, but now that I was here, I'd have to deal with it.

"So, are you staying?" McGill asked as we returned to the main floor.

"I am." Did I really have any options, now that I had given up my life in New York?

"For how long?"

"I don't really know yet." And I didn't.

Chapter Three

❊ ❊ ❊

I T WAS MID-MORNING, and the village had come to life, shrugging off the torpor of a lazy day at the end of summer, and beginning the bustle that would become the "back-to-work" attitude of September, once Labor Day weekend had passed. Even in Autumn Vale, there was a "back-to-school" rush, I guess, and I saw a mom tugging two kids into the general store, a tall, narrow building with poster-obscured windows. I parked at one end of the main street and walked down it, watched by a trio of old men sitting on a bench outside of Vale Variety, a convenience store.

If I was going to stay for a while, I needed supplies: food, toiletries, cleaning products. McGill had assured me I could go to Rochester, about thirty-five or forty miles away, but there is nothing that gains you friends in a small town like spending your money there. That was true in Italy, France, Germany, and the good old US of A. I needed to scope out the town and learn a little about it, if I was going to figure out how best to sell Wynter Castle.

I dawdled around town for a while, but the residents seemed to shy away from me. Oh, they watched me all right. I felt the blaze of scores of steady gazes as I sauntered by. I ambled past the one antique store that appeared to still be open for business, Crazy Lady Antiques and Collectibles, but the sign noted it had limited hours, on Friday and Saturday only. There was apparently a tiny Autumn Vale Public Library, accessed by a ramp and a side door off one of the alleys, but the hours were Monday, Wednesday, and Friday, noon to five. Autumn Vale Community Bank was an interesting little building, dark-red, shiny brick, situated right on a corner and with a curved face and doors set into the curved corner, but I didn't feel like going in to the bank just yet.

The "all you'll find at Wynter Castle is death" comment made to me by Binny the Baker echoed in my brain. Did she honestly think my uncle had killed her father? But you know, a woman who loved teapots that much couldn't be *all* bad. I stopped in front of her shop, noting the customers coming out with paper bags full of the most incredible-smelling focaccia. I was hungry! Okay, so I would buy bread and try to make a fresh start with Binny. If her dad was missing and presumed dead, I felt for her. It was hard losing a parent at any age and in any way.

I entered, and waited my turn. Every woman in there was watching me, as long as they thought I wasn't looking at them. Gossip, McGill said, about old Mel Wynter's niece's arrival, had gotten around. That's what had brought him out to the castle; someone saw me talking to Virgil Grace and called Binny Turner, found out who I was, and then called the realtor.

I turned and looked around the shop, noting that opposite the shelves of teapots was a wall of photos. There was one of Binny and an older man, both dressed in camouflage, and holding guns. There was another of the same old man and a blonde, middle-aged woman, again, both in camo and both holding guns. Sheesh . . . was Autumn Vale the kind of place where everyone hunted? I'm no hunter, except for great bargains on shoes, but I was going to stay out of the whole judging-someone-based-on-their-pastimes thing. That had been one of my mother's failings. Instead, I sidled up to the glass case and said, "Everything looks wonderful!"

Binny served every single person in the bakery, then turned and looked at me. "Can I help you? Again?"

She hadn't helped me the first time, but I was not going to point that out to her. "I feel like we got off on the wrong foot, Ms. Turner," I said in a conciliatory tone. "I'm Merry Wynter, Melvyn Wynter's niece. I was sorry to hear that your father is missing. I know how hard it is to be in that kind of pain."

She froze, and glared at a spot above my head, but didn't answer. The bell above the door tinkled, a sign that someone else was entering. Not the time to pursue this. "Uh, well, I'd like a half dozen of the panini, a few ciabatta, and one of those marvelous focaccia, please," I said.

The baker silently put the food in a couple of paper bags, took the money, gave change, then turned to the other customer, an older woman who stood looking over the items in the glass case. There were biscotti and pfeffernüsse on the top shelf, and an assortment of sweets, buns, and breads on the others, all exotic and beautiful.

"Binny, I know we've had this argument before," the customer said, looking at the glass case and sighing, deeply. "But I simply don't understand why you won't make muffins and cookies. This is Autumn Vale, not New York City, you know."

"Mrs. Grace, how are the folks around here ever going to refine their palate if I let them buy muffins and cookies instead of croissants and biscotti?" the baker said, wiping her hands on a wet cloth. "I didn't study under Alfred Bannerman just to come home and make cookies, like some small-town housewife. I'm not forcing anyone to come in here, you know."

I smiled, appreciating her tough-mindedness. She was prickly, but at least she knew what she wanted to do.

The woman sighed again and closed her eyes, briefly. "Binny, dear, I'm grateful for all you've done for Golden Acres—the day-old bread, all the freebies—but my oldsters want muffins. The other day I asked Doc English if he wanted focaccia, and he said he ought to wash my mouth out with soap."

I snorted in surprised laughter, and the woman glanced back at me with a smile, but continued talking to Binny Turner.

"I want them to eat well. I've tried sourcing muffins and cookies out of town, but all I get are stale, cardboard imitations, and they won't eat them. I want good, nutritious, *fresh*, homey food that eighty- and ninety-year-olds will enjoy, and I would like to buy local, if I can."

The baker's face was stony, and she replied, politely enough, but with finality, "I don't have time or resources enough to do everything, Mrs. G."

"I appreciate that, Binny. I'll take a half dozen of the cannoli."

While they finished their transaction, I examined the rows of teapots—I loved one cheeky teapot shaped like a roly-poly baker—then followed the woman out. "Excuse me," I said. "I couldn't help but overhear you in there."

The woman turned to me with a frank expression of interest. "You're Melvyn's niece, aren't you? The one who inherited the castle."

"I am."

"My son told me about you."

"Your son?"

"Virgil Grace, the sheriff. I'm Gogi Grace."

I shook her outthrust hand. "Of course! I had a feeling I recognized your last name. Well, anyway, I wanted to say, if you have a kitchen at the old folks' home, muffins ought to be super easy to make. They're so simple even I can't foul them up. It's pretty much the only pastry I can make—well, that and cookies—but with older folks, try something standard, like banana-bran, or apple spice."

Mrs. Grace raised her perfectly trimmed eyebrows. "Do I look like I cook?"

I looked her over, biting my lip, from the silver-tipped mane of perfectly coiffed curls to the toes of her bone-colored Ferragamo pumps. "No, you look like you just walked out of Saks."

"So do you," the woman said, eyeing me up and down. "We have a cook, but she's got all she can handle with three squares a day."

"Oh."

"You're not at all what I expected," Mrs. Grace said, pointing to my top. "Anna Scholz, am I right? Fall 2013 show?" she asked, about the print tunic I wore.

My eyebrows rose. She was dead-on. I had changed into the Scholz print tunic and DKNY jeans for the trip back into town. My generous wages with Leatrice had allowed me to purchase designer clothes, discounted appropriately, of course. I am what Shilo calls "plush-size," but plus-size does not mean unfashionable anymore. "Good eye. Do I pass muster? Despite what Sheriff Grace probably said?" Yes, I was fishing for information, and maybe a compliment.

"How do *you* know what he said? Besides, he only noticed . . . ah . . . *one* aspect of your figure," the woman said, with a wicked twinkle in her brilliant blue eyes. "My son *is* a man."

"I noticed."

"Anyway, you were talking about muffins. I don't cook and my hired cook doesn't have time; can you make me some to try? Say . . . two dozen?"

"Two . . . what?" A few morning walkers, two women and three kids, bustled past, their beady eyes staring us down until they parted like a wave around us. One woman even looked back. I wondered what the conversation would be at the local watering hole. Did Autumn Vale even have a local watering hole? I shifted my gaze back to Mrs. Gogi Grace, who waited, a polite smile on her carefully made-up face. "So let me get this straight; you want me to make two dozen muffins for your seniors."

"That would be wonderful!" she cried, touching my arm with a practiced club-lady grip. "Thanks, darling, for offering. The oldsters will love them, I'm sure! I'll be in touch. I'll come out to the castle tomorrow, shall I?'

"I beg your pardon?"

"You *are* staying at the castle, correct?"

"Yes, but—"

"Then I'll come out tomorrow . . . oh, say in the early afternoon. I'll pick up the muffins and you can give me a tour. I'm dying to see the place!" She sailed off down the sidewalk, waggling her fingers in the air behind her.

I stared down the street as some of the locals watched. Binny was in the bakery window, too, and I thought, uh-oh. If she overheard Gogi Grace asking me to bake for her . . . but there was an amused smile on the woman's face. I smiled back, and Binny chuckled, then moved farther into the dim reaches of the bakery. Why did I have a feeling I wasn't the first person to be manipulated by Mrs. Grace, when it came to taking care of her "oldsters," as she called them?

I could have ignored her manipulation. I wasn't afraid to. But it struck me that Mrs. Grace would be a valuable ally in the clannish town of Autumn Vale. She was the only person who had talked to me with any openness, besides McGill. She probably had a lot of connections in town. And she might even have answers about my uncle and Wynter Castle.

I finished up my shopping in the general store, buying way more than I had intended. Of course I tried to make a friend of the clerk, but she was polite and that was it. As I left, lugging several bags of stuff, I saw the clerk reach for the phone, and wondered if my complete shopping spree would be dissected over coffee among the locals. I wasn't sure what they would make of muffin tins and maxi pads, but they could have at it.

When I returned "home," I marched straight to the cavernous castle kitchen, depositing the bags of baked goods, and shopping bags filled with cleaning supplies, overripe bananas, muffins tins, paper muffin liners, and a heap of other staples. On my first tour, McGill had assured me that all the appliances worked, but other than the dirty microwave they didn't look like they had ever been touched. With an order for two dozen muffins, I would put the oven to the test.

Hands on my hips, I looked around, studying the long expanse of galvanized steel countertop, punctuated by a professional-grade butcher-block section and a deep sink with sprayer attachment. The fridge, empty until now, was a huge, double-door model, probably only three or four years old. "What on earth were you planning, Uncle, and why didn't you ever do it?" I said out loud. Trying to get into his octogenarian mind was impossible. Maybe the castle would eventually reveal his plans. I shivered. It was going to be strange living alone in this monstrosity. In fact, a lot of things were going to be strange, including trying to adjust to the enormous space. I was accustomed to a New York studio apartment of four hundred square feet. The castle kitchen alone was probably more than that, and the appliances were commercial grade. Maybe Melvyn was planning to convert the castle to an inn similar to what McGill and I envisioned?

The kitchen, at least, had been what was called in city lingo "sympathetically restored," meaning the exposed stone wall had been left as is, and the fabulous, two-hundred-year-old features had been restored. It was longer than it was wide, and at one end was an enormous fireplace, original, I would bet, judging from the darkness of the bricks. The fireplace was surrounded by bare shelves, painted an antique blue sometime in the last twenty years; the shelving arched up over the empty mantel. But it all looked naked, and seemed soulless to me. The empty shelving was just one part of it, I supposed. What was a kitchen without food? Just another room.

I stared at it for a long minute, considering; what it needed was a seating area, somewhere to cuddle up to the warmth of the fire on a cold day. I would explore the castle and see if there were any suitable chairs, or a settee. If I was going to live here for a few months, I'd need to be comfortable. The shelves needed some rustic touches, maybe oil lamps, some pottery, even old cookbooks, as did the mantel. The working part of the kitchen was more modern: it had to be, for anyone to cook there. In the middle of those stainless steel appliances and work area, was a long, raised worktable with a pot rack overhead. Though it took up too much space in the center, it would be a useful work surface.

Suddenly overwhelmed, I slumped down on a stool and glanced around, tears filling my eyes. I was probably just tired and hungry, but all of a sudden I wondered how I was going to do this. What the hell was I doing in the middle of nowhere, in a castle that I had to find a way to sell? At thirty-nine, I was starting over with no clue of what I was supposed to be doing for the rest of my life, now that my career was busted and no one in the fashion industry would even trust me in their homes, much less working for them. I wasn't being melodramatic in thinking my career was over, it was simple fact. Leatrice, spiteful and angry, had poisoned the fashion industry well. Even those who didn't believe her lies just didn't need to take that chance. I was alone, almost penniless, with a behemoth of a building as my only asset.

I shook off the weariness and depression, slipped on my loafers, and headed outside; fresh air or tea are my cure-alls.

Defeat was not an option. Wynter Castle was amazing, but to be sellable it had to present as a viable property with great potential. The more I did to it, the more likely I would be to get a decent payday. With at least a million dollars or so that the castle *could* fetch if I worked hard, I could head back to the city and maybe start my own business. What kind of business, I wasn't sure yet, but something.

The double oak door creaked shut behind me and I strolled to the edge of the flagged terrace, looking out over my land. *My* land. Weird. The castle grounds consisted of several acres (by my questionable judgment) of open land, surrounded by forest on all sides. The only exposed vista was down the laneway, but the lane then curved around a grove and disappeared in the trees.

I tried to visualize this landscape without the holes, but it was tough. I crossed a patch of the long, weedy grass and sidled up to one of the pits, staring down at the dirt and roots. It was at least six feet deep. What on earth was someone looking for? McGill theorized that it had to do with Binny Turner's missing father, but could she really believe that Rusty Turner's body was buried on the castle grounds? And that eighty-year-old Melvyn Wynter had managed to kill and bury the poor guy by himself? Sounded far-fetched to me.

And even if all that was true, how could Binny Turner be responsible for digging all of these holes?

As I glanced around, I noticed a pair of glowing eyes trained in my direction. Something moved on the edge of the forest, an animal watching me. I squinted and shaded my eyes with my hand. Whatever "it" was, it was orange. How many native animals are orange? I took a step in that direction, wondering what it would do; it melted back into the forest. Just then I heard rumbling in the distance. Earthquake? As I stared down the lane, a small excavator appeared from around the bend, followed by a disgraceful, rattletrap vehicle that I immediately recognized.

"Shilo," I shrieked, jumping up and down in glee. I tore off toward the car, trotting to it, then alongside it as it made its way up the lane. My dearest friend in the world—well, one of just two or three—was waving and chirping happily as she tootled up the drive.

Chapter Four

�֎ ✖ ✖

SHILO DINNEGAN HALTED her creaky, old vehicle on the weedy, flagged drive and leaped from the ancient Ford; she threw her skinny arms around me, hugging hard. Despite the fact that we had just had dinner three days ago—during which I wanted to tell her my plans, but was afraid I would burst into tears—it felt like I hadn't seen her in months.

I hugged her back, then held her away from me. "Shilo, what are you doing here?" I asked, shaking her.

"You invited me to come stay," she said calmly, cocking her head on one side, her black eyes snapping with good humor.

"I . . . but . . ." I spluttered, then broke into laughter. "Shilo, you know that's not quite true, but I'm *so* glad to see you. And you know you're welcome to stay." My depression vanished like mist, as I considered what a difference having Shilo around, even for a little while, would make. Arm over her shoulders, I turned to the Bobcat driver, and found it was Jack McGill, wearing battered blue jeans, a soft, old, plaid shirt, and a huge grin. "So you're the cut-rate hole filler?" I said.

"Yup, I am. Borrowed this machine from a friend. I'll get going. I want to get these filled for you so you won't break your neck."

He started work immediately, and Shilo linked her arm in mine and tugged me away. "Isn't he cute?" she said, watching him over my shoulder.

"You think he's cute?" I glanced back at McGill, who had begun at the hole closest to the castle. *Really?*

"SO YOU WERE LAST HERE WHEN YOU WERE *HOW* old?" Shilo asked.

"I was about five, I think," I said, pulling a boho-chic dress out of one of Shilo's many suitcases and shaking the wrinkles out of it.

The room I had chosen for myself was one with a "Jack and Jill" bathroom and a room on the other side. I had vaguely thought I might make the other room an office, of sorts. Instead, I put Shilo in it, figuring that would be only one bathroom to clean rather than several. The castle already felt smaller because of her boundless energy and enthusiasm. The cage with Shilo's bunny, Magic, was on top of a dresser, and the rabbit stared at me with witless focus through the square mesh.

While McGill worked steadily on filling holes, a gentleman in overalls had arrived—summoned by McGill, who knew exactly what needed to be done—and turned on the boiler, lit the pilot lights, and explained how it all worked, checked that everything was functional, then tipped his John Deere hat and left. I had sheets and blankets in the laundry, not trusting my uncle's housekeeping, and would be able to make up our beds with fresh linens shortly. The washer and dryer were industrial-size, so it was all in one load.

"Why didn't you look up your uncle, after your mom and grandma died?" Shilo asked.

I sat down on the mattress as Shilo finished her unpacking and talked about my family, something I rarely did. "I didn't remember the trip here very well. Still don't. And I only have a dim memory of Uncle Melvyn. We came here by train, I remember, and Uncle Melvyn met us at the station in an old car, something that looked like it was from a forties gangster movie, the kind my grandmother liked to watch on TV." I wondered if that car was still in one of the outbuildings that dotted the landscape, and that I had yet to look into.

Why had Mom come all the way to Autumn Vale, I wondered. I told Shilo the rest of the story: It was a long trip and I was tired, which is why I don't remember much of the castle, I guess. I tumbled right into bed, which I shared with Mom, but I woke up the next morning alone. A little scared by the movie-set weirdness of the castle, I found my way down to the kitchen. Mom and Uncle Melvyn sat in the kitchen talking, and I remember the smell of strong, burnt coffee. I lingered at the door of the kitchen, shy, I suppose, as the conversation between the two of them became an argument. I don't remember what they said, but the tone of an adult argument is familiar to any child.

Mom stormed out of the kitchen, grabbed my arm, and hauled me upstairs. I sat cross-legged on the bed while she packed our bags and called for a cab to take us back to the train station. Though I was hungry, there wasn't even time to eat; I remember that vividly. The cab pulled up, honked its horn, and we stormed out of there, followed by my shouting uncle. I knelt on the seat of the car and looked out the back window. Uncle Melvyn stood at the huge oak double doors, shaking his fist.

"What did they fight over?" Shilo asked, shutting a drawer now filled with her confused jumble of clean underwear.

"To this day, I don't know. My mom wouldn't tell me. But we never came back here, and she never mentioned him again. You didn't know my mother, but she had those kind of arguments with people all the time. If someone didn't share her political views or her moral ideals, then they were the enemy."

"Wow. Judgmental much?"

"I know. She said compromise was for those who couldn't stick to their ideals. I mean, she was right, usually, about the stuff she was passionate about, but it didn't make it any easier to have friends. I don't think I ever had a friend with Republican parents. Mom wouldn't stand for it.

"Anyway, I asked a few times about Uncle Melvyn, but finally stopped after the umpteenth dirty look from Mom. We moved to New York and lived with Granny, Mom's mother. You know the rest; when I was twenty-one Granny died, and Mom just months later. I never even thought of looking up Uncle Melvyn. I supposed I didn't realize he'd still be alive. He seemed ancient when I was five, though I guess he must have only been in his fifties."

Shilo danced into the bathroom with her cosmetics bag and dashed back out without it. "We met when you were . . . what?"

"I was twenty-eight." That was the year I'd met Miguel Paradiso. Everything changed when I met Miguel, a photographer who confessed, on a Lane Bryant shoot in St. Tropez, that skinny girls frightened him. Hunger of any kind frightened Miguel, except for the hunger for love he saw in my eyes, he said to me.

It was a *great* pickup line. He was such a romantic, and had a genius for flattery, useful in his work as a photographer. Every woman felt more beautiful around Miguel, more womanly, softer, vulnerable. Cared for. I fell in love almost that same moment and couldn't believe my good fortune when he fell in love with me, too. We got married just six months later in that Connecticut castle, which Miguel knew from a shoot. We had two glorious years together before he died in a car accident while on his way to a job in Vermont, leaving me a widow at the age of thirty-one.

Shilo reached out and touched my arm. "You're thinking of Miguel."

"How do you always know?" I asked, the view of my friend shimmering through the veil of tears.

"It's not hard to figure out," she said, her pixie face drawn down in a sad expression. "If you're crying, you're probably thinking of him. We all loved Miguel," she said, referring to the community of photographers, artists, stylists, designers, and models who made up our friendship circle.

Most of whom had now abandoned me. The Leatrice effect, again. Even those who didn't believe the woman's outrageous claim thought I had sold out by going to work for her, instead of continuing my work as a stylist. "I know," I said. "I still miss him."

After a brief pause, she said, "So seriously, dearie; what are you going to do with this monstrosity of a castle?" Shilo got up and twirled around in the room, her arms spread wide.

"It's either a godsend or a death knell," I said, getting up and wandering the room, touching the furniture, comprised of both beautiful and ugly old pieces in the Eastlake style. "I thought I could just sell it and move on, but it seems like the universe wants me here for a while, anyway. My idea is to fix it up enough to unload it, and get the heck back to NYC."

"But we'll see what the universe has in mind for you, right?"

"Right." I glanced over at Shilo and frowned. "By the way, how did you find your way here so quickly? I got lost a dozen times. It took me forever!"

"Gypsy blood, my dear," Shilo said, waggling her fingers near her eyes, veiling them mysteriously, then peeping at me. "It's not that far from the city, as the crow flies. I'm part Roma, and part Irish Traveler, you know, and both sides can find their way anywhere by intuition."

"Okay," I said.

"I did get lost outside of Autumn Vale," she admitted. "But darling Jack was just leaving a construction lot with that machine. I flagged him down, and when he said he was coming here, I followed him."

Darling Jack? "This is a weird place," I said. "This whole valley is distinctly odd. Like, Shirley Jackson odd. *Stephen King* odd!" I told her about my GPS acting up, and about my dubious welcome, the "Wynter Castle is death" refrain from Binny the Baker. I mused about my quirky cell phone reception, and also told her about Gogi Grace, the retirement home owner.

Shilo laughed. "You actually let her rope you in to making two dozen muffins? On your first day in a new town?"

"She seemed nice, and she looked like she might be a valuable contact."

"Method behind the madness?"

"You bet!"

Once Shilo was settled in, and Magic had a carrot to chew on, we went down to the kitchen and I familiarized myself with the appliances by making lunch, one of my favorite soups, Gouda and Harvest Vegetable Chowder. I was starved, having only munched on one of the buns I bought from Binnie that morning. I went outside while the soup simmered to see how McGill was coming along. He was making progress, but slowly, and he looked unsure of the machine a good deal of the time. I caught his eye and waved him down.

He moved the Bobcat away from a hole and shut it off. "How's it going?" he asked, climbing out of the machine.

"Good. Want some lunch? I've rustled up a little food."

He enthusiastically agreed, and followed me through the big front doors. "There's another way in, you know, right to the kitchen instead of going all the way around," he said, his voice echoing in the big hall.

"I thought I saw another door, but I've lost track. It's taking me a while to find my way around. You'll have to show me."

He showed me the door, off a long hall lined with cup-boards behind the kitchen, a butler's pantry, I think it's called. While he washed up, Shilo and I found a few chairs and moved them into the kitchen. We set the worktable, using the oddly assorted dishes that my uncle had left, then I brought the big pot of soup to the table and pulled a batch of cheddar-bacon muffins out of the oven, dumping them into a big bowl, with a stick of real butter and a knife alongside.

McGill came in, wiping his hands on a towel and sniffed the air. "Wow, something smells great!"

"Merry is the muffin queen!" Shilo said. "Miguel said that he fell in love with her because of her muffins . . . and her buns!"

"Shi!" I said, giving her a stern look. *That girl has no boundaries*, I thought, but did not say aloud.

Chastened, Shilo said, "Sorry."

Of course that necessitated an explanation as to who Miguel was. I found out that McGill had lost his wife not long after they were married, and after some mutual com-miseration we were devouring lunch and chatting like old friends.

"So, was anything ever resolved between my uncle and the Turners?" I said, turning the conversation to business. "What were they fighting over?"

He shrugged, dipping a big chunk of savory muffin in his soup. "Bad business blood," he mumbled, around a mouthful of muffin. "When Rusty disappeared, everything screeched to a halt. There's a lot more to it than that, but I don't know everything."

I exchanged a glance with Shilo. It seemed like McGill was avoiding the subject, or trying to pass over it lightly. "Did he just disappear? What do you think happened to him? Is he really dead?"

McGill shrugged yet again, as he chewed and swallowed. "I just don't know. There was so much going on. Rusty Turner . . ." He shook his head and made a sound between his teeth. "He was a contentious sort. Melvyn wasn't the only one he was having trouble with."

"But Binny clearly thinks he's dead," I insisted, refusing to be sloughed off.

"Tom's got her convinced that Melvyn killed him, and—"

"Tom?"

"Her older brother. He worked for both Turner Construction *and* Turner Wynter, their construction partnership."

"I didn't know my uncle and Rusty Turner were in business together!"

"Oh, yeah! I guess I didn't exactly say that. They had a company together, and Rusty's son, Tom, worked for them. So did Dinah Hooper, Rusty's sorta girlfriend. Rusty and Tom had Turner Construction, too. Anyway, Turner Wynter was working on the castle, as well as on developing other properties."

"What other properties?"

He shrugged. "They had a few interests."

"If they had a company together, that's more than just a few common interests." Was he being evasive or just noncommittal? "I don't want any more trouble. If they keep digging holes . . ." I shook my head.

"Hey, I'm just *guessing* that Binny and Tom are behind the holes," McGill said, holding up both hands. He pushed away his bowl. "I don't have a scrap of evidence to back that up." He glanced down at his watch and leaped up. "Shoot! I gotta go." His cell phone wouldn't work—service in Autumn Vale and environs was spotty, at best, he admitted—so he made a quick call using the castle landline for someone to pick him up. It was fortunate that he had left the landline hooked up for just that purpose, in case he got stuck out at his most remote listing without cell coverage. He then said, "Got a client from outta town meeting me at a house, and I'd better go home and clean up first. I'll be back tomorrow to fill in more holes. Thank you, ladies, for the lunch. Those muffins . . ." He shook his head and rubbed his stomach, where a half-dozen cheddar-bacon muffins now lived. "*So good!*"

"I made a lot. Do you want to take some with you?" I asked, and laughed at the hopeful look on his face. I popped another half dozen in a big baggie and handed them to him. "They're best while they're fresh. You can warm them up in the microwave."

Shilo and I washed up the mismatched jumble of bowls, mugs, and cutlery, then took a ramble around the castle. It was soon clear that the pattern of the building was a *U* shape. The kitchen and pantry was on the end of one prong, with a neglected kitchen garden behind. The entrance McGill had shown me in the butler's pantry opened right out onto the huge swath of land where he was working, filling in holes.

But I hadn't slept since the day before, and Shilo was always ready to snooze, so we both hit the hay early. I fell asleep right away, then awoke in the pitch black of night, feeling confused and scared for a few minutes. I finally figured out where I was, and once I fully came to, my mind began to teem with questions and ideas. I peeked in Shi's room, but she and Magic were curled up together, deeply asleep.

As I padded downstairs in my slippers and robe, carrying a notebook and pen, it finally, truly hit me; I owned a castle, the real deal, almost two hundred years old! It was the middle of the night, but inspiration flooded my mind as I put the kettle on for tea, which I would either have to make in a mug (shudder) or in a saucepan. I chose a saucepan and poured boiling water over a tea bag and set the lid over it to steep as I sat down at the table, one low light illuminating my notebook.

McGill had told us a little about the castle during lunch. It had been built in the 1820s by Jacob Lazarus Wynter, an early nineteenth-century building baron who made his fortune constructing mills for the Indian bands along the various rivers emptying into Lake Erie and Lake Ontario. That was already more information about the paternal side of my lineage than I had ever known. I was descended from a robber baron? I vaguely remembered that phrase from school, but wasn't sure Lazarus Wynter fit the mold. This place had real historical significance, and it made me sad that instead of a thriving family inheritance there was just poor little old me, who had to sell it to live. The least I could do would be to get some kind of historical designation for it, and maybe a plaque relating both what McGill had told me and whatever other family history I could dig up.

I made a note of that idea, then jotted down a few ideas for the inn, possible places to advertise my inheritance. Everyone I have ever known in the business world dreams of one day retiring from the rat race and opening a little inn in the country. Well, for the right price I could help them fulfill their dreams. I started writing down names of people; modeling agency owners, models, actors, caterers, anyone I could think of who might be interested, or know someone who would be.

Tapping the pen on the page, I looked around the dark, spartan kitchen. The joint lacked charm. McGill told me he and his mother had cleaned up somewhat after Melvyn died and was buried, because he knew if he was going to sell it, it would need to be at least clean. But the guy had certainly not put any imagination into it, nor had he staged the castle to sell. Who could blame him? He had other fish to fry, no doubt, and easier sales to make. I should bring my stuff out of storage, I thought. It would be nice to have all my things around me for once. I'd had to keep some of it boxed up and packed away at all times, since Miguel's death, after I lost most of my savings and was forced to downsize. I shied away from the thought, because getting all my stuff meant going through old photos of Miguel and me in happier times. I didn't want to face that yet. It had been seven years though; when would I be equipped to handle it?

Not yet.

For the time being, I would just live there with whatever

I could scrounge among the stuff left by my uncle. I wondered if there were any mugs that I had missed stuffed away in the butler's pantry, so I sidled in to that room, turning on the light and scanning the high, glass cabinets, which were mostly empty.

I heard a noise, and quickly turned out the light, peering out the window that overlooked the land where McGill had been working. Was that the Bobcat I heard? McGill, working in the middle of the night? I squinted into the darkness, and saw the faint illumination of the excavator cab. Yes, someone was operating the machine, but instead of filling in, they had moved to a fresh patch of land and were digging!

Chapter Five

❈ ❈ ❈

"FOR THE LOVE of Pete," I yelled, annoyed. This was exactly what I had been concerned about. If it was Binny or her brother, I wanted them to know this was not acceptable, and without a thought for my safety, I flung open the butler pantry door and bolted outside into the dark, toward the roaring machine. The interior light showed some jerk in the driver's seat manipulating the gears and digging. Grr!

As I was crossing the wide open space between me and the Bobcat, I saw something—some creature, a streak of orange by the light of the excavator—launch into the open compartment at the operator. There was an unearthly screech, a howl of pain, and then the man bolted from the driver's compartment and stumbled toward the woods, pursued by the animal. I followed as well as I could in slippers and a housecoat, but I tripped, went down hard, and by the time I clambered to my feet, all I could see was the fellow disappearing into the woods.

"Merry! Where are you?" Shilo was at the door, backlit by the overhead light.

I limped back to the door of the butler's pantry and gasped, "Call the cops!"

Shilo had her cell phone, and dialed 911—she got a connection, miracle of miracles, maybe because it was the middle of the night—and told the operator we were at Wynter Castle, and relayed in brief what I said had happened. We then sat in the kitchen with the door locked, and waited. And waited. Long enough that the excavator sputtered to a stop, out of fuel, I suppose. Gradually my anger and panic turned to just anger at the lackadaisical attitude of the local constabulary, so when the sheriff's car finally pulled up to the castle, I strode outside to the lane.

As Virgil Grace climbed out of the car, I stormed over to him and said, "What exactly is the point of coming now, an hour after the hole digger left?"

"Pardon me for not coming immediately, Miss Wynter, ma'am," he said, with a laconic, weary edge to his voice. "But I had a domestic, and trying to convince a beaten, frightened woman to file charges against her drunken boyfriend took precedence over a phantom hole digger."

In the light from the open doors I could see that he had scratches across his cheek near his hairline, and he looked exhausted. "Okay, all right. I'm sorry for snapping at you. You're here now," I said. I told him what I had seen, and we went to look at the machine.

The sheriff played his flashlight over the Bobcat, and noted some blood on the seat. "Well, whatever that animal was, it sure left a mark!"

I looked at the scratches on the sheriff's cheek and down at the drop of blood, and said, "It sure did!"

THE NEXT DAY MCGILL, AFTER GASSING UP THE excavator with fuel he brought with him, was back at it, filling in holes—the sheriff didn't swab the blood he found or check for fingerprints, since there was no way the county was going to do blood testing or any other forensic examination for the "crime" of someone starting up an excavator illicitly, he said—and I knew I had to get down to work if I was going to have a couple dozen muffins for Gogi Grace when she came that afternoon.

"I wish I had Granny's cookbooks here," I said, standing at the counter and looking at the pile of ingredients uneasily. "The bacon and cheddar muffins yesterday were easy; just a basic, savory muffin recipe. I vaguely remember the proportions necessary for bran muffins, but I wish I was sure."

McGill came to the door, rubbing his hands together. An unseasonable cold snap had taken hold of the valley. "I smell coffee. Mind if I grab a cup?"

I waved at the percolator on the stove, and Shilo got him a chipped mug from the meager store of dishes.

"We can't disturb her," Shilo whispered to him. "She's trying to figure out a recipe. She promised Mrs. Grace two dozen bran muffins for the old-age home today."

"Ah, muffins! For Golden Acres? That's swell."

Shilo stared at him. "Did you say that was 'swell'? I feel like I just stepped back into the fifties."

McGill grinned at her, then sidled up next to me. "Say, Merry, I've always wondered, what's the difference between a muffin and a cupcake?"

Shilo groaned, hand on her head in dramatic fashion. "Oh, you've started her up now! Prepare to be lectured. You've just enrolled in Muffins 101."

"Huh?" he said, looking back and forth between us.

I bit my lip to keep from laughing at the tragic look on my friend's face. *She's just heard the lecture once too often,* I thought. "You go feed your bunny, or something, while I tell McGill all about it." I got the other three sets of my brand-new muffin tins out of the bag—I think I had wiped out the town of Autumn Vale where muffin tins were concerned—and washed them, then dried and lined them with paper cups as I answered McGill. "It's easy. Most people think that if it's frosted or iced, then it's a cupcake, but that's not so. Some muffins can be frosted, too. Instead, think of the difference between a banana cake and a loaf of banana bread."

"Okay," he said. "I got that."

"Well, with the batter of a banana cake, you can make cupcakes, and with the batter for banana bread, you can make banana muffins. You can do the same with any cake batter or quick-bread batter."

"Ah!" he said, his eyes lighting up. "Cakes are to cupcakes as, uh, what did you call it?"

"Quick bread," Shilo, who had not gone to feed Magic, filled in.

"Right . . . cakes are to cupcakes as quick breads are to muffins!"

"Correct!" I scanned my pile of ingredients. I hadn't been able to find bran at the general store, so I'd bought a big box of bran cereal. "In general, muffins are denser and a little less sweet. They're a whole lot easier and less finicky than cupcakes, let me tell you, but right now I'd give my right arm for my cookbooks." Why hadn't I thrown them in the car instead of in a bin at the self-storage? Because I hadn't foreseen a retirement home full of seniors needing bran muffins. "Well, here goes."

"Feel free to experiment on me," McGill said. "But right now, I'd better get back to work."

For a few minutes, Shilo was my assistant, but eventually she wandered off, and I was left to work alone. I like it that way, when I'm baking. One batch came out too coarse and dry. I hadn't let the bran cereal soak up the moisture for long enough, I thought, so I increased the milk content and waited a little longer for the next batch. They turned out a lot better, and I tried another recipe that I vaguely remembered from my grandmother's handwritten recipe cards, locked in a storage container in Manhattan at that moment. In the end, I had two dozen each of banana bran and peanut butter–bran muffins, and a whole bunch suitable only for the birds. It had been good to cook again, even in the huge unfamiliarity of the castle kitchen, and I had gone overboard, as usual.

Once more I offered McGill lunch, and as we three ate at the long table, I pumped him for information on Sheriff Virgil Grace and his mother, the elegant Gogi Grace.

Gogi, he told me, was a local who had left Autumn Vale to go to college in the sixties; she did the hippie-chick thing for a few years—and had been at Woodstock, it was rumored—then came back to town and married a local boy. She would have loved my mother, I interjected. Mom always claimed she was at Woodstock, too, but then, there were a million or so people there, right? Anyway, McGill went on to explain that Virgil was her youngest, the only one of her kids who stayed in town. With Rusty Turner's help, she had bought and renovated Golden Acres, a century-old house that had been completely redone, with modern lifts so her oldsters didn't have to climb stairs.

"What about the sheriff?" I asked, still wondering about those scratches on his face and the long time it took to respond to our call the night before.

"Yeah, is he married?" Shilo, said, leaning against McGill's arm and batting her long eyelashes up at him.

McGill looked down at her, his mouth pursed, and said, "No, he's not. Why, you interested? You wouldn't be the first outsider to try to get him."

Shilo reared back and frowned. She looked especially pretty today, her long, black hair tied up in a ponytail with a paisley scarf. "I'm not interested," she sniffed, her dark eyes snapping with irritation. "I was asking for Merry!"

"Don't do me any favors." I said. "I'm just curious about him, McGill. How well do you know him? What's he like?"

He shrugged, his favorite evasion. "I've known him our whole lives. He's divorced, owns his own house, which I sold him, and works a lot. When his mom had breast cancer . . . whoops!" He looked stricken. "That's private info; I shouldn't have said anything."

"It's okay. Consider it forgotten," I said.

"Well, when she was sick, he looked after her. Her other kids don't get back to Autumn Vale much, but he's stayed."

"He sounds like a good guy," I mused.

McGill shifted in his seat. "He is," he said shortly. "I gotta go back to work. See you gals later."

"Swell," Shilo said softly, grinning up at him.

I showered and dressed carefully, choosing a soft, gray jersey Kiyonna wrap dress and letting my long, dark hair flow over my shoulders. I scanned myself in a cheval mirror in my bedroom, when a wolf whistle made me whirl around; Shilo stood at the door, grinning.

"Who are you dressing up for?" she asked. "Some man coming that I don't know about?"

I laughed and turned back to the mirror, making sure the dress tie was properly draped. "Don't you know? Women dress mainly to impress other women. You have to see Gogi Grace. That woman is stylish, and I don't want to look frumpy." I hooked sterling silver hoop earrings in my ears, slipped an art-glass pendant over my head, and stood looking at myself. It was good to have an occasion to dress nicely for, and I was glad I'd thrown the Kiyonna dress in my bag at the last minute.

"And she's the mother of that good-looking Sheriff Virgil Grace, right?"

"Yes, but that has nothing to do with anything," I said primly, slipping my feet into red Marc Jacobs pumps. "You were way out of line with what you said to McGill earlier. I'm not interested in him or anyone else. Let's go downstairs. If someone knocked on that gargantuan door, I wouldn't hear a thing from here."

"Doesn't the doorbell work?"

"I don't know, I never thought of—"

Just then a sonorous gong sounded.

"It works," we both said at once, and laughed.

I clattered down the stairs and across the flagstone floor, followed by Shilo, then threw the door open for Mrs. Grace, who entered bearing a large box with a huge bow on top.

"Housewarming gift, my dear," she said, as she handed it to me and walked past. "Or should I say castle-warming?"

I handed the box to Shilo with raised eyebrows, and followed Mrs. Grace, who had strolled into the middle of the great hall and was looking around.

"I haven't been in here for years," she said, slipping off her violet cashmere wrap. "Melvyn got a little . . . odd . . . these last few years."

"Odd? In what way?" I folded her wrap and put it on the side table in the entryway.

Gogi met my eyes and smiled. "Patience, my dear. I have a feeling that there is a lot you would like to know about your uncle, and Wynter Castle, but one step at a time."

I watched her eyes, veiled today by a fringe of soft, silver bangs. There was something there beyond what she was saying. I remembered what I had said to Shilo about the woman being a valuable ally, and nodded. I could be patient. But still, I was curious. First things first: I introduced Gogi to Shilo, and both women looked each other over.

"Jack McGill told me about your friend," Gogi said, taking Shi's hand and giving it a gentle shake. "He mentioned how beautiful you are, Shilo. I haven't heard him say that for a long time."

My friend smiled, then pardoned herself to go clean Magic's cage.

As Gogi and I started up the stairs for her tour, I said, "I hear that Rusty Turner did the renovations on your retirement home."

"True. There are a few handymen in Autumn Vale, and they can do things like installing a toilet or painting a room, but Turner Construction was virtually the only game in town for large operations."

We walked through the castle, but she clearly knew it a lot better than I did. I felt like I was being guided the whole way, by how she turned into a room I hadn't intended to enter, or walked along the gallery, showing me the view from above of the gigantic crystal chandelier that was still draped in what she called a "Holland cloth."

"When I was planning my wedding," she said, leaning on the oak railing, "back many years ago, I always thought I'd like to be married here. I'd have a harpist up here so the sound would float down, like it was coming from heaven."

When we descended the stairs to the main floor, she headed for the breakfast parlor, one of the two turret-shaped rooms in the front corners of the castle. She flung open the double doors and walked into the middle near a cloth-draped dining table. "I always pictured this as a tearoom."

Shilo had rejoined us, and followed her in, while I was last. My brain flooded with images as I slowly walked around the circular table in the center . . . I could see it. Shelves with my best teapots covering one wall . . . the antique sideboard— it was covered in a Holland cloth right now, but Shilo and I had peeked under the cloth, and it was a gorgeous Eastlake beauty—adorned with silver trays of treats . . . small tables dotted around the large room, and lots of people at the tables, enjoying tea and muffins.

Gogi was smiling as I looked up into her eyes, and nodded. "Jack is right about you," she said. "You've got the vision."

Shilo and I exchanged glances. "I was only here once, when I was about five," I said.

"I know."

"You . . . know?"

"Melvyn and my husband used to drink together at the tavern. Mel was upset about something that happened between your mother and him. He wanted to make it up to her, but she would never take his phone calls, and sent back letters with 'deceased' written on them."

Why had my mother shut out my father's only living relative like that? Life had not been easy. We had to move in with Grandma because Mom just could not make ends meet on her own. She was a typist for many years at a law firm that took on a lot of pro bono civil rights cases, but eventually arthritis crippled her hands and she couldn't work. So why had she shut out the one family member who may have been able to help?

I had been assuming it was some kind of argument related to my mother's quixotic sense of right and wrong, but it could have been other things, things I didn't know about. It could even have had to do with my father, or his inheritance, or . . . who knew? Had Mom gone to Uncle Melvyn for financial aid, and he refused? I asked Gogi that.

"I don't know what happened," she said with a sympathetic smile. "I wish I did. I can see you've got a lot of questions."

"Why didn't Uncle Melvyn come see us in New York, if he was so concerned?"

"I think he did, but Charmaine still wouldn't see him."

"Maybe we should go to the kitchen. I have a few muffins for you to taste." I felt numb, flooded with strange new insights about my father's side of the family. I had been relatively content for the last thirty-four years with not knowing anything concrete about this part of my past. But by coming to Wynter Castle I had pried the lid off a can of worms, the story of the Wynter side of my DNA.

I needed time alone to process what I was learning. In all the months of having this inheritance, I had never once thought that coming to Autumn Vale would answer some decades-old questions. And pose a whole lot more.

McGill came in from the butler's pantry just as we entered the kitchen from the other direction. "Hey, Mrs. G, Shilo! I got five more holes filled in, Merry," he said, eyeing Shilo with a bit of a smile. "I've got to go, but I'll be back tomorrow. I've locked the Bobcat; maybe that will keep your late-night gopher out of it."

Gogi looked from one of us to the other, and I told her what had happened the night before, surprised that her son hadn't filled her in on the event.

"And you say something attacked your hole digger?"

"Some kind of cat, I'd say."

"Becket!" Gogi exclaimed.

"Do you think so?" McGill asked.

"What are you two talking about?"

The realtor said, keeping his eye on Gogi, "Melvyn had a cat named Becket, but that animal disappeared the very night after Mel died. I thought he got himself killed."

"This was no housecat," I demurred.

"Oh, there is nothing ordinary about Becket," Gogi said. "He's a big fellow, a ginger tom."

"Ginger," I said. That was another word for orange, like the flash of orange I had seen at the edge of the woods and in the attack on the unknown hole digger. But still . . . "No housecat could survive in the woods for almost a year, and all through the winter," I said, shaking my head. "We'll see you tomorrow, McGill."

"Right-o. Gotta go. See you, Shilo!" He exited.

"Isn't he cute?" Shilo said, racing to the window to watch him leave, her black ponytail swinging. "He rhymed everything with my name!"

I ignored her odd infatuation with the lanky realtor and turned to the muffins on the worktable. "I'd like you to try these, Mrs. Grace," I said. "Let me know what you think."

"You're to call me Gogi, my dear, everyone does." But the woman obediently tasted one of the buttered bran muffins. "Mmm!" she said, nodding, her mouth full. "These are splendid!"

"I can give the recipe to your cook."

"She won't have time to make them," Gogi said with regret, brushing crumbs from her fingers. "I simply couldn't ask it of the poor woman. She's already overworked. And any new staff I hire has to be for the guests' health care."

She squinted over at me, a calculating look in her blue eyes. "How much would you charge me for, say, ten dozen assorted muffins a week?"

"Ten *dozen*? As in one hundred and twenty muffins? Every week?"

"Sure."

"But I'm not staying here!" I exclaimed.

"You're staying long enough to fix the castle up and sell it, right?"

"Yes, but—"

"Then you'll need something to do." The woman took a calculator out of her shoulder bag, slipped on a pair of glamorous, rhinestone-studded cheaters, and tapped at the number keys. "It's just for the short term, until I can source muffins and cookies. You'll need to get the kitchen inspected so I can buy the muffins from you."

"I beg your pardon?"

"State rules. I can take *these* because they are a gift," she said, fluttering her hand at the muffins. "But if I buy muffins from you for the oldsters, they need to be made in a commercially licensed kitchen. This one is fitted with everything it needs, you just have to have it licensed."

Shilo snickered, and I threw her a warning glance, before saying, "Mrs. Grace . . . Gogi . . . I have no intention of going into the muffin business, so there is no need to get the kitchen commercially licensed. Period." I was putting my foot down. She was not going to run me over again.

"Maybe I misunderstood," she said, head cocked to one side. "You're thinking that this place could be sold to become an inn or event venue, right? That's what Jack McGill told me."

"Yes, I'm hoping so."

"If the kitchen is already commercially licensed, that's one step toward selling it for one of those uses."

It made a dreadful kind of inevitable sense. "I'll think about it."

"Per dozen, times ten," Gogi said, and showed me the sum on the calculator.

It wasn't a fortune, but it would help pay the utility bills while I stayed. "I'll make coffee," I murmured, a little stunned at the way things were moving along.

She slipped her glasses and the calculator in her shoulder bag. We sat, ate a couple more muffins with steaming coffee, and she told me about Turner Wynter, the development company Rusty Turner and my uncle had co-owned. It employed both Tom Turner, Binny's brother, and Dinah Hooper, Rusty's girlfriend.

"Turner Wynter was a real estate development company," I reiterated. "Was it going well? This is kind of the boonies for development, especially with the economy the way it's been for the last few years."

"I won't say they got along well," Gogi, said, her well-shaped brows raised. "There was quite a bit of trouble in the last little while before Melvyn died, some lawsuits about the business. Most of the townsfolk sided with Rusty because no one got along with Melvyn except me and Doc English, one of my residents."

"Things got that bad?"

"Two men like Rusty and Melvyn were never going to work together well. Things got pretty heated. Virgil had to step in a couple of times, because the two old fellows got into fisticuffs."

"Fistfights?" I said. "*Really?* What did they do, a swing and a miss, or was it walkers at dawn?"

Shilo snorted, but Gogi only smiled. "You'd be surprised the damage a couple of old guys can do to each other. Believe me, I've had to deal with it at my home. And even though Rusty was not as old as Melvyn, he's the one who ended up on the short end of the stick. Your uncle was not afraid to whip out a rifle to defend his property. That's one of the things that made me wonder . . ." She shut her mouth and shook her head. "Never mind."

"No, go on . . . what were you going to say?" I asked.

She stared at me for a moment, but when she spoke again it was about the night Rusty Turner disappeared, and how my uncle Melvyn died, exactly one month later. Rusty was just there one day, and gone the next, she said. All kinds of rumors swirled, but his girlfriend, Dinah, appeared heartbroken and said she didn't know where he went. One story was that he had removed a large amount of cash from the bank, and called someone he knew from the city; he was on the run, some said. But no one knew for sure. Tom Turner swore Melvyn had murdered him, at last, after all their fights, and buried him somewhere on the property.

Then on an icy day in late November, an early frost slicking the road on the rocky ridge, Melvyn was driving; no one ever knew where or why so early in the morning. It was thought that he lost control on a bend and went off a cliff, his car exploding in flames when it hit the bottom, near the river.

"But I knew Melvyn fairly well," Gogi said, leaning across the table. "Why was he driving that time of morning? Even though he'd gone a little peculiar, he still knew he was getting on, and that his skills weren't what they used to be. And where was he going? I just don't believe he was out there alone. Or if he was, that he went off that cliff by accident."

"Are you implying that he was *murdered*?"

She nodded and pursed her lips, sitting back in her chair. "But no one, not even my own son, will take it seriously."

Chapter Six

❊ ❊ ❊

I HATED TO say it, but had to. "Maybe that's because it's not murder."

Gogi shrugged, an elegant insouciance in her manner. "I suppose no one will ever know, but I'll always believe Melvyn's death wasn't an accident."

There was no real answer to that, and we sat in awkward silence for a long minute. "I'm curious about Binny Turner, the owner of the bake shop," I finally said as I got up to make a pot of tea. I was coffeed out, and needed my caffeine in a gentler form. "I get the impression she won't make anything she deems 'ordinary.' What gives with that?"

"What are you talking about?" Shilo asked.

We both explained Binny Turner's bake shop to Shilo, who said, "She made the focaccia we had for breakfast? Why doesn't she just open a bakery in New York? I'd sure go there." Shilo, like many models, loves to eat, and irritatingly does not gain an ounce. Superfast metabolism, she's always said.

"She seems to have a mission to get the people of Autumn Vale to broaden their tastes."

Gogi smiled and nodded. "Her dad put her through cooking school and she apprenticed for a year in Paris. But she'd get a lot more people in if she made some other goods, like muffins and peanut butter cookies."

"She seemed pretty busy."

"Only because she sells her wares for too little. If she sold them for what they were worth, no one would come in."

"Hmm, you're right there," I agreed. "But costs must be a lot lower here than if she had a shop in Manhattan."

"Maybe. She lived with her mom for most of her life, but after her dad offered to put her through school, they got closer."

"And then he disappeared. Must be tough on her."

Gogi shook her head, and said, "I feel for the girl, I really do." She watched me get up and toss a tea bag into a saucepan, and said, "Merry, why don't you open that housewarming gift I brought?"

"Okay," I said, and retrieved it. I set it on the table and took the gorgeous, pink gauze bow off the large robin's egg–blue box, then lifted the lid. There, nestled in pink tissue, was a teapot—and not just any teapot, but a real Brown Betty. I lifted it from the box and smiled.

Shilo stared at it, her forehead wrinkled in puzzlement, while Gogi watched.

"Thank you," I said, not trusting the steadiness of my voice to say more.

"Do you like it?"

"I do. So much!"

"Do you know what it is?" she asked.

Shilo laughed out loud. "Who doesn't know what a teapot is? Do you think we're from the Antarctic or something?"

Gogi stifled a laugh while I shot my friend a look. "It's a Brown Betty," I answered. "It looks just like the one my grandmother used to make tea for all her Village cronies in our apartment in New York. Every Friday afternoon, her old friends would come around and they would have tea and 'muffings,' as I called them when I was little." My vision blurred, and before I knew it I was sobbing, great wrenching, embarrassing sobs.

"Oh, no, what did I . . . is she okay?" I heard Gogi say.

"I don't know," Shilo said. "I've never seen her do this before, not even when her husband died!"

Two sets of arms were soon around me, and I just let it all go, the years of pent-up anguish that I had been holding onto even through my most recent tribulations, the accusations of theft leveled at me by someone I had once considered a friend. Stupid that a teapot finally broke my control, but that's what happened. To my surprise I could feel and hear that the other two women were sniffling and sobbing, too.

After a minute, I blindly reached out and someone— probably Gogi, because Shilo was never prepared for anything—pressed a tissue into my hand. I dabbed my eyes, carefully pressing the tissue under them to staunch the flow of tears and keep the inevitable trails of mascara to a minimum, then blew my nose.

"Feel better?" Gogi said, her lovely pale eyes on mine. She smiled gently.

I could see no evidence that she had wept, and wondered if I was wrong after all. Shilo had tears still pooling in her eyes as she mournfully gazed over at me. I took a deep breath, cradled the Brown Betty in my arms, and said, "You know what? I *do* feel better."

"I'm so glad you didn't apologize for crying," Gogi said. "I've always wondered why men think of crying as a weakness, when it is what helps women vent, then stand up and do what needs to be done. It's a sign of strength, not weakness."

"Then I must be a *really* strong woman," Shilo said with a long sniff.

Gogi handed her another tissue, and my friend blew her nose. "So what happened to your grandmother's Brown Betty?" the older woman asked.

"It broke the day she died. My mother dropped it while she was trying to make tea. I think she was stifling how awful she felt, and she was shaking from the effort. I didn't know what to say; she just seemed to not want me to help, or comfort her, or anything."

"I think it's hard for a mother to let her kids see her cry," Gogi said. "Virgil hates it, but he's good about letting me do what I need to do."

I knew she was likely referring to grief and pain during her battle with breast cancer, but didn't say anything. If she wanted me to know, she'd tell me. I made tea in the lovely pot, poured for us all, and told Gogi about my teapot collection, and how I had felt a kinship for Binny the moment I saw her cool collection of teapots.

Shilo said. "You mean there is another woman in the world obsessed with teapots? And I thought you were the lone lunatic!"

I smiled. "Nope, there are a lot of us."

"Merry, since you're here for a while, I wonder if you'd consider doing something?"

I was wary immediately; Gogi Grace already had me agreeing to make 120 muffins a week, and that was about the limit of what could be expected from me, I would hope. "Uh, I don't know. Do you need a kidney?"

Her eyes widened and she was startled into laughter. "No, I have very healthy parts, thank you very much, and the ones that weren't healthy were lopped off."

Again, I caught her wry reference to breast cancer, but I wouldn't have understood it if McGill hadn't already spilled the beans.

She drank the last gulp of her tea and stood. "I want you to think about something you could do while here. Since I can't get my darling son to take me seriously, I wonder, would you sniff around and see if Melvyn's death seems on the level to you?"

I was not expecting that and I laughed, thinking she was

joking. She apparently wasn't. I coughed, shrugged, and looked to Shilo for help.

But she was watching me, too, and said, "Maybe you should, Mer. I mean, he was your uncle, and he left you this big, beautiful castle! Poor guy . . . hey, maybe *he* could tell us what happened?"

I gave her an exasperated look. "Shi, really? Do you remember what happened the last time you tried to hold a séance?"

She had the good grace to look embarrassed. I turned to Gogi, who had a definite question in her eyes. "Shilo fancies herself a gypsy. We held a séance to contact my grandmother at Shi's place. Shilo invited some friends, and the lights were out."

Shilo snickered, and I threw her a dirty look.

"What happened?" Gogi said.

"My friend Gregory got fresh with Merry," Shi said, giggling. "She decked him, and at the same time my bunny—his name is Magic—had gotten loose and hopped up onto the table, turned the candle over, and sent my neighbor shrieking out of the room and down to the superintendent to tell him my apartment was possessed."

"And the candle set fire to the tablecloth and we had to put it out with the wine I'd brought," I finished.

"But you had enough left to throw some in Gregory's face," Shi finished, still giggling.

"And your neighbor was *really* scared because you kept yelling 'Magic! Magic!' like a maniac, and she thought you were out of your gourd, when you were just yelling at your rabbit."

Gogi Grace laughed heartily, but then finally said, with a sigh, "I have to get going. It's getting toward supper, and some of the oldsters need help getting to the dining room. I'm always there at dinner."

"I'll bag these muffins for you," I said. "And maybe pop them in a box; it might make them easier to carry. Four dozen muffins are kind of heavy. We'll bring them out to the car for you."

She graciously accepted our help, and Shilo and I followed her out to her car, parked by my rental in the weedy driveway. She put the muffins on the passenger seat and slammed the door. She surveyed the potholed land with her hand shading her eyes from the slanting sun, then her gaze settled on me. "You didn't answer my question. Will you at least think about looking into Melvyn's death?"

I felt uneasy, and I wasn't sure why. An old man had died going off a slippery highway. There didn't seem to be much of a mystery there, but then, Gogi Grace knew my uncle, and I didn't. "Your son is professional law enforcement; if there was something there, I'd think he'd know."

"He thinks I'm imagining things, but there were so many people who didn't like Melvyn. And with his dealings with Rusty . . ." She shook her head. "The whole thing has upset me."

"I'll think about it."

"Promise me you'll *really* think about it, not just let some time lapse then say no."

I shifted from one foot to another. She had certainly caught me at what I was planning. "I will seriously think about it, I promise," I said, meeting her gaze.

She came around the car to me and enfolded me in a warm hug. "Thank you, Merry. And you, too, Shilo. You know, you're right about Jack McGill," she said, winking at my friend. "He is cute, and he's a very smart fellow. A good catch!" She waved, popped into her car, and drove away.

As I watched her go, I had the troubling thought that maybe I *would* have to look into my uncle's death. If it had anything to do with the Turners' obsession with my property, and even, perhaps, their father's disappearance, I might need to know so I could protect myself and my inheritance.

Chapter Seven

✳ ✳ ✳

T HE NEXT MORNING I left Shilo to "supervise" McGill's hole filling. I was going to need to take back my rental car eventually, but not yet. Once I did, I would be relegated to borrowing Shilo's rattletrap ancient vehicle, which I didn't relish, or buying a car, which suited me even less, so for the next little while I'd stay with the rental.

I drove into Autumn Vale, intent on a few errands. Ingratiating myself to the locals was on my list, but first I was going to visit the lawyer. I had talked to Andrew Silvio many times over the last few months as he probated the will, but I had never met him. Gogi had given me directions to his office, and I found it with relatively little trouble. It was on the first floor of a beautiful, old house that had been converted to offices.

The central foyer, from which an impressive staircase wound up to a second floor, had a brass plate announcing whose offices were in the Autumn Vale Professional Suites. There was a doctor, a dentist, a chiropodist, and a licensed private investigator, among other professionals. I entered the glass door that had "Andrew Silvio" etched on it in gold, and as I did, a buzzer sounded somewhere close; a short, stocky man barreled out of an inner office. He looked around and saw me standing by the door.

"Miss Wynter, right?" he said, his voice gruff. "C'mon in. Nice day, huh? Take off your sweater. Want a coffee?"

I followed him into his inner sanctum, but didn't take off my sweater. I slung my bag over the back of a chair and took a seat across the mahogany desk from him as he sat, donned close-up glasses, and shuffled through papers on his desk. "No coffee for me, Mr. Silvio. I came just to introduce myself in person, and ask for some advice."

"Legal?" he asked, looking over the rims of his glasses at me.

"Not exactly." I put both hands on the surface of the desk and composed my thoughts. Wow, I needed a manicure. That's the first thought I had. Then I thought some more. "You knew my uncle."

"I did. I was his legal representative in estate matters."

"Why did he leave the castle to me?"

Silvio shrugged. "You're his niece."

"I know, but my mom had been estranged from him for well over thirty years. I'm just surprised that he still wanted me to have it." I watched his face as his gaze shifted away.

He leaned back in his chair and plaited his fingers over his paunch. "One thing you may not know about Melvyn: the family name was important to him. He had me do research. He was pleased that despite your marriage, you kept the name Wynter."

"But I didn't. Not really. I took my husband's name, but when he died I went back to Wynter." I would have kept his name—I had loved being Mrs. Merry Paradiso—but I went back to my maiden name at the request of his family, who had never been fond of me. His mother blamed me for his staying in the States and dying here.

He shrugged. "Same thing."

"If he had you do research on me, why didn't he contact me? I don't get it."

The lawyer gazed at me for a long minute. "You know, death catches us all unaware, even an eighty-something-year-old man. I think he planned to contact you once he got a few things sorted out."

"A few . . . what, like the lawsuits between him and Rusty Turner?"

"You've heard about that, huh?"

"Did you represent one of the men? Which one?"

"I was not able to represent either gentleman, since it would have been a conflict of interest in this particular case," he said, threading his fingers together, the heavy ring on his wedding finger tripping up the action.

"Why?"

"I drew up the partnership papers, so it would have been deemed that I had special knowledge of Rusty's business that would not necessarily be the case in the general run of things."

"Who *did* my uncle use?"

"He retained a lawyer from Ridley Ridge, a very competent fellow . . . can't recall his name right now."

"Okay," I said, disappointed. I had hoped for some information on the state of the lawsuits. Well, I had yet to go through my uncle's papers; maybe I'd find more information there. "What was the nature of my uncle and Rusty Turner's partnership?"

"Pretty simple, kind of an exploratory company to figure out if it was worthwhile to develop your uncle's land for a condo neighborhood. That's all I know," he said firmly.

Given his desperate plans to try to monetize the Wynter estate, probably so he could keep the castle running, I wondered how Uncle Melvyn would feel about my plan to sell it. Nothing I could do about that, though. I couldn't keep it. "I'm curious about Wynter Castle. If I'm going to sell it, it might help to write up a little history, you know, of anything important or interesting that happened there. Do you know anything about it?"

"Not a thing. I married into Autumn Vale; my wife is from around here, but I'm not. If you want to know more, maybe you should go to the library. The girl who runs it is a local."

Now to broach a more delicate subject. "Mr. Silvio, I have heard some local talk that Melvyn was responsible for Rusty Turner's death, or at least his disappearance."

"Pfah!" he said, with a wave of one broad, ringed hand. "Gossip. People like to speculate, you know? Melvyn would never have done something like that."

Okay, now for the even touchier part. "It has been suggested, too, that maybe Melvyn was murdered by the same person responsible for Mr. Turner's disappearance."

He sat up straight and glared at me across the desk. "Miss Wynter, I think you've been listening to a lot of small-town folk who are bored and find that speculating about murder makes their day more interesting. End of story. Poor old Melvyn was heading to Rochester. He told me he was going to go one day, and I told him to wait until the weather got better, but he was a stubborn old bird and his eyesight wasn't so good."

He could be right about bored locals speculating. Even Gogi Grace, as levelheaded as she seemed, could just be in it for the titillation. How much did I truly know about anyone in Autumn Vale? I stood and stuck my hand out. "Thank you for your time today, Mr. Silvio. May I come back if I have further questions about the estate?"

"Sure!" he said, reaching across and taking my hand. "Come back any time. I always like to see a pretty face."

I smiled automatically at the intended compliment and showed myself to the door. I walked out of the house slash office building and looked up and down the street. I was just steps away from Abenaki Avenue, so I strolled toward it, getting my bearings as I went. Autumn Vale was indeed a "vale," located in a valley between two rocky prominences. Maybe that was why cell phones did not seem to work, nor did the GPS in my rental.

Or maybe it was just that Autumn Vale is a truly weird little place. I stood at the corner of Abenaki and Wallace and watched the locals go by. There was an assortment of colorful individuals. One elderly fellow wearing an obvious yellowish wig came out of a variety store with a pack of cigarettes. He lifted the wig, balanced a few dollar bills on his bald pate, and plopped the toupee back down. Cool wallet.

I also recognized the old guy I had frightened the first morning in the village, when I mentioned Wynter Castle. He shuffled along, this time wearing a woman's straw sun bonnet and a pink plaid sweater. I wondered if he was one of Gogi's folks.

As I stood observing, I saw a big guy in a red-and-black-plaid jacket and unlaced boots strolling down the street. I was close enough that I had a good look at his face, and could see some long, angry-looking scratches from his temple down across his cheek. Interested in anyone showing such wounds, I sprinted to the sidewalk and followed him right up to Binny's Bakery and inside.

"Binny!" he yelled, and hammered on the counter.

I turned my back and examined the wall of teapots as a group of elderly ladies, all bundled up in woolen coats and hats—overkill on a coolish but still mild September day, but then, I wasn't eighty years old—entered and crowded around the pastry counter, oohing and aahing over the selection. Maybe Binny had something there about refining the locals' palates, one pfeffernusse at a time.

The baker came out from the back, politely greeted the group of ladies, and then said, "Tom, do you have to yell and beat on the counter? What do you want?"

"Dinah left me a message; she said to tell you that she lost her key to the office, and could you lend her yours?"

"Why?" Binny asked. "She's not even working there anymore."

I half turned around and watched.

"Don't ask me why she needs it. She just told me to get it." He put out his hand, palm up, and waggling his fingers. "Hand it over!"

"No! Tell her she can ask me herself if it's that important." She turned to her customers and began to help them choose their treats.

The penny dropped and I got who this was. I said, "You're Tom Turner!"

He looked me over, with a frown. He was a big enough fellow, dressed in stained work pants and dirt-encrusted boots. "Yeah, who are you?"

"Merry Wynter; I own Wynter Castle. Let me guess," I said eyeing the long, red scratches down his face. "You got those lovely marks when you started up an excavator on my property to dig some more huge holes, and got attacked by a cat!"

His face got red enough to match the scratches and he loomed over me. "What are you talking about?"

"Tom, don't talk to her!" Binny said, her voice shaking. She watched me, her dark eyes wide with fear. "Don't say anything."

"Why not? Afraid he'll incriminate himself?" I said, trying to egg him on into a confession. "What are you guys looking for on my property? You don't *honestly* think my ancient uncle Melvyn did away with your dad and buried him there?"

"You better shut up," Tom bellowed.

The old ladies clustered together and watched, breathless, clutching each other's arms in ghoulish delight.

"You going to make me?" I asked, in my best New York voice.

Binny had the phone in her hand and was dialing a number.

"I wouldn't push me, if I was you, lady."

"I'm not," I said, backing down a bit and making my tone reasonable, as common sense prevailed. No real point in goading him to violence. I took a deep breath. "But I know for a fact that you're the one damaging my property. I don't know *why* you're doing it, but I suggest you stop, now, or I'll have you arrested for trespassing next time."

"Tom, you keep your big mouth shut!" Binny warned, her hand over the phone receiver.

"*Or* just tell me the truth," I said. "Why are you doing it?"

"You can't prove *nothing*!" he said, his hands clenching into fists.

Only guilty people say that, and it made me mad. He was costing me a bunch, when all I wanted to do was sell the darned castle and scoot on back to New York. I got real close to him and looked up into his pouchy, red-veined eyes. Anger won out over common sense this time. "Look, you big goon," I said, jabbing his chest with my pointed finger. "You come out to my property one more time and I will not be responsible for what happens!"

He sputtered and made inarticulate noises in the back of his throat, but nothing else.

"I'm calling the cops!" Binny said, watching us both.

"Good," I said, moving toward the door. "Then I can tell Sheriff Grace exactly what I just told your brother, and *he* can look at those scratches."

She slammed the phone down and glared at me, saying, "Maybe you had better go."

Tom moved toward me slightly with a kind of growl in his throat, and I bolted outside. Heart pounding, I leaned against the brick wall. I hadn't meant to get so worked up, but when I thought of how scared I was in the night, and how much it was going to cost to fix up the damage he was doing, I just lost it. When Tom stomped out the door, I don't mind saying I hightailed it down the street, not wanting another confrontation. It was stupid to anger a guy who was that big and that short-tempered.

I strode down the sidewalk, heading who knew where, and dashed down a side street when I saw the sheriff's car cruising toward the bakery. I didn't know how to defend what I'd said, and didn't want to deal with Virgil Grace at that moment. I walked along for a short way, leaving behind the clustered stores and buildings of downtown Autumn Vale, such as it was. I was fuming mad, at first, and didn't much notice my surroundings, but the fog of fury began to dissipate.

I stopped and looked around; I was in a residential area now. The sign in front of me read Golden Acres. It was a lovely old manor, but didn't look big enough to be a rest home until I started to walk up the angled drive. As I got past some of the century trees that shaded the grounds, I could see that a small, modern addition had been built behind the house. The drive sloped up to a prominence, where several park benches were set in the shade of a grove of maples along a smooth pathway. Some of Gogi Grace's 'oldsters' were basking in the autumn sunshine, their faces turned upward like sunflowers, as the sound of warbling birds filled the air.

I nodded to them as I passed, and felt their eyes on me as I approached the door. I entered into a wide hallway, where a set of stairs ascended ahead of me and to the left. There was a reception desk, and the phone was ringing nonstop as the young woman who appeared to be the receptionist blocked the hallway.

"Mrs. Levitz, you can't go out right now," she said to an elderly woman. "It's almost lunch. Don't you want to stay and have lunch?"

The woman, wheeling along using a walker for support, had an angry look on her wrinkled face. She tried to dodge the girl, bellowing, "I'm going to see my mother. She's waiting for me. School is over, and she always walks me home."

"No, Mrs. Levitz, school's not over yet," the girl said, glancing to the left and right, probably looking for help.

"Yes, it is. You're lying. If there's anything I can't abide, it's a liar!" The woman plucked a stuffed animal out of the basket of her walker and chucked it. When the young girl dodged aside to pick it up out of the path of another resident, Mrs. Levitz rolled her walker around her and headed to the door.

I got in her way. "Ma'am, can you help me?"

The receptionist dashed behind her desk and hit a buzzer and another button. I could hear the lock on the front door *snick* into place.

"Who are you?" the old woman asked, glaring at me. "Are you one of the teachers?"

Just then, a big fellow in scrubs dashed down the hallway, and gently took Mrs. Levitz by the arm. "Dotty, your son is coming to see you this afternoon. Don't you want to stay in? He's going to come visit, and then he'll take you for a long walk." He gave the receptionist an apologetic shrug, and muttered, "She got away from Angie and we didn't notice. Sorry, Jen."

He got Mrs. Levitz turned around, confusion now wrinkling her brow as she plaintively asked, "I have a son?"

The receptionist swiftly answered the phone, transferred the caller, unlocked the door, and then smiled at me. "Thank you."

"It was nothing," I said. "Does she really think she was going to meet her mother? She must be about ninety!"

"Ninety-six and still hell on walker wheels," the girl said and laughed. "Heavens . . . her son is over seventy! The dottiest ones are the most able to get about."

She had a lilting Irish accent, and I smiled. "And Dotty is dotty, it seems."

"Can I help you?" she asked.

"I was wondering if Gogi Grace is here?"

The receptionist hit a buzzer, and said, "Mrs. Grace, someone to see you. Your name?" She looked up at me.

"Merry Wynter," I said and she repeated it.

My new friend, today dressed in a soft-purple suit with businesslike gray pumps and a purple paisley scarf draped around her neck, emerged from a door down the hall and beckoned to me. "Come along, Merry. I'll give you the tour."

The modern addition was small, but clean and bright, with bedrooms off a square, open area centered by a nurse's station. There were two dining rooms, she told me, one for the mobile folk, and another for those who needed more room and more help. The second floor of the new section was much the same as the first; an elevator with wider-than-normal doorways and a deeper cabinet accommodated motorized wheelchairs, and could even be used for transporting patients who were bedridden. "Turner Construction, Rusty Turner's company, did all the work on this seven years ago," Gogi said.

"It turned out well!" I replied, impressed by the neat, simple layout.

She took me out a side door on the main floor and showed me the protected garden, cradled in the *L* shape between the modern addition and the old building. "Rusty did this a couple of years ago," she said, pointing out the six-foot-high privacy fencing, safe even for those with dementia who might wander off, since there was no external access except a locked gate.

"So all of this is in the newly built area; what's in the older section?" I asked.

"I'll show you that now."

I followed Gogi, who was talking as she went; upstairs in the old section were suites for those who could manage stairs and were more independent. We descended the wide, sweeping staircase, as she explained that on the main floor were the social rooms. She led me to what was probably once the dining room and parlor, linked by pocket doors, which were open. There were tables set up sporadically, and settees and shelves with books lined one wall. A few gentlemen and ladies were seated in some of the comfortable wing chairs near the fireplace and by the front window. Some were reading, others chatting, and one was just watching everyone else.

"We call this the library."

A pudgy teenager with dark, frizzy hair pulled back in a tight ponytail carried in a tray laden with cups, sugar, milk, and spoons. She set it on the table in the corner. When she straightened, she noticed Gogi, and her sullen expression, mouth turned down in resentment, changed to one of uncertainty.

"Pardon me a moment," Gogi said, then crossed the room and took her aside, speaking to her for a few minutes. The girl nodded, wiped away a tear, and nodded again. When they were done, the girl impulsively reached out and hugged Gogi. After that, her expression lighter, she went to each lady and gentleman in the room and offered tea or coffee.

"What was that all about?" I asked.

Gogi watched the girl for a long moment, then drew me aside. "I wouldn't normally say anything; I try not to let people become prejudiced before they meet her, you know. She's here on community service," she murmured. She met my gaze, and answered the question in my eyes. "Graffiti. She was caught in the cemetery spray-painting awful slogans on gravestones."

"Is this the right place for her?" I asked, a little shocked that they would put her with the elderly.

"Oh, I think so, with careful supervision, of course. In fact, I asked for her. I followed the case in the local paper, and when I learned that she had been abandoned by her mother and left in the care of her grandmother, who no longer could control her, I knew she was going to end up in a group home. I was afraid she'd never learn or understand why she was angry. She needs to figure that out if she's going to get past it."

I was silent for a long minute as I watched the girl caught by one old gentleman, who grabbed her arm and asked her something. She looked like she was ready to flee, but one look from Gogi kept her in place. She sat down, and before long the old man was talking to her intently, and she was listening. *Truly* listening; I could tell.

"That's Hubert Dread. He has the most interesting stories. Not all of them are true, but they are interesting."

"So, you think her graffiti problem was a result of . . ." I raised my eyebrows, a question in my tone.

"Fear. Anger. She was raging against living with an old woman who didn't understand her, and yet at the same time she was afraid of losing her grandma." Gogi sighed and shook her head. "That's an oversimplification, and I don't mean to play armchair psychiatrist, but it's a beginning. She seems a little better already. It was a gamble; working here could have made her more angry, but it's turning out the way I hoped."

As Gogi led me to an alcove to sit, an old man wandered in, the one wearing the sunbonnet.

"He *does* live here!" I said. "Who *is* that fellow?"

"Well, actually, that is someone I'd like you to meet," Gogi said. She went to him and took his arm, saying something as she led him over. "Merry, this is Doc English. Doc, this is Merry Wynter, Melvyn's niece, the one who inherited the castle."

His pouched blue eyes, filmed by cataracts, lit up and he put one gnarled hand on my arm. "Hey, I've seen you before. You're the one asked me where Wynter Castle was a few days ago. Scared the crap out of me; I thought you were a ghost, that early in the morning."

I glanced at Gogi, then back at the old guy. "Doc, you do know you're wearing a lady's straw sunbonnet, right?" I said. I didn't mention the pink-plaid sweater.

He grinned, his own real teeth a kind of yellow and spotty collection in his mouth. "I sure do. Nice girl, the nurse this morning, but she said I'd get a melanoma if I didn't wear a hat. So I grabbed the first one I saw. *Then* she said I'd catch cold if I didn't wear a sweater, so I borrowed hers. Then I headed out for my constitutional. If I walk every day," he explained to me, "I'll never lose the ability."

I chuckled. He had a point, and an interesting one it was. That explained the random selection of headgear.

"You're the one made us the muffins, hey?" he said, eyeing me. "You making more?"

"I am."

"Bran's good . . . keeps the pooper working . . . but what about carrot?"

"I love carrot! I'll make some for the next batch."

"Doc, Merry had some questions about Melvyn. Could she ask you about her uncle?"

"Sure. Get me some coffee instead of that colored water the girl is bringing around, and I'll tell you anything you want to know."

Chapter Eight

✖ ✖ ✖

"I'LL GET HIM some of my private stash," Gogi said. "We share a love of cappuccino!" She trotted away, her paisley scarf fluttering behind her.

"What do you want to know?" Doc asked, after I made sure he was comfortable in an armchair by the wall of books.

I thought about it for a minute. What *did* I want to know? "What was my uncle like? I only met him once, and that was just for a few minutes."

"Yeah, your mother was a pip, hey? Didn't take to old Mel too good."

"So you knew about my very brief trip here," I said, and he nodded, his expression neutral. "Do you know why they argued?"

He shrugged. "Maybe. Maybe not."

The young girl, done with her conversation with the old fellow, brought the tray of mugs around and asked if we wanted a drink. I said yes, but Gogi came back into the lounge at that moment with a special mug for Doc.

"Here you go; don't say I never do anything for you," she said, dropping him a wink. "You two okay here?"

I nodded as the girl brought me a mug of coffee. "Thank you," I said, and she offered a hint of a smile. "What's your name?"

"Lizzie," she said.

"Well, thank you, Lizzie, I appreciate the coffee."

The girl went on to the next set of folks. Gogi nodded. "Okay, I've got a lot to do before lunch; if you two are comfortable, I'll see you again, right?"

"I'll have another batch of muffins for you tomorrow," I said. "Two dozen carrot and the same of apple spice, maybe."

Doc sipped his coffee and closed his eyes. "Good stuff. Just what the doc ordered," he muttered. When he opened his eyes, he fixed his gaze on me. "You look a lot like your mother."

"You saw her?"

"Nah, saw photos. Mel kept one in his room of you with your mom and dad."

I knew the photo he meant; there weren't that many. It was of me and my parents on the observation deck of the Empire State Building. My father I only remembered vaguely as a shadowy, comforting figure. "My dad spent time at the castle, didn't he?"

"He was a great kid," Doc said with a reminiscent grin, showing his yellowed teeth. "Broke his arm jumping off the parapet once; thought he could fly."

"Honestly?" I was uneasily aware that my knowledge of my dad was so sketchy, I didn't even know whether he was normally a daredevil kind of guy. A little overwhelmed, I blinked back tears, which had begun to well.

Doc regarded me with sympathy in his old, rheumy eyes. He had surrendered the sun hat, but still had on the pink-plaid sweater. I cleared my throat, but found I couldn't say another word for the moment.

"You know, we don't hafta talk about it all at once," he

said, and patted my hand. "You can come back and ask about your pop another time. 'Bout Melvyn, too. Why don't we talk about the castle, first? You planning on keeping it?"

"I don't see how I can. What would I do with it? How could I afford to keep it?" Even if I wanted to stay in remote Autumn Vale, I thought, but did not add.

"You think that hasn't dogged the last four generations of Wynters, how to keep the castle running? Ever since your family lost all its money—"

"All its money?" I blurted out. "Were we rich?"

"Now, how do you think that castle got built in the first place?"

He had a point. At one time the Wynters must have been very rich, but like me, they had been foolish and lost their money. Seems it ran in the family. "You're right. I guess I knew that. How did that come about? And how did we lose the money?"

He waved one hand. "You want the castle history, you go talk to that little gal who's set up the library. She's got all kinds of info there, some useful, most not. But I can tell you about Melvyn, if you like."

And he did just that for the next hour. I heard about the hijinks back in the day; he and Melvyn were school buddies. They went off to university together, then served in "the big one," as Doc called World War II. Doc came back to Autumn Vale, married, and had a bunch of kids, while Melvyn . . . well, he just started working on converting Wynter Castle into something that could make money rather than lose money. I was left with a sad sense that I would have liked Melvyn, if I had ever gotten to know him.

"But my dad, he was Melvyn's brother's kid, right?"

Doc slurped back the last of his cappuccino, smacked his lips, then burped. "Yup. Your daddy was the only son of Murgatroyd Wynter, Melvyn's younger brother by about three years. Murg was a good kid. Married a local girl, had one kid—your pa—but his wife, your grandma, she died real young. Anyway, Murg and Mel started working on Wynter castle, and planting trees, with your daddy running after them on his short little legs. Mel always said there was money in trees."

"What did that mean?"

"Damned if I know." He yawned mightily, as a buzzer sounded somewhere. At once, the old folks all got up and headed out of the room. Doc got up, too, and picked up his empty cup.

"What's going on?"

"Lunch, my girl, lunch. No old person misses a meal if they can help it. Never know when it's your last, I guess. You should see some of these genteel old biddies scarf down their food. 'Specially dessert."

I jumped to my feet. "But . . . but I want to find out so much . . . like, how did Murgatroyd, my grandfather, die? And when? And what about my grandmother, Murgatroyd's wife? What was she *like*? And what did Uncle Melvyn plan for the castle? And my mom . . . what did she and Melvyn argue about? You said you might know."

He shrugged and yawned again. "I'm gonna eat, then have a nap. Nothing like an after-lunch nap to get you through the day."

Subtle but effective, that stopped me in my tracks. "Well, it was nice meeting you, Doc. May I come back?"

"Come back all you want! And next time I see you while I'm out for my walk, we'll walk together."

I picked up all the ingredients I'd need for the next day's muffins, and headed back to the castle, to find that my handyman-slash-real estate agent had gotten another few holes filled, and Shilo had made him a lunch that was more fit for Magic than McGill. Rabbit food, in other words. He was picking away at his salad when I came in, and looked up at me with hope in his eyes. I shook my head, and he sighed, a sad man doomed to a veggie-heavy lunch. I took salad, too, and we chatted for a few moments, but he had to get going to show a house in another town for a fellow real estate agent.

I had phone calls to make, one inspired by the fact that I now knew, after talking to Doc, that I wanted to stay at Wynter Castle long enough to get a sense of my father's side of the family. I missed out on time with Uncle Mel, but maybe I could learn a little and fill in the gaps in my family history. I'd never get a better chance. After I sold the castle, I didn't imagine I'd be coming back to Autumn Vale. I called the storage facility where all my stuff was, and asked about a mover who could pack it up and bring it to Autumn Vale for me. They assured me they knew just the fellow, and could supervise it for me.

Over dinner, I told Shilo about my decision and she hopped up and down in her place, as Magic scoured the table for more carrots and lettuce. But a moment later, she got a pensive look on her face.

"What's up, buttercup?" I asked as I finished the last of my soup.

She gave me her trademarked "underlash" look, gazing up at me from behind a fringe of bangs and eyelashes. When I was working on the open market—in other words, before I fell under the Leatrice Peugeot spell and ruined my life and career in New York City—I occasionally styled Shilo for shoots, and had taught her that her "look" was irresistible to the public in the same way that Princess Diana's "Shy Di" look was. She was an eighteen-year-old model when I first met her, but she had not gotten a day older looking in the eleven years since.

Now she was using "the look" on me. "Tell me what's wrong; you only use that look on me when something is worrying you."

"Mer, what about me?"

Maybe I was having a dim moment, but I didn't get it. "What do you mean?"

"Can I stay and help?"

"Stay . . . what, here? Why would you want to?" I saw in a flash that I had hurt her feelings. I reached across the table and took her hand, squeezing gently. "Shi, you know you can stay as long as you want. I just meant, I'm not sure if that is what you'd really *want* to do."

She looked startled. "Don't you know? You're my best friend. You're the one who makes me feel good about myself, even when I'm having a bad day. You're my . . . my BFF."

Yeah, I teared up. I squeezed her hand again and released. "If you and Magic want to stay, I'd love to have you. You're free to hang out here as long as you want, or go whenever you want."

"That's why I love you," she whispered. "I've never had anyone say that I'm free, before."

I swallowed hard. To know why, you have to understand Shilo. There is much about her past that is a mystery to me, and I have never pressed her on it. She'll tell me when she feels like it. When I met her she had no apparent family, and shared an apartment with six other skinny, frightened, teenage models. She had come so far since then that I didn't realize, sometimes that the skinny, frightened girl was still inside her.

We went for a long walk after dinner. It was a beautiful evening. In the cavernous wilderness of Manhattan, one could forget (if you never made it to Central Park) that pavement and concrete were not natural walking surfaces. We wove between the holes, some filled, most not, and waded through the weeds. The ground had been warmed all day by the sun, and as a cooler breeze puffed to life, I could feel Mother Earth radiating back that warmth under me.

We walked the entire open portion of my property, and even explored some of the outbuildings, like little kids looking for a playhouse. There was a huge garage, which the lane that circled the castle led to. Its big, double doors were locked, but when I stood on a cinder block by a window and cupped my hands around my eyes, I could barely make out that there were a couple of vehicles inside, one that looked like a gangster car—you know those long, low-slung forties cars with a running board, the ones you see in gangster movies? It might even be the one I remembered Uncle Mel picking us up in, from the train station, on that long-ago day. Would it still work, I wondered?

There was a falling-down ramshackle shed; when I sidled up to it while Shilo picked wildflowers (aka weeds), it was clear that the shed had not only been broken into, but it looked like someone had been camping out in it. Could be kids from town, or transients, but either way, it was going to stop. I made a mental note to ask McGill where I could get a heavy-duty padlock. Even farther from the castle there was a big barn, almost on the edge of the woods. I was not going to explore that; not today.

The woods were like walls around the castle, a long, straight line, a right angle, and another long straight line, the same over and over. The castle was boxed in by dense forest that was made impassable, in most spots, by thick, tangled weeds and vines along the perimeter. It was like a fairy tale, *Sleeping Beauty*, I think? The one with the impenetrable thicket of thorns. Once I got closer, I was eerily aware of something watching me, and I saw a spot of orange that melted back into the gloomy gray and green. The attack cat again, supposedly Becket, Uncle Melvyn's faithful companion. But I was too distracted by the magnificence of the forest, and by a realization that struck me as I stood and stared. A pattern emerged in my vision. The trees were mostly lined up in perfect rows, like marching soldiers. "I wonder if the Wynter family planted all of these trees," I said, pointing out the straight lines to Shilo.

"That sure doesn't look natural." She shivered.

Doc English had said my grandfather and Uncle Melvyn had planted trees. Could this forest be the results of their labor? "Someday I'd like to take a walk in there."

"Some*day*," Shilo agreed, "but not tonight."

It was getting dark and the moon was rising. The cool breeze had become cold. "Okay," I said and laughed, linking my arm through hers. "We'll head back now."

I made us cocoa, and we drank it, then headed upstairs. As we got ready for bed, I told her about my day—we kept both ends of the Jack and Jill bathroom open to talk to each other, then closed it at night—and my run-in with Tom Turner. "I don't know what is up with him. Big galoot." Uneasy, I looked out my window at the Bobcat excavator, and beyond to the black woods. "I wish McGill wouldn't leave the excavator here. It's like an invitation."

"Can't be helped," Shilo said. "It's too slow to drive it back and forth from town, and he doesn't have a trailer to carry it. He's locked it down. That's the best he can do."

"I know. Good night, sweetie." I waved to her, grateful beyond words for her companionship, and closed my door, collapsing in bed and burrowing my face in sweet-smelling linen. It was weird living with someone else's stuff, but in a week or so I'd have all my belongings from the storage locker in Manhattan. The castle, as big and cavernous as it was, was beginning to feel like home, since I had constructed a bedroom "nest" with some of my familiar stuff around me, and was working on the same for the kitchen. I was undecided if my increasing comfort in Wynter Castle was a good thing or a bad thing.

Despite the peace of falling asleep after a vigorous day, my dreams were tumultuous; in them I confronted various weird folks, asking them about my father as a child. Then I was running across the lawn of the castle, dodging huge holes made by giant badgers. I could feel them underground. It was like a scene from *Tremors*, a movie that always makes me laugh when I catch it on late-night TV.

And then I woke up. I could still hear and feel the rumble. I dashed to the window, but didn't see anything. Was it an earthquake, maybe? It wasn't loud, just a faint vibration. I flung on a housecoat and slippers, and dashed downstairs, through the kitchen and out the pantry door. It takes a lot longer to do that than it does to say it in such a big place. "Darn it!" I yelled. The Bobcat was in action, and someone was digging another damn hole!

I raced back into the kitchen, fished around in my purse to find my cell phone, realized it was either dead or not getting a signal, and grabbed the wall phone receiver, dialing nine-one-one. I yelled my location and emergency, and said that Virgil Grace, sheriff of the Autumn Vale police department, was well aware of the problem. I slammed the phone down and dashed back to the door.

The Bobcat motor was still going, but the operator had stopped digging. Fury was building up in me. Had the coward taken off, leaving the vehicle running? I stood in the open door. No movement. I heard a loud caterwauling a ways off. Maybe that was my feline stalker.

I waited and watched. Still nothing. Finally fed up, I stormed outside toward the excavator, the scent of newly turned earth strong in the air. "Tom Turner, come on out and fight like a man!" I yelled like an idiot. I stopped a ways away. There was no one in the driver's seat. What the heck?

Just then, the sheriff's car screamed up my drive, emerging from the woods. He parked it facing the Bobcat, and the bright, halogen headlights illuminated the scene, throwing long, weird shadows over it. Virgil Grace, dressed in a uniform jacket, plaid jammie pants, and little else, bolted out of the car leaving the engine running and lights flashing. "Stop, Merry! Don't move another inch. Let me handle this."

"There's no one in it," I said, waving my hand toward the machine.

He threw open his trunk and emerged from it with a big, square flashlight, then trained the light on the scene. "Tom, you there?" he called out.

Aha! So he *did* think it was probably Tom Turner! "There's his red-and-black-plaid jacket, on the edge of the hole!" I said, as we walked toward it.

The chug of the motor and the smell of the raw earth he had just opened will forever haunt me and take me back to that moment. Together, Virgil and I looked over the edge of the hole, where Tom's jacket lay, and the sheriff shone his flashlight down into it. At the bottom was the still form of Tom Turner, dressed as I had seen him earlier that day. Shilo, in her robe and slippers, was loping toward us asking what was going on.

"Oh, no!" I cried, hands over my mouth.

"Damn it!" Virgil shouted. "Tom? Tom, you okay?" He whirled and handed me the flashlight. "Shine this down in the hole and don't waver." He grabbed a handful of weeds at the top of the hole and gingerly lowered himself near the guy, kneeling at his side as I tried to angle the flashlight beam as best as I could so Virgil could see what he was doing. I couldn't get close enough, and picked up a long piece of metal, which threatened to spill down on the cop and Turner, tossed it aside, then shone the light on the guy's face.

There was blood, I could see that, as Shilo picked her way close and grabbed my arm, trembling. Virgil tried to rouse Turner, but then looked up. He shook his head. "He's dead. Murdered."

I was shocked, and stammered, "M-maybe he just fell and hit his head."

Virgil grabbed a hank of roots and clambered up out of the hole. "No," he said tersely, dusting the dirt off his hands. "You two, come with me," he said, and headed toward his car.

We followed, holding onto each other like frightened bunnies.

"What's going on?" Shilo whispered.

"I don't know," I muttered.

"Sit in the back for a few minutes," he said, opening up the back of his sheriff's car and motioning us to slide in. "You'll stay warmer."

"We could just go back to the castle." I said.

"Not yet."

"Why?"

"I can't let you go until I get your statement, check your hands for defensive wounds, and fingerprint you."

"Defensive . . . fingerprint . . . what?" I was stunned. "What's this all about?" I was not going to be cowed into acquiescence.

Virgil faced me, his expression grim in the shadowy flash of the roof lights. "Look, Merry, everybody in town has been talking about how you threatened Tom Turner in Binny's Bakery today. She called me to complain."

"But Merry was just telling him to keep off the castle property, or else!" Shilo cried, clinging to my arm.

"Exactly," Virgil said, over the thrum of the excavator engine. "And tonight he came back. And now he's dead."

Chapter Nine

✼ ✼ ✼

T HE NEXT HOURS were a nightmare, and I pretty much mean that literally. Virgil ordered backup, and they taped off the "scene of the crime." I say that guardedly because from what I could tell it just looked like Tom had climbed down from the Bobcat, looked into the hole, lost his balance, and fell in. Maybe he hit his head on a rock or something, but why was that murder?

I thought Virgil was being ridiculous *until* I caught sight of one of the investigators picking up a long, iron rod with plastic-gloved hands from the grass near the hole. He held it up to the light and called Virgil over, pointing to something on it. Like a movie replaying in my mind, I remembered picking it up from the edge of the hole, a long iron rod that was in my way. I had tossed it aside, leaving, no doubt, a nice copy of my finger- and handprints on the thing.

Sugar.

A chill crept down my spine. These people didn't know me, didn't know that violence is not in my nature. All they knew was that I had threatened Tom Turner, and now he was dead.

We waited for hours in the police car. One of the police technicians had already photographed our hands, and examined them. I had a couple of scrapes on my palms, probably from clearing weeds away from the garage windows earlier that evening; what would they make of those? Should I explain them, or would that seem suspicious? I stayed quiet. Being examined so closely would make anyone nervous, I say.

Virgil came over at one point and asked for permission to search the castle. If I said no, they'd keep me out until they had a warrant, which, given the circumstances, they would have no trouble getting. I told them to go ahead, but to mind Magic. I had to explain that I meant to be careful that Magic, the bunny rabbit in Shilo's room, didn't escape. Finally the sheriff opened the police car door and told us they had bagged some things for evidence, but we could go back in. He was stomping away when I caught up with him and grabbed his arm. I could see the weariness on his stubble-lined face, but he looked at me with grim resignation. Gone was the flirtatious, young guy I had met that first day. I didn't think I'd see that flirtatious fellow ever again.

"What could you possibly have taken from the castle?" I asked.

"Mostly paperwork. We'll give you an official receipt. You can get it when you come to the station to sign your statement and give us your fingerprints. That goes for your friend, too."

In my statement I had already told him about tossing aside the iron bar, which, it turns out, was a crowbar and possibly the murder weapon. My fingerprints were going to be on it, guaranteed, and may well have irrevocably smudged the actual murderer's prints. "This doesn't have anything to do with me, Virgil," I said, tension tightening my voice.

"You know Tom Turner was the kind of guy who made enemies wherever he went. I can't be the only person who was at odds with him."

He glared down at me. I'm a fairly tall woman, but he was taller. "Look, Merry, I can't discuss this. I know in the TV shows the cop always speculates on what is going on and shares his feelings with every civilian who'll listen, but in real life, that would damage the case. It's for your protection."

Great. I was being kept in the dark for my own protection. Moodily, I watched him walk away, back to the scene, as the sun climbed and peeped over the top of the forest. Shilo came up and put her arm through mine.

"I'm tired and hungry, Merry. Can we go in and get coffee and food? Poor Magic is probably freaked right out by all the people stomping around."

And so my day started.

By now, the kitchen almost felt like home, despite its size. Shi and I had dragged some overstuffed wing chairs in and created a cozy nook by the fireplace, which would be lovely on cool, autumn evenings if I ever had the nerve to try to light a fire. New York apartments with real, working fireplaces were well beyond my standard of living, though if you want me to bleed a radiator, I can do that. But the working end of the kitchen was just as it had been. I couldn't wait until I got all my old baking stuff out of storage and could liven the dull place up a bit.

I mixed up the carrot and apple muffin batters, then began baking. Soon enough I had my four dozen muffins ready to go in the cheap plastic wear I had bought in town, and Shi and I munched a couple of the extras. They were *so* good; surprising, since I was just estimating the ingredients.

Shilo was going to go into Autumn Vale with me later in the day, but first, despite the tragedy we had witnessed in the night, I wanted to begin evaluating the castle, and figure out what needed to be done. My warm feeling the day before about getting to know my lost family had dissipated; I suppose a dead body in a hole on your property has a tendency to dampen enthusiasm. I now just wanted to sell the darn place and move back to civilization. I know that sounds snobby, but *you* try being woken up at three am by a lunatic on an excavator who then has the bad sense and worse taste to get murdered.

I felt horrible about Tom Turner, but I hadn't done anything to him, nor did I know who did. I was nervous, frightened, and worried. And all of that emotion was punctuated by anger. I hadn't asked for *any* of this. All I knew was, I needed to get on with the business of getting rid of Wynter Castle.

We stood in the main hall, our voices echoing in the cavernous space as we talked about how to best show the place off to make it saleable. It needed to be warmed up considerably, but I didn't want to get in the way of its natural beauty. We fell silent as the sun ascended and beamed through the rose window, sending blades of colored light streaming, piercing the gray shadows of the hall.

"Wow," Shilo said.

I wanted to weep, because that simple ray of light had reminded me of how amazing an experience this was turning out to be. So much beauty and I couldn't keep it, could never afford to live in this gorgeous place. "I guess I should enjoy it while it lasts," I said quietly. "It'll be even better once the rose window is cleaned up." I made a note to find someone to do that task—there was no way I was going to try cleaning a window twenty feet off the floor—and also to see if I could hire someone cheap to do the yard work. I wondered how much this was all going to cost. Gogi, had been right: if I was going to stay any length of time at all, I needed to get a flow of income going.

We worked for a few hours removing Holland covers, rearranging furniture and assessing the castle's strong and weak points. The biggest task was finding a way to get the Holland cover off the chandelier, but at long last we managed it with minimal damage to ourselves and the long-handled pruning shears I discovered in the pantry. As the fabric cover floated down to the hall below, we stood for a long moment, looking down on the chandelier from the gallery. It was amazing, hundreds of crystal shards dangling from gilt-coated brass. I'd have loved to turn it on, but thought I should get an electrician to look it over first.

Then I went to my uncle's desk, which was in the smallest extra room on the second floor. He had a cluttered, dusty, old rolltop desk with an array of nubby pencils, inkless pens, stained erasers, and rulers from a variety of commercial sources, including "Autumn Vale Community Bank; Where Your Hard-Earned Dollar is Safe and Secure!" It looked to me as if someone had rustled through it lately, and I thought that this was probably one spot the police had checked.

I was going to have to go through all the junk piece by piece, but not today. I idly sifted through, noticing Autumn Vale Community Bank check records and account books, bills from local utilities, an unopened envelope addressed to Turner Wynter Global Enterprise, and one curious little torn memo in scrawled handwriting . . . someone had written "Call Rusty about mobi . . ." and the rest was illegible. It had to be my uncle's handwriting . . . who else would leave a handwritten note in his desk?

I couldn't do any more though. Time was flying.

Shilo and I got into her rattletrap—the miles were adding up too quickly on my rental, especially for someone who didn't have an income—with the four dozen muffins for Golden Acres. As Shilo drove, I pointed out the by now well-known way into town. The castle was above the town, to some extent, and when we rounded a curve I told her to pull off to the side for a minute.

I got out and walked to the edge of the road, where there was a break in the tree cover. Shilo joined me. The town was laid out like a little animated map, the main street, Abenaki Avenue, pretty much a straight shot through town, and the streets off it curving along rising elevations. This was the place I had stopped the morning I arrived; I had been just a couple of miles from the castle and hadn't known it. A distance away along the valley, I could see some kind of industrial business: an office trailer, a big warehouse, a machine yard with lots of heavy machinery lined up, and stacks of construction materials. I wondered if that was Turner Construction, or Turner Wynter, whatever it was called. What was going to become of that business now? It must already be in tatters, with my uncle gone, Rusty missing, presumed dead, and now Tom gone, too.

I shared my thoughts with Shilo, and then said, "Poor Binny. She lost her dad, and now she's lost her brother." I got back in the car and we made our way into town. I directed her to Golden Acres, and dashed in to give the muffins to the kitchen staff to disperse. I'd visit with Gogi and Doc another day. As we then drove down Abenaki Avenue, I saw that the bakery was actually open.

"Should I go in and say how sorry I am to Binny?"

Shilo guided the car to the curb and parked. "I'll go in with you."

I felt trepidation as I entered. There were a half-dozen people already in there. Given what had happened to her brother, I was surprised Binny was there and open for business as usual. Her relationship with her brother was something I knew little about. The baker was serving customers and she didn't seem any more or any less grumpy than she had the last time I was in there. I waited my turn, and, with Shilo by my side, came up to the counter. "Binny, I just . . . I wanted to tell you how sorry I am about what happened to your brother."

She swallowed, and tears welled in her eyes. She simply nodded. I was relieved. I'd been afraid, after the confrontation I had with her brother, that she'd think I did it. Her face was white, though, and it looked like she was just holding herself together by a thread.

A hunched-over fellow of indeterminate age, thin as a rail, and with a sparse, fine covering of hair on his head, said, "I bet it was them two guys who showed up last year asking all kind of questions. That was just before your dad disappeared, Bin."

I watched him with interest; he was young, probably about Shilo's age, but had the stature of a little old man, and I wondered if his hunched look was a congenital condition or just a mannerism.

"Gordy, that was a year ago," Binny said. "You can't possibly think they did something to Tom."

"But they were real suspicious, asking all kind of questions about your dad's business, and even about Tom."

She shrugged helplessly. "I don't know," she said, her voice thick with unshed tears. "I don't understand what's going on anymore."

Another local who had just entered, a fellow about the same age as Gordy, chimed in, "You gotta know it was probably Junior Bradley who did Tom in."

"What are you talking about, Zeke?" Binny asked sharply. "Tom and Junior were best friends."

"Who is Junior Bradley?" Shilo said.

Gordy, who had been watching Shilo with that hopeless admiration most men felt for her, said, "Junior is the zoning commissioner in town. Him and Tom were good buddies, but they had a big fight the other night at the bar up Ridley Ridge."

"What was the fight about?" Shilo asked.

"A girl," Gordy said.

Zeke chimed in. "Yeah, Tom and Junior were both after Emerald, one of the dancers at the bar. They got into it, and Junior threatened Tom. Said he'd better leave Emerald alone if he knew what was good for him."

I had been right; there were others out there who had been less than thrilled with Tom. "Were you guys there?" I asked.

Both men turned crimson.

"Uh, nope. I heard about it from a friend," Zeke said, his Adam's apple bouncing up and down his throat, his gaze turned away from all of us women. He stared steadily at the wall of teapots.

"Or, the awful event could be connected to . . . the *Brotherhood*," Gordy said, his tone sententious.

Both Zeke and Binny rolled their eyes.

"The Brotherhood?" I said.

"You've got to get off that kick," Zeke replied to his friend, with the air of someone who has said the same thing many times before. He turned to me. "The Brotherhood of the Falcon is a bunch of old farts who sit around and make exclamations, or declamations, or whatever they do."

"Declarations," Binny said. "The last one was something about keeping the Brotherhood all male, as if any women would *want* to join! Zeke's right, Gordy. Those are just a bunch of old guys drinking beer and remembering their glory days."

"I don't know," Gordy said, his tone slow and doubtful as he nodded and winked with that knowing expression of someone who is in on a deep, dark secret.

"For God's sake, Gordy . . . Dad was a member!" Binny said.

"Well, *I* heard they're connected to the Freemasons, and you know who *they* are!" He was clearly waiting for someone to take the bait, but no one did and he looked disgruntled.

"Anyway, I've got work to do," Binny said, and whirled around, stomping back to her ovens without another word.

Shilo and I stood and stared at each other for a moment, uncertain of what to do. I wished I could help, but I was the last person who could offer Binny comfort. I looked to the two locals. "Well. I guess we'll be going."

"You're old Mel Wynter's niece, right?" Gordy said. "The one who's inherited the castle."

"And you were there last night when Tom was killed, right?" Zeke said, looking me over closely.

"Uh, yes."

"What'd you see?" Gordy asked softly, glancing over at the kitchen.

"Not a thing," I said, using the tone that forbids further discussion. "Did you guys know my uncle?"

"Nah," Zeke said. "But every kid in school snuck out to the Wynter estate and tried to look in the windows. I got chased away from there a couple of times by old Mel with a shotgun."

Lovely. "We have to go," I said. But I didn't move. These guys probably were my best source for local info at that moment, I realized. It would be stupid to ignore that. "As we were coming in to Autumn Vale, we noticed a warehouse property just past the edge of town. Is that where Turner Wynter is located?"

"Well, it's Turner Construction, yup," Zeke said.

Binny started banging pots around in back, and I heard one loud sob. If I was a friend, I'd barge back there and comfort her, but I didn't quite know what to say to a girl who didn't seem to want or need consolation, preferring to hide in her kitchen and cook. Or maybe I did know too well what that was like. I had done the same when Miguel died. Gordy gave a look, then hitched his head toward the door. Shilo and I followed him and Zeke out to the street.

"Don't go mentioning Turner Wynter around Binny," Gordy said, joining us at the curb.

"There's a lot of bad feelings there," Zeke added. "Tom was sure in a tizzy about it all, the lawsuits and such. Don't know what'll happen now that they're all dead."

"I've heard about the lawsuits; what were they about?" I asked, interested in the gossips' take on the situation.

Gordy and Zeke explained in their tag-team manner that there was once a plan for Turner Wynter to develop Wynter Acres, using some of the land attached to Wynter Castle. It devolved into lawsuits slung at each other, with both Rusty Turner and Melvyn Wynter claiming that the other man had cheated him. Other than that, they didn't appear to know the details of who sued who, or about any possible resolution.

"Y'know, *you'll* probably have to settle the lawsuit," Zeke said, hitching his thumbs in the belt loops of his jeans. "Along with Binny."

"Me?" I squawked, taken aback. "It has nothing to do with me."

"Your land now, your lawsuit," Gordy said, rocking back on his heels.

"But there's no one left to continue against!" Shilo exclaimed.

I saw both young guys shutter like blinds, and their gaze became shifty.

"I guess that's so, isn't it, Zeke?" Gordy said.

"Mighty interesting, that," Zeke said. "Mighty interesting."

And with that, the two cast me one long, thoughtful look, and ambled off down the sidewalk with their heads together, chattering like gibbons. Great. I felt like I was now back in the center of some kind of local suspicion.

"We're going to visit a certain lawyer," I said to Shilo.

Silvio was in, and Shilo and I entered, but this time he seemed out of sorts. "What do you want this time, Miss Wynter?"

And he had been so friendly last time! "I take it you've heard about Tom Turner's death in my yard?" I said, steeling myself against hurrying in the face of his irritation.

He nodded.

"People are suspicious, it seems, of my connection to the whole case because of those darned lawsuits. Can't we resolve things, now that it's all water under the bridge?"

He sighed heavily, very much the put-upon legal eagle. "There is nothing I can do about it, I told you. Nothing to do with me."

"The point is, it is a complication in the estate."

"Yes. It's unfortunate. Rusty and Mel started out working together on Wynter Acres, and it all seemed so promising. It was to be a housing development meant to attract retiring baby boomers who wanted to live in the country but have the convenience of condo living. Then Mel accused Rusty of cheating him and it all went to hell in a handbasket. Though I could not get legally involved, I *was* trying hard to mediate between those two bullheaded, old men."

"Until Rusty disappeared and Melvyn died."

He nodded. "I don't even know where everything stands. It's all in limbo until we know the legal determination in Rusty's death or disappearance."

"In other words, it could go on forever," I said. "What does that mean to my wanting to sell the estate?"

He shrugged.

Anger was building up in me. "So you can't even tell me if I'll be *able* to sell the estate, is that it?"

"Oh, you should be able to sell, but there will be conditions attached to the sale."

Great. Buyers just *love* conditions. His next appointment, a young woman, entered, and we were forced to leave, me feeling kind of huffy about the whole thing.

"We may as well find this library folks keep telling me about," I said. Shilo and I walked the streets of Autumn Vale, the locals watching and whispering about our every step.

Finally, along a side street in the downtown section, up a sloped alley, I saw the sign I had noticed before, hanging out from the building. Autumn Vale Library it read, in curly script that looked hand painted. According to the placard attached to the wall it was open, so Shilo and I strolled up the wheelchair access ramp to the door and entered to the sound of weeping.

Shilo gripped my elbow, as full of consternation at the

woeful, echoing sounds as I. It was like the place was haunted by a mournful ghost. As my eyes adjusted to the dim light, I looked around the cavernous, gray room lined with bookshelves, most not above shoulder height, and finally saw what looked like a desk.

We approached. Behind the desk was a girl in a wheelchair. I say "girl" because at first glance she appeared to be no more than ten or eleven. But on closer inspection, as she turned red-rimmed eyes—beautiful, luminous, *huge* eyes—toward me, I could see within them a woman's full measure of pain.

"Are you okay?" I asked my voice faltering.

She stared at me for a long moment, then said, "When one man dies, one chapter is not torn out of a book, but translated into a better language."

Shilo said "Huh?"

But I'd heard or read the quotation before. I closed my eyes; it took me a moment, but I finally replied with the next, more famous part of it, my voice softly echoing up into the gray shadows of the library's upper reaches. "Any man's death diminishes me, because I am involved in mankind, and therefore never send to know for whom the bell tolls; it tolls for thee." It was from a prose piece written by John Donne, and was the source of Hemingway's most famous title.

The girl bowed her head for a long moment, and we were silent. But she looked up, and said, "It's true, isn't it? He's dead. Tom Turner is gone."

"You were friend of Tom's," I said.

She nodded, her large, gray eyes fixed on me. "He was a good man, despite what others say. Despite what *you* may think."

"You mean because of my run-in with him?"

She nodded.

"You know who I am."

She nodded again.

"I just wanted him to stop digging holes on my property," I said, on a sigh. "I really wish it hadn't ended this way. I'm sure you feel the same."

"I do . . . I'm so s-sad! That's where he died, isn't it?" Her breath caught on a sob, but she was trying to be brave. I could tell.

It was my turn to nod.

Shilo was looking back and forth between us. "I think I'm going for a walk," she said.

Once Shi was gone, the girl said, "I suppose you're here to learn about the Wynters of Wynter Castle."

"I'm in no hurry," I said. "That can wait. Why don't we talk about Tom Turner, first. I know so little about him or anyone here. You know who I am, but I don't know who you are. What's your name?"

"Hannah," she said. "It means 'God has favored me.'"

She smiled through tears, and she was beautiful. I pulled a chair over to sit beside her, and we talked. Hannah was a little person, tiny of frame and fragile as a bird, with pale skin like bone china. But her heart was huge, too big for her small frame, and she seemed filled with an eager grace. I don't know how else to express it. A beautiful yearning poured from her, expanding to fill the dim recesses of her library.

"How did you come to work here, in the library?"

"It's *my* library; I applied for a grant, I talked them into it, and I got the place renovated. I've always loved reading," she said. "When I was a kid, I read a book *The Little Lame Prince and His Traveling Cloak*. It opened up the world to me. I've been to Cameroon with Gerald Durrell, and to Yorkshire with James Herriot. Isak Dinesen showed me Kenya. I've been around the world with books as my traveling cloak."

"I know exactly what you mean," I said. "I've lived and breathed in Regency England with Jane Austen. I've walked the Yorkshire moors with Emily Brontë and the streets of Victorian London with Charles Dickens. Books are a marvelous transport. Tell me about why you were crying for Tom Turner."

Her smile illuminated the shadows. "We were going to be married."

Chapter Ten

❈ ❈ ❈

"**M**ARRIED?" I STARED at her. Was she serious? I examined her serene face. Yes, she was serious. "Uh, did he tell you that?"

"No, of course not. He didn't know it," she said, her head tilted to one side, her huge gray eyes dreamy. "But it would have happened. I was the only one he told things to, you know? He talked to me."

"It sounds like you were friends," I said carefully.

"We were. Good friends. And he loved me." Her eyes flooded, and one big drop fell on her hands, which were folded in her lap. "Eventually he'd have seen that no one would have . . . no one . . ." She sniffed and shook her head, looking down at her hands, struggling with her emotion.

"I'm sorry, Hannah," I said, gentling my tone. "He was lucky to have someone in his life who loved him so much." It seemed an impossible match to me, this little, bookish miss and the hulking, angry Tom, but perhaps she would have been the making of him. That she loved him so fiercely changed how I saw him and strengthened my sorrow at his death.

She told me good things about Tom Turner, that he was the one who had built the wheelchair ramp for her and all the shelves for the books, many of which were from her own collection. The library truly was hers, supported in part by the Brotherhood of the Falcon that Binny made such sport of, and with other grants that she zealously pursued. She was quite accomplished, I gathered, at writing grant proposals. As Hannah spoke, I thought about how a person could be so many things at once, good and bad and sometimes ugly. I recalled what Gordy and Zeke had said, about Tom and Junior Bradley fighting over some bar dancer named Emerald. Which Tom was the real deal, the one who hung out in bars looking for a fight, or the one who built shelves and a ramp for a sweet-faced librarian? I guess he was both.

"I want to know who did this," Hannah finally said.

"Me, too."

"Then let's figure it out."

I gaped at her. "Let's . . . you mean you and I?"

"Why not? We're both smart women, right?" Hannah smiled even as tears welled in her eyes. She sobered, and said, "I won't rest until I know who killed him. He didn't deserve it."

I stared at her for a moment, then said, "You know, some are probably going to think I killed him. In fact, I know they do."

"Did you?"

"Of course not."

"Good. Then let's get started figuring this out."

But how to do that? Maybe if I got to know Tom posthumously, it would help. "What was he like? From your viewpoint?"

"Rough around the edges," she said, staring off into the distance. "I've known him a long time. Mrs. Turner used to babysit me before she left town."

"Mrs. Turner?"

"Binny's mother."

"She left town? When? Why?"

"She took Binny and left . . . oh, let's see . . . Binny was about ten, I was fifteen, so I guess about fifteen years ago or so? No one knows why."

"Hmm. Odd that she took just her daughter and left town." It seemed to me in a small town, someone should know why, unless it was something so breathtakingly horrible that no one wanted to be the first to say it.

Her eyes flashed, and she fastened them on me. They glittered strangely in the shadowy dimness. "And don't you go thinking anything nasty. It wasn't *anything* like that."

My eyebrows climbed. She was not quite so sheltered as I had thought, if she had picked up on the direction of my wandering musings. But then, a voracious reader does learn much of the world, if only through books. "I'll take your word for it." I hadn't truly thought the woman had taken Binny away to avoid some kind of abuse by father or son anyway; it had been a possibility, though not high on the list. There were dozens of other explanations, most of which didn't involve anything sinister at all. "How did father and son get along after Tom's mom left?"

"She actually wasn't Tom's mother . . . Rusty's wife, I mean, which I guess was why she didn't take Tom with her when she left; plus he was, like, nineteen or so. Tom was from Rusty Turner's first marriage. His mom died soon after having Tom."

"You do know a lot about folks, don't you? What do you know about my uncle Melvyn?"

She waved one delicate hand airily. "Tom's murder first. Focus, Merry."

What would have been annoying from anyone else, was charming coming from her, and she knew it. I had to smile. "What was Tom looking for on my property? Do you know?"

"He *said* he was looking for his father's body—and that's what he told Binny—but that wasn't true." She hesitated.

"And . . . ?"

She shrugged, and engaged the joystick of her wheelchair, whirling around and wheeling to one of the bookshelves. I followed. Her mood had changed abruptly. She looked at the spines of the books at her eye level, pulled one out, and handed it to me. "This will tell you more about Autumn Vale and your ancestors. The town is called Autumn Vale because of them, you know."

"What do you mean?" I asked, looking down at the plain, hardbound book.

"The town was supposed to be called Wynterville, but one of the earliest settlers was dead-set against it. Said the Wynters were already too powerful. He got folks on his side, and the town was named Autumn Vale, it is said, so it would never be Wynter."

"Wow." It sounded like the kind of story that gets started when a town mythologizes its past, but it could be true. I paused for just a second, but then charged ahead. "Hannah, do you *know* what Tom was digging on my property for?" It had not escaped my notice that she had avoided the question neatly.

She pressed the joystick and returned to her librarian desk. "I don't know, exactly, but I'm pretty sure he didn't really believe that Rusty's body was buried there. He had Binny convinced, though, at least for a while."

"So what *was* he looking for?" I insisted. "Come on, Hannah, if you have any idea, please tell me!"

She sighed. "I don't. Truly, Merry, I would tell you if I could." Her shadowed face was marked by an expression of indecision.

"Okay. Who disliked him enough to kill him?"

Hannah grimaced. "Poor Tom. He was good at making people dislike him. I don't know why."

"Then where should I start?"

"Well, two places. I heard he had a fistfight with Junior Bradley, the zoning commissioner. They were childhood friends. Tom wouldn't tell me why they fought."

I'll *bet* he wouldn't tell her why. The girl adored him, and he would have shattered her view of him if he told her that he and his friend had come to blows over a stripper. I'd definitely have to check out that dancer *and* Junior Bradley. "And who else?"

"Well, you should probably consider Dinah Hooper."

The name sounded familiar, but with all the locals I had been meeting, I was momentarily stumped. "Who is she?"

"She is . . . was . . . Rusty's girlfriend. She works at Turner Construction. Her son, Dinty, worked there, too, but he left town some time back."

"How is Dinah dealing with Rusty's disappearance?"

Hannah looked pensive. She angled her face upward, and a ray of light shone in one of the few high windows in the dim library, catching her eyes, beaming brightly in the luminous gray depths. She was like a faery, sometimes fey, sometimes grave, looking like a child but speaking like a woman. I'll admit, among the many characters of Autumn Vale, she fascinated me most.

"I feel sorry for her; I'd say she's truly upset and worried. It's difficult for her, I imagine. But . . . I won't say anything else. You should talk to her yourself."

"I will. Is Dinah Hooper in a position to inherit anything, now that Tom is gone, and Rusty probably, too?"

She didn't flinch from the question, and in fact I could tell she had already considered it. "I don't think so. She didn't live with Rusty, and they weren't married. If anything, I think it kind of exonerates her, you know? Because if she was out for money, it would have been better for her if Rusty had stuck around and married her."

"The son, Dinty . . . when did he leave town? Before or after Rusty disappeared?"

"Uh, after. A few months, actually. Why?"

I shrugged. It could mean nothing at all, or it could have been guilt that sent the guy away. I didn't know him, but I'd bet that Gordy and Zeke did. I'd have to tap into those two guys' knowledge at some point. Should be easy if I used Shilo as a lure.

"I don't care what happened to Rusty," Hannah said, her fine-boned face holding a grim expression. "We're trying to figure out who killed Tom, and why."

"I know. I'm just trying to find my bearings. Could it all be tied up together?"

"I suppose."

Shilo came back in to the library, a poorly hidden expression of excitement on her face.

"Shilo, this is Hannah," I said. "Hannah, this is my best friend, Shilo."

"Shilo . . . that means peaceful."

"Bad name for me!" Shilo said with a laugh, plunking down in a chair by the librarian.

"You're so beautiful," Hannah said, gazing at her steadily. "You look how I always imagined Rebecca from *Ivanhoe* would look." She reached out and touched Shilo's long, dark hair. She fingered the curled locks with a wistful look. Her own hair was thin and mousy, lying flat on her narrow skull, parting around her ears like a stream around a rock.

"And you make me think of the pixies," Shilo said, touching Hannah's hand gently. "I believed in pixies when I was a kid. I played with them, out in the forest. Always my favorite faery folk."

I could see they would be friends, each a little odd, each willing to say exactly what she thought. Hannah nodded, as if reading my mind.

"I saw Jack McGill," Shilo said, her eyes sparkling, as she turned back to me.

"McGill?" Hannah said.

I whirled around and looked at Hannah. "You call him McGill, too?" I said.

"Sure," Hannah replied. "Jack is too common a name for him."

"I know. Even though he is a Jack-of-all-trades, in a

sense. He's filling in the holes that Tom dug." That sobered me, bringing me back to Tom's death. I could see it had affected Hannah similarly. "How did you happen across him, Shi? What did McGill have to say for himself?"

"Well, he was showing an empty storefront to a prospective tenant. The tenant was Dinah Hooper."

"Dinah Hooper?" Once you hear a name, I thought, you just keep hearing it! "Rusty Turner's girlfriend. Why would she be renting out a storefront?"

"He wouldn't tell me," Shilo said. "But it's interesting, right?"

I chewed my lip. It was certainly interesting.

There was probably more I could have asked Hannah, but a local library patron came in, an odd woman, heavyset and with a determined frown; she wore a red hat and purple dress, and pushed a rolling walker along the shelves, but didn't seem to depend upon it for support. She grabbed books as she went, tossing them into the basket of her walker.

"Hey, do you take book donations?" I asked.

"We do!" Hannah said, luminous eyes glowing. "Do you have any?"

"I sure do. I have my mother's books, which have been in storage since she died; a lot of classics and poetry. I also have my grandmother's. She favored kids' books and classic mysteries. Lots of hardback Agatha Christie novels. All my boxes are coming from storage, and I could sure use a home for the books . . . that's *if* they're in good shape. They should be. Can you use them?"

"We definitely can. Whatever we can't use, we sell to raise money at the annual Autumn Vale Harvest Sale." Her smile died. "Tom always takes the books to the auditorium for me." Tears welled up.

"I bet Jack would help out with that," Shilo said softly, smiling down at Hannah.

The girl brightened just a shade. "Do you think so?"

"You *know* he will," Shilo answered. "He seems to be

very civic-minded, and the book sale . . . I'm sure lots of folks count on that every year."

Hannah colored faintly and nodded. "Thank you."

I told Hannah I'd be back another day, and she said she was often at Golden Acres for their Book Hour. She took in coffee table–type books for some of the old folks to look over and reminisce about. She was something of an amateur historian, it seemed, and talked to the oldsters about their early years in Autumn Vale and made up trivia games. She had heard about the muffins I was supplying, she informed me, and approved.

"I like muffins," she said. "Take the book I gave you; it will give you some information on Wynter Castle. And come back in and check out more of the local history books sometime."

As Shilo and I left, the purple-dressed woman eyed us covertly, using the brim of her red hat to shield her interest. Not very successfully, I might say. "Maybe I'll see you at Golden Acres, then, or I'll come back here!" I said as I waved good-bye to Hannah.

As we emerged out to the main street, I felt like I'd just left a dream. Hannah was an odd, little creature, full to the brim with emotion and tremulous longing. I wondered how hard that would be, to have people dismiss you because of your stature or disability when inside you were an adult woman, yearning for love. But she filled the library with her personality, making a gray, dull interior into a faery land.

"Do you want to see the store Dinah Hooper was looking to rent?" Shilo asked.

Tucking the book into my voluminous bag, I replied, "Yes! I do." I didn't know Dinah Hooper, and so couldn't conclude that she had anything to do with Tom's murder on my property. I was grasping at straws, but it was worth a look.

We strolled along the main street, as I tried to get used to being stared at. It was natural, I suppose; I was a stranger, and the owner of a notorious plot of land. I was a Wynter. But a local had also been murdered on my property, after vandalizing it repeatedly. I smiled and nodded at those who met my eyes, and ignored those who didn't.

"This is it," Shilo said as we came up to a small storefront.

A nicely dressed older woman trotted toward us, concentrating on the tiny screen of her cell phone and tapping away at a text message. She stopped abruptly as she looked up and saw us watching.

"Hi," I said, striding toward her, arm outstretched. "My name is Merry Wynter. This is my friend, Shilo Dinnegan."

The other woman awkwardly shuffled her armload of papers, Prada handbag and cell phone, and put her hand out, grasping mine in a warm grip that almost hurt because the number of rings on her fingers. "Binny told me all about you." She eyed me up and down, then turned her attention to Shilo. "But she didn't mention you."

"I'm just here as support," Shilo said. "Are you Dinah Hooper? Jack McGill mentioned he was meeting with you, and that you were looking to rent a storefront."

"I *am* Dinah Hooper," she said. She looked up at the storefront with a worried expression. "This place is going to be my new business. I need to have something to do since . . ." She broke off and shook her head, her eyes tearing up. "Since poor Rusty disappeared, and now Tom is gone, too. I just don't know what's going to happen with Turner Construction. I guess I don't have a job anymore! Not that I've been doing anything there for a while. I'm going to do *something* with this place; maybe open a flower shop."

"This must all be so difficult," I said. "Was Tom like a son to you? Were you close?"

"Close? No. But I don't know how Rusty is going to feel about all of this."

"You think he's still alive?" I blurted out, then clapped my mouth shut.

"I'm sure of it!" she said fervently, fingering the strap of her purse, pulling at a loose thread. "He just *has* to be. I will *not* believe that he's dead."

I didn't know what to say to this. It sounded like she was in denial.

Shilo glanced at me sideways, then said, "Do you think he just left town, then? Why would he do that?"

The woman frowned as her cell phone chimed with a dance tune. She looked at the screen, and said, "I have to take this. To answer your question, Rusty was not well. He was upset by some stuff at work—Tom, God rest his soul, was giving him no end of heartache—and I think he just took off. I didn't think he'd be gone this long, and I wish I had a way to contact him."

"But Tom and Binny seem to think their father is dead!" I said.

Dinah shook her head, her blonde hair stiffly resisting any movement. "They just don't want to believe that he would purposely leave them alone, that's all. They don't understand their dad."

"Who do you think killed Tom?" Shilo said.

"If I knew, don't you think I'd have told the cops by now?" Dinah answered smartly, and then punched a button on her cell phone. She said hello as she got her keys out, entered her new storefront, and closed the door behind her.

We stood staring after her. "That was sudden," I finally said.

"I guess she didn't appreciate being questioned by strangers," Shilo commented with a wry tone. "Who could imagine that?"

"I guess you're right," I said. "We were a little nosy and pushy with her. Let's find a restaurant in this town and have something to eat." It was early afternoon, and I hadn't eaten anything but muffins since earlier in the morning.

Shilo moved the car closer, locked up as best she could—her car is in bad enough shape that the locks only work intermittently—and we began looking in earnest for some place to eat. Most small towns have that one place, usually a down-home kind of café or restaurant, where everyone gathers to gossip. As soon as I saw it, I knew that Vale Variety and Lunch was it. I had passed it several times in my hunt for muffin ingredients over the last few days, thinking it was just a mom-and-pop variety store, but now I noticed the "Lunch" part of the sign. When Shilo and I entered, I saw that beyond the variety store at the front was a lunch counter and café area, which was quite deep.

Gordy and Zeke were there, and greeted us as long-lost friends. It seemed some kind of badge of honor that they could introduce us to others, among them, significantly, Junior Bradley, who had been Tom Turner's friend before having a fistfight with him over a dancer named Emerald, as the story went.

Junior looked up, briefly, but then hunched back down over his grilled cheese sandwich and Rochester newspaper. Various others included the odd-looking woman in the red hat and purple dress, whose bag full of books was now on the floor near her walker, beside her tiny table at the back of the diner. She was reading a romance while she slurped tomato soup through her teeth. At another table, studiously ignoring her, was a woman of about the same age—late fifties/early sixties, at a guess—wearing a dress made out of cotton with multiple, humorously positioned cats all over it. She was rigidly upright, and stared straight ahead of her as she sipped a cup of tea from a thick, white, porcelain, restaurant ware cup.

Shilo and I sat at a table near Gordy and Zeke, our two personal informants, and a waitress slouched over, handing us a menu and mumbling the specials: tomato soup with grilled cheese sandwich or tuna salad on an English muffin. I noted "Breakfast All Day" written on the chalkboard above the counter, and ordered two eggs, sunny, with whole-wheat toast. Shilo ordered breakfast too: eggs, bacon, toast, but with sausages and a stack of pancakes as well. The Hungry Gypsy's Special, I guess.

"What do you think of Dinah Hooper?" I asked Gordy, who was staring at Shilo with an intensity that most would find unnerving, but didn't seem to faze her in the slightest.

"Dinah?" Zeke answered, instead of his bewitched friend. "She's a good egg. She's involved in everything: annual fall fair, hospital committee, reads to the old folks at Golden Acres . . . lots of other things."

The prim woman in the cat dress slammed her teacup down on the table in front of her and stood, her pale-green eyes bulging with emotion. "That woman! That woman is the devil's pawn . . . you mark my words." With that, she gathered up her things and marched out of the café.

Chapter Eleven

WE ALL WATCHED her stomp out of the place, and though I can't speak for the others, I was stunned by her pronouncement.

"Who the heck is that?" Shilo asked.

"Isadore Openshaw," Gordy said.

Shilo burst into laughter, and I snickered, too. Both guys looked confused, so I said, "C'mon, guys . . . Isadore Openshaw?"

They exchanged looks. "I don't get it," Zeke said.

"Never mind."

The woman in purple rose up, and said, "It's funny . . . 'Is a door open, Shaw?' How can you rubes not get that? That's why Isadore doesn't speak to me. I laughed at her name once. Woman's got no sense of humor. I guess that's what happens when you work in a bank too long." She turned to me and nodded. "I was hoping you'd be smart. Guess you are. If you're smart, then you'll be looking at the whole ball of wax. What happened to Rusty Turner? What happened to Melvyn Wynter? And now Tom Turner?"

I glanced at Shilo, and said, "It seems like an awful lot of intrigue in such a small town."

The purple lady made her index finger into a gun, her thumb the hammer. "Bingo," she said, cocking and firing the little finger gun. She then grabbed her walker and strode out, leaving a trail of cracker crumbs in her wake.

"Wait, what do you mean?" I called, half rising from my chair.

"Don't bother," Zeke said. "She won't tell you. She fancies herself a kind of oracle, or something. Likes to make mysterious pronouncements, then never explains 'em."

"Who *is* she?" I said, watching her weave expertly through the variety store at the front and toward the door.

"Janice Grover," Gordy said. "Her husband is Simon Grover, the Grand Tiercel of the Brotherhood of Falcons." He nodded slowly and winked that slow wink of his that indicated a fount of secret knowledge.

Zeke rolled his eyes.

"Is she . . . reliable?" I asked, not quite sure how to phrase my real question, which was, is she a whackadoodle?

"She's got three grown kids," Zeke said, frowning.

I wasn't sure if that was an answer to the question I was truly asking, or his own interpretation, but decided not to pursue that line of investigation. "So what about this Openshaw woman . . . what's she got against Dinah Hooper?"

"Now, that's a good question," Gordy said. He furrowed his brow, indicating deep thought, then said, "I bet it goes back to last year's fall fair catnip mouse incident."

"Do tell," I said. I couldn't wait to hear this.

Zeke nodded and his Adam's apple bounced up and down his throat. "That's prob'ly it. At last year's Autumn Vale Harvest Fair, Miss Openshaw set up a booth selling catnip mice to benefit the kitty cat rescue organization she's trying to start, you know."

Silence. "And?" I prompted.

Gordy took up the story. "Well, then Mrs. Hooper, who

was the organizer, you see, told her she couldn't collect money for a charity if it wasn't registered, and made her close up her booth. Miss Openshaw was left with 227 catnip mice and nowhere to get rid of 'em. Ended up giving 'em to the shelter over in Ridley Ridge to give away with every cat adopted."

"Is that it?"

Gordy and Zeke both looked surprised at my comment. "Caused quite a kerfuffle at the time," Zeke said, and Gordy nodded in agreement.

Still, the devil's pawn? Wasn't that a little harsh over catnip mice? Maybe I just didn't get the complicated nature of relationships in small towns.

Shilo and I ate our lunch, my head swimming with all the oddball people I was meeting. Autumn Vale was turning out to be one strange little burg, more entertaining than any street corner in the weirdest section of New York. Was it something in the water? Maybe I'd better stick to Perrier, I thought, pushing away my glass of tap water.

"Zeke, back to Dinah Hooper . . . I understand her son, Dinty, lived here with her for a while. When did he leave? And why?"

Gordy sniffed and crossed his arms, while Zeke ruminated for a long moment, then said, "You had to know Dinty. He was a troublesome sort. Him and Tom . . . they didn't get along at all. Not at all."

"Okay, so they didn't get along. Is that why Dinty left town?"

"You could say that. I heard it all," Gordy said. "Tom, in front of everyone, told Dinty he better keep his shifty eyes off Binny, or he'd give him what for. Dinty called her a name, Tom lit into him, and the next day Dinty packed up his Jeep and headed out of town. Dinah said he had talked about heading out west to Denver to get a job in construction. Autumn Vale didn't have the right kind of opportunities for a guy like him."

Zeke rolled his eyes. "Otisville is the only place with opportunities for a guy like that."

"Otisville?"

"Federal prison," Gordy filled in.

As Shilo chased down the last scraps of her pancakes, spearing them with little grunts of satisfaction, I rose, strolling over to Junior Bradley. I had no idea how to approach him, but didn't want to miss the opportunity. "Hi," I said, then had a brainstorm. I'd ask about my uncle's desire to create a condo community, and whether zoning had been approved! It seemed like a great conversation starter. "I understand that you're the local zoning commissioner. My name is Merry Wynter, the new owner of Wynter Castle. I was wondering if I could talk to you for a moment." I was about to slide into the empty seat opposite him when he abruptly stood up, folding his newspaper and tucking it under his arm.

"I don't talk business in public. Call and make an appointment," he said, towering over me. He was a big guy. He thrust a card at me just before striding off, weaving through the variety-store section at the front.

Business card in hand, I stared off after him. What a grouch! I had hoped to start with the zoning, then slide in a couple of questions about his relationship with Tom Turner, but maybe it would be better if I did so in private. Hannah had presented him as a possible killer, though, so I sure wasn't going alone. I'd drag someone with me, preferably male; maybe Jack McGill.

Junior Bradley didn't look like someone I wanted to mess with, but I could understand why he didn't want to talk in the local luncheonette. Talking business in the open in a small town was probably not a good policy unless you wanted that business spread through the gossip mill. Anyway, I was sure that Virgil would have heard about the fight between him and Tom, and questioned him about it. But it still would be worth my while to talk to Junior. I returned to my table but just shook my head when Shilo asked me what happened.

Gordy and Zeke ambled off, stopping at our table to say an awkward good-bye, as Gordy ogled a final eyeful of Shilo. Zeke angled for an invitation to the castle, and I brushed off his hints by saying that once I had some of the changes made and the cleanup accomplished, I'd be inviting the whole town to come have a look.

After lunch we headed back to Wynter Castle. Virgil and the team were still there, and I didn't even want to think about what they were doing, or if they had removed Tom Turner's poor, broken body. It was like this sore spot that I was avoiding touching or acknowledging, too awful to even think about. But as Shilo turned off the car—it always stuttered and yammered and banged before it actually shut down—Virgil headed toward us. We got out and waited, leaning on the hood.

"Your car is still hammering away," I commented to Shilo. "You ought to have that thing looked at."

She frowned and squinted at the car. "It's getting worse. Oh well, if it breaks down, it breaks down." Her insouciance was part of her charm.

"Ladies," Virgil said, striding up to us. "I need to ask you a few questions." He frowned and looked over at Shilo's car. "You realize your car is making a funny noise?"

"Ignore it," I said airily. "It always makes funny noises."

He cocked his head. "Does it always yell 'Help, help, help'?" He raced around to the trunk. "Open this up!" he yelled.

Shilo, eyes wide, got out her key, dashed to the rear of the car, and jiggled it in the lock. I joined them just as the trunk lid sprang open and we found a girl curled up in the trunk, gasping for air.

She clambered out and blasted us with an icy look. "I almost died in there!" she yelled.

Fists on his hips, Virgil glared at us. "You want to explain this?"

"I know you!" I said, pointing at the girl. "You're Lizzie; I met you at Golden Acres. Shilo, why did you have Lizzie locked in your trunk?" I know I shouldn't have said that; it made Shi look bad. But it wouldn't have been the weirdest thing she's ever had in her trunk. I'm just saying . . . you never know with Shilo.

"I didn't put her in there," she said pointedly, and switched her glare to the girl. "Why were you in my trunk?"

Note she did not ask her *how* she got in there, she asked *why*. I told you about her car being a rattletrap, and that extended to the anti-theft system; a teething two-year-old could pop that lock.

"How should I know you didn't have one of those lock-release thingies that are supposed to prevent people from dying in freaking car trunks," Lizzie grumbled, brushing off her plaid skirt and black leggings. "You should clean it out, you know," she said, pulling a wad of old gum out of her frizzy, dark hair. She tugged her hair back into an elastic. "It's like a landfill site in there, and smells like a petting zoo."

"Well, pardon me! I didn't know anyone was moving in."

Virgil had been monitoring the exchange with a wary look, which had now turned weary. "Lizzie, why did you climb in the trunk?"

The girl sighed and rolled her eyes. "Well, duh . . . so I could come out here and get a good look at the castle. I've been out walking in these woods a lot," she said, waving her hand around to take in the whole of the Wynter Woods, "but I've never been able to break into . . . uh . . ." She trailed off, and shifted gears, finishing with, "That is, I've never gotten to see the inside of the castle."

She had a camera around her neck, a really *good* camera. I squinted at her with, I'll admit it, some suspicion. I was remembering Gogi's story about the girl having to do community service because she spray-painted on grave-stones. "Why didn't you just ask me if you could come out and have a look?"

She shrugged. Virgil's puzzled gaze shifted from one of us to the next.

"Shi, why don't you take her inside and feed her muffins," I suggested, "while I talk to the sheriff."

"Sure. Want to meet my bunny?" Shilo said, leading the girl away.

"As long as that's not code for something weird," Lizzie said, trudging after her.

"I'll be in soon," I yelled after them. Shilo waved without looking back. "And don't let her out of your sight."

"I won't," Lizzie shot back.

I chuckled and shook my head. "I know a bit about her story," I said, turning to Virgil. "Gogi told me she was caught spray-painting gravestones."

He nodded. "Yeah, not good, I know; her mom is a piece of work. Just showed back up in Autumn Vale a year or so ago with Lizzie in tow, after being gone for years. Lizzie will not say why she was vandalizing tombstones."

I turned and watched Shilo and Lizzie as they entered the castle. "I heard that she's living with her grandmother?"

"Yeah, her mom's mom. No one knows who Lizzie's dad is, or even if he's local. The dad could be some dude her mother picked up wherever she took off to after high school."

One more mystery in a town that seemed to offer them by the gross. "What do you want to know, Sheriff?"

He took me back through my interaction with Tom, and even my brief encounters with Binny, giving me no hint what he was looking for. I also told him all that I'd heard in town, about Junior Bradley and Tom Turner's fight a while ago. When I was done, he shook his head.

"Keep everything locked up tight, okay? There was another break-in last night not too far from here, just a farmer's shed, but I want you to be careful."

"Maybe that was Tom's killer, have you thought of that?"

With a disgusted look on his face, he said, carefully, "Well, Miss Big City, no, gee golly gosh, I never would have thought that a break-in and a murder the same night might be connected. Thank you *so much* for pointing that out."

Okay, he had a point. He turned and started walking away.

"Hey, wait a minute!" I called after him. "Do you have any leads? Are you going to interview Junior Bradley? What's going on?"

"I can't comment on that," he said.

"What do you mean, you can't comment?" I raced after him and caught his sleeve. "I'm not a reporter, for crying out loud; I'm the one who found Tom's body."

"All the more reason." And he was gone, off talking to the team, which appeared to be wrapping up. I watched as they moved Tom's body, bagged in black, into the hearse and cleaned up the area of all of their tools. It was sobering, and left me with the familiar desire to leave, to run away from sorrow. It tugged at my heart, urging me to abandon ship. So far, life in Autumn Vale had been such a mixed bag of fear, sadness, and bafflement that I just didn't know what to make of it all.

Just as the hearse started to clear out and the cops looked like they'd be doing the same soon, Jack McGill booted up the lane in his Smart car. Together we watched the hearse drive off, then I said, "Want to come in? A teenage girl named Lizzie is here; she kind of hitched a ride with us. Maybe you can take her back to town."

"Lizzie Proctor? I know who you mean." He looked toward the castle. "Troubled girl. Doesn't get along with anyone."

"Neither do I," I grumbled. I was tired and completely worn out. "You people have the strangest little town I've ever seen."

As we walked toward the castle, I asked him about Dinah

Hooper, telling him what Isadore Openshaw had said. "But Dinah seemed like an okay woman to me. What does Isadore have against her?" I could not believe their feud was over catnip mice.

"Beats me. Isadore is a little odd. Never married. Has cats. Lives alone."

"And that makes her odd?" I challenged. "Good lord, McGill, I thought better of you than that."

He held up both hands in protest. "That's not me!" he protested. "I'm just repeating what the locals have been saying. Even folks at the bank find her odd. My mom knows her from book club and says she's kind of got a conspiracy-theory paranoia. Thinks people are watching her home. She moved here about ten years ago to take care of her brother, and when he died, she stayed."

"So she's not a born-and-bred local?"

"Not exactly."

"Could've fooled me. She certainly has the Autumn Vale stamp of peculiarity." I glanced over at McGill, but he didn't seem offended by my grumpy honesty. We circled the castle and entered through the butler's pantry door to find Shilo and Lizzie sitting together companionably, eating muffins and drinking milk. McGill's eyes lit up when he saw Shilo, but first he said, "Hey, Lizzie. How's school going this year? You're a junior, right?"

"I'm just the belle of the ball, y'know? Half the boys in love with me, the girls all jealous bitches. Five dates lined up for junior prom already. Which lucky guy shall I choose as my escort? And gee whiz, will he bring me a wrist corsage?"

I cocked my head and examined her. She had a definite edge to her, but I'd bet she was smarter than any of the kids in her class. If I didn't watch it, I'd find myself liking her. "Why aren't you in school today?"

"Got suspended."

"Already?" I exclaimed.

"Yup. New record."

"Hi, McGill," Shilo said, throwing him a muffin. "Sit. Eat!"

"Be honest," I said, sitting down. "Why did you hide out in Shi's trunk, Lizzie?"

She chewed and swallowed a bit of her muffin, drank some milk, made a face, and set her glass down carefully. "I think I know who killed Tom Turner."

Chapter Twelve

❊ ❊ ❊

OF COURSE WE all shouted at once, but since we all
shouted different things it was kind of a scramble of
"Who?" "How do you know?" and "What did you see?"

I was the one who shouted "Who?"

Lizzie looked a little scared, and Magic, the bunny, who
had been sitting quietly munching on a carrot—I didn't mention that before, did I?—squeaked and jumped off the table.

I put up my hands for silence, let Lizzie finish her last
bite, and said, calmly, "Who do you think killed Tom
Turner?"

"That weirdo Gordy Shute," she mumbled.

"Gordy?" I was puzzled. "Why would Gordy kill Tom
Turner?"

Lizzie looked calmly across the table to McGill. "Why
don't *you* tell her?"

The real estate agent looked puzzled. "I don't know what
you're talking about, Lizzie."

She rolled her eyes. "Oh, come *on*! I've only been here
a year, and I know about this old crap. Everyone knows that

Tom was always a big old bully, and that he used to pick on Gordy back in high school."

"Where did you hear that?" I asked. "That was forever ago, if they were teenagers."

"It's a small town," Lizzie said. "People still talk about the earthquake of 1957 as if it happened last week."

I blew air out through pursed lips. The amount I didn't know about living in a small town . . . well, it was a tonnage. I eyed her with some respect; the kid was smart. Could a grudge live that long in the incubating atmosphere of Autumn Vale? Did proximity fester rage?

Shilo was staring at McGill. "Did you go to school with them, Tom and Gordy and Zeke?"

He was kind of pinkish as he said, "I went to school in another town, a . . . a religious school."

He seemed embarrassed. Maybe in Autumn Vale that made him an oddball? In New York, every second kid went to Hebrew school, a Roman Catholic academy, or a new age arts school. "Just because Tom bullied Gordy," I said, "it doesn't mean that Gordy would want to kill the guy, Lizzie." To her, high school was the current state of her suffering, but about fifteen years later? Folks might remember that Tom was a bully, but the feelings from past events could not be running as hot. It was possible though, that there was a more current tension between them.

"Whatever," Lizzie said, shrugging her shoulders. "Are you going to show me around this place, or what?"

I stared at her, bemused by her moodiness. "How old are you?"

"How old are *you*?" she shot back.

Shilo suppressed a snort.

McGill, two spots of red on his gaunt cheeks, said, "Lizzie, you might want to try being polite for a change."

"She has a point," I said, watching her. "Why should she answer, unless I'm willing to do the same? I'm thirty-nine. And three-quarters."

Her eyes widened. "Geez, my mom is only thirty-two. I turned fifteen a month ago."

"Happy belated birthday. Was the camera a gift?"

"You could say that."

Not exactly a straightforward answer, but maybe it was none of my business. I was not going to be bullied in my own castle, however, by a teenager with bad manners. "Lizzie, you might want to consider this; you have a long life to live ahead of you. At the rate you're offending people, you're going to run out of folk to talk to before you're twenty."

Shilo snickered and McGill smiled.

"That doesn't matter because I'm going to be out of this hick town the moment I turn eighteen."

"Where are you going to go?" Shilo asked.

"New York, where people actually have lives," she grumbled, slumping down in her chair.

"Look, I know being fifteen can suck at times," I said. "Been there, done that. But like it or not, you're stuck here for at least another three years, right? Not everyone is out to make you miserable, and it's up to you to figure out who might be an ally, and who just needs to be ignored."

She was silent, for once, and looked like she might actually be thinking about that.

"Gogi Grace is an ally; you've already figured that out, I think."

More silence.

"Besides, even in New York you have to be nice to people sometimes," I said. "Now, do you want to rephrase your request for a tour?"

She watched my eyes, fiddling with her camera. "Okay. Can I see the castle? Please?"

"That's better. Sure." I left McGill and Shilo to flirt cautiously in the kitchen, and I took the kid on a tour. I even let her take photos. As we left one of the bedrooms—not mine or Shilo's . . . I left those out of the tour—I said to her, "No Facebooking them, okay? No sharing them at *all* without

my permission, and that goes for anything on my property."
I thought it best to lay the groundwork so there would be no
misunderstandings later.

She shrugged. "My grandma doesn't have Internet
access," she said, "and no one will buy me a cell phone. So
I don't have Facebook or anything. I'm a pariah."

A pariah . . . how did she even know that word? What an
odd girl! "Just putting it out there. What do you photograph?"
I asked as we moved back down the stairs to the main
hallway.

She didn't answer until she had framed and taken a photo
of the rose window, and the double oak doors. Then she sat
down on the steps. "Wanna see?" I sat beside her and together
we scrolled through all the photos on her SLR digital camera.
She took all kinds of pictures . . . people, places, and nature.
She was pretty good. Better at framing photos than me, that
was for sure.

"Where is that?" I asked, as she scrolled to a photo of a
wooded area, and a sad, leaning tent spotted with mildew.

"That's in your woods . . . or I think it's *probably* your
woods," she said. "I don't know where the property line is,
or anything. There's a few trails. I followed one, and then
there's kind of a clearing beneath a hill; that's where this
camp is. Creepy. All kinds of crap there . . . old tins, clothes,
other stuff." She brought up an interesting photo of a burned-
out fire, with a can of beans, the label charred and the lid
half opened.

I made a mental note to walk through the woods sometime. If there was an old encampment, that was the kind of
thing I wanted cleaned out, so it didn't encourage trespassing. "Can you show me where this is sometime?"

"Sure. If I remember. Like I said, there's a kind of path
to it, but it's overgrown and weedy. This picture was from,
like, June or something."

"Do you ever come across other camps?"

"Sometimes," she said.

"If you do, I want to know. I'd appreciate it." Of course, I didn't want her to be wandering in my woods alone, but that was a conversation for another day. If I had made enough of an impression, she might just ask me when she wanted to explore, instead of sneaking around.

She nodded, but was silent. She was a complicated girl. Chatty and gushing while I showed her around the castle, she had now clammed up and become broody again, as moody as fifteen can be. She clicked through to another photo, and I yelped. "Hey, that orange cat," I said, pointing to the picture on the screen. A big orange fluffy cat was sitting on a stump, staring directly at the photographer. "Do you see it often?"

"Sure. Whenever I'm in the woods it follows me, but I can't get close to it, I don't know why."

I stared at the photo, wondering if it was indeed my uncle's cat, Becket. I was going to have to remember to take treats in my pocket when I went for a walk in the woods. If it was Melvyn's cat, I wanted to rescue it.

McGill came out to the entry hall, with Shilo trailing behind him.

"McGill, is this my uncle's cat? Show him the picture, Lizzie."

He bent over and looked at the photo. "Yup, that's Becket all right."

Wow. The cat had been living in the woods for so long? Amazing.

"I gotta get going," McGill said, straightening to his full height. "Come on, Lizzie, I'll give you a lift back to town."

She rose and nodded. She turned to me and said awkwardly, "Thanks for showing me the castle. It's cool."

"You're welcome," I said. "If you'd like to come out again, let me know. Just don't stow away in a car trunk."

Her eyes lit up, but she merely nodded, and trailed McGill to the double oak door.

"McGill, would you have a moment free tomorrow?" I asked.

"I might. How can I help you?"

I was aware that I was seriously imposing on his time, but there was so much I needed to know about Autumn Vale, and people I needed to talk to. "I have to talk to Junior Bradley about the zoning for this real estate venture my uncle and Rusty Turner were involved in. Would you go with me to talk to him?"

"Well, sure, I can go. But Junior's an okay guy. He's just got a lot on his plate lately."

"You think it would be all right to talk to him alone?"

"Yeah," McGill said. "I have to deal with him all the time, and he's fine, once you get past his attitude. All business when it comes down to it."

"Okay."

"But if you still want me to go with you, just give me a call." McGill said he'd be back to continue filling in holes when the cops released the site, and then he and Lizzie left, the Smart car tootling down the winding laneway. McGill beeped the horn just before they disappeared around the bend.

Shilo said she was going to find Magic, who had hopped away after being startled in the kitchen. I stood looking out over the scene, leaning against the door frame. I was so tired, for a moment I felt like I was floating away above the grounds, looking down the hole to poor Tom at the bottom. It was a nightmare vision, and I shook my head, trying to rid myself of the lingering impression. Whatever he had done in life, he hadn't deserved to be murdered.

Who wanted him dead? I had a host of possibilities.

Junior Bradley had to be at the top of my list because of his fight with Tom at that bar. Dinah Hooper, his father's girlfriend . . . well, I didn't actually know of any reason, but there were such close ties there. One man in her life was missing and one was dead. She had to be a suspect.

I guess I had to add Gordy Shute to the mix, given Lizzie's description of the torment Tom had inflicted on him, and even Binny made the list. She didn't appear to be on particularly close terms with her brother. Neither of those seemed likely to me, though.

This was ridiculous. I squeezed my eyes shut. Why had I promised Hannah I would try to figure out who did it? I had a feeling that whenever Hannah wanted something, she would just turn her luminous gray eyes on the person, and they would agree to anything. Even *she* hadn't been able to answer the one outstanding question that was bugging me the most; what was Tom Turner digging on my grounds for? It was absurd to think he was looking for his father's body. Only Binny apparently believed that.

And I had told Gogi I'd try to find out if my uncle was murdered. Melvyn was eighty and driving along a treacherous, icy road. Why did it have to be murder? And was I really going to play Nancy Drew?

When I opened my eyes, it was to find Virgil Grace standing before me, a mixture of sympathy and weariness on his face. "Hi, Sheriff. Sorry. I guess I drifted off for a moment just standing here."

"I don't blame you. We're pretty much finished there, but I'm putting crime-scene tape around the hole and I'd appreciate it if you could keep away from it until I say different. I know Jack wants to get going on filling it in, but he's going to have to find another excavator for now, and work on other holes."

"Another excavator?" That was bad news. I was prepared for a delay, but not the barring of the little excavator's use altogether. "For how long?" I asked, dismayed.

"Can't say," he grunted, his tone clipped. "Until I say so." He turned to go.

"Sheriff, hey! I'm sorry, you know . . . about Tom Turner. Were you and he friends?"

He had turned to watch me, and shrugged. "Kinda. I mean, we were on the high school football team together.

We hung out, but not in recent years. He passed his time with a different crowd."

"With guys like Junior Bradley?"

"What do you know about that?" he asked, squinting at me as the sun set behind him, the gleaming shards of light streaking his dark hair with silver. It made him look older and, to me, more attractive. He moved back to stand in front of me, looking down into my eyes with his curious, flat gaze.

Behind me, in the house, I could hear Shilo clattering up and down stairs, yelling, "Magic! Magic!" like a demented conjurer. The sheriff had lines under his eyes, and I almost reached out to smooth his ruffled hair back from his temple. I shivered. "What do I know about Junior Bradley? Just what I told you earlier, that I heard he and Tom got into it at some sleazy dive bar. Why?"

"Nothing."

But there was something, and I'd swear it was more than just a bar fight over a woman. I stared at him, unblinking.

"Look, I know this is awkward for you, being new here, and the owner of this place," he said, waving to include all of Wynter Castle and its environs. "But just let me do my job, which is to figure out who killed Tom Turner. Believe me, I want to know. Tom was a good guy. You didn't know him that way, but I did."

"I heard he was a bully in high school."

Virgil shrugged. "High school was a long time ago. People change."

"One more question," I said as he started to walk away, and he turned back again. "Do you think that Tom's murder has anything at all to do with his father's disappearance?"

"Disappearance? You mean Rusty? So you believe that story that Dinah's spinning, that Rusty just up and disappeared. He left his son and daughter and business and just evaporated, poof, into a puff of smoke."

That statement told me more than anything about his

own beliefs on the matter. "Okay, so you think Rusty Turner is dead. Is Tom's murder a part of the whole mess? Do you suspect Dinah?"

"Not specifically. And I don't know where Rusty is, dead or alive. Other than that, I can't comment," he said, turning away and stalking toward his cruiser. "Lock your doors at night," he hollered back at me, then got in, slammed the door, gunned the motor, and skidded out of my weedy drive with a screech of tires. Was he angry? At what?

"Man, he was pissed," Shi said from behind me.

I turned around, and she was holding Magic. The bunny was nibbling at her chin. "I know. But why? Is it because he hasn't got a clue who killed Tom Turner, or because he thinks he may know, and doesn't like it?"

Chapter Thirteen

❈ ❈ ❈

I CALLED HANNAH and asked her—since she had a computer and Internet access—to do research for me on New York State rules and regulations as far as making food for a nursing or retirement home. She called me back and confirmed Gogi's statement that I needed a licensed, inspected premise to bake the muffins. I was skating on dangerous ground by making them in the castle kitchen without a permit. She gave me a list of phone numbers to call to ask about getting the official paperwork I needed.

I made calls to the state licensing board and set up a preliminary inspection, just to tell me what I needed to do before getting a permit to make muffins in my kitchen. Of course, the end result of that was a stiff warning not to do any baking for the public until I received a permit. Which meant that I needed to find a kitchen to work in immediately if I was going to keep supplying Golden Acres with muffins.

It was a good excuse to visit Binny again, since that was one of the few places that had a license to make food, but there were a couple of other possibilities that Hannah suggested, among them the nursing home itself. She also said the Brotherhood of Falcons hall had a permit. Of *course* the men themselves never cooked, but they did rent it out for weddings, and the local women's guild borrowed it for dinners and events. I just didn't know if I could deal with a group of men who actually had a meeting to discuss a formal order to bar women from the premises. I concluded it was too risky—to their genitalia, such as it was—and mustered up the fortitude to call Binny, not sure what the reception would be like.

To my surprise, she asked me to come in the next morning to talk.

Shilo and I spent the rest of the day planning the work the castle needed, while I tried to avoid thinking about Tom Turner, and the fact that there was a murderer out there. After the last twenty-four hours, we were both exhausted and turned in early to read, my selection a book of poetry, Elizabeth Barrett Browning's *Sonnets from the Portuguese*. My uncle, surprisingly, had an extensive collection—Keats, Longfellow, Blake, Tennyson, Shelley, Coleridge—but it was all over the place in a tiny, airless dungeon of a room with bad lighting. That was one big change I planned. Books deserve better conditions, and there was a library downstairs that would be perfect once cleaned and aired.

I was up early the following morning, and sat at the kitchen table with my notepad and a cup of coffee, planning my next few days and all I had to do. I got the surprise of my life when Shilo joined me. She is a lay-abed, as I call her, loving to sleep in, cocooned in blanketed comfort. But there she was, dressed and ready for coffee, appearing in the kitchen doorway, Magic in hand, while I was only on my second cup.

While I made her some coffee, she grabbed lettuce and carrots out of the fridge and set Magic on the table with his vegetarian munchies. Magic was just a plain bunny, kind of a brownish-gray color, completely undistinguished, but Shilo loved him with a fierce protectiveness that was almost maternal.

Maternal. I cocked my head and watched her. My funny friend had always flitted from man to man, as if she were a butterfly in the garden of love. But did the ever-increasing noise of the female's biological clock sound *tick-tick-tick* even in *her* ears? Was her interest in McGill more than as another fleeting romance in a long string?

Nah. Impossible.

"What are you going to do today?" I asked Shilo as I got ready to head to Autumn Vale.

"I'm coming to town with you," she said.

I was surprised, but glad of the company. She confined Magic to his cage, and we set off in my car. As soon as we hit town, however, Shi headed off alone to "explore," as she called it.

I had timed my arrival at Binny's Bakery to be after the morning baking was done, but before the customers started arriving. As suggested by Binny, I went to the back, where there was a steel door off the alleyway. I rapped on it and was admitted, the warm, yeasty air flooding over me in waves and taking me back to my grandmother's kitchen. My mom wasn't much of a cook; she had been too involved in social committees and action plans, marching and protesting and burning her bra in public places, much to my teenage mortification. But my grandmother more than made up for it. Taking in a good, deep sniff of the air, I happily followed Binny through the bakery kitchen, lined with stainless steel, commercial-size ovens, to a little table in the corner, where she had a French press coffeemaker and chocolate croissants on a platter.

For little old moi? I felt like crying. It was like being back in the Village at a favorite coffee shop. Why was she being so nice, especially since her brother and I had had a heated disagreement practically hours before his murder? But I would take whatever I could get.

Once we had steaming cups in front of us, and I had devoured a chocolate croissant, I regarded her with interest.

Her hair was flyaway in the steam-bath atmosphere of the kitchen, and her cheeks were red, but she seemed serene, not at all as testy as she had been with Gogi and with me. It was odd, considering her brother had died just the day before.

"You do love baking, don't you?" I asked, to break the ice.

She nodded. "I call it dough therapy. When I'm baking, I let go of everything: every stress, every pain, every rotten memory." She paused, then continued. "It's the one thing my dad really came through on, this bakery," she said, waving her strong hands around at the kitchen. "He sent me to culinary school, and paid for this place."

"What about your mom? I hear that she left your dad when you were a kid." That was a little personal, but I was still trying to figure out what was the best way to deal with someone as prickly as Binny. Would she freeze up under direct questioning, or was she the type who liked straightforward talk?

"I still talk to my mom often," she said. "She was dying in this little town. I didn't see it that way at the time, but now I know that she and Dad weren't getting along, and she had to leave. My dad is a huntin', fishin', woodsy kind of guy, you know? Guns and camo and outdoors stuff."

"I've seen the photos of you with your dad, and Dinah with your dad, too. I was surprised Dinah would go hunting. She doesn't seem that kind of woman."

"Everyone in this town hunts and fishes . . . well, pretty much everyone, anyway. Even Mrs. Grace. You'd be surprised, but she wins the lady's target shoot at the fall fair every single year."

"Wow. Gogi Grace?"

Binny nodded.

"I would have taken her for the uptown kind of woman," I said, thinking of my new friend's elegance.

Binny returned to the subject of her mother. "Anyway, she hated Autumn Vale. We went to Chicago to stay with her mom and dad. I'm glad we did because I learned to bake from my grandmother."

"Me, too!" I said, surprised by some of the weird connections we had. I shared my own upbringing, which was, in a way, similar to hers, and then silence fell between us. I was just about to discuss my proposal that I use her ovens, when she burst into speech.

"Okay, so here it is," she said, rapping her knuckles on the tabletop. "I was wondering . . . I mean, you're new in town, and I was thinking . . ." She shook her head.

I was intrigued. "What's up, Binny? Talk to me."

"I don't know what to think," she said, staring into my eyes. "Tom said he thought Dad was dead, and that Melvyn killed him and buried him at the castle. But that's dumb. Melvyn Wynter was, like, a hundred years old." She paused and screwed up her mouth, before saying, "Dinah thinks that Dad is alive, and just took off. But she can't tell me *why* she thinks it."

Her voice had clogged with tears. I thought of all I had heard, and how everyone assumed that her dad was dead. But what if he wasn't? "So what if Dinah is right, and your dad isn't dead, just missing?"

"*Exactly!* What if he's alive but just staying away from Autumn Vale for some reason?"

It seemed a little far-fetched. "Why do you think Dinah is saying he's still alive? What is going on that she thinks he might purposely disappear like that?"

Binny was silent for a long minute. "Look, can I trust you?" she finally asked.

How do you answer a question like that? It seemed to me that faint hope of her father being alive was distracting her from her brother's death, so I'd play along. "You can trust me to keep my mouth shut unless what you have to tell me is about something illegal, immoral, or fattening," I joked.

She clapped her mouth shut. And it stayed shut. "You need to use my ovens," she finally said. "That's why you're here, right? You can use them any afternoon, because I do all my baking in the early morning."

I had clearly put my foot in it. Which was it, I wondered, illegal or immoral? Fattening was clearly not a problem. I took another bite of chocolate croissant, chewed, swallowed, and said, "Binny, you have to know I was joking."

She examined me for a long minute. There were so many pauses in our conversation it was the word equivalent of Swiss cheese. "I just don't know who to turn to," she said, her voice thick with tears. "It's all such a mess. Dinah has been the only one . . . I mean, she's at least someone who cared for Dad. If she honestly thinks he's alive . . ." She shook her head and clamped her lips shut, though they still trembled. "I think she's trying to protect me somehow. But from what? And then, I found . . ." She stopped and shook her head again.

"Found what?"

But she was mute, just shaking her head. I was touched and sad for her. When my grandmother died and then my mom, six months later, I was a mess. Virtually the same thing was happening to her now at just a little older than I had been. "What did you find?" I urged again. "Something that leads you to believe your dad is alive? Why don't we talk about this whole mess?"

The shop door jangled, indicating customers. She grabbed a rag and blotted her eyes, settled her expression, and headed out to the shop. I could hear her talking, and then the door jangled again a couple of times, quickly. I tried to imagine what it was that had suddenly given her hope that her father was alive. When things quieted down, she came back to the kitchen, more composed. I stood, but just then the bells over the door jangled once again. She headed to the door.

"Look, Binny," I said, stopping her by putting my hand on her shoulder. "I know what you're going through. Or at least . . . I know some of what you're going through. I have a lot of questions, but you're getting busy." I felt her tense, needing to tend to her shop. "Why don't you . . . would it be too hard for you to come out to the castle after the shop closes? Come out for dinner?" Tom's body was gone, but I wasn't sure she could handle coming to the site of his murder.

She nodded. "Yeah. Okay. I will. I know the way."

We set a time, and I left the shop with an agreement that I would come out the next day to use her ovens to bake muffins.

But I wasn't heading home. I took out my cell phone and miracle of miracles, it decided to work! I punched in a number from memory.

"Jack McGill here," came the real estate agent's voice.

"Hey, McGill, it's Merry Wynter. I wanted to check . . ."

"I'm not available right now, but if you leave your name and number, I'll get right back to you!"

Darned voice mail! I hated the kind that fooled you into thinking you'd reached the person you wanted. I clicked my phone off and stuffed it back in my purse. McGill had said that Junior Bradley was fine, and who would know better? The township zoning offices were on a short, dead-end street off Abenaki, so I walked there after stopping back into Binny's Bakery, leaving word with her where I was headed in case Shilo stopped by looking for me.

The door listed office hours as eight a.m. to four p.m.; I rapped and walked in. It was a dusty, dank, little space, no light, little air. Junior Bradley sat at the only desk, a metal monstrosity from the fifties or earlier, and glared at a computer screen that showed a FreeCell game in mid-play.

"Hi," I said brightly, determined to be friendly even though his expression as he looked up at me was as if he had bitten into a lemon. "We haven't formally met yet, but I'm Merry Wynter," I reminded him, "Melvyn Wynter's great-niece and heir." I moved forward, hand stuck out, but he ignored it.

"Okay, so what do you want?"

He wasn't going to be polite. All right, kill him with

kindness, as my grandmother used to say. "I'm *so* sorry. I know you must be devastated, having just lost your best friend, Tom Turner. And how sad that your last dealing with him was a fistfight!"

His face turned bright red, but he only sputtered and shook his head. I sat down in the uncomfortable, rickety chair across from him and crossed my legs. The chair wobbled precariously, and I quickly uncrossed my legs and sat straight. I did not want to end up on the floor, legs in the air; *so* undignified. "Look, I'm not here to talk about Tom Turner or his death," I said. Mendacity suited me at that moment. "It's none of my business. But I *am* here to find out some information about my property. I understand that Turner Wynter Construction had some kind of plan to build a subdivision, or neighborhood . . . or something, on the castle property. I've begun to look through my uncle's papers, but they're a mess, and it's going to take me a while. Can you tell me anything about it?"

He stared at his computer screen for a long minute, then pasted a weak smile on his pale face. "I can try to help," he said. "I'm just real torn up about Tom. We were kids together, you know?"

My bull-crap radar was beeping loudly, and I never ignore that. "I had heard you were best friends, but that things had changed between you lately."

He sighed. "Yeah, we were friends, and rivals. We dated the same girls, played the same games, sometimes on the same side, sometimes against each other. It was never serious, you know, when we fought over women."

"Like the last time?"

"The last time?"

"The last time, when you had a bar fight, reportedly over a girl named Emerald?" I watched his expression.

His face was lined beyond his years, and he had pouches under his weak eyes. He rubbed them and pinched over his nose. "Uh, that was just . . . a misunderstanding."

"On whose part?"

"Mine. I . . . uh . . . I thought the girl was, uh . . . trying to tell him to get lost and he wasn't listening. Look, what's that got to do with anything?" He squinted across the desk at me and leaned over on his elbows. "Didn't you say you wanted to talk about your uncle's zoning problems?"

"Problems? I didn't actually know there were problems."

He picked up a pencil and began tapping it on the desktop. "Well, yeah, you know, Melvyn and Rusty . . . not the two sharpest tools in the shed. And always at cross purposes. One would file a paper and the other wouldn't know a thing about it." He shrugged. "They would have worked things out eventually, I guess."

Helped by him? In a town as small as Autumn Vale, you wouldn't think two partners could be working so determinedly at cross purposes. Something didn't seem right. "But there were lawsuits in the works, then Rusty disappeared and Melvyn died."

He nodded. "Yup."

"Where does that leave me?" I asked, curious about what he'd say.

He colored pinkish. "What do you mean?"

"How can I clean up my zoning problems?"

"You mean, you intend to go ahead?"

I narrowed my eyes and watched him for a moment. He seemed panicked. What about? "I haven't decided yet. But one thing I know for sure: the zoning still being up in the air is not good news for a potential buyer. I'd like to get everything sorted out and resolve the lawsuits that were in play at the time of my uncle's death. Can I see the paperwork?"

"What paperwork?"

I was losing patience quickly. "The paperwork having to do with the zoning of my uncle's—and now *my*—acreage." I thought *way* back to my few months working in a zoning and planning permissions office in New York. "I'd like to see any plans that were filed, as well as the paperwork that went with it, any zoning change requests, building permits, lot subdivisions, *anything.*"

"I'll . . . uh, well, geez, I'll need a while to pull everything together," he said, rising and walking over toward the door. "I'll give you a call when I have it all ready, okay? I got work to do, now, so you run along and I'll give you a call."

I didn't get up to leave, I just turned in my seat to watch him, standing there, the door open to the outside, where autumn sunshine was flooding the street. A breeze fluttered in the open doorway, clarifying the musty air. "You're playing a computer game, Mr. Bradley. Surely you can pull away from that to get me some paperwork."

"Uh, I don't even know if I can show it to you, you know," he said, and cleared his throat. He rocked onto the balls of his feet and back. "It's, uh . . . well, I don't know. You know, it was Rusty's project, too, and with Tom gone, maybe Dinah is in charge."

"Or maybe Binny is," I said.

He was getting redder by the minute. "Binny doesn't know a damned thing about her father's business."

"Is that why Tom is dead and Binny's alive?" I asked. It just popped out. It was a dumb thing to say.

"I don't know what the heck you're talking about," he said.

His mystification *seemed* genuine. I got up and strolled toward the door, stepping through and turning back. "When can I come to look over the paperwork?"

His expression hardened. "When you've got a court order." He slammed the door in my face and I heard the lock *snick.*

Jerk.

I rounded up Shilo, who had been shopping in a couple of places, and we got groceries and headed back to the castle. About six, Binny Turner rolled up to the parking area in a white van that read Binny's Bakery on the side. She strode up to the castle with her gaze resolutely turned away from the hole that was still cordoned off with police crime scene tape. I met her at the door and showed her around the place, then we sat in the kitchen and ate dinner. I'd made chicken spaghetti, which went nicely with the focaccia she had brought and the bottle of merlot I found tucked away in my uncle's wine cellar. I was definitely going to have to explore the cellar a little more thoroughly, because the merlot was not half bad.

Over dinner, I told her and Shilo what had happened with Junior Bradley in the zoning office.

"What is his problem?" Shilo said, indignant on my behalf.

"He and Tom really were lifelong friends," Binny said, doubt creeping into her voice. "He's probably just reacting, you know, to Tom dying."

Her voice broke on the last word, and I impulsively put out my hand, covering hers on the table. I shared a look with Shilo, who got up, collecting our plates.

"You've gone through so much," I said softly, leaning toward her. "I want you to know, I understand. I *do*. I've lost a lot of people in my life, and grief changes you, at least for a while. And sometimes for always." My voice caught on the last word, as I thought of Miguel.

"I just . . . I don't want to wallow, you know? I called my mom last night. She's going to come to Autumn Vale next week and spend a couple of weeks here to . . . to help plan the funeral. I mean . . . I don't know when I can hold it because the police haven't released the b-body yet. But I'm all Tom had left, with Dad who knows where, so I'm going to have to take care of it."

She broke down and cried then, her head cradled in her arms on the table, and I was glad. She had been holding it all in, determined to be strong, but strength doesn't come from suppressing emotion. I knew, because I had gone that route and all it led to was an emotional collapse. I went around to her side of the table and sat beside her, at first rubbing her back, but then talking about Tom, and her complicated relationship with her brother.

She seemed grateful to speak with someone who had no personal feelings in the matter. They had been apart for a significant portion of her childhood, so when she came back to Autumn Vale she had had to forge a new relationship with her brother. That had been complicated by her father's disappearance just months after she opened the bakery. She and Tom had gotten along all right, but were not close, and she still felt like an outsider in Autumn Vale, even though she had been born here.

"I didn't know what to think, at first, when Dad disappeared. I mean, Tom seemed certain Dad was murdered, and by Melvyn!" She sighed. "I just didn't know what to believe. He knows everyone so much better than I do."

I remembered what she said in the bakery when she asked if she could trust me. What had she been about to tell me when I made that ill-timed joke? A direct question would probably just scare her off. "But you see how ridiculous that is, right, to think that Melvyn could have killed and then buried your father?" I asked, as Shilo ran water and squirted detergent in the sink. When Binny nodded, I said, "*I* think Tom never actually believed that your dad was buried on the Wynter property, it was just an excuse to justify to you why he was digging." I paused to let that sink in. "But if that's so, then what was he looking for here? And who else knew he'd be here digging?"

She looked thoughtful, but shook her head. "I just don't know. I wish I did."

I wished she did, too. Shilo sat back down opposite me and we exchanged glances. "Did your brother have any enemies?" I asked. "Was he involved with anyone?"

"He didn't have a girlfriend. I know people said stuff about some dancer, but I don't think that was serious, just guy stuff, you know? Between him and Junior? He had a serious girlfriend a long time ago, but then she left town and that was it. He said he wasn't the marrying kind."

"What about work?"

"Work . . . you mean the company? Turner Construction? Him and Dinah have been trying to keep it afloat since Dad disappeared."

"Is that why she asked for the key to the office?"

She had a blank look for a moment, then said, "Oh, the other day, in the bakery before . . ." Tears welled in her eyes. "Tom said she'd lost her key, but she hasn't been working there for a while, as far as I know. There wasn't much to do. Tom just wasn't able to keep Turner Construction going like Dad did." She sniffed, and Shilo handed her a paper napkin. "She probably just wanted in to collect some of her personal stuff."

Or maybe Tom wanted the key himself for some reason. It was all a jumble in my head. But my mind kept returning to the zoning problems and Junior's evasion. Was there something there? Did it all come back to that, something about the Wynter property?

"Binny, this is going to seem like an odd request," I said. "But could you get me into the Turner Construction offices to look around sometime?"

"Well, sure." She blew her nose. "How about tonight?"

Chapter Fourteen

AN HOUR LATER, Shilo and I, in her rattletrap vehicle, pulled into the yard by the makeshift offices of Turner Construction behind Binny's van. It was starting to get dark, and the yard was a place of long shadows and murky corners. Before Shi turned off her headlights, I saw the Turner Construction sign looking the worse for wear, a random pattern of holes scattered over it as if it had suffered target practice.

Binny was already at the door of the trailer riffling through a ring of keys and trying them. "I don't know what key works," she lamented. "These are Tom's keys; the cops gave them to me."

"But you have a key to the office yourself, right?" I asked, remembering her refusal to give Tom the office key for Dinah.

"I did have one, but I've . . . uh . . . misplaced it," she said.

Misplaced it?

"Let me try," Shilo said. She took the ring and studied the keys by the yellow bug light over the trailer office door, then she bent over and stared into the lock. She took one key in hand, inserted it, and voilà, the door opened.

Binny gaped, mouth open. I shrugged and said, "Don't ask, because I don't know how she does it."

"I'm a gypsy," Shilo said, her grin wide. "We're good with locks."

We entered, and Binny flicked on a light switch; fluorescents shuddered and blinked into wavering brightness. The place was a mess; papers everywhere, trash bins overturned, surfaces heaped with junk. "Somebody has trashed the place," I said, aghast.

Binny looked around. "No, this is pretty much how it always looks."

Her voice sounded a little odd, and I shot a quick look over at her, but her face was blank. "Dinah Hooper worked here, right?"

Binny nodded. "She was the office manager; took care of day-to-day stuff."

"And she was okay with this mess?"

"She had her hands full lately just trying to keep the company going. Dinah and Tom . . . since Dad has been gone, they didn't work together too well, you know?"

There was an old sofa bed in one corner, and it looked like someone used it to sleep on. I hoped some bum wasn't using the place to hide out, but there was no evidence of that. I suspected Tom had been using it as a crash pad. As far as that went, I didn't even know where he lived, or if he used the office as his full-time apartment. "Had your brother been sleeping here, do you think?"

Binny seemed reluctant to answer, but she nodded. "I think he may have been. He was living at the house with Dad, but then Dinah kind of semi-moved in, and he started to bunk out here, sometimes."

"I thought Dinah and your dad didn't live together?"

"They didn't officially live together, but she stayed there sometimes."

"Do you live in your father's house?"

"Nope. I live over the bakery. It's more convenient. Dad's house is in town, but it's a ways away, at the other end. We own the building my bakery is in, so I took one of the apartments upstairs. Gordy and Zeke share the other one, a two-bedroom over the back."

"So . . . no one is living in your dad's house right now."

She shook her head. Tears began welling in her eyes, and I knew I had to back off. Shilo, meanwhile, while Binny and I were talking and looking around, had sat down at one of the desks and turned on the computer. She was a card game addict, so she was probably taking the opportunity to play solitaire.

"What were they doing businesswise before Tom died?" I asked, scanning the junk, trying to make sense of the place.

"I *think* they were doing work for the Brotherhood of the Falcon. They needed the roof fixed on the hall and some other repairs."

"Really?" I remembered Gordy's wild theories about the Brotherhood; should I be dismissing out of hand what I didn't know a thing about? Then I recalled a random comment made by someone or other. "Your dad was a member, right?"

She nodded, her eyes filling with tears. Again. She turned away and stood, clenching and unclenching her fists.

I hastily moved on. "They weren't doing anything else? Did Tom work with anyone?"

"Not lately," she said, turning back to me, having mastered her emotions. "Not as far as I know. I think they used to hire guys as they needed them. Neither he or Dad talk . . . talked . . . about the business with me."

I looked around. The faux wood–paneled trailer itself was long and narrow, with two desks right near the door, and an area at the back that held a washroom, a kitchenette, and the ratty sofa bed. In between there was a drafting desk by the only window, and along one wall a large, wooden cabinet with shallow drawers that I knew would hold blueprints, maps, and plans. I worked in a planning office when I was a teenager, just as a gopher. For a while I even wanted to be an interior decorator, and thought getting the job at the planning office was a first step. Fetching coffee didn't teach me a whole lot, but snooping did.

"I want to see the plans for the development of Wynter Acres. Do you know if Turner Wynter ran their business out of these same offices?"

"I suppose so," Binny said, looking around dejectedly. "I mean, this is the only office that I know about. I wish I could help more."

"No, it's okay," I said. "You've helped a lot just by letting me in here." More than Junior Bradley had with his obstructionism, I thought.

"Well, if there was—or is, rather—a Turner Wynter Construction Company, then you and I might end up being co-owners of at least part of this mess. I'm going to need help to figure it out."

That wasn't a welcome prospect, because it tied me more firmly to a place I needed to leave, sooner rather than later. But if there really were lawsuits filed, maybe that could be resolved by the two of us more equitably than if Tom had still been involved. "Let me just riffle though the plans, see if I can come up with anything." I pulled a stool over to the cabinet and read the labels, looking for anything that referenced Wynter property. None of the labels made any sense to me, so I just started at the top.

I soon figured out that most of the big jobs had been done years ago, and that lately—whether it was because of the economy or something else—the jobs had been getting smaller and smaller. The most recent big project appeared to be Binny's bakeshop remodel. Turner Construction had redesigned and rebuilt the place to include room for the ovens and front shop area. The upstairs apartment had been renovated. Other than that, there were some sloppy-looking drawings for an addition proposed to the Brotherhood of the Falcon clubhouse, and a proposal for another addition to Gogi Grace's Golden Acres.

I was vaguely aware that Binny was looking over Shilo's shoulder, and I wondered what they were up to. I was about to ask when I suddenly came across charts and drawings that appeared to reference Wynter Acres. I pulled them out of the drawer and rolled my chair over to the drafting table, turning on the powerful light over the desk.

My first impression was that whoever had done the plan was a rank amateur.

First, the plat. A plat is a scale map showing the proposed subdivision of the land, and often includes vegetation and other considerations. This plat was crude; barely legible; and with few markers to show landmarks, elevations or even the lot sizes. It didn't look like they had had a surveyor do the necessary work to mark out the proposed subdivision of the land. If this was the plat registered with Junior Bradley's zoning office, it should have been rejected immediately. Would my uncle have understood enough to know that?

I sat and stared at it for a long time, trying to figure out what was going on. There was no way they could have intended to proceed in subdividing the Wynter land using this plat as a planning device. It was impossible. There wasn't even a compass indication on it, or access roads marked. Why would Rusty's office draw this shoddy plan up in the first place? And it was while Rusty was still in the mix; I could tell by the date, which indicated the plan was from the previous spring. *If* that date was legit. Careless work like this could have numerous mistakes or deliberate errors.

There were so many considerations if they planned on

subdividing Wynter land into a community; what about water? Roads? Drainage? Electricity?

And what about buyers?

The town of Autumn Vale was barely viable as it was, with empty storefronts along Abenaki, and more houses for sale than anyone could ever want. Who did my uncle and Rusty Turner think was going to buy these condos at Wynter Acres? Silvio had claimed the idea was to attract aging boomers who wanted to live in the country but have the convenience of condo living, but the plans I saw were for sizable, single-family dwellings, not condos.

It was ridiculous. Maybe my uncle had been a pie-in-the-sky dreamer, but from all evidence Rusty Turner had been a pragmatic man with many years of experience in the building and development business. He had sent his daughter to culinary school. He had taken whatever small jobs were available in their town. Why have this shoddy plat drawn up? To fool Melvyn?

But . . . *why*?

I remembered something Andrew Silvio had said; Melvyn accused Rusty of cheating him. Based on the plat I had examined, that could well be, if Mel was paying to have the advance work done, and this pathetic piece of crud was what Turner had come up with.

I rolled back to the drawers and leafed through anything else I could find, and concluded that there was no way anyone had had serious plans to develop Wynter Acres. I had gone through a few of my uncle's papers so far, and hadn't come across anything to indicate some long-term strategy . . . unless . . . I cocked my head as I remembered the envelope I had found in my uncle's desk to Turner Wynter Global Enterprises. Was that related to the real estate development? It had to be; it was the only thing the two men were involved in together, as far as I knew.

But had Virgil Grace taken stuff out of the castle when

they searched it? He said he did, but I didn't have the receipt yet, so I didn't know what. That was going to be my first order of business the next day. Did items taken away by the police have anything to do with Wynter Acres?

My head hurt. I was confused, even worse than I had been before this little field trip. I stared at a map of Autumn Vale and followed the valley until I got to a road that rose up to a town on a ridge . . . ah, Ridley Ridge. There was a bar in that town where Tom and Junior Bradley had fought.

Maybe I would need to talk to Emerald and find out a little more about Tom Turner and Junior Bradley and the truth behind the fight. So far he was my star suspect for Tom Turner's murder. Why? I didn't have a clue at this point, except that I was following the violence.

I had one more thing to do. I looked up, but Shilo and Binny were still engrossed in something on the computer, so I went back to the drawers. I began searching through, and found that all of the old stuff was properly drawn up. When Golden Acres was redesigned, for example, it had been perfectly planned and executed, judging by the professional-looking drawings I came across, which included site elevations, blueprints, and drainage locations. Zoning permissions were all in place, as were building permits, with official seals and the zoning office stamp of approval, though the zoning commissioner at the time must have been Junior's predecessor, since the signature was different.

That was the last indication I needed that Wynter Acres, no matter what Uncle Melvyn thought, was never a serious plan, at least as far as Rusty Turner was concerned. Was it possible that my uncle had found this out and turned nasty? I didn't believe for a second that he had killed and buried Rusty on the property, but had he killed him and dumped him somewhere else?

"You done yet, Mer?" Shilo said, her eyes shining with excitement.

"Uh, yeah . . . what's up with you two? What have you

been doing?" Though Shilo looked excited, Binny appeared troubled.

"I think . . . I think my father and my brother were involved in something shady," Binny said.

"I was just coming to the same conclusion," I said. "Why do you think so?"

"The figures don't add up," Shilo said.

Oh, did I forget to mention that Shilo, among her other talents, can look at a list of figures and add them up in her head at warp speed? She can also see anomalies, little things that don't make sense in the numbers. She's an odd duck, to be sure.

"There is a heck of a lot of income coming in," she continued, "but almost no work done to account for it. And there are, like, shadowy references to other accounts, but nothing to back it up. There might be something I'm missing, but I doubt it."

"What could that mean?" I wondered out loud.

Binny spoke up. "The logical explanation, I guess—the *legitimate* explanation—is that if Dad and your uncle were going into business together to develop your uncle's land, maybe they had started up accounts to use for equipment purchases and rentals."

That actually made a lot of sense, and if it was true, then the accounts could have to do with that, and there would be no mystery. "Who did the bookkeeping for your dad's company?"

"Lately? Dinah Hooper."

"Then I think we'll have to ask some questions of Ms. Hooper tomorrow," I said. "I have some of my own for Mr. Silvio and Sheriff Grace, too."

IT WAS ONE OF THOSE SLEEPLESS NIGHTS FOR ME. The next day was going to be full, and the anxiety of unanswered questions, financial worries, and a plethora of other problems had me awake at three a.m. I brewed tea made in my new Brown Betty teapot and filled a mug. As I stood in the pantry doorway, a cool breeze wafted in, the smell of night-scented phlox drifting toward me from the weedy yard, as well as the comforting chirp of crickets. Disregarding the *necessity* of selling this property—I honestly did not see anything changing that—if I could, would I stay here at Wynter Castle? If it were financially feasible, would it be my choice?

Though I had been a city girl most of my life, settling in at the castle had come surprisingly easy. I loved the place; it suited me somehow. Oh, it was *way* too big, and in winter it was going to be hell to heat, and if Shilo hadn't happened to stalk me all the way to upstate New York I would be hideously lonely. But right now, leaning in the doorway of the back door and drinking tea, I was weirdly content for someone who had found a dead body just a couple of nights before.

I had my notebook in the kitchen and I returned to the table and began doodling, which soon enough became a list of ideas that would let me keep the castle. It could become a rest home, a retirement home, an inn, or an event venue, if I chose to run it as one of those things. I could sell off some of the land—if anyone would buy it—or I could . . . I ran out of ideas, and my wayward mind began roaming over random thoughts.

Those random thoughts began to settle around the enigma that was Sheriff Virgil Grace; what did I make of him? He was good-looking in a surly way. Kind of scruffy, but a manly man, to be sure. I do like a manly man. When you're a big girl, being held by a big guy makes you feel fragile and feminine. Dumb, right? But I can't help it! I'm a modern woman with retro hormones.

I recalled a little tidbit that McGill had let slip; Sheriff Grace had other siblings, but when his mom was sick, he was the one who looked after her. Tears welled and one dripped onto the notebook page, smearing my ink; I thumbed the droplet away, which smudged the page even worse. That was my Miguel, all over. When his mom came down with a virulent form of influenza in the first year of our marriage, he flew back to Spain to be with her for six weeks. It had been our only source of contention, but looking back, I was being petty and selfish. If I could only turn back the clock, I would have behaved much differently. If only. I wished with all my heart I could tell him now, that what I had complained of then made him a very good man, and I wouldn't have wanted him to do anything different. Miguel's selflessness and nurturing ability was some of what made me love him so much.

Was Virgil Grace another very good man? I had not been in love, or had a crush, nor had I even kissed another man in seven years. Erotically charged dreams of the past had been my only outlet. Would I ever love again? Would the part of me that died the night Miguel crashed his car ever come back to life?

I sniffed back tears and abandoned that morose nighttime melancholy. I couldn't undo the past, and I couldn't live in it. Picking up and petting Magic—he had somehow, as his name suggested, escaped Shilo's closed room—I reflected on the changes Wynter Castle had worked in me. I felt, like the night-scented phlox that bloomed in wild profusion among the weeds, that I was opening up, blooming to new possibilities in my life. Leatrice's betrayal of me and the friendship I had thought we had was a closed book. Her treachery had poisoned the well of the New York fashion world in a way that hurt to my core, but it had shown me who my real friends were.

When I thought of real friends, Pish Lincoln's name popped into my head. Pish was a brilliant, witty, intensely alive older gentleman who had been a money manager for many a lucky model of my acquaintance. If I had trusted

him with my investments I would not now be broke, but I had
stubbornly thought that the insurance money from Miguel's
death was like funny money to be played with. I tossed it
willy-nilly like confetti, drifting toward stocks in companies
that sounded good to me, or whose products I liked. Pish
had tried to steer me, but I hadn't, to my current chagrin,
listened.

When I figured out more of what Turner Construction was
involved in, maybe he was someone who could answer a few
money questions for me. I trusted him implicitly, and missed
his daily dose of calm, good sense. In fact, a need for information or not, I was going to call him. When I left New York,
I hadn't been sure I could handle all the fond and teary fare-
wells my friends would have foisted on me, and I had slipped
out of the city like a thief in the night. He was going to be
angry, but he never stayed angry for long. Not with me,
anyway.

I set Magic down on the table and wrote a list of things
to do on the morrow. Lists are my thing. I love lists, so making one felt like I was returning to some semblance of my
former self, the self before Leatrice stabbed me in the back
and twisted the knife.

The list:

1. Call Pish Lincoln and throw myself on his mercy.
2. Go to the police station and demand to know what
   they took from the castle.
3. Question Dinah Hooper about the financial dealings
   of Turner and Turner Wynter Construction.
4. Find someone to mow the freaking field that's growing
   up around the castle.

Seriously, Wynter Castle was beginning to look like an
abbey abandoned during the Reformation, only not as neat
and tidy.

Oh yeah . . . I jotted one more thing down on my list.

5. Go for a long walk in the woods with Lizzie, and get
   her to show me the abandoned encampment.

I wanted that torn down, removed, cleansed. Picking up
Magic again, I went back upstairs and actually slept for three
hours, waking up feeling more like myself than I had in
years.

Chapter Fifteen

�֎ �֎ ✖

THE LIST WOULD need to be tweaked, I discovered. I got a call first thing in the morning from Sheriff Grace asking me to come in and sign a statement. If I was going to be out and about, then I may as well do the things on my list that required a trip to town.

Shilo and I, following directions—turn left off Abenaki at the Autumn Vale Community Bank—found the tiny police station. Located at the end of obscure and brief Valley View Avenue, the sheriff's department was a small, modern building with a barracks-like look, narrow, slit windows, and overall gray, drab appearance. I left Shilo in the car, went in past the big, glass, double doors, and was guided to Sheriff Grace's office by a young female deputy. I sat down in an uncomfortable chair across the desk from his leather swivel chair. He joined me moments later, but not before I examined his walls, the "artwork," such as it was, included local citations for his coaching of the town's Little League baseball team and an honorary membership in the Brotherhood of the Falcon. They had made him an "Eyas," which

I guess was a fledgling falcon. Other than that there was a pleasant if nondescript watercolor of an autumn forest.

As he took a seat across the desk, I remembered my late-night thoughts and blushed. I don't blush. Ever! But he was very good looking: dark, wavy hair, thick enough to catch your fingers in, and just that bit of shadow along the jaw, very much like Miguel always had five minutes after shaving. *I have been alone a long time,* I thought. Nothing wrong with a little late-night fantasizing if it was left to late at night. I took a deep breath as he slid some paperwork across the desk to me, regarding me with that steady, unsmiling look he had perfected.

"This is the list of what we took from the castle," he said. "It's mostly paperwork, anything with Tom Turner's name on it."

"Was there a lot with his name on it? Why would there be?" I squinted and examined the paper. Pretty soon I was going to have to admit that I needed close-up glasses—cheaters, my mother had called them. Oh, joy. Anyway, it was a simple list, though from it I could not tell what each document pertained to.

The sheriff shrugged. "Old Melvyn and the Turners were involved in some real estate deal that went bad, and there were lawsuits, so there was a fair bit of paperwork and we just wanted to look it over more closely, see if we can find anything that has to do with Tom. It's a mess of bank loans, defaults, zoning problems, and missed deadlines."

Bank loans? *Oh, lord,* I thought, *I hope that the estate is not saddled with a mountain of debt, undiscovered until now.* I was going to have to take this seriously and untangle the mess before the property was actually salable. I felt like I had been wearing blinders, and they had just fallen off. Lawyer Silvio, among others, had some 'splainin' to do.

"Your uncle also wrote nasty notes to the Turners, and vice versa," the sheriff went on. "I know about a lot of this because I was occasionally involved, called in by both parties at different times. I know very well what those two old men were like."

"But they're all dead now," I said, glossing over the fact that no one truly knew what had happened to Rusty. Despite Binny's and Dinah's hopes, I figured the old guy had probably died, and his body just hadn't been discovered yet. Maybe he went for a walk and fell off a cliff. Who knew? "What does this have to do with Tom's murder?"

"We don't know. But there were things mentioned in the letters . . ." He stopped abruptly.

I was intrigued. "What kind of things?"

He regarded me calmly. "Tom was well-enough liked by many, but he had his peccadilloes."

Peccadilloes; is that what they called them in a small town? I smiled inwardly. "Such as?"

"Girlfriends he had cheated on. Friends he had betrayed in some way or another. Don't we all have those dark spots in our past?"

I stiffened. It felt like his comments were aimed at me. It would only take a phone call or two to come across Leatrice's accusations of thievery against me. Maybe he already knew about it. But that had nothing to do with this. "What's your point, Sheriff?"

He leaned across the desk. "Now, locally, folks are kind of looking at you oddly because you threatened Tom Turner, and then he winds up dead in your yard."

"That's ridiculous. I'm not the kind of woman who goes around bashing people over the head!"

"Maybe so, but folks around here don't know you, right? And you must admit—"

"I don't have to 'admit' anything," I snapped. "I didn't kill him, but I sure would like to know who did so I can sleep better at night."

He thrust his fingers through his hair, and it stood straight up. Combined with his dorky uniform, a dark-blue shirt done right up to his neck and adorned with a clip-on tie, it made him just *too* cute in a way my perfect, suave, dignified Miguel never was. Come to think of it, that was Miguel's only fault, his lack of a sense of the ridiculous, especially about himself.

"Look, I'm not accusing you, all right? I'm worried. There have been break-ins all over the county lately, and you and your friend are alone out there at that castle. If I thought you'd do it, I'd say find someplace in town to stay." He paused, eying me and narrowing his eyes. "You wouldn't, would you?"

"No. Mostly because that doesn't make a bit of sense to me." I shifted my purse on my lap. "Sheriff, I don't mean to be difficult, but you're not going to find evidence of whomever killed Tom in my uncle's papers. Surely you have leads? Personal issues?" His stony expression told me that if he did, he was not going to share them with me. There was more I should ask, more I wanted to know, but he wasn't going to tell me anything. I took the receipt and stood. "If that's all . . . ?"

"We'd like to take your statement now," he said, his tone expressionless. He pushed a button, and the female officer came in and sat in the spare chair. "We'll be taping the interview, and you can sign the transcript once it's done."

"I did give a statement that night," I said, keeping my tone carefully neutral. I really wasn't trying to be difficult, but he grated on my nerves.

He met my eyes. "That was preliminary in nature. Miss Wynter, please . . . I'd appreciate your cooperation."

I nodded, and he took me through the evening one more time. It was like reliving it, especially looking down into the hole and seeing Tom at the bottom. I made sure to be clear about the crowbar, which I had found at the lip and tossed aside. By the time I was done, I was shaking, emotions rising within me that I thought I had tamped down and conquered. Death is wicked, and a purposeful death—robbing someone of all the potential life he had left to live—was evil.

I had one last thing to say on the record. "I want whoever

did this found and prosecuted. I want them to spend the rest of their life in jail. It's horrible to think that there is a killer out there, and he or she could be watching me, or have some reason to want to hurt me." My voice was trembling. I steadied it, as I finished. "It was on my property, and I won't rest until the killer is out of circulation."

That was the end of my statement, but not the end of my visit with the sheriff. I had been ready to walk out before, but calmer now, my flare of anger gone, I remembered that I had questions, too, and a promise to fulfill. As the female officer left the room, I stayed in my seat. "Sheriff, I would like to learn more about my uncle's death, the car accident. Do you have a moment?"

He hesitated. "Not really, but shoot."

"What happened? All I know is he slid off the road on an icy, November morning."

"That's pretty much all we know, too. Old Mel was in his eighties, and his eyesight was not the best. Regardless, he seemed to have taken it in his head to drive the highway at six or so in the morning."

"It would have been dark at that time."

Virgil nodded. "We were having a cold snap. The road was practically frozen over."

"Do you know where he was going?"

"Silvio mentioned that Mel told him he was heading to Rochester for some reason. That's all I know."

"So it was just an accident?" I thought of Gogi's suspicions, and wondered what was behind them. It seemed simple enough to me; an elderly man with poor sight on an icy highway in the dark. It sounded like a recipe for trouble.

"I have no reason to think it was anything else."

"Where's the car?"

"Our impound lot. It's damaged beyond recovery."

"How did the call come in? What time of day was it?" I asked.

"Early. It was about six a.m. when we got the call from a

citizen who was passing by and saw a car off the road. They were concerned, and told us where to find the car."

"Who was it who called?"

"Not my place to tell you, Miss Wynter. The caller wished to remain anonymous unless called to give evidence at an inquest."

"And? When is the inquest?"

"We haven't scheduled it yet. I haven't gathered all the information I need."

"Why not?"

No answer from the stone-faced cop. He was being deliberately difficult, and I eyed him with suspicion. Something else clicked in at that moment. I didn't recall any mention of an insurance settlement in the accident case, so it was not closed, not by any means. "You're not convinced it was an accident," I said, suddenly sure of my conclusion. "And you don't want an inquest until you know the truth. Why? Was there any damage not accounted for by the accident?" I saw by his expression that I had nailed it.

"We're investigating. I haven't closed the books on it yet."

"So there is something about the car-accident theory that doesn't ring true to you."

He sighed and closed his eyes. "Miss Wynter," he said, his tone frosty, "I *said*, I'm still investigating. I have no concrete proof that it was anything more than an accident, but there are a couple of minor scrapes of black paint on the back bumper that trouble me. Mel was not a great driver, however. For all I know they could be from a fender bender in the parking lot of a Wegmans in Buffalo!" He stood and walked to his office door, holding it open for me. "And that is all I have to say."

But as I passed, he grabbed my elbow.

"Merry . . . Miss Wynter, please be careful," he said, his gaze intense, his voice a growl that sent shivers down to my toes. "I don't like the idea of you out there at the castle with a killer on the loose. Please reconsider staying in town."

I pulled away from him, tugged down my jacket—I was dressed for professionalism in a skirt suit—and headed out to the car, where Shilo, out of the car now, sat on a curb, waiting. We got back in and I let Shilo off at Jack McGill's office—she and the lanky Lothario were getting along like a house afire, it seemed to me—and found a parking spot outside of Binny's Bakery.

Okay, I thought, gripping the steering wheel a little too tightly, *so I had gone to the police station and demanded to know what they took from the castle.* Check that off on the list, and note a big, fat nothing beside what I had learned, other than the fact that Virgil Grace was cute, in uniform or out, and had a sexy voice. Oh, and that my uncle may have been murdered in a hit-and-run accident. Maybe Gogi was right after all, to be concerned.

I stopped at the bakery and told Binny I would be back later to bake—I was going to try some chocolate-walnut and prune Danish muffins—but right then I was going to track down Dinah and find out what, if anything, she could tell me about the financial troubles between my uncle and Rusty Turner. Binny gave me Dinah's address.

She lived in a little apartment over Crazy Lady Antiques and Collectibles, one of the shops on Abenaki, Binny had told me. I walked down the street toward it, not even sure of what I needed to know, or what to ask Dinah. I guess I was trying to figure out where everyone fit in the scheme of things in Autumn Vale, New York. It was as if three jigsaw puzzles had been tossed into a box together, and none of the pieces I was collecting came from the same one.

As I remembered from my first morning in Autumn Vale, Crazy Lady Antiques and Collectibles was the last shop in a line of conjoined downtown building faces, all brick, some painted, some left natural, and most windows boarded up this far down the block. I had never stopped to look in the window. Wow. I stared in open-mouthed awe. There was a jumble of stuff packed into the store window, from petit point dining chairs to a gigantic plant stand in the shape of a dragon. There was new junk, old crap, antiques, and kitsch all sharing space, jammed cheek to jowl as my grandmother used to say.

But I wasn't there to browse, I was looking for the door to Dinah Hooper's apartment. I searched to the right and to the left on the old, brick building facade, where there ought to be a door opening to reveal a staircase. In fact, there should be a mailbox or buzzer or something indicating the upstairs apartment, shouldn't there?

From what Binny had told me, Dinah Hooper had shown up in Autumn Vale two years or so prior. Binny was not in town then; she was still exploring the world of baked goods by apprenticing in a Paris *boulangerie*. Dinah, following a friend, had come to Autumn Vale looking for a fresh start, apparently, and soon found work at Turner Construction as office manager. She had swiftly moved on to become the boss's girlfriend, and made new friends in town.

Binny appreciated the kindness she saw in Dinah, and the good care she took of Rusty, who was on several different types of medication. Dinah regulated them, and made sure he kept his doctor's appointments. In the months before he disappeared, his health had actually improved considerably, Binny said. That was why she was having so much trouble figuring out what had happened to him. Dinah was firm in her belief that Rusty was not dead, but had just left town for some reason, though she claimed not to know why.

Stymied, I stood and frowned at the storefront. Darned if I could find a doorway. I was being watched, too, not just by some of the fine citizens of Autumn Vale from across the street, but also by a woman in the window. Aha! It was the odd woman in purple, Janice Grover, the woman I had first seen in the library and then later at Vale Variety and Lunch. She gestured to me to come in. I stepped up and opened the door, a chime hung over it announcing my entry.

"I'm looking for Dinah Hooper," I said, as I squeezed

past a shelf that was in the way. "I was told her apartment is above the shop?"

"Sure is." The woman eyed me up and down. "What do you want with her?"

"Why?" I asked.

She grinned. "Now, that isn't supposed to be what you say. You're supposed to answer me. Most people do, if you surprise them with a direct question."

"I'm not most people." I looked around the shop. It was as crammed full as the front window. "Where did you get all this?"

"Estate sales, closeouts, bargain-basements. Liquidations. Garage sales, flea markets, the dump." She adjusted a stack of dusty teacups on a shelf. "My husband says I never saw a sale I couldn't wipe out."

"Your husband . . ." I searched my memory. "Oh yes! Your husband is the Grand T-something of the Brotherhood of Falcons."

"Grand Tiercel. And the head of the local Old Duffers chapter—though they never get off their fat behinds to golf—and bank manager. Man never stops going to meetings. You'd think he was afraid to come home!"

One look at her formidable person, today clothed all in fuchsia, her shelflike bosom jutting like a magnificent ship's prow, and I wondered, was her husband as afraid of Mrs. Janice Grover as everyone else seemed to be? I remembered her remark about Isadore Openshaw's lack of a sense of humor; she had said maybe that's what happened when you worked in a bank too long. Was her husband as humorless as Ms. Openshaw? Or just terrified of the indomitable Mrs. Grover? "Bank manager," I mused, and I remembered the stodgy little edifice I had passed. "Is that the Autumn Vale Community Bank?"

"That is the one and only bank in this town, in case you hadn't noticed, and the one everyone uses. Most don't want to go all the way to Ridley Ridge, where there are a couple of branches of the major banks. Autumn Vale is kind of . . . insular."

"That's one thing to call it."

"Weird being another? I thought that when we moved here twenty years ago," she said, moving a poodle figurine an inch on a piecrust tabletop, leaving a clean ring in the dust. "But since then, I've come to embrace its oddities. It's freeing in a way," she said, adjusting her parrot earrings. They matched the fuchsia dress nicely. "You're the Wynter heiress, right?"

Heiress? *Moi?* I had never thought of myself that way. Could you be broke and still be an heiress? "I guess you could say that. I'm Melvyn Wynter's great-niece, and his heir." She was someone else in town I thought I'd enjoy getting to know. I do enjoy the offbeat. Maybe it was all those years living in Greenwich Village, though the neighborhood had become awfully stodgy of late, not like it was when I was a teenager. Perhaps I did belong in Autumn Vale, where weird was a way of life. "You seemed to feel, when you talked to us in the restaurant the other day, that Melvyn's death, Rusty's disappearance, and Tom's murder are all connected. Who do you think did it?"

"Not a clue, my dear girl. Not a clue! But it seems like an awful lot of tragedy for one small family and business, unless you're in the middle of a Greek drama or a Shakespeare play. Or one of those cozy mysteries, where the residents of a tiny town are bopped off one by one, and yet no one gets the willies and leaves."

"Do you know anything about my uncle Melvyn's accident?"

"Not much. It was Simon—my husband, you know—who called the police."

Chapter Sixteen

I WAS SHOCKED by that, but tried not to show it. "Really?"

"It was early in the morning, about six or so, and Simon was just coming back from the city, where one of my sons had some kind of crisis. He saw poor old Mel's car off the road and down the embankment. Well, he got out and shouted down, but no answer. He came home and asked what he ought to do, and I said 'Call the police, you idiot'!" She laughed, a great honking hoot that was out of place given the subject matter. "For all he's a good, solid guy, Simon can be a bit of a dope."

My mind whirled with thoughts; had Simon Grover been the one who forced my uncle off the road, by accident or on purpose? I mean, who comes back from a trip to see their son at six in the morning? Was he drunk? Was he out to get Melvyn?

What color car did Simon Grover, solid citizen, drive?

"So, your husband was coming back from seeing your son?" I asked slowly, watching her face. "Weird time of day, wasn't it?"

She shook her head. "Not at all. Booker is a good boy, but he was having girlfriend troubles and called, upset, wanting to talk. Simon drove up to Rochester to see him but didn't want to miss work, so he started back early."

"He must have been tired, and then to see Melvyn's car off the road . . . did he stop to try to help?"

"Well of course! I said that already, right? He shouted. But Simon's in no shape to scale down an embankment. He came home and we called Virgil." She paused and eyed me. Slowly and with great emphasis, she said, "The sheriff told us there was no way poor old Melvyn would have been alive, even if Simon *had* been able to make it down the embankment."

Well, that was clear enough, but still . . . how could I ask about her husband's car color? There didn't seem to be any way without showing my suspicion, but it was the kind of thing I ought to be able to find out fairly easily. Gogi might even know.

Simon was the local banker. I pondered the anomalies we had found in the business dealings between the Turners and my uncle, and the large cash infusions Turner Construction had been receiving. Would the bank manager know where the money in the Turner accounts came from? At this point, I wasn't ready to go into those oddities with a stranger whom I didn't know if I could trust. I wanted to ponder it and talk to my financial-whiz friend, Pish, first; he was as trustworthy as a locked diary. "I'd better get moving. As much as I'd love to look around your store, I'm just looking for Dinah Hooper's apartment right now. How do I get to it?"

"Around the corner you'll see a nondescript kind of door. There's a buzzer beside it, no name, though. Don't know if she's home."

I paused. "What do you think about Dinah? She's kind of new in town, right?"

Mrs. Grover shrugged. "Seems all right to me. She moved right into town, joined clubs, volunteered, made friends. Not like Isadore; when Isadore Openshaw came to town seven or eight years ago to look after her brother, she just kind of hid away. After he died, everyone thought she'd open up, have more time for folks, but once a grump always a grump. Set in her ways."

Speaking of grumps set in their ways . . . "Did you know my uncle?"

"Weeeell, kinda. He wasn't a big fan of mine, if you know what I mean."

I looked at her, eyebrows raised, inviting her to continue.

"I'd been out to the castle a couple of times, just to look around, you know. He chased me off the property and told me never to come back."

I bit my lip, trying not to giggle.

She eyed me with a smile. "Oh, don't worry . . . once I got home, I laughed plenty. Must have been quite the sight, an old curmudgeon chasing a large lady in a floral muumuu, boobs bouncing like basketballs, down the driveway, shaking his shotgun and yelling, 'Get off my property!' at the top of his lungs."

I *liked* Janice Grover! I couldn't help myself. "I guess my uncle was a mean old man."

She shrugged, her parrots swinging merrily. "I hear he wasn't so bad if you knew him well. Gogi Grace swears he was once quite affable. But I was a newcomer, see . . . only been here twenty years."

A newcomer. I blew air out of my lips, my bangs fluffing out, and she grimaced in sympathy. "I guess I'd better go and find the other newcomer in town," I said. I took a last look around at the boxes and tables and shelves jammed with junk. It was so packed in the shop, I was on sensory overload, and I'd need a day or more to explore. "I'm going to have to come back and look around. You might even have some stuff I need."

"You bet! That place needs dressing up. Say, I have a storage place—kind of a warehouse on the outskirts of town—where all my big stuff is stored, like outdoor stuff. You need to have a look. I'm usually here, even when the sign says Closed, so just bang on the door anytime and I'll take you there." She sighed. "It's my hobby and my addiction, I suppose."

I went out and circled to the side of the building, on a narrow lane, finding the door right where Janice had said it would be. I hit the buzzer, and after a few seconds, a window slid open above me. The nicely coiffed Dinah stuck her head out.

"Good morning," I said, looking up. "Can I come up and talk to you?"

"I was just on my way out," she said. "Do you want to meet me at my new shop?"

"Sure," I said. "Would you like coffee, or something from Binny's Bakery?"

Her expression brightened. "That would be nice! Meet you there in ten minutes!"

Food smoothed social communication, I've always thought. There was a reason many deals were done over lunch at nice restaurants, and it wasn't just the booze. I got a selection of pastries from Binny's and two coffees to go from the Vale Variety, and headed to Dinah's storefront.

The door stood wide open, and she was inside, moving a couple of folding chairs to a small, teetery, wrought-iron table. I "hallooed" and entered, carefully navigating through boxes with the cups, box of pastries and my purse.

"Here, let me help you!" she said. She took the box and trotted back to the table, propped it open, and set a stack of paper napkins beside it.

I put the coffees on the table, as well as the creamers and sugar packets, then tucked my purse under one of the chairs and sat down.

"This is nice!" she said with a bright smile. She eyed my skirt suit, pointed, and said, "I love the color!"

It was a robin's egg blue, not perhaps very fallish, but it

was a lovely cut and fit well. I had put my hair up and was
wearing gray pumps and chunky jewelry to make the color
seem less out of sync with the season. After all, it was after
Labor Day but not quite autumn yet. "Thank you! Loeh-
mann's Back Room," I said with a grin.

She sighed. "I miss shopping. I only make it to the city
once or twice a year. Rochester and Buffalo are okay, but
they are not Manhattan!"

She was stylish, like Gogi was. I wondered if the two
women were friends, being of similar age and tastes. I wondered why Dinah stayed in Autumn Vale, now that Rusty
and her job were gone. I wondered a whole lot of things, but
didn't want to rush the inquisition . . . er, chat. "You do manage to find Prada, though," I said, pointing my spoon at her
handbag. "And Balenciaga!" I shifted my pointer to her
shoes, chunky-wedge platforms.

"Rochester has a *few* good shops. I'll take you there
sometime, maybe?"

Having bonded over a similar taste in nice clothes, hand-
bags, and shoes, we continued over awful coffee and wonderful French pastry. "Binny is wasting her talents here," I
mumbled around mille-feuille, which crumbled in my mouth
and showered my lap with crumbs.

"That is God's own truth," she muttered. "She should
still be working in New York City."

As we drank coffee and ate pastry, I mentioned my problems with cell reception. She nodded. Autumn Vale itself
was kind of a dead zone, she said, because of its location in
a deep valley with few towers close by. It was definitely
underserved.

"Your best bet is to switch providers."

She went on to advise me that if I didn't want to do that or
didn't think it would help, I could have Wi-Fi installed at the
castle and have my cell phone jigged to ping off it, or some
such nonsense. I'm substituting words; it was all too technical
for me. "I am impressed, and a little in awe," I admitted.

She shrugged. "I have to deal with stuff like that all the time, so I've worked out the bugs."

I looked around the empty, uninspired space, wondering what Dinah would do with it. But I had other fish to fry, as my grandmother used to say, and many questions to ask. "So what is a nice, stylish woman like you doing in the cultural desert that is Autumn Vale?"

She shrugged and took a sip of coffee. "It's as good a place as any, I guess. Cheaper than a city."

"I'd take you for a Florida sort," I said. It was true; she looked like a Boca Raton real estate agent, or a senior sales associate at an upscale boutique catering to wealthy retirees.

"Can't stand hot weather," she said with a laugh.

"I still can't imagine why you came here to live, of all places!"

"I knew someone who lived here, and it seemed like a nice area. Then I found a job, and just . . . stayed."

"Who did you know in town?"

"It was an old friend, but she died a year ago," she said, her eyes watering. She ducked her head down and dabbed at her eyes with a napkin.

"I'm sorry," I said. I gave her a moment, then asked, "What do you plan on doing with this shop? Have you decided?"

For the next ten minutes, she sketched out her plans for a florist-slash-design boutique. It sounded like the kind of place I'd shop, but I had to say, "Do you think that will fly in Autumn Vale?"

"I hope so," she said. "I need to find some way to make money. I have a little cash to set up with, but if it goes under, I'll be broke. I've tried looking for a job, but there's nothing. Since Rusty disappeared, most of Turner Construction's jobs dried up, too, and I didn't even take a salary for the last three months or so. Tom just wasn't like his father, you know? The boy had no hustle."

Rusty's disappearance had hurt her in more ways than

one, it seemed. "I don't want to probe a delicate subject, Dinah, but you seem sure Rusty is alive. Where do you think he went?"

"I wish I knew."

"Then why do you think he's still alive?"

She set her lips in a straight line and frowned, wrinkles gathering on her forehead, below her fluffy, white-blonde bangs. "He left a note, see."

"He did?" That was the first solid evidence I had heard that he had skipped town and not died. Binny hadn't said anything about a note.

"He did. He went to the bank and withdrew ten thousand dollars, and when I went to work the next morning, I found a note on my desk."

"What did it say?"

"It said he had business to take care of, and not to worry, that he would be back."

"He didn't say how long he'd be gone?"

She shook her head. "He didn't say anything to his kids, which surprised me. Him and Tom had been fighting, so I guess I shouldn't have expected Rusty to say anything to him, but Binny . . . Lord, the sun rose and set by that girl, according to Rusty. He would have done anything for her. Him not telling *her* . . . well, it's odd. I've been wracking my brain trying to think why he up and left like he did."

She sniffed and reached into her bag, drawing out a packet of tissues and blotting her mascaraed blue eyes carefully. "He's been gone so *long*. I have to . . . I'm starting to think something happened while he was away. If I knew where he was going, I could check with the police there and hospitals, but . . ." She trailed off and shrugged. "That sheriff is no good at all. I keep hounding him to try to find Rusty, but he's not doing a darn thing. I just don't know what to think! And now, with Tom dead . . . poor Rusty! He's going to be devastated with how he left things with Tom. When . . . *if* he comes back."

"What did they fight over?"

"I just don't know. I think it was business, but I'm not sure. There was something going on between Rusty and Melvyn. I knew that, but I didn't think Tom was involved, other than it had to do with his father. There were lawsuits and bickering and turmoil. Gosh, it was nasty! Old Melvyn came out to the office with a double-barrel shotgun one day and called Rusty a low-life, lying snake." She shook her head, but there was a faint smile curving up her lips.

"Did he mean it? I mean, my uncle, with the shotgun?"

"Well, the hole in the side of the trailer would seem to suggest he was serious!"

Chapter Seventeen

"YOU MEAN MY uncle actually shot the place up?"

"Oh, he wasn't aiming at anyone," Dinah assured me. "He shot over Tom's head, but said next time a Turner would pay."

Holy crap, I thought. He had waved a shotgun at Janice Grover, too. Maybe old Melvyn was truly nuts and *did* kill Rusty. But he didn't kill Tom Turner, and that was the murder I was hoping would be solved pronto. Was it all tied in together? Did the "something funny" going on have to do with those poorly drawn up plans for Wynter Acres I found? "Dinah, were you in on any of the discussions between Rusty and Melvyn about subdividing the Wynter land to build condos?"

"I came in on the tail end of it. It didn't make a bit of sense to me," she said, eyes wide. "I asked Rusty, who would buy a condo out in the middle of nowhere?"

"My thoughts exactly! What did he say?"

She rolled her eyes. "Men! He said to keep my pretty, little nose out of it, that Melvyn had hidden assets and the only way to get them out of him was to go along with the old fool." She gasped. "Oh, dear. He was your uncle, and . . . I'm so *sorry* for how that sounded. Rusty wasn't the easiest guy to deal with. It sounds bad, but he didn't mean it . . . well, I'm not sure exactly how he meant it."

"It sounds like Rusty was using Mel," I said, my tone blunt. I didn't want to reveal that I had seen the shoddy plats and subpar plans.

She put one hand on mine on the table, and said, "Merry, I don't want you to get the wrong impression about Rusty. He's a great guy, honest! Except he sees the world in terms of black and white; he seemed to think Mel owed him. He was worried, and had some kind of plan in mind to keep the company afloat."

Uh-huh, a plan to cheat old Melvyn, maybe. Was that where the money in the account came from? And who else was he swindling? "You did the bookkeeping for the company, right?"

"I did."

Interesting; she had just implied that Rusty, her boss and boyfriend was trying to cheat my uncle, but had no problem admitting she did the company bookkeeping. "Was everything aboveboard and square?" She looked a little offended. I hadn't worded that very well. "I didn't mean about your bookkeeping, Dinah. I guess I meant the books from *before* you took over."

Mollified, she sighed and said, "They were a terrible mess! I started out as just a kind of office manager and receptionist, you know, but Rusty was in over his head. He used to have a gal who came in two days a week to do the deposits and payroll, but she quit. She had messed things up so badly, I didn't even know where to begin. There were checks that hadn't been deposited, bills that hadn't been paid . . . it took me a year to get things straightened out, and I'm not positive that I did get it all square and shipshape. I wasn't a very good bookkeeper myself when I started, but

I took a correspondence course, and a lot of it is common sense along with the ability to look up state and federal regulations and apply them."

"Who was it who used to come in to do the bookkeeping?"

"I . . . don't remember the name," she said, her gaze shifting away. "Is it important?"

"I guess not." I had a sense that she did indeed remember very well but didn't want to implicate someone.

She stood and shook crumbs off her lap. "I had better get down to the nuts and bolts. I have to measure this place and figure out what I'm doing. Gogi Grace is going to give me a hand."

"She's great, isn't she?" I said, standing and likewise scattering crumbs from my skirt.

"She is, honest to God, like the sister I never had."

I walked to the door, my heels clunking on the board floors and echoing in the empty place; it was a bland space right now, plain-board floors, white walls, dusty from disuse. It needed a lot of work before it could be a design store, and I hoped she knew what she was up against. I turned before I got to the door. "By the way, do you know anyone who does yard work or anything like that? I can't seem to find any listing for a landscaping company in Autumn Vale, and I need the Wynter property taken care of on a regular basis."

"What, you're not going to mow it on your own?" she said with a quick grin. "I say just put up a notice at the Vale Variety. Rusty used to find day workers that way, for when we needed site cleanup." Her grin died, as she talked again about her missing boyfriend.

"I'll do that. Thank you, Dinah. I hope this place does great guns!"

"Me, too, *if* I ever figure out what to make it!"

I left the pastries behind for her and Gogi. On the street, I looked up and down as a young woman with a stroller passed me, a determined frown on her face. I had a lot to think about and even more to figure out. The last few days had revealed that the odd little town of Autumn Vale had seen some swirling controversies and issues over the last few years, some of them to do with my late uncle.

Was it unusual in that respect? Probably not. Get enough quirky characters together in one small space, though, and you had a recipe for disaster. The economic downturn could not have helped. Small towns across the country had been hit in a frightening way, that much I knew from reading the news. Just looking at the main street in this town you could see it had once been a thriving downtown that was now largely vacant. And it wasn't just that people were now taking their hard-earned bucks to Rochester or Buffalo, it was that anyone left in town probably didn't *have* any bucks, hard-earned or otherwise.

I was slowly redefining my economic situation as measured against the townsfolk of Autumn Vale, New York. My small heap of savings seemed like a larger pot than I had once considered it. I suddenly realized that Jack McGill had not given himself the job of filling the holes in my yard just to be nice to a newbie, it was part of a financial-survival strategy. Real estate in a small town as depressed as Autumn Vale had to be tough.

My eyes were open. I walked down Abenaki feeling raw and vulnerable. The boarded-up stores now represented failed dreams, lost livelihoods. Where did anyone work in Autumn Vale? There was no industry, that I could tell. Turner Construction was probably once the beacon of prosperity by the town's modest measure, but it was history now, with no one to run it. A group of teenagers hung out in front of Vale Variety, their faces wan, smoking cigarettes and muttering to each other. They were going to have to leave town to get jobs, probably; would they ever come back? Was the lifeblood of the town leaking out, one young drop at a time? Was I just tired and edgy and making a mountain out of a molehill that wasn't even *my* molehill?

Gordy and Zeke were coming out of Binny's as I

approached. What did they do all day? They were both in their early thirties, I figured, because Gordy had been in high school at the same time as Tom Turner, but neither appeared to work. "Hey, guys," I said. "How's it going?"

Both nodded. "Not bad, I guess," Gordy said.

"I have a problem, and I'm wondering if you guys know a solution."

They eyed me warily.

"You know the castle property," I said. They exchanged glances and nodded. "Well, it is a massive headache to me. I can't take care of it all. The property looks like a field, and if I'm ever going to get it back in shape, I need to start with a good cleanup. Do you know, or know *of*, anyone who does that kind of thing? Landscaping, I mean? Just basic stuff like mowing down the tall grass, and pulling weeds. There's a lot of work to do before winter."

They exchanged glances again. It was Zeke who spoke up, eyeing me with doubt in his squinty eyes. "You mean, you'd pay?"

"Of course!"

"We could do it." They spoke at the same moment; it was eerie.

"Could you? It wouldn't take you away from . . . from other things?"

"Nah, stuff can wait," Zeke said, shoving his hands in his saggy-jeans pocket.

I was truly relieved. "You would be doing me a huge favor," I said, and meant every word of it. "But I don't know the first thing about machinery. It is a really *big* property, and . . . what about a mower? What kind would you use for a property like that?"

"We might be able to come up with something," Gordy said. "My uncle's a farmer out your way, and I could borrow his hay mower, if the grass is that long."

"It is. I don't think it's been cut all summer. The place looks abandoned." I quickly pulled a card out of my purse and wrote my cell phone number on the back as well as the castle landline. I handed it to them, and Zeke took it.

"What day of the week is it?" I asked, suddenly aware that I had, in the twilight zone of Autumn Vale and Wynter Castle, lost track.

"Friday," they intoned together.

"Okay, call me," I said. "I appreciate your help, guys!" I had a few more things to do in town, among them a visit to the post office to arrange continued forwarding of my mail. The post office building, one of the streetscape oldies squashed in together along Abenaki, was opposite Binny's Bakery, so I strolled across the quiet street and walked in, a buzzer triggered by my entrance sounding somewhere.

There was a counter across the room, and along one wall a bank of post office boxes stacked from small at the top to large at the bottom. Dinah Hooper was there, pulling a wad of envelopes out of one of the medium-sized post office boxes. She turned and smiled. "Hey, fancy meeting you here!" she said.

"I just left you waiting for Gogi!"

"She was delayed at the home. One of her clients is very ill," she said. Her expression saddened, and there was a glimmer of tears on her face. "I don't know how she manages it—emotionally, I mean. I do what I can at Golden Acres, read to some of the residents and help them with their taxes, but it's hard for me. My mother passed away five years ago this week, and I still think about her every day. Being there reminds me of her."

"I know how you feel. My mom and my grandmother died within six months of each other. That was eighteen years ago, and I still miss them."

"Oh, I'm so sorry!" she said, stuffing the envelopes in a cloth bag and touching my arm in a gesture of sympathy. "And here I am moaning about losing my mother when I was in my fifties!"

"It's hard no matter the age," I said.

"I'd better go," she said with a watery half-smile, "before I get any more morose!"

As Dinah exited, I turned to the woman at the postal counter, who had been listening in with unabashed curiosity. "Hi. How are you today?" I asked.

"I'm just great," she said with a huge grin plastered on her broad face. She leaned on the counter, her plump arms folded. "You're the girl who inherited the Wynter Castle, right?"

"I am."

"Figured you'd be in here sooner or later. Everybody comes to see the postwoman, you know."

Minnie, a woman in her mid-sixties, I judged, and as broad as she was tall, befriended me swiftly; she seemed hungry for a fresh face, and gossiped relentlessly about many of the folks I had come to know. Doc English was a hoot, but a lot smarter than anyone took him for. Dinah Hooper was one of those women who seem doomed for unlucky lives. Virgil Grace was a mama's boy, and his mom was a bad woman to cross.

"Gogi Grace? What do you mean?" I asked, startled by her assertion.

She looked from left to right, as if there was a crowd waiting to listen in, and leaned across the counter, fixing her gaze on mine. "The woman's got money. How do you think she came into it?"

I shook my head.

"Inherited. Husbands number one and two!" She held up two fingers like a peace sign.

"I didn't know that. Which one did she have her kids with?"

"Husband number one. He didn't leave her a lot of dough, but the insurance after he died? *That* paid for the big house. It was husband number two who had the money. When he died . . ." She let out a low whistle and widened her pouchy eyes. "How do you think she afforded the renovations for

Golden Acres? That cost *mucho dinero*, inherited from *numero duo*."

I felt bad gossiping about Gogi; I've been on the nasty end of tittle-tattle. Taking a deep, cleansing breath, I said, "I'm here to see about having my mail forwarded from my old address for six months. I figure I'll be here at least that long fixing up Wynter Castle."

She straightened and instantly became professional. I filled out the forms and paid with my debit card, finishing up just as another customer came into the post office. I slipped out with a wave good-bye, figuring I'd be the next topic of conversation. Minnie was a talker, and I'd make a mental note to remember that. I wasn't sure what she was implying about Gogi, but I was going to erase the postmistress's insinuations from my mind.

With renewed energy and determination, I headed off to the library. I got lucky; as I had remembered, Friday was an open day, and not only were there a couple of patrons, one of them was Lizzie. Perfect. "Hi, Hannah," I said, to the diminutive librarian. She waved, then went back to her conversation with Isadore Openshaw, who was piling books up on a table. Lizzie was covertly watching me, as she leafed through a magazine featuring Amy Gulick photographs. I sat down at the table opposite her. "Still suspended?" She nodded. "You busy tomorrow?" I asked, noting the kohl around her eyes, and the bloodred lipstick. The girl was going emo, it seemed, if that's what they still called it. It was called Goth, when I was a kid. If she was trying to frighten folks away, she was probably in the wrong town. Weird was a way of life in Autumn Vale.

"Why?" she asked, staring down at the page.

Good for her; she had learned to be suspicious of open questions like that. It took me a long time to learn they usually preceded requests to help someone move, or bury a body. And yes, I did get asked to help someone bury a body once; a friend's beloved dog had died, and she couldn't bear to do it alone, and yes, I did help her. We cried and drank wine together afterward. If I ever needed help burying a body, she promised she'd come through for me. I had her phone number with me at all times.

"I was wondering if you would come out to the castle tomorrow and show me where that abandoned camp in the woods is. You can take all the pictures you want, I just need you to guide me, since you obviously know the woods better than I do."

"Sure," she said with a shrug. "But I'll need a ride out to your place."

"If I can't get Jack McGill to do it, I'll pick you up myself. You don't mind McGill, do you?" I suddenly remembered that she was fifteen, and might have an opinion on her chauffeur.

"No, he's cool."

So far, my day was proving to be useful, more than I even imagined in my midnight maunderings. I turned my attention toward Isadore Openshaw and Hannah. I wanted to ask Hannah some questions about Tom, but they would just have to wait. Ms. Openshaw, morose bank teller, was piling books up at a crazy rate. Was she really going to read them all?

I examined the spines. *The Tao of Meow. The History of Greed. Women Who Love Too Much. The Seven Habits of Highly Effective People. The Secret.*

Wow, what a mixed bag! Maybe Isadore Openshaw was a self-help junkie. I've known women like that, who seemed to think all they needed was one more self-help book and they'd be happy. Just one more book and they'd discover what was wrong with *them*, why people kept crapping on *them*. I could have told her there was no "secret." Mostly we create our own reality, it was true, but not always. Sometimes bad stuff just happens, and the only thing you can do is try to move on.

Which was what I was doing after the crapstorm that was Leatrice Peugot. I looked up from her stack of books to find

Isadore staring at me with a weird, focused look. Should I befriend her, I wondered? I might need an ally at the bank if my uncle's finances were as twisted as I feared.

I smiled. She grabbed her stack of books and shuttled awkwardly to the checkout desk. Lizzie, who had noticed the interaction, snickered, and I gave her a dirty look. "What are you, Miss Charming all of a sudden?" I said.

The teenager made a face and bent back over her magazine.

After the bank teller left, Hannah motored over to our table. "How are you two doing?" she asked. "It's Lizzie, right?"

The girl nodded, her gaze sliding back to the magazine. I got a feeling she felt awkward with tiny, wheelchair-bound Hannah, but I couldn't be sure. Lizzie seemed to be awkward with most people, except Gogi Grace.

"Lizzie is a talented photographer," I said to Hannah. "She's taken some interesting shots of my property. In fact, she's going to come out tomorrow and take more pictures and show me around in the woods."

Hannah's narrow face lit up. "Would you show the photos to me? I'd love to see modern pictures of the castle and the grounds. I've read so much about it, but I've only seen old photos from the fifties, and driven past it once or twice."

Lizzie agreed to bring her camera back to the library to show Hannah whatever photos she took of the castle and grounds. "It's the *best* place for pictures!" she enthused. "I used to sneak onto the property and take all kinds, especially last winter, and just before a storm. The sky behind the castle . . . too much!" She sighed, her artistic fervor leaving her speechless.

"So next time, bring your camera with you here and show Hannah!" I said.

"Sure." She stood and picked up the magazine. "I have to go to Golden Acres now," she said, and left.

Hannah and I were alone in the gray confines of the

library. We talked about Lizzie for a moment, then I told
Hannah what I had so far learned about Tom's murder,
which was almost zero.

She was one of those people who asked just the right
questions at just the right moment. "Who feels like the killer
to you?" she asked.

"If I had to guess this moment, I would say Junior
Bradley."

"Why?"

"He was the last known person to have a violent confrontation with Tom."

"Hmm. I wouldn't get attached to that one theory, though,
right?"

"I won't. I'll keep looking."

"Merry, I know you worry that I have Tom on a pedestal,
and that I don't know much about life, but I know more than
you might think. Tom was upset about his father's disappearance, yes. He and Dinah were arguing a lot in the last
few months. But there were *other* things going on in his life,
too, something from a long time ago that he had just discovered was not quite as he thought it was."

"What does that mean?"

"I don't know," she said regretfully. "He looked ashamed,
and wouldn't tell me what had happened."

He knew about her hero-worship of him, probably, and
didn't want to tell her unsavory details that might damage
how she saw him. I thought for a long minute. "Was there
anything else you were talking about at that point?"

"I was, uh . . . wait! I remember!" Her small face was
turned up into the light, long lashes fluttering as she closed
her eyes. "We got into a conversation about parents, and I
was telling him how much I appreciate mine. I don't know
what I would have done in my life without such a great dad.
Tom looked . . . ashamed." She cocked her head to one side.
"I don't know why."

"Maybe he was ashamed of something to do with Rusty?"

I thought about it. Had Rusty's hasty disappearance had to do with his own son?

"There's something else," Hannah said, eyeing me with discomfort.

"What is it, Hannah? You can tell me anything."

"Tom was working for someone, doing something he wasn't proud of, but he needed money, he said."

This sounded promising. "What was it?"

"He was following someone for a lawyer. But he wouldn't tell me who he was following."

"What lawyer? Andrew Silvio, maybe?" I asked, but she just shrugged. Were there any other lawyers in Autumn Vale? Was I limiting myself by only considering this town? I remembered my conversation with Silvio, who told me about a lawyer in Ridley Ridge with whom Melvyn was working on the lawsuits between him and Rusty. "He didn't give any indication who he was following, or why? Or what he found out?"

She shook her head.

"Can you think of anything else at all?"

"No. I'm going to ask around, though. I see lots of people every day, and no one will think twice about me asking questions, because everyone knew how I felt about Tom."

The wistfulness in her voice about broke my heart. "Be careful, Hannah," I warned. "Maybe it would be best if you just left this up to me. There is a killer out there, and we can't let ourselves be blinded by anyone."

"I'm not helpless," she said with a frown.

"I know you aren't. Just be careful." I stood and said, "Is there somewhere here I can change my clothes? I have to go bake muffins, and a skirt suit just doesn't cut it, so I brought jeans and a T-shirt with me."

A few minutes later, dressed down for baking, I decided to call Shilo. I stood out on the street and held up my cell phone. Not working today. I eyed the sky, noting the low ceiling of clouds that obscured the ridge above Autumn

Vale, and wondered if that had something to do with the spotty reception. Dinah had suggested Wi-Fi for better cell reception, but I wasn't sure that would help me. In truth, I didn't really understand anything about it. I'd need her to write that stuff down so I could ask an Internet representative without sounding like an idiot.

I walked toward Binny's Bakery, just as someone whooshed past me on a bicycle. Isadore Openshaw? It was indeed her, heading toward the bank, her books piled in the wicker basket of her bike and a white paper bag from Binny's Bakery on top. It reminded me of the scene from *Wizard of Oz* with the mean woman on the bicycle threatening Toto.

While Binny served her customers, I tried to get accustomed to using commercial ovens and baking all my muffins at once. It was faster, but I had to watch them the whole time, because I just wasn't sure if the temperatures were the same as using a home oven. I let them cool and tried to get ahold of Shilo again. I finally got her using Binny's store phone. My friend sounded chipper. She was in Ridley Ridge, helping McGill stage a house he was trying to sell. I told her I was going to deliver the muffins to Gogi then head back, and she said she'd meet me at Golden Acres.

But first, I'd drop in at the bank and look around. Autumn Vale Community Bank was a squat, two-story redbrick building on the corner of Abenaki and Mohawk Road. It had dentilated ornamentation at the top and a rounded corner where the glass door was. It was a charming, old building, and the plaque attached read that the bank had been in existence since the early 1800s. I stepped inside. There were only two wickets—the old-fashioned kind like out of an old movie, with brass bars and a marble countertop—and a manager's office at the back, with Simon Grover's name in gold, Gothic lettering.

Isadore Openshaw was at the only open teller's spot, and I approached the wicket. She would have to speak to me there. She looked up and I smiled. Her expression soured, like she had a tart candy in her mouth, which was, by the way, ironically coated with powdered sugar.

"Hi, my name is Merry Wynter, and I just thought I'd stop in to introduce myself."

"What can I do for you?" She had a surprisingly husky voice, scratchy, as if it wasn't used often.

"Well, I would like to inquire about my uncle's affairs here. I'm not sure if he had an account with you?"

"You'll have to speak to Mr. Grover. He's busy right now. May I make you an appointment?"

"No, I don't think—"

"Then I can't help you," she said and turned away.

Sheesh! "Okay, all right, I'll make an appointment. How about . . . tomorrow morning?"

"Tomorrow is Saturday. The bank is closed on Saturday."

"Uh, Monday, then?"

She narrowed her eyes and glared at me through the brass bars. "He's busy Monday morning."

Frustrated with her stonewalling, I said, "How about any morning for the next—"

"Izzy, where the hell is my coffee? I asked for it a half hour ago."

She jumped and hustled away to a coffeemaker in the back corner, poured a cup, and took off with it to Grover's glass-doored office, sidled in, and then came back out. I tried to imagine Janice Grover hustling like that when her husband roared. Nope, wouldn't happen. Good thing he had "Izzy" at the office. Izzy? I shook my head as the woman hurried back to her neglected window. I could not think of her as anything but Isadore Openshaw.

A customer entered the bank as I tried one more time to convince her to let me in to see Grover. No go, and the elderly woman behind me, leaning heavily on her walker, should not have to wait just because Miss Openshaw was being a pain in my rear.

I considered marching back and thrusting myself into his

office, but I decided that likely wasn't the best way to introduce myself to the banker who might be able to help me. I'd simply call him directly for an interview. I returned to the bakery, retrieved the cooled muffins, and headed to Golden Acres. Had I ever been this busy working in New York?

Doc English was sitting outside of Golden Acres in the one single ray of sunshine the clouds were allowing through, wearing a flowered sunbonnet and a goose down vest. I was starting to think he dressed as he did to get a rise out of people, which was confirmed to me when I commented on the hat; he just smiled like the Cheshire cat. I delivered the muffins to the kitchen, but when I asked after Mrs. Grace they told me she had just gone out, so maybe she and Dinah had finally managed to get together.

I then asked about Shilo, and was told she was playing checkers in the social room. As I entered, Mr. Hubert Dread, the old fellow with the war stories, had just finished beating her hands down and with a great flourish, but she told him she'd be back for a rematch. She appeared to be adjusting nicely to life in Autumn Vale.

We loitered around town, had a very late lunch at the Vale Variety, did a little shopping, and then headed home. I told her about my appointment the next day with Lizzie, and she offered to call McGill to ask him to pick Lizzie up. He was already booked to come out and continue filling the darned holes in, she said, since he had called the sheriff and asked about the rest of them apart from the one Tom had been found in. Virgil Grace had okayed him resuming his duties, as long as he stayed away from the murder scene.

The dark clouds had thickened, and rain spattered on the windshield as we began to climb the ridge out of town. My tires crunched on the gravel at the edge of the road and I straightened the wheel. As my gaze flicked along the side of the road, I noticed a bike and slowed. It was just resting on a grassy, weedy patch, looking like the rider had either ditched it or . . . or what?

"That wasn't there this morning. I hope no one's hurt!" I pulled over and Shilo and I both got out and trotted over to the embankment, looking up and down the road in both directions. We were along a forested stretch, with a steep decline on one side and a sharp rise on the other. The decline side was where the bike was, and there were broken saplings and trees with the bark broken off. I got a bad feeling as we approached the roadside, but the damage to the trees didn't look fresh.

I hustled over to the edge, but just as I was about to look over, I heard a rustling sound, and clambering up the steep embankment came none other than Miss Isadore Openshaw.

Chapter Eighteen

❈ ❈ ❈

"IZZY . . . UH, MISS OPENSHAW," I cried in surprise. "What were you doing down there?"

Shilo stared at her, openmouthed. The woman tugged her shapeless dress down over her hips and clumped over to her bicycle, kicking up gravel.

"What *were* you doing down there?" I repeated.

"This is where your uncle died, you know," she said, pointing down the hill, her mousy hair fluttering out of a tight bun. "Now, you tell me *why* his car went off the road right there?"

"It was early morning, still dark in November. He was an old man with bad sight. The road was icy—"

"No it was not! It was *not* icy!" Her voice shook.

"Okay," I said, puzzled by her vehemence. "What are you trying to say?"

She righted her bike and got on.

"Wait! Don't go yet," I said, standing in front of her, both hands out in a "stop" gesture. I wasn't going to let her put me off with her verbal surprise attack. "What are you

implying? Why are you here? Were you looking for something down there?"

"No," she said, hopping off, wheeling the bike around
me, and hopping back on—she was very agile for an older
woman wearing a dress—and cycling down the hill, back
toward the village.

"What is going on?" I yelled after her. She picked up
speed and disappeared around the bend of one of the switch-
backs in the road. "This whole town is wacko," I grumbled,
moving over to where she had emerged. I looked down the
hill and saw nothing but her path, and the broken saplings.

"What do you think she meant, talking about it not being
icy on the morning your uncle died?" Shilo came up beside
me and stared down the hill.

"Good question." I thought about it. Someone—who was
it?—had said that Melvyn was headed to Rochester that
morning. But if he had been headed to Rochester or anywhere away from town, he would not have been on this winding road heading *into* Autumn Vale. Where was he going in
town? And why? "I just don't know." We headed back to the
castle.

It rained heavily overnight and into the morning, but it
finally began to clear midmorning. It was almost noon when
I took a cup of coffee out to survey the property, before
McGill and Lizzie arrived. In the distance I saw that spot
of orange again, closer this time. And he wasn't moving. I
watched for a while but the animal still didn't move.

I'd seen the orange cat often enough since I'd been at the
castle, but never for too long. He had come closer each time,
but never close enough for me to go up to him. He usually
melted back into the woods, as if he wanted me to follow
him. If it really was Uncle Melvyn's ginger cat, Becket, then
he was one remarkable dude to live for ten months on his
own. My friend joined me outside.

"Shi, do you think that's Becket?" I asked, pointing to
the lump of orange. Suddenly it did move and it sat up,

staring toward me. I handed my coffee cup to Shilo. "Just wait . . . don't follow me. I'm going to try to get closer." Over the next twenty minutes, I approached ever nearer to the cat, inching closer and closer. He looked like he was ready to bolt, but he didn't.

McGill roared up to the castle in his Smart car and screeched to a halt. Lizzie bolted out of the car, whirling and yelling—loud enough that even across the field I could hear her clearly—at McGill, "You're an idiot, you know that?" She stomped into the castle.

The cat streaked away, limping. Damn! There was probably something wrong with his paw or leg, and that was why it had stayed as I approached. I returned to the courtyard in front of the castle where Shilo and McGill were in conversation. "What the heck happened?" I said, now in a peeved mood.

McGill shrugged. "I was just telling Shilo, I don't have a clue. I was making conversation, and she suddenly howled like a banshee!"

"What exactly did you say?" Shilo asked.

"I don't know."

"Come on, McGill, you have to remember," I pleaded.

"He asked me if I was planning on taking photography in college," Lizzie said. She had emerged from the castle and stood on the top step, arms crossed, a sullen look on her face.

Shilo, McGill, and I exchanged puzzled looks. I piped up, "And that was a rotten thing to say because . . . ?"

"Well, duh! I'm *never* going to be able to go to college. How will I? My grades suck, my grandma is old and poor, and my mom is a whore. It's never going to happen!"

That was a whole lot of trouble unloaded right there. But I picked the one thing I did know about. "Lizzie, hold on!" I said, hand out in a pacifying gesture. "You say your grades suck? How bad?"

"Some Bs, more Cs. Why?"

I hesitated, then said, "You know, those applying for arts scholarships don't always need great grades in academics. Art schools are more focused on performance. If you're good—and I already know you're a great photographer—they will primarily consider your portfolio of work when determining scholarships. And you've got time to think about it and plan."

"Really?"

"Really. Come on in, both of you, and have lunch before we get started." I cast one look at the field, but Becket was gone. Now I was worried about him. If he had an injury and it got infected . . . well, it didn't bear thinking about.

We had soup and muffins, my go-to meal for any occasion, and then McGill powered up the Bobcat—Virgil had cleared the way for him to use the excavator rather than trying to get another one—and moved across the open section of the property to the back edge of the field. He was starting with the farthest holes this time and moving back toward the castle. At least now I knew there would be no new holes. I chastised myself as soon as I thought that, but it was true.

"Are you coming with Lizzie and me, Shi?" I asked.

She bit her lip and cast her gaze out toward McGill. I was surprised. My friend was quirky and flighty. No man had ever been able to pin her down, but in this case, McGill didn't even seem to be trying. He was smitten, clearly, but she was, too. I didn't see the attraction, but she knew him much better than I did by now.

"Decision time," I prompted.

"Nah, I'll stay and do the dishes. You two go on."

We set out across the field, wading through the long grass that I hoped would soon be gone, the growl of the Bobcat fading as we got to the woods and moved past the damp, tall weeds along the edge. Lizzie hadn't said a word for a half hour. I told her about my uncle's cat, and my fear that he was hurt.

"If you see him, tell me. I'm worried about him." There appeared to be a couple of old paths through the woods—they branched out and zigzagged across each other—and Lizzie hesitated, frowning and bringing her camera up to her eye. Then she set off down one path. I doubted she knew where she was going, but I made a mental note of where we had come in, and followed.

Some trees had tags, I was surprised to see, and some even had plaques down at their base, obscured through the years by plant material. I knelt and uncovered a few, as we went. The variety was astounding, with several different types of each species of tree. There wasn't even just one kind of oak; according to the plaques, there was burr oak, black oak, English oak, and more. Who knew? But the arboretum, if that's what this was, was badly overgrown; even I could tell that. And the trees had been planted too close together, it seemed to me, as if the planner hadn't considered the size of the trees as they grew. There were dead trees that would need to be cut down and removed.

After a half hour of walking and no talking, I finally asked, "Do you truly know where we're going?"

"Yeah."

We wandered for another twenty minutes though, before I finally had a sense that she was following a path she recognized. It had probably taken her time to get her bearings, because she would not have ever entered the woods from the castle grounds before. There was a path from the road, she said, and that is how she always got in. The forest thinned, more light from overhead leaking through the canopy. We came to a small clearing, and there, as she had said, was a wretched, moldy, nylon tarp half fallen over a thick, mossy log. A mildewed and broken tent was on the opposite side of a fire pit from the tarp. The fire pit—just a ring of rocks—held the remains of charcoaled logs, burned tins, and other refuse.

I glanced over at her. "Do kids from the high school come out here for parties?"

"Do I look like the kind of girl who would be invited to a bush party, if there was one?" she said, sending me a withering glance.

"I'm never going to be able to find my way here again," I said, looking around, feeling the sense of isolation and quiet. "I was hoping to hire someone to clean up this crap, too, but I'd be afraid they'd get lost."

She wasn't listening anymore, off in her own world of camera angles and light. I regarded her with interest, as she positioned herself low and snapped a photo of the moss-covered log, with the forest in the background. "You're a long way from home. How did you get up here so many times to explore? You needed a ride up here today."

"I have a bike. It's not that far."

"For a fifteen-year-old," I said, then thought of Isadore. She had clearly made it up here by bike, too. I still couldn't figure out why, and what she'd meant when she made such a point of the spot where Uncle Melvyn went off the road. "Is this the only encampment that you know about?"

She frowned, looking around. "I saw another one once, but I've never been able to find it again. It's not in a clearing like this is. It's in an evergreen part of the woods. And it looked like someone was using it. Creepy. I didn't stick around."

"I've got Gordy and Zeke coming out to mow my property, and I was hoping they could clean up this campsite, too, but I'm afraid they'd get lost." She snickered, and I cast her a look. "Hey, be nice."

"I'm sorry, but those two couldn't find their way out of a paper bag."

I tried to hide my own smile. "So judgmental," I murmured. "Would you show them where it is, if I get them to do it?"

She shrugged but said, "Sure." She eyed me, then added, "You know, I could help them, too, if you're paying."

"You'd do that kind of work?" I was surprised; it's not my kind of thing, clearing brush and trash, but Lizzie was, in many ways, tougher than I.

"It's better than scrubbing floors. Grandma and I have an agreement: I do all the outside work, and I don't have to clean inside."

"You'd be willing to show Gordy and Zeke the way here *and* help them clean up?"

She paused and eyed me. I got the same feeling I did when a salesman had his sights on me. I knew the question she was going to ask before she even spoke.

"What's it worth?"

I had to admire her sense of timing. In the dense isolation of the woods, I was more sure than ever that she was the only one who would be able to guide the intrepid duo this far. "Look, if you can find the other encampment, too, it'll be worth a lot more. You find me that other encampment, and guide and help Gordy and Zeke, and I'll . . ." I eyed her as she fiddled with her camera. "I'll buy you a new gadget for your camera. How would you like a panoramic lens?"

Her eyes widened. "And a macro zoom?"

"You're pushing it, kiddo, but maybe."

She got down to business right away. "Look, we need to go back soon, right? On our way, I'll try to find the other encampment."

I was glad I had worn a pair of my oldest jeans, as well as hiking shoes borrowed from Shilo's wardrobe. The girl had the same shoe size as me, luckily—the only size we have ever shared—and never traveled without an abundance of footwear. I followed Lizzie, weaving through the woods and stepping over fallen trees. It was exhausting, and I knew I was going to ache the next day, but Lizzie never seemed to tire. Oh, for the stamina of fifteen.

A couple of times, I thought I heard a motorcycle engine.

Were we near the highway? Or was someone trespassing in the woods, zooming around on the trails? It would be tempting, I supposed for a dirt-bike rider. Lizzie stopped a couple of times and cocked her head. I took the opportunity each time to catch my breath and look around, finally tuning in to what I had missed until now: birdsong. A harsh screech, discordant and echoing, trilled to me. The bird alit on a low branch, watching us with an unnerving stare. It was a blue jay, and it was curious about our incursion into his territory. The next time we stopped the blue jay was there again. Was it the same one, and was it following us?

Lizzie paused, looked around and nodded. "I know where we are, now. I've only been this way a couple of times, but I think we're almost there."

Close to us was the sound of water, and soon we stepped over a trickling stream that bubbled and chuckled along a winding trail. I stopped and cupped some of the water in my hand. It was frigid cold and clear, and tasted clean when I sipped it from the cup of my hand. My fabulous woodswoman skills told me it was springwater. My spirits lifted. I could not believe that this was my land!

Lizzie led me up a path that was even more treacherous because it was on a slope. She scrambled ahead of me, and I heard her cry, "Aha!"

I scaled the last bit, huffing and puffing, and looked down over a crude encampment with another half-collapsed tent. The fire pit was like the other one, a simple ring of rocks. Lizzie took photos, as she had of the other encampment, searching for unusual angles and zooming in on things, while I looked around.

Finally, I sat down on a log near the fire pit and picked up a stick, while Lizzie wandered, taking close-ups of the tent. I was about to tell her we ought to get going, when I heard an involuntary exclamation from her and turned to find her backing away from the tent, her expression blank, her whole body trembling.

"What's wrong?" I said, standing. She just pointed.

I strode over to the tent and looked in. Then I turned around and raced to the edge of the woods to throw up. I still contend that is any sane woman's reaction to finding a very, *very* dead body.

Chapter Nineteen

❈ ❈ ❈

I'M ASHAMED TO say that I did not hold it together as well as Lizzie did. That fifteen-year-old girl led me out of the woods and back to the castle, where I babbled to McGill and Shilo about the awful scene we had discovered. McGill called Virgil, and before long the cops were at the castle yet again, this time in the bright light of day. Fortunately, Lizzie, her face white, her lips compressed, assured them she was able to guide them back to the scene—I would have had no clue how to find the encampment again—but I made McGill go with them, so he could make sure *she* was all right.

My story this time, as related to a sheriff's deputy, was brief, because the body had been there awhile before we arrived on the scene. We found it, that was all. I paced after that, then went to the kitchen to make a big pot of coffee. Shilo and I had discovered a commercial coffee urn in one of the closets in our perambulations of the castle, and it was about to come in handy. I made several dozen mini muffins, too, with the mini-muffin tins I had bought the day before, and heaped them in a basket and set them on the kitchen table. I set out as many coffee cups as I could find, then called Janice Grover at Crazy Lady Antiques to see if she had a box of old mugs I could buy or borrow. Unfortunately, all I got was an answering machine. It was just make-work anyways, something to keep my mind busy as it shied away from the terrible sight I had seen in that tent.

Who *was* the dead body in the tent? Had he or she died alone, or been killed?

I paced along the flagstone terrace of the castle, as Shilo tried to make me feel better by avoiding the topic. A cold breeze swept up the lane, tossing the tops of the trees, and clouds began to scud along the vaulted blue, closing the scene in with ominous darkness, very Hollywood horror movie like. All we needed was a crypt, a coffin, and thunder to make it complete. But through it all, as I paced, Shilo talked about McGill, Ridley Ridge, and then McGill some more.

I whirled and gazed steadily at her. "Do you think that body is . . . could it be Rusty Turner?" Had he gone no farther than the woods near the castle and died of a heart attack or stroke? Or had old Uncle Melvyn murdered him and left his body there to rot? Given the conflict between them, it was a legitimate concern.

"We don't know anything yet," Shilo pointed out.

Finally McGill and Lizzie emerged from the woods as a light rain began to spit down. I hopped down off the terrace and raced to them, hugging Lizzie. She rocked back on her heels and stared up at me, a question in her eyes. What the question was, I couldn't say. "Are you okay, Lizzie?" I asked, staring down at her. "You don't need to be strong, or anything, just tell me how you feel."

"She was great," McGill said, one hand on her shoulder. "She led Virgil and his boys right to the spot, and told them what she found and how, and pointed out where you had thrown up. We stayed a few minutes, and then I asked Virge if it was okay if we came back here."

She shrugged, more to get McGill's hand off her shoulder than anything else, I thought.

"Do you want to go home?" I asked. Her face looked a little pinched and white, and she nodded. "I'll drive you." I turned to Shilo. "Can you tell the sheriff where I've gone, if he asks?"

She nodded yes, her arm through McGill's, her head on his shoulder.

I retrieved my keys—I had already changed my clothes, so I was fit to meet a grandmother—and pointed out my rental car. "You'll have to guide me," I said, sliding in to the driver's seat as she settled in on the passenger's side.

She didn't answer. I glanced over as I started down the long, curved drive. Tears were rolling down her pale cheeks. I let her silently cry, concentrating on driving in the brief shower, until we reached the turn-off to her grandmother's home, which was on the outskirts of Autumn Vale. "Are you going to be okay?" I asked, glancing over at her.

"Yeah. I'm fine." She sniffed. "It was just . . . when I thought about someone dying all alone in that tent, just lying there . . . it was awful. Do you think he was old or young? Did he suffer?"

I pulled the car over onto the shoulder of the road and turned to face her. "It's one of those things that we might never know. It's a terrible tragedy, but it's just as possible the person died in their sleep, and didn't even feel a thing." I didn't think so, but there was no point in saying that to Lizzie.

Her tears had dried, and skepticism was back in her eyes. "Right. Not likely."

I shook my head. "Just trying to make you feel better." I stopped, and realized that was what someone had once tried to do for me, and it didn't help a bit. The night my grandmother died, I was at a party. I knew she was in the hospital, but didn't think it was anything serious, so I went out with my friends. I was doing shots while my grandmother lay dying in the hospital. An earnest, young nurse tried to make me feel better later, when I found out she'd died while I was getting drunk, but I saw right through her, like Lizzie saw through me.

But this was not about my haunting guilt, my sense that I had let my beloved grandmother down, this was about Lizzie. And she had no guilt to feel, no reason to let it affect her beyond the human kindness that allows us to feel empathy for our fellow creatures. "I guess what I'm trying to say is, this was that person's path in life. There is not a thing you can do about it. If you want to talk about it, I'm here." She was tougher, in some ways, at fifteen than I had been at twenty-one, but I wouldn't take that for granted. I vowed to myself that I'd check in with her often over the next few days. I wondered if the local police department had a victims' services or social worker to deal with the traumatized.

We drove on, and she indicated her grandmother's home, which was a tiny bungalow on a narrow street that angled up toward the ridge above town. But when we approached, she suddenly said, "Why don't you just drop me off? I'm fine."

"Lizzie, I'm going to speak to your grandmother. Number one, I want her to know about that poor soul we found in the woods, and that we're taking care of it, and number two, I want to be sure it's all right that you come out to the castle again."

She shook her head, tight-lipped, but I was not going to be swayed. She was very young, and even asking her to come out to the castle could be misconstrued. I should have checked with her grandmother before asking her to guide me through the woods. No one in Autumn Vale knew me from Eve. What was I thinking? I pulled into the driveway, where a beat-up Cadillac sat, parked on a crazy angle. Lizzie flung herself out of my car and stomped up the drive, with me following as quickly as I could. She disappeared around the side of the house, toward the back, but I was going to knock on the front door like a civilized human being. I heard the shouting before I even got up to the porch.

"I don't care what you say, Lizzie is *my* daughter and I can take her back any time I want."

"Not without CPS getting involved!"

Lizzie's mother and grandmother?

"You don't have a court order, Mama, so don't try to fight me on this."

"You are *not* gonna take that child back to your house; not with all manner of things going on!"

I hesitated, not sure what to do. I stared at the screen door and willed the arguing to stop, so I could knock.

"*What* things? You don't know a damn thing about me. You *think* you do, but you don't. I don't even drink anymore!"

"Stop it, both of you!" That was Lizzie intervening.

"Honey, I didn't know you were home. Your mom and I are just . . . we're talking about where you're gonna live, and I told her you're staying here until she can . . . until she gets herself straightened around."

"Listen to me," Lizzie pleaded. "Both of you shut up for one minute!"

But I didn't want her to have to explain me. I knocked.

"Now who the heck is that?" came the grandmother's worried voice.

When she came to the door, I introduced myself. She was a plump woman, probably in her sixties, with a worried round face much like her granddaughter's, and faded blue eyes under a fringe of gray. "If you don't mind, I'd like to come in and talk to you about Lizzie's day."

Looking confused and uncertain, she stood back and let me in.

Lizzie had disappeared. I entered the living room, a tidy enough space with a sagging couch and big-screen TV, on which a game show on mute played across the screen. A woman stood by the front window; so this was Lizzie's mother. She was slim and attractive, with dark hair tied up in a ponytail, and she was wearing jeans and a jean jacket.

I explained why I invited Lizzie out to the castle in the first place, and apologized, acknowledging that I should have asked her grandmother first. I then told them both what we had found together. "I'm so sorry," I finished, wringing my hands. "I just wanted you to know that if she seems quiet or upset, she may need to talk to someone. That sight . . ." I shuddered. "It's not something anyone should ever see."

Lizzie's mother had seemed pensive until now, but there were tears standing in her eyes by the time I finished. She had her arms folded over her chest, and she was chewing on her fingernail. I suspected that she had recently quit smoking, or was trying to refrain, since I'd seen other ex-smokers nervously biting their fingernails. She turned away and stared out the front window. "Poor Lizzie," she said, a catch in her voice. "Mama, I want her to come home with me."

"Why? So you can leave her alone while you go off to do whatever it is you do?"

"I work, Mama, I work!" She sobbed, and headed for the door. "She's fifteen, not five . . . she can stay alone sometimes." Shaking her head, she cried, "It's no good; I don't know what to do anymore. I just don't . . ." She flung the door open and stomped out onto the tiny, cement porch, then stood staring at the Caddy, which was blocked in by my rental. The rain had stopped for the moment, but the sky was still a leaden gray.

"You can have your daughter back when you stop working at that awful place," the older woman yelled after her.

"I'd better move my car," I said, and headed to the door.

"You're never going to understand what I've been through!" the younger woman hollered back at her mother from outside.

"You'd better not say that again, Emerald Marie Proctor, because I understand more than you'll ever know."

I stopped stock-still on the bottom step and stared at Lizzie's mom. "Your name is Emerald?" I asked stupidly.

"Yeah. Why?" she growled at me. "You going to move your car or what? I need to get out of here and get ready for work."

But I couldn't move. Emerald was Lizzie's mother, and Emerald was the woman over whom Junior and Tom Turner had fought. There could not be two women named Emerald in or near Autumn Vale, could there? She was agitated, I could tell, but I needed to ask her a couple of questions. "Hey, I was just wondering . . . I know you and Lizzie are having a tough time right now—"

She snorted. "Yeah, a tough time because my own mother is turning her against me!"

I remembered Lizzie's remark about her mother being a whore. Emerald might be right. My mind was working a mile a minute, and I thought a shot in the dark may be required. "It must be difficult, especially with . . . especially since Tom Turner died recently."

She whirled to face me, her expression one of terror. "What are you saying?"

"You and he were . . . you had a relationship, right?"

She nodded, tears welling up in her eyes. She jangled her keys in her hand, and said, "Yeah, a long time ago. Then I took off. I just came back to Autumn Vale a year or so ago. Thought I'd reconnect with my mother! Ha! Then Tom started coming around again, and he got to wondering . . ." She trailed off and shook her head, the tears streaming down her cheeks.

"He got to wondering if he was Lizzie's father, is that right?" I said it softly, but she nodded. "Was he?" She nodded again. "But you haven't told Lizzie."

She shook her head, and choked back a sob. "What's the point *now*?"

"What were he and Junior Bradley fighting over at the bar you work at that involved you?"

"Nothing!"

"But I heard . . ." I paused, remembering what Zeke had said. "Someone in town told me that Junior told Tom to keep his hands off you."

She frowned and shook her head. "Where do people get that garbage? That never happened. The fight was not about me at *all*. Look, I can't do this right now. I have got to go. Move it or lose it, lady!" She got in her car, slammed the door, and gunned the motor. When I hustled to pull out, she screeched down the drive, backing up as skillfully as a NAS-CAR driver, and took off out of town, perhaps toward the bar at Ridley Ridge to work.

I decided to check on Lizzie, but when I went up to the door, I could see her sitting on the sofa with her grandmother, who had her arms around her grandchild. It was a complicated situation, and I didn't think I could help, at least not today.

Instead, I headed back into the heart of Autumn Vale and Crazy Lady Antiques, parking along the side street that intersected with Abenaki behind a dirt bike that was taking up an on-street parking spot. Janice was in her shop and answered the door when I knocked. I told her my need for serving coffee to the masses, and she located a big box of oddly assorted mugs, most with funny and/or inappropriate sayings, and I carried them outside and around to the side street, with her following me. She threw in a box of odd plates and serving pieces she obviously wanted to get rid of. I asked, "You knew the Turners, right?"

"Of course."

"Did Tom ever get married?"

"Nope. That boy could never settle on one girl. My Jackson is about the same age—Jack moved to New York for school and never came back—and he said that Tom was serious about some girl in high school, but she broke up with him and broke his heart."

Was that Emerald, I wondered? "What do you know about Junior Bradley?"

"Never trusted that boy. He cheated my boy Booker out of some money once." She cocked her head as I shoved the box of mugs in the backseat of the car, and turned to take the box of serving pieces from her. "Are you trying to figure out poor Tom's murder?" she asked. "Better leave that up to the cops."

I straightened. "It happened right outside my door, Janice. I'm unnerved. I want it solved. Is that so strange?" I wasn't about to talk about the dead stranger in the woods, not before we knew who it was.

"Virgil Grace is a good investigator, Merry. Leave it alone."

"I would think you would subscribe to that old adage, Janice, that no woman who ever got anything done did so by listening to people telling her not to do things."

She chuckled and patted my shoulder. "But in this case, there's danger afoot. And you've got enough to do sorting out your family estate without getting involved in murder."

It was good advice that I wouldn't be taking. The bakery was still open, so I stopped in and bought up her stock of end-of-the-day rolls and sweets. I don't know why I was bulking up my store of coffee mugs and treats as if I expected a horde, but from the number of cars that had been at the castle when I left, I wanted to be prepared. Anything I didn't use I could toss in the commercial freezer.

I saw through Binny's sullen facade now that we were friends, and I was dreadfully worried about the body in the woods. Odds were it was her father, and who would break the news if it was? I'd *have* to be there for her, if it proved to be true. Losing her brother had been tough, but if the body in the woods was Rusty, it was going to be doubly hard on her. On the other hand, she now had a niece she had not known about before. But none of that news was the kind of thing I could pass on at the moment, so I kept my mouth shut.

I pondered the whole mess as I drove back to the castle. Should I be leaving well enough alone, as Janice suggested?

Virgil Grace was investigating Tom's murder, and he knew the town and its people better than I, but I couldn't just forget about it. As I had said to Janice, it happened right outside of my door, and the killer was still out there.

When I returned, the investigation was in full swing, with a state police command center vehicle now parked in my weedy drive. The clouds had cleared enough that a ray of sunlight peeped through. I called McGill over to collect the box of mugs, and commandeered Shilo to help with the bags of treats. I carried the smaller box of plates and serving pieces; together, we hauled them to the kitchen, and Shilo and I washed and dried all the dusty mugs, setting them out on trays on the long kitchen table.

The afternoon sun was lowering in the sky by the time we were done, and I strolled over to where Virgil was talking seriously with a woman in state police khakis. When she cast a glance at me and strode away, I approached the sheriff. He looked worried and tired and none too pleased to see me. Couldn't blame him. On the other hand, it wasn't my fault the body was in my woods.

"We've made a big urn of coffee, and I have some muffins and other things for folks to eat. If you would like to spread the word, everyone is welcome."

He eyed me and nodded. "Okay. That's real nice of you."

"But?"

"Look, I know you've been asking questions in town. Stop. Now."

I watched his eyes, trying to decide what to say. "Maybe you'll answer a couple of questions for me; then I won't have to ask other people."

He sighed and looked skyward. I'd swear there was a hint of a smile on his lips. He looked down at me, his expression softening. "You can ask, anyway."

Which of all the jumbled thoughts and questions in my head were most important? Maybe if I was a real investigator, those things would fall into order. First things first. I took a deep breath. "Is that body in the tent Rusty Turner?"

"It's male, that's about all we know."

"So it's possible. Is there anyone else local it could be?"

"No one has been reported missing."

"Oh." But I squinted up at him, realizing he hadn't really answered my question and wasn't going to. The state police female deputy strolled toward us. Darn. I had a lot more questions.

"Sheriff Grace, we need you for a few minutes," she said.

"I had a couple of more questions," I said. "Can we talk later?"

He nodded, then walked away with the deputy.

McGill knew all of the Autumn Vale deputies and even some of the state police officers, and he was introducing Shilo around to them. I should probably join them, I thought, but remembered I had not yet checked off one more thing on my list. I went inside, grabbed the cordless phone, and curled up in one of the cozy chairs Shilo and I had hauled in to the kitchen by the fireplace. I dialed a number from memory, a sudden, desperate need to hear one voice making my movements hasty.

"Hello?" came that familiar, dear, warm voice on the phone.

I burst into tears.

Chapter Twenty

❋ ❋ ❋

"WHO IS THIS? What's wrong?"

I hadn't expected to react like I did, and I could hear the panic in my dear friend's voice. "Pish, it's all right, it's me!" I burbled, my tone thick and strange.

"Who . . . Merry? Is that you?"

"Yes!"

"Are you okay? Where *are* you? I've been trying to call you for a *week*! The stupid phone company keeps saying your line is disconnected. Then I tried your cell phone, but it kept going to voice mail or saying you were unavailable. I tried calling Shilo, but she's gone, too. I thought an alien had kidnapped you both. Or one of her gypsy relatives. Are you *okay*, sweetie?"

I took a deep breath, put my head back and closed my eyes, bathing in the flood of his concern. "Yes, Pish, I'm fine. You know the castle I inherited? Well, that's where I am. I gave up my apartment in the city and moved here."

"And you didn't *tell* me? How *could* you? Oh, Merry, I thought we were better friends than *that*!" He always spoke in italics, and in person the emphasis was exaggerated by fluttering hands. All designed to disarm and disorient, I believe, because his laser-focus, blue-eyed gaze is enough to alarm the unwary.

Pish is one of the sweetest people I have ever met, but his goodness is enhanced by a tart sense of humor and well-developed regard for the ridiculous. He'd adore Autumn Vale. What the good people of this town would think of him, I didn't know. I could picture him in his beautiful Central Park West condo, which he shared with his querulous, elderly mother. He'd be sitting in front of a fireplace as I was, on a cool, September evening, but there would be a crackling fire in his; he'd be drinking cognac and reading Faulkner, or quaffing brandy and chuckling over Tennessee Williams, or sipping pinot noir and leafing through Escoffier. I could hear a recording of Domingo's version of "Nessun Dorma" in the background, the rich voice rolling through the airwaves.

I sighed. "Darling, it is because I love you that I couldn't tell you I was moving out of New York. It would have broken my heart to see you upset. It was a mistake. I'm sorry."

"What about Shilo? Do you know where she is?"

"I called her the morning I arrived, and she took it as an invitation, so she tootled up here in that dreadful vehicle she calls a car." There was silence for a long moment, and I knew his feelings were hurt that I had called her and not him.

"That is just like our darling scatterbrain," he said, his tone dry. "I suppose I'll have to forgive you, though I'll hold a grudge for a while and make you suffer."

"I miss you," I said, realizing how true that was. I met Pish through Miguel. He was my husband's financial advisor, a wise decision that had left me a wealthyish widow, which I reversed with my own stupidity. However, my bad-decision days were over. I was not one of those sad folk who stagger from awful situation to awful situation. "I wish you were here right now."

"Describe the castle, darling. I have been *dying* to hear about it ever since you inherited it! The real estate listing did it *no* justice, I'll bet," he said.

He, dear man, had advised me right away to go see my inheritance, but I was in the middle of the Leatrice drama at that point, and couldn't leave New York. That was my excuse, anyway. I was just stunned by the development and afraid of what I'd find. I told Pish all about the castle, and my multitude of troubles, from Tom Turner's murder up to and including the body in the tent in the arboretum. As I talked, police officers and professionals came and went, grabbing mugs of coffee and handfuls of muffins and treats from the baskets of Binny's Bakery items. I waited until the kitchen was empty of others, then finally said, "Pish, I called you to check in, and I'm sorry you've been worried, but I also have some questions."

I filled him in on our trip to the Turner Construction trailer, and my discoveries about the shoddy plat and grade school–level renderings of the Wynter Acres plan. Then I told him about what Shilo had discovered: the regular large cash deposits to Turner Construction accounts in the Autumn Vale Community Bank that had no discernible source, given that work had all but stopped in recent months.

"Who would have had the ability to deposit in the account?" he asked.

"Since Rusty's been gone? Probably just Tom and Dinah."

"Dinah was not married to Rusty Turner, is that right?"

"No, nor living with him," I said, beginning to see what he was asking. I thought about our conversation, how Dinah had more or less given up on working at Turner Construction since before Tom died. She seemed a little desperate to find a way to make money. And yet she said she hadn't been taking a wage from Turner Construction in the last few months. Why, if there was a large amount of money there, as there seemed to be? Did she know where it came from or not? Did she refuse to touch it or take her wage because of the money's origins? If it was Tom's, I supposed that would make sense. I shared my thoughts with Pish.

"I don't want to say too much, my dear, but it sounds to me as if Tom Turner had found a way to make money that had nothing to do with construction, and it may have led to his death."

"What do you mean?"

"Well, drug peddling is one possibility, I suppose. But maybe he was involved in some kind of money-laundering scheme. And if he was, the kind of folk he would have been dealing with . . . well, he wouldn't be the first who thought he was smart and ended up dead."

That gave me pause, and I remembered someone—was it Gordy or Zeke?—had said something about a couple of scary guys in town late last year, about the time Rusty disappeared and my uncle died. I had a lot to think about. Pish told me to give his love to Shilo, and that he would be in touch—he was going to see if there was any information he could dig up—and that he hoped I'd take pictures of the castle and send them to him. As soon as I got my digital camera out of storage and my laptop working and got Internet service out in the boonies, I would.

I sat for a while staring at the empty fireplace. Someone cleared their throat behind me, and I turned to see a big-bellied fellow draining the last of the coffee urn and snagging two muffins.

"You Mel's niece?" he asked. He was dressed in overalls and a plaid shirt, but the getup didn't quite look natural on him.

"I am," I said, rising and going toward him. "Merry Wynter," I added, sticking out my hand. I recognized him, but waited for him to introduce himself.

"Simon Grover," he said, juggling the muffins and coffee, then clasping my hand in a firm grip. "You been talking to my wife."

"You're the bank manager, and head of the Brotherhood of the Falcons!"

"Yup. Not here because of that, though; I'm captain of the Autumn Vale Volunteer Fire Patrol. We're providing backup to the state police and Virgil's boys and gals."

Making a quick decision, I motioned to the comfortable chair by the empty fireplace. "Would you like to sit and have your coffee in comfort, Mr. Grover?"

"I sure would," he said with a sigh of relief. "My dogs is barkin'! These boots *ain't* made for walking." He spoke with a folksy air, maybe one he had developed since coming to manage a bank in a small town in rural upstate New York.

Grover waddled over to the fireplace and I let him sit with his coffee and muffins while I put the urn on to perk again. Then I joined him and we sat in companionable silence for a long moment, while I tried to figure out how to introduce the topic of my uncle's dealings at the bank. In one sense, it was my business since I was the heir, but what went on *before* my uncle's death could be deemed private, I supposed.

"You know," he said, "I liked your uncle. We were brothers, in a sense, and Rusty Turner, too; us three were the founding members of the Brotherhood of the Falcons. Now I'm the only one of the three founding members left. The three amigos."

Mad thoughts of a tontine-like arrangement flitted through my mind. But *was* it so mad? "I didn't know my uncle was part of the club."

"When my wife and I first moved here, I went out of my way to be pals with Melvyn. He was getting to be a crusty old fella even then. Not many friends."

"He *was* friends with Gogi Grace's husband, though, I understand. And Doc English."

He shrugged, his bulky shoulders rolling. When he didn't answer, I wondered if I had offended him by naming Melvyn's buddies, right after he had said my uncle didn't have many. He didn't look offended, though. He was holding his empty coffee cup, glaring into it with a sad expression.

"Let me refill your cup with fresh coffee," I said. When

I came back and handed him the fragrant steaming brew, he sighed in contentment.

"Your coffee's better'n my wife's."

"A lot of people like perked coffee better than drip." How could I talk to him about my uncle's affairs, I wondered. To make conversation, I said, "It's great of you and your volunteers to come out this afternoon." I wasn't sure how they could possibly help or what they were doing other than standing around talking, drinking coffee, and eating muffins. It was more likely that he had come out for one more excuse to avoid his wife's company, although maybe that was unfair. "I got the mugs from your wife's shop," I said, testing the waters.

"Bunch of old crap she's got there. Never makes a penny," he grumbled.

Okay. "It must have been awkward for you, with both Melvyn and Rusty as founding members of the Brotherhood, and them being at legal loggerheads."

"It sure the hell was! Pardon my French. Those two old arseholes—again, pardon the French—were getting more and more cantankerous. I tried to get 'em to see sense, but they just . . ." He trailed off and shook his head. "Couldn't get 'em to stop feuding."

"Toward the end, was my uncle okay?" I still feared that the body in the woods was Rusty Turner, and that my uncle had gone off his rocker and killed him.

"Okay, as in, all his marbles?"

I nodded.

"Well, yeah, I'd say your uncle was sharp as a tack and just as painful, if you sat on him."

I pondered what that meant. "In other words, he was fine, unless you crossed him?"

"Yup. Then he was like a wasp, wouldn't let you out of his sight until he'd given you what for."

His chagrined tone made me wonder if Simon Grover, bank manager, had crossed Melvyn Wynter before he died.

I knew too well that Rusty Turner had, repeatedly. "Did he, uh, come in to the bank ever?"

Grover shrugged. "Sometimes. Not often."

"Was my uncle worried about anything? Before he died, I mean."

"He was mad as hell that Rusty had disappeared. Said the old coot was trying to avoid the lawsuit."

I pondered my discovery that Uncle Melvyn had been heading into town that fateful morning when he went off the road. "Was he angry enough that he'd be confronting someone about it?"

The banker frowned into his empty cup. "Like who?"

A sudden inspiration made me say, "The lawyer, maybe? Mr. Silvio was trying to get them both to agree, though, right? Like you were. He was trying to solve things between my uncle and Rusty Turner?"

The man snorted into a chuckle, then a wheezing, coughing guffaw. "Have you ever heard of any lawyer trying to settle out of court unless there was a wad of cash involved? No way! Silvio was lining his pockets from the money two old men with grudges brought him. He wasn't mediating; hell, he was exacerbating, egging each one on to file more and more lawsuits!"

I heard a noise behind us, but it was just McGill, filling a couple of mugs with the fresh coffee. He had an odd look on his face, one that I couldn't translate.

"Merry? Virge wants to see you outside."

"Yeah, okay."

Grover heaved himself out of his chair and set his mug in the sink as he waddled past. "I guess I'd better go home, see what the little woman's got for supper," he grumbled, heading for the door. "She can't make coffee worth a damn, but at least she can cook." He lumbered outside.

Darn! I had just been about to ask him about finding my uncle's car off the road, hoping to quiz him on what he had seen. It still seemed odd to me that he was returning home to Autumn Vale at six in the morning! And I hadn't had a chance to inquire about my uncle's bank dealings and what was up with Isadore Openshaw. That would all have to wait.

I took my time, delaying going out to see the sheriff. Instead, I stacked dirty mugs in the sink and ran soapy water, then washed them and set them on the drain board to air-dry. I had a lot to consider, and what the bank manager had just said about the lawyer made me wonder. The tangled mystery of who killed Tom Turner in the middle of the night on my property had many threads. Who wanted him dead being the central thread, of course, or even, who *needed* him dead and why? I knew so little about the local dynamics that I was afraid I was missing much of what could help me figure it out. But then, Virgil Grace was local, and he might even now have a solid idea of who killed Tom. I wouldn't discover that until he made an arrest. I sure hoped it wouldn't be *me* led away in handcuffs. I had to believe Sheriff Grace would realize that an argument in town in front of witnesses did not make me guilty of murder.

But Mr. Lawyer Silvio . . . I hadn't even put him in the mix until now. Far from trying to put a stop to the back-and-forth lawsuits between the two old men, as he said he was doing, it appeared—or so the bank manager said—that he had been spurring both men on. But why? The answer that made sense was, to make as much money as he could with the fees he would accrue from one or the other. But Silvio had already told me he represented neither man in the lawsuits, since that would be a conflict of interest.

Did I believe him? It should be easy enough to find out the truth. Or maybe he was making money off the discord somehow. Could I really see Silvio creeping across my property in the middle of the night wielding a crowbar and cracking Tom Turner over the head? I wouldn't put it past him, especially the creeping part. One thing I had to keep in mind when dealing with anyone was, there could be motives that I just wasn't seeing because I had not been in town long enough. That went for Mr. Silvio, too. He had not always been an Autumn Vale citizen, but maybe he had been there long enough to have a grudge against Tom Turner. Hannah had said Tom was doing something for a lawyer. If that was Silvio, maybe whatever it was went wrong? Did Tom find something out and threaten Silvio with it?

I had a lot of questions, and very few answers. I wandered outside. McGill was still hard at work, despite it getting darker by the minute and the grim scene of police vans and patrol cars. Shilo talked earnestly to one of the investigators, Miss State Police Khaki Uniform.

The sheriff saw me and approached, full tilt. "Didn't McGill tell you I wanted to talk to you?"

"Yes, he did." I looked up at him, examining the line of scruff along his jaw. "If this is twenty questions, it's my turn. Did you know that you constantly have an unpleasant look on your face? One of these days, you're going to turn into a grumpy old man with a peptic ulcer."

I turned away and watched McGill push dirt into a hole not that far away from us. He had been working steady, making progress while I mooned around weeping to old friends on the phone, talking to a hypertensive bank manager, and washing mugs.

The sheriff settled his expression some, and said, "Well, I just thought you'd like to be the first to know. We don't think the dead body is Rusty Turner."

I actually felt a leap of joy at that; one thing poor Binny would not have to deal with. But the question remained. "Who else could it be?"

"We're still working on that. The medical examiner might be able to tell us more."

I watched Sheriff Grace's profile; he was a good-looking man, no doubt about it. But his permanent scowl damaged that, and I was serious about him ending up with a peptic ulcer if he didn't watch it. Looking at it from his viewpoint though, this was serious business and nothing to smile about. And these folks were his friends and neighbors. "You know, it's probably just the body of some hiker who got lost, set up camp, and had a heart attack in his sleep."

"I wish I thought that," he said. "But he has blunt-force trauma to the head, from what the ME says, and in his pockets he had some stuff that makes me think he's local. I just can't figure out who the hell it could be."

Local, and not Rusty Turner. "What did he have in his pockets? A card from a local business? A takeout menu from Vale Variety and Lunch? He could have that kind of stuff and still just be a transient passing through."

Virgil shook his head, and I knew he wouldn't or couldn't answer me.

"It's getting too dark to do anything, so we're packing it in. But we came across the other site you and Lizzie found, and we've got it cordoned off. We'll have a team here tomorrow morning to investigate it, in case it holds any answers."

"Okay." I watched as he stalked off.

Shilo joined me as the officers packed up and departed.

I told her I had spoken to Pish, and she was happy about that. I then threaded my arm through hers and we reentered the castle. "You and I have a lot to talk over," I said. "Starting with the fact that I have discovered who Lizzie Proctor is, or at least, who her father is, supposedly. Shilo, Binny Turner has a niece."

"What? You mean . . . ?"

"Yup. Tom Turner was Lizzie's father."

"Wow. Didn't see that one coming."

"Neither did I."

Chapter Twenty-one

✖ ✖ ✖

I WOKE UP the next day sure of a few things. First, I needed to speak to Junior Bradley again and try to find out what he and Tom Turner had really been fighting about. At the same time, I needed to know about the faulty plats and plans I found at Turner Construction. Who approved them? Who loaned the company money for construction based on them? What lawsuits were truly extant when Melvyn died? Did it have anything to do with those faulty plans, I wondered.

I also needed to get a handle on who I thought *might* have killed Tom Turner. Despite everyone's belief in Virgil Grace's ability to solve the murder, I could not just stand by and wait. After all, nine months later he still had not figured out if my uncle's "accident" was really an accident. Maybe I could even help, with an outsider's viewpoint. I wondered what the buzz was in town, especially now, with this body we found yesterday.

As Shilo snored on the other side of the Jack and Jill

bathroom door, I showered and dressed comfortably in jeans and a soft, V-neck T-shirt. Then, cup of coffee in hand, I exited the front door, descended from the terrace, and walked down the weedy drive to try to get a better view of the castle and decide what needed to be done first. I turned and squinted, looking over my inheritance. As I had begun to realize, I was going to be at Wynter Castle longer than I had anticipated, and had better start planning for a winter spent in upstate. But I had a couple months of outdoor time left before the unpredictable winds of November set in.

The exterior itself was attractive: old, cut stone, square facade with a turreted look to the rounded extensions at either end, and Gothic-arched windows. The entrance, centered on the long, flagged terrace that wrapped around the ballroom on the west side of the castle, was bland, though, even with those amazing oak doors. It needed something to set it off, to make it stand out. Maybe gardens or potted plants and statuary. The terrace, I had discovered, extended all the way along the far side, and the ballroom's French doors opened out onto it. That, too, needed something to break up the long expanse.

How was I going to afford any of the upgrades needed? I had to make or borrow enough money to bring Wynter Castle up to a degree of attractiveness for potential buyers. The property would only appeal to someone who could afford to gamble. Wynter Castle was too far away from New York City to make it a spa retreat, and there was absolutely nothing nearby to make it a desirable destination from a tourist's aspect. Investors would cringe. It needed a buyer with imagination and bucks.

I turned away and wandered the property near the castle, avoiding what I now thought of as the death hole, where crime-scene tape still fluttered from hastily erected fence posts. It was only early September, but after a couple of very cool nights the leaves were beginning to get that desiccated look from late-summer stress and nearly autumn change coming on. A blue jay shrieked at me from a cluster of brushy shrubs that had grown up in the long grass.

When was my grounds crew going to show up? They never did phone me. Had I done the right thing, hiring Zeke and Gordy to mow the fields? They didn't strike me as the brightest bulbs in the package, maybe twenty-five-watt in a hundred-watt world, but how bright did you have to be to mow a yard? That sounds snooty, but I was getting irritated at the slow pace of life in Autumn Vale. No one seemed to be ready to hustle. The grass, or hay, or weeds—whatever the mess was— had to be taken care of and soon, because . . . well, because I needed to see progress.

I walked past the excavator parked among the filled-in holes, thinking of all the damage Tom had done, and wondering why. He could not possibly have believed that old Melvyn Wynter had buried his father, not when he was digging all the way out to the edge of the property. It didn't make a bit of sense!

Sipping my coffee as I scanned the edge of the woods, I thought I saw a patch of orange. Was Becket back? In all the flurry of the day before, I had almost forgotten the poor, limping cat! I edged closer, but the animal didn't move this time. My heart started pounding, and my stomach lurched. I walked faster, speeding to a trot. It was Becket; it had to be!

It was. He wasn't moving, but he was still breathing a labored, slow pant. As I knelt by him, he opened his eyes, meowing fiercely, then wailing and thrashing about. As I leaped to my feet and backed off, he focused and met my gaze; his meow gentled to a question. I hadn't had a cat in years, but I knew that sound. He needed help.

Tossing the junk-store coffee cup aside, I knelt again, and scooped him up. He was wearing, amazingly, a collar, with a cheapie plastic tag attached; incredible that it had survived nearly a year! "Becket" was written on the cardboard insert. "You poor fellow," I murmured. There were no cuts or bites that I could see, but he didn't look right. He was a big cat, long-limbed, but skinny, *far* too thin, and his orangey fur was matted and dull looking. As I carried him, his head lolled over my arm, his eyes open but filmed.

The next hour was a blur. I took Becket in to the kitchen and laid him on a towel in one of the chairs by the fireplace, then got Shilo up. We gave him a drink of water, which he lapped at thirstily before collapsing again in exhaustion. I got ready to go, organizing my day as quickly as I could as I worried about the cat.

Even through the thick walls of the castle, I could hear the heavy engines of police vehicles arriving; they were coming to finish up with the encampments, as Virgil had promised. I wrapped Becket in the towel and carried him outside to the car, as the sheriff and his crew set up their base of operations, but I didn't have time to talk. I handed Shilo the keys to the rental and we took off, with me holding Becket and Shilo driving. Shi had been able to get ahold of McGill, who told her where the only vet in town was located. She had explored a lot already, more than I had, mapping out the town in her retentive brain, and she brought me to a little clinic that took up one end of a redbrick, modern strip mall that also had the town waterworks department and other municipal offices in it.

The vet was a young Asian-American woman, Dr. Ling. After she heard my remarkable story and confirmed that though he was not my cat, I was going to be responsible for the bill, she ordered me to leave Becket there in the treatment room. As we left, I heard her call out to an assistant to start a fluid IV. Becket was in good hands.

Again, life in Autumn Vale had changed up my day in weird ways.

Shilo told me she was going to hitch a ride back to the castle with McGill, who was headed out there to fill in more holes—at the rate he was going, he'd be done by the next day—so I was free to do what I needed to do. I had at least thought well enough ahead to throw my muffin tins in the car, so I headed down to Binny's Bakery to see if she would mind me starting the muffins a little early.

I entered to the now-familiar clang of the bell over the door and was once again taken by the collection of teapots, which I examined with interest. It wouldn't be long before I had all my stuff from storage, and then I was going to have to deal with my own dozens of boxes of teapots and teacups. Binny came out from the back, wiping her hands on a towel, and said, "Oh, it's you!"

"Yeah. Could I start my baking a little early?" I explained why.

She had an odd look on her face, and nodded. "Sure." She paused, tapping on the countertop and biting her lip. In a rush, she said, "Maybe you can do me a favor?"

"No problem," I said. "You've been so generous, I'd love a chance to do you some payback."

"Would you mind the store for an hour while I run an errand? You know how to use a cash register, right?"

I didn't then, but I soon learned. A half hour later, she threw some goodies in a bag and took off out the back door. No explanation. Boyfriend, maybe? Not my business. I made two large batches of muffin batter—banana bran and apple-sauce, since those two seemed to be going over best—popped them in the oven, and set the timer, as a couple of customers came in. It just happened to be Isadore Openshaw and another, middle-aged lady.

"Hi, what can I help you with?" I said, in my brightest customer-service voice.

Isadore looked like she'd swallowed an air bubble, kind of pained and grimacing, but the other woman smiled and cocked her head to one side. "Who are you? Where's Binny?"

I explained who I was as Isadore stared fiercely at the goodies in the bakery case. "I've met a lot of folks, including Miss Openshaw," I said, "but I haven't met you yet." I stuck out my hand over the counter.

"Well, isn't this fascinating! I'm Helen Johnson of the Autumn Vale Methodist Church," she said, taking my hand in a firm, if clammy, clasp. "I visited your uncle many times, to take him soup and ask him if he'd like to join our congregation. We have such wonderful seniors' programs, with euchre nights, shuffleboard, and bus trips to Amish country!"

I stared at her for a long moment, nonplussed, wondering what kind of reception she'd gotten from my cantankerous uncle. Hopefully she wouldn't have a story about being chased away by a rifle-wielding madman. She was one of those born church ladies, but in tweed capris instead of the expected skirt, topped by a silk blouse and pearls. Sensible sandals and socks, visible under the counter's pass through, finished the ensemble, and a hat topped her billowy nest of gray hair. "I'm pleased to meet you. How did the visits with my uncle go?"

Isadore snorted and stared ferociously over my head.

Helen glanced over at her with a frown, then looked back to me. "Well, he was not pleased to see me. Tell me . . . was he suffering from Alzheimer's, perhaps? Every single time I went out, he asked the same question; what did I think I was doing there? He was so terribly confused. I never knew what to tell him."

I took a deep breath to keep from laughing. The timer dinged, and I rushed to pull the muffins out, then returned to the counter and explained to the ladies what I was doing there: making muffins and minding the store. Helen clasped her hands together. "Oh, muffins! My darling mama told me about your wonderful muffins. She lives at Golden Acres, you know, and feels fortunate. Mrs. Grace is such a wonderful woman, a real social leader in this town. Even though she doesn't go to church."

I was exhausted by her relentless cheerfulness, and relieved when she bought two ricotta-stuffed pastries, while Isadore chose a gooey éclair. I boxed them up.

"One day when I was out there," Helen said, lingering

while Isadore waited at the door, tapping her patent leather shoe on the step, ". . . at the castle, you know, there were two strange men, but I didn't see Melvyn. I wondered and wondered about those men, you know, and I heard rumors they had been in town that day, but I never saw them again." Her dark eyes were bright with curiosity, the perfect image of a nosy Nelly.

"When was that?" I asked.

"Oh, Lord, let me see; when *was* that?" She looked up in the air and cocked her head. "Was that before the fire in the woods behind the church, or after? After, probably. No, before." She paused and frowned down at her sandals. "No, it had to be *after* the fire. I remember now! A week or so *after*. So that would have been, let me see . . . last October? Almost a year ago." She nodded sharply, triumph on her round, cheerful face. "Late October of last year."

I was exhausted with her thought process, and Isadore was clearly ready to go out of her mind, but I wasn't done yet. "What did the men look like?"

"Well, now, they weren't very friendly. They had on suits, *black* suits, and they had a black car."

"Old? Young? White? Black? Tall? Short?"

She shrugged. "I don't remember, dear."

"I have to go to work, Helen. I'm late! Mr. Grover won't have a clue how to open."

"Hey," I said to her, "your employer came out to the castle yesterday, Miss Openshaw. Simon Grover was with the volunteer fire department, giving support to the police."

Isadore didn't answer, but Helen's eyes widened. "Oh, my, yes! I heard about the corpse in the woods near you. Was it Melvyn's body?"

Taken aback, I said, "Uh, no, Melvyn's body was never missing."

Isadore was practically dancing in place. "It's ten-o-seven, Helen! I'm late. I thought you needed money at the bank, and then had to get to choir practice?"

Why didn't she just head on to the bank and let Helen follow? Maybe it was like women in a bar who needed to go to the washroom; they traveled in duos. Or . . . maybe Isadore didn't want me talking to Helen alone?

"Oh, heavens, yes! Well, I'm glad the body wasn't your uncle's, dear." With that, both women left the store, and Isadore took her friend's arm as they marched off down Abenaki.

I pondered that weird conversation as I packaged up my cooled muffins. Was it my imagination, or did Isadore get even more agitated when the two men at my uncle's place came up in conversation? I was now certain she knew something, but concerning what? My uncle's death? Both she and Gogi had questioned how it happened, but would Isadore have even talked to me about it if I hadn't caught her examining the scene?

The bakeshop got busy, and more than two hours dragged by, with me having to figure out what every item was priced at, and where a fresh supply of bags was, and how to construct the bakery boxes. When Binny slogged into the shop at almost one, I was tired, grumpy, and puzzled.

She held up her hand, as she came from the back room tying a fresh white apron on. "I know, I know; I was gone longer than I expected. Sorry. Hope you weren't swamped."

Mollified, I replied, "Well, it was longer than I expected. But I sure met a lot of locals! If you need help, I'd be happy to fill in for you sometime. I was going to offer rental money for the use of your ovens, but maybe you'd consider a trade of services, your ovens for my time?" It had just come to me that moment, and since my mouth often moves as quickly as my mind—or even quicker—I made the offer as I thought of it. It would save me money I could use toward the castle refurbish.

"That would be good."

She looked tired and bewildered, and I wondered what that was all about. Maybe she had a boyfriend she wasn't talking about, and she had met him but they had had a fight.

That was a whole lot of "ifs," though. Dinah Hooper walked in the door at that moment, and Binny watched her.

I hung about for a few minutes, and we chitchatted, but neither woman said much of interest. Dinah was talking about her decision to open a floral and décor shop, while Binny was feverishly dashing around, clanging pans together, as customers came in to the store. I couldn't spend too long, not if I wanted to do everything that I needed to do, so I left.

I was mystified.

Something had upset Binny. Whatever it was, it wasn't anything she could share with me. I went and had a bite to eat at the Vale Variety. My sometimes working/sometimes not cell phone kicked in with a text message, telling me that Shilo and McGill had had lunch with his mom, and were now on their way out of town to the castle. Lunch with his *mom*? Wow, talk about speed dating. In all the years I had known Shilo, she had never latched onto a guy so thoroughly. And McGill seemed to return her interest in spades.

During our many conversations, I had learned that McGill had lost his wife around the same time I had lost Miguel. He seemed to be open to new romance though, while I was mired in the past, swallowed alive by my sense of loss, still, after seven years. How was McGill managing, even with a girl as extraordinary as Shilo? *Most* widows and widowers that I knew of moved on more quickly than I was able to, though. All around me, folks were getting together and going on with their lives, while I still mourned the only man I had ever loved. Miguel was going to be a hard act to beat, and maybe that was my problem. I still measured every man I met and had a passing interest in against his perfection.

I checked in with the vet's office after lunch, but though Becket was doing better, he wasn't quite ready to leave. I could practically hear dollar bills winging their way out of my wallet. I decided I may as well take the muffins to Golden Acres, so I drove there and parked on the sloping road, then circled the building to the back, where I delivered the baked goods to the kitchen.

Then I went through to the old section of the retirement residence. There was some kind of event going on in the community room; I could tell by the laughter. I followed the sound, and entered through the pocket doors. Hannah was sitting in the middle of the room surrounded by old folks. Books were piled around, and she was clapping at something someone had just said.

"Merry!" she cried. "You're just in time! It's Random Quote Day."

"I beg your pardon?"

"It's a game," she said, her huge eyes sparkling.

Lizzie was sitting in the corner talking to Mr. Dread, and ignoring everyone else. I let her be for the moment, and joined the turmoil that swirled around Hannah, a virtual senior tornado of oldsters grabbing books, showing them to others, tottering around the tiny librarian with wheelchairs and walkers.

"It's your turn," she said, and tossed me a book. She named a page and line number swiftly. "Read it now!"

I didn't have time to protest, nor did I notice the book title, so, with everyone eyeing me, I opened to the page and scanned down to line seven. "'It is not time or opportunity that is to determine intimacy; it is disposition alone. Seven years would be insufficient to make some people acquainted with each other, and seven days are more than enough for others,'" I read out loud. How apropos of our fast friendship! And I recognized the quotation. I closed the book: *Sense and Sensibility*, Jane Austen. Of course. I eyed Hannah suspiciously and she beamed a bright smile in my direction. That was no random quote; the minx had planned it in case I showed up, knowing my love for classic English literature, and zeroing in on the appropriate quotation.

"Who's next?" she said.

I wanted to find Gogi, but I murmured to Hannah, as I passed, "Can we talk before you leave?" and she nodded.

In the reception area the same girl I had met before—and whose name I had forgotten—was ably filling her post as combination watchdog and phone answerer. "Is Gogi Grace available?" I asked her.

She turned her brown-eyed gaze on me, and tears welled. "I'm sorry," she said, her light Irish accent soft and vibrant. "She isn't able to see anyone at this moment."

"Is everything okay?" I asked, a little alarmed by her evident sadness.

She glanced around and leaned forward. "Everything is just fine, but . . . she's . . . she's having a vigil for a terminally ill patient right now, someone who has no family. She's asked not to be disturbed."

"That's so *sad*! Who is it?"

She shook her head. "It's no one you would know. The lady has been confined to her bed for years; she's 103. No one left even remembers her. But Mrs. Grace won't let her leave alone."

"Thank you. I . . . I wish her well." I turned away and spotted Lizzie, standing partly shrouded by the potted fern by the door. She stared at me, her eyes dark and red-rimmed. The girl had been crying, and I wanted to know why. "Do you want to talk?" I asked. She nodded. "Let's go outside."

Chapter Twenty-two

❋ ❋ ❋

WE WALKED OUT to the benches out front; that was as good a place as any, since I hoped to catch both Hannah and Gogi, should she become free. The clouds had gathered and concealed the sun, with an ominous darkness in the distance. I wished I had a sweater. A cool breeze swept up the sloped road. But Lizzie—wearing a sweatshirt that was emblazoned with a slanted, homemade logo in fabric paint asserting that "AVHS Sucks!," probably a reference to her high school—seemed comfortable. We sat down on one of the empty benches and she thrust her legs out in front of her, slouching back with her arms folded over her chest.

"How are you doing?" I asked, to kick-start the conversation. With a moody teenager, I could wait all day before she would do it.

She shrugged.

"You going back to school yet?"

"Still suspended."

"What did you do, anyway?"

"They didn't like my sweatshirt."

Surprise, surprise. "How'd you sleep? I hope it wasn't too bad, thinking about what we found in the woods."

She shrugged again. "I don't care about that." She paused, but then went on, saying, "My mom came back to the house this morning."

"Oh?"

"Why is she suddenly pretending like she cares?" Lizzie asked, kicking at the grass that edged the walkway.

"Maybe she really does care, Lizzie. I know it doesn't feel like it, from your aspect. Has she messed things up between you?"

"We were doing fine until she hauled us back here. Then she just handed me to Grandma and took off."

I didn't know what to say to that, because it wasn't my place to defend either woman, nor did I know enough of the story to know who was in the right or who was in the wrong. "Was she trying to straighten things out, maybe? Did she figure you needed a safe place to live until she could do that?"

"Yeah, well, she said she'd be back for me and that we'd be able to live together again, and then she just . . ." Lizzie glared up at the sky.

I stayed silent, not sure if pointing out that her mom seemed to be trying to keep her word would help. From the conversation I had overheard, it appeared that she had come back and wanted Lizzie to live with her, though the grandmother was blocking the effort.

"Did they find out who that guy in the woods was yet?" she asked.

"Not yet. They've eliminated one local guy, Rusty Turner, but haven't nailed down who it is." I waited a moment, then said, "I'm sorry for dragging you into it, Lizzie. If I had known . . . but of course, I didn't. We never would have found him if it wasn't for you. It was a good thing to do."

Watching my face, she said, "That cop, he wondered if you, like, led me to the place with the body."

I was taken aback and put off. "Sheriff Grace thought I led you to that place?"

"I know, right? I hate cops." She slouched down further. "He wondered if you had already found it, and were just trying to . . . what did he call it?" She screwed up her face in thought. "Were you trying to have me coronate your story, whatever that means."

Coronate? Oh! "Corroborate?"

"Yeah, that's it," she said, her puzzled expression clearing. "Like, trick me into being the one who found the dead guy. But I told him no way. I told you about the camp, not the other way around."

"I appreciate that. I'm new here, so no one knows what to think of me."

"Yeah, you're kind of different."

The way she said it was a compliment. I think.

I told her about finding Becket and taking him to the vet, but I was thinking all the while. Would her mom ever tell her who her father had been, I wondered? Lizzie was owed the truth so she could at least have her aunt, Binny, to get to know. It would be good for Binny, too, I thought, since she appeared to have no one but her mother. But it wasn't my place to interfere. Contrary to what some of my friends say, I do not think I know what's best for everyone but myself.

After another half hour, Hannah trundled out the door and down the walk toward us. "Hey, there," she said as she approached. "How are you girls doing?"

Lizzie, still a little shy with Hannah, ducked her head and said hello back. Hannah grabbed a book from the bag hanging off her wheelchair handle and gave it to the teenager. "I saved this for you," she said.

The teen took the book and looked at the title, her face turning red.

I glanced at the cover. The book was entitled *Uglies* by Scott Westerfeld. I gaped at Hannah with horror, and she caught my look.

"What's wrong?" she asked, glancing between me and Lizzie.

I glared at the title of the book and raised my eyebrows.

"Oh, my goodness, you don't think . . . Lizzie," she cried, stretching out her delicate hand. "I didn't give you the book because of the title! Good lord . . . you're a *beautiful* girl," she said, wistfully stroking the teen's hand. "I never even thought you could take it *that* way. I gave you the book because . . . because I wish it had been around when I was a teenager. It would have helped me understand how it's good to be unique, and how no one should think they're wrong for being different than her peers. You have a brain. You have a heart. That's not always easy in this world, because they'll try to stifle your smarts and crush your spirit." Her chin went up. "I know that from experience."

Lizzie smiled a crooked grin, then, and said she had to go, so she dashed off, book under her arm. I asked Hannah if she had another copy, because I knew I wanted to read it myself.

"I do. Come down to the library sometime and I'll loan it to you. It's a great book about thinking for yourself. Not something you've ever had a problem with, I'd bet." After a pause, she glanced over at me, and said, "You do think it was okay that I gave her that book? Lizzie believed me, right? It never even occurred to me that she'd think the title was referring to her!"

"She believed you," I said.

"I hope so. If she likes it, there are a couple more books in the trilogy."

We were silent for another moment, each lost in our own thoughts. If there was anyone who would want to know about Lizzie's paternity, it would be Hannah, who loved Tom so, but did I dare tell her? I didn't know her well, despite our quick empathy. "Have you thought any more about the complications in Tom's life, and who may have wanted him dead?" I asked.

"I have." She folded her small hands together on her narrow lap and looked down at them, twisting a filigree silver ring around on one finger as she spoke. "Tom has not always been . . . circumspect. He's made a lot of people angry."

"Junior Bradley, for one."

"Right, but others, too. I didn't remember this until just yesterday, but he and Dinah Hooper had an argument one day in the middle of the street."

"What about?"

"I don't know," she said, distress on her pretty, little face. "They were too far away, and there was no one around them."

"Okay, anyone else?"

She glanced up and down the walk, and leaned toward me. "He . . . he had a big fight with Mr. Grover, the bank manager."

"Really?" I thought about the genial Simon Grover, who had not seemed the type for a heated disagreement. I hadn't seen him crossed, though. "Did you hear any of it?"

She nodded vigorously. "I didn't remember until just yesterday—I've been so upset—but it was something about Turner Construction's account at the bank, and Mr. Grover was telling him that it must have been a mistake on Tom's part, because his bank didn't make errors."

That sounded kind of innocuous, and not like a fight that could lead to murder. She may have read that in my expression, because she shrugged. It was all she had. I considered something Pish had said to me, though, about the funny business with the accounts at Turner Construction; he had said it sounded like either drug peddling or a money-laundering scheme. I knew that some small businesses had made their revenue stream more robust by using their accounts to launder money.

So, was Tom involved in the funny business going on at Turner Construction? From my brief acquaintance with him, he seemed more the drug-peddling type than a money-scam guy, but there was no saying he hadn't been doing both. Was he fiddling with the accounts in concert with Dinah Hooper? Or had he and his father been doing it behind her back, and she found out, but was trying to distance herself? Was Mr. Grover upbraiding Tom about the problems with the bank accounts? Confusing.

"Hannah, can I ask you a few questions about people you might know?"

She brightened. "Sure!"

I pondered for a moment. Where to start? Somewhere off the beaten path. "Do you know Lizzie's mother?"

She turned pink and ducked her head. "Uh, I know *of* her. Tom knew her."

How much did she know, or guess? "Did he . . . know her well?"

Hannah put her chin up and, soft gray eyes glittering, said, "Why don't you come right out and ask, Merry? I don't know for sure, but . . . but I think Lizzie might be Tom's daughter. Is that what you're fishing for?"

I was stunned into silence.

"She looks so much like him!" Hannah continued, a soft smile lifting her lips. "And even her expressions . . ." She trailed off and looked away.

I nodded. "Lizzie's mom pretty much confirmed that yesterday when I took the kid back to her grandmother's place. But Lizzie doesn't know it yet. And I don't think anyone ought to tell her until we know who killed Tom, at least."

Hannah sighed and slumped a bit. "I'm glad," she said. "A bit of Tom will still be in the world." Her eyes welled, but she dashed the tears away with her finger, then fished around for a tissue, blotting her eyes. "What else do you want to know?"

"What does Isadore Openshaw have against Dinah Hooper?"

"What do you mean?"

I told her about Miss Openshaw's anger toward the woman, expressed in the Vale Variety and Lunch.

"I don't know," Hannah said with a frown.

"Has Dinah ever done anything to her? Other than the catnip-mice incident at last year's Autumn Vale Harvest Fair, I mean?"

"I don't know Mrs. Hooper very well. She comes to Golden Acres sometimes. She used to have her son take people for walks . . . you know, push their wheelchair down the block and back." Hannah chuckled. "That was no fun for Dinty, nor the resident!"

"Why not?"

"You had to know Dinty Hooper. He was a grumpy guy. When he finally took off, everyone in Autumn Vale heaved a sigh of relief."

"You must talk to Miss Openshaw quite a lot, given all the books she borrows. What do you know about her?"

"Let's see, she lives alone since her brother died, except for her cats. She works at the bank, pretty much the only teller other than a part-time girl who works on Fridays."

"Does she drive?" I asked, remembering her on her bike up near Wynter Castle.

"She rides a bike everywhere."

"But you don't know for sure that she doesn't know *how* to drive."

"I guess not."

I watched a pair of elderly women stroll arm in arm down the sidewalk, one with a cane. My mind wandered, and I wondered what my mother and grandmother would have been like had they lived. Would my grandma be one of these octo- or nonagenarians, living for muffins and tea, and Random Quote Day? I'd love to be able to visit my grandma, do crafts and drink tea with her, take her for car rides.

My mother would be in her sixties, and probably still

protesting. What would she think of my inheriting Wynter Castle and trying to maximize some profit from it? I wish she were around to tell me what it was she had against Melvyn Wynter. Once things settled down—and by "things" I meant two murder investigations on my property—I wanted to talk to Doc English again about my uncle, learn more about him.

A van pulled up to the curb and a middle-aged woman hopped out of the passenger side and waved.

"I have to go," Hannah said. "That's my mom."

I probably had more to ask her, but my mind was fuzzy and I was confused. "Bye, Hannah. I'll talk to you again soon!"

"Call me if you have any more questions!" She motored down the sidewalk and around to a lift in the back, waving as she centered herself on the lift and trundled into the back of the van.

As Hannah and her parents headed off, Gogi Grace came down the sidewalk and sat down beside me. She looked calm and serene, but I wasn't sure what to say.

"Are you okay?" I asked, watching her face.

She nodded. "The doctor is coming to pronounce death. I'm keeping an eye out for him."

"So . . . the patient died?"

"It was just a matter of time. She slipped away peacefully ten minutes ago." One tear escaped and raced down her cheek, marking a pale trail in her matte foundation.

"Do you want to talk about it?"

She shook her head. "I'm all right. Let's talk about something else, shall we?"

We spoke of my and Lizzie's discovery of the body in the woods, and she frowned over that. Autumn Vale had occasional missing persons, she said, and those who just left town for greener pastures. That was a fairly common occurrence. But she agreed with me that it was more likely that the dead fellow was a hiker who had either run afoul of a friend he was with, or died of natural causes. The sheriff had told me his head was bashed in, though, so definitely murder. I also told her about meeting Helen Johnson in the bakeshop, along with Isadore.

"They're both in my book club," Gogi said. "Helen goes for Christian and Amish romance novels."

"Amish romance novels?" I said, eyebrows high.

"Oh, yes, they're very popular with the ladies of the Methodist church. Isadore, on the other hand, reads a bit of everything, kind of a literary omnivore."

"I noticed. What is that woman's deal?" I asked. "She always seems so . . . tense." I explained about my visit to the bank.

"She has a lot of responsibility on her plate. I think she takes her job very seriously."

"She pretty much said that Simon Grover wouldn't know how to open the bank without her there."

"I don't doubt it."

"I want to find out about my uncle's dealings with the Autumn Vale Community Bank . . . you know, whether there were any outstanding loans, or anything like that. Isadore is either stonewalling me, doesn't like me, or . . . I don't know."

My cell phone chimed and I jumped. It wasn't a sound I was used to hearing in the dead zone that was Autumn Vale. It was Dr. Ling, telling me that Becket was going to be all right. He was exhausted, dehydrated, and hungry, but recovering rapidly. I could take him home.

I sat staring at the phone for a moment. "I guess I have a cat," I finally said.

"Let me think about things," Gogi said, "and try to figure out if there are any details I should have shared with Virgil. He really is trying to solve this, you know. Tom was his friend. He doesn't show it, but this has upset him badly."

A big, black car pulled up to the home, and an older gentleman got out, grabbing an old-fashioned doctor's bag from the backseat along with a briefcase.

"That's the doctor," Gogi said. She stood, and I did, too.

She reached out and pulled me into a hug, then held me away from her. "I hope you figure out a way to stay in Autumn Vale, Merry. This is a good place to live. It took me a while to see that, but I finally did."

As she met the doctor, hugging him briefly—she was definitely a hugger—and then walked up the path with him, I remembered what the postmistress had implied, but dismissed it. Gogi Grace had *not* knocked off her husbands for the insurance money and inheritance. It was patently ridiculous.

Chapter Twenty-three

✳ ✳ ✳

AT THE VET'S office, I was given Becket's collar and the bill. I paid Dr. Ling's assistant using a credit card; I needed to save my cash to pay for local labor, because I didn't think Gordy and Zeke—if they ever decided to come out to work at the castle—would take MasterCard. I bought a case of cat food, too, and litter and a box. It was all in the backseat, while Becket snoozed on the towel on the passenger seat. The vet said he was still weak and would need several days to fully recover. I petted his head and he opened one eye, meowing weakly.

As I drove through town, I noticed Simon Grover getting into what I presumed was his car. It was a vintage, black Lincoln with some dull-black paint concealing what looked like old damage on one side. Damage, on Simon Grover's black car. It gave me food for thought, I can tell you, since I was still puzzling out the first assignment given to me in Autumn Vale by Gogi Grace: to find out if my uncle was murdered.

I followed Simon out of town—not on purpose, but we were evidently both going the same way—wondering where he and his wife lived. We ascended up and out of Autumn Vale, me following him, still not on purpose. When he finally turned off the highway, though, I was curious, so I turned, too, and followed him at a discreet distance. After a while I wondered, was he even going home? I could be following him all the way to Rochester to visit his troubled son, Booker. That was not a good idea with a sick cat on the front seat. I was slowing, ready to do a U-turn, when I saw him pull into a drive some distance down the road.

This was where the bank manager and Janice lived? It was a side-split ranch house with a double garage, tidy and modern. I had pictured a woman like Janice Grover rattling around in a great, shambling Victorian, stuff everywhere, her love of junk evident in her home, as it was in her shop.

But wait . . . someone was coming out of the house, and it wasn't Janice. The hefty bank manager heaved himself out of the car and another man approached, took a briefcase from Grover, and the two men shook hands. The other man was Andrew Silvio. They strode into the open garage together.

I had no excuse for going up there, and had a sick cat that was beginning to wake up and meow. So I eased back onto the road and drove past the house, looking for a place to turn around, as I pondered what I had just seen. There were a hundred innocent explanations, I supposed. Grover could easily have retained Silvio for some legal work. Silvio could be legal counsel for the Brotherhood of the Falcon. Or he could even be a member of the organization. Wasn't that what businessmen did, join fraternal groups to make contacts, network?

I turned and cruised back past the house, but there was no activity that I could see. What I kept coming back to was the badly repaired damage to Grover's black sedan. Did it mean something, or was that pretty normal? In the past week or so, I had noticed a lot of cars with damage on them. One local was driving around with a smashed windshield, the result, I was told, of a run-in with a deer. I just didn't know.

My uncle's accident was nine months ago; if Grover had been the one to push him off the road, surely he would have gotten the damage to his car fixed right away? And though I had the feeling that Virgil had left the casebook on my uncle's accident open for a reason, he must have noticed the bank manager's damaged front panel.

As I pulled up my weedy lane, some uniformed officers were packing it in, closing the doors on the back of the state police van and winding up electrical cord. Virgil Grace was talking to a couple of detectives, but it had the appearance of a conversation that was coming to an end. McGill was, to my surprise, filling in the last hole, except for the one poor Tom Turner died in. He and Shilo had made great progress.

I didn't know what Shilo and I would do without McGill around. He jumped down from the excavator, and grabbed the crate of cat food and other stuff while I carried Becket into the house, gently toting him upstairs, and doing the necessary things, like setting up the cat litter box I had bought, putting down bowls of food and water, and making a bed for him near the radiator in my room, where it was warm. I made sure he was comfortable, then closed the door behind me and descended.

Outside, it looked barren. Deserted. "Where's the sheriff?" I asked McGill, who was locking down the excavator.

"He's gone."

Gritting my teeth, I slapped my thigh. "Darn! I wanted to talk to him." Really, I had wanted to tell him what I had seen, but what did I have to report? That I had seen the bank manager and the local legal eagle together? Big whoop, as Shilo would say.

Speaking of . . . Shilo came floating out of the castle, a skirt and pretty, gauzy top on, with a jacket over it and a scarf fluttering from under the lapels. She took McGill's hand and he stared down at her with a goofy smile. "We're going to have dinner with McGill's mom. Is that okay with you, Merry?"

"Of course, sweetie." I could not believe the change in my friend. What would happen if McGill was the one? Could I picture her becoming an Autumn Vale businessman's wife? Maybe even a mother?

"Are you sure? I don't want to leave you alone with a sick cat."

"You two go on. Have fun."

Still, my friend hesitated. "Do you want to come with us?" she asked. "We can fit you into the car. Or take mine."

"No, I'm beat. I think I'll go to bed with a book."

"You go on to the car, Shi. I'd like to talk to Merry," McGill said.

Shilo smiled and floated over to the car, leaning against it, elbows on top of the tiny roof, staring off to the woods.

Tugging at the cuffs of his jacket, the real estate agent looked uneasy. "Merry, I need to ask you a couple of questions. And . . . and to say something."

I matched my expression to his serious tone. "What is it, McGill?"

His lean face, beaky nose, and too-full lips combined in a look that was earnest and honest and wholly adorable. I understood Shilo's attraction; McGill was the kind of guy you just looked at and trusted. Trust was a big deal for Shilo.

"Shi and I have talked a lot, but she keeps avoiding the subject when I ask about her parents." He glanced back at her. "Are they dead?"

"Not that I know of. I've known her a long time, McGill, and she rarely mentions them. I have a feeling they're alive, but she's estranged from them."

"That doesn't seem possible! She's such a sweetheart."

"I know, but there are reasons a girl might cut off contact with her parents. I figure she'll tell me about them when she's ready."

He nodded. "You're right. I just don't know what to say to my mother. She'd like to know more about Shilo, but there isn't much to tell."

It must be quite an adjustment for a small-town parent, accustomed to knowing something about the girls her son dates. "You'll have to get used to that. Her life started when she came to New York at eighteen to become a model. That's about all I know. But I can tell you a lot about her life since."

He smiled as he watched her. "I feel like I know everything I need to know."

"Then what else did you want to ask?"

Turning his gaze back to me, he said, "What kind of ring would she like? Elaborate or simple? I don't know much about stuff like that. I only did it once."

"Are you . . . are you sure?" I gasped, my breath knocked out of me. I knew what he was really asking, but I composed myself. This was important. "Are you sure you're not moving too fast?"

"I'm sure here," he said, hand on his heart. "My mind hasn't quite caught up yet."

My eyes burned, and so did my heart. I wasn't sure if it was joy for Shilo over what she'd found, or jealousy, or a sense of loss, a fear that I might never feel that emotion again. "Pretty . . . a heart-shaped stone, maybe, as unusual as she is. Not a plain white diamond, but maybe a pink diamond, or something colorful. Anything you like, she'll love."

"Thank you," he said, taking my hand in his and squeezing it. "I'll have her home late. I want to show her all my hideouts from when I was a kid."

I sighed as he hopped in the car and drove away, and sent a wish after them, that their love was true, and happiness would follow them wherever they went. Instead of looking through the library, I spent a couple of hours going through more paperwork, and searching through my uncle's stuff, trying to understand his relationship with Rusty Turner. Not a lot to go on there. I checked in often on Becket, following doctor's orders, which were to feed him and give him water, as much as he wanted, but in small quantities often, rather than letting him gorge himself. He seemed to want out, but I kept him in my room to keep him from doing too much too fast.

My supper was solitary, a grilled chicken breast and salad eaten at the big kitchen table with a book of poetry propped up in front of me. It gave me a good sense of what my life would be like if Shilo married McGill and moved in with him. The castle was far too huge and echoed at night, making weird noises that had me on edge. I was tired and weepy and feeling sorry for myself. What was I going to do with Wynter Castle, being that I was the last remaining Wynter? I was about to turn out the lights and go upstairs when the phone rang. I picked it up, said "Hello?" as I flopped down in one of the chairs by the fireplace.

"Merry? It's Hannah."

"Hi, Hannah! Nice to hear your voice."

She said much the same back, a very polite girl, then told me that over supper, she had asked her mother some questions. Her mom was the Lady's League organizing chair, and she knew Isadore Openshaw and Dinah Hooper quite well. When Hannah mentioned Isadore's trouble with Dinah, her mother told her something important.

"It all goes back to Dinah taking her job away at Turner Construction," Hannah said.

"Dinah doing *what*?" I said.

"Dinah got a job there as kind of office manager, mostly because Rusty was hot-cha-cha in lust with her," Hannah said on a cute giggle. "But Isadore did the bookkeeping for the company . . . you know, taxes, payroll, that kind of thing. It was just part-time, in addition to her job at the bank, which was just part-time at that point, too. I forgot that there used to be a lady named Mrs. Murphy, who was like the dragon lady of the tellers. Isadore supplemented her teller's job with doing bookkeeping for folks. Anyway, that all changed when Dinah took over at Turner Construction."

I thought about it for a long moment. That explained

Isadore's venom toward Dinah, but it didn't explain why Dinah had claimed not to remember who used to do the books for the construction company. Although . . . if I had had to get someone fired because they were doing a lousy job, I might avoid the whole question, too. "Wait . . . how did Isadore get out to Turner Construction? It's a ways out of town. She couldn't have ridden her bike out there all winter."

"Wait a sec, I'll ask my mom," Hannah said. When she came back, she said, "Mom says Isadore used her brother's big, old car to drive out there. I guess she can drive, but leaves the car in the garage most of the time."

Except when she was running my uncle off the road? Okay, so that was a stretch, but it was possible. "You have been a busy little bee, haven't you, to find all this out?"

"I have! Oh, and one more thing I found out," she said. "Tom was following someone for a lawyer, right, but we didn't know what lawyer? Well, I know Mr. Silvio's secretary, Chrissie; in fact, we went to school together when we were just little kids, and she comes in to the library all the time. *She* says that Tom was following a woman because Mr. Silvio suspected her of something, she wasn't sure what."

"What woman?"

"She didn't know," Hannah said regretfully. "She might be able to find out, though, tomorrow, when she's in the office."

"Why wouldn't he hire the private investigator who has an office in the same building, if he wanted someone followed?"

"I don't know. That guy doesn't spend a lot of time in Autumn Vale, I think. Plus, Tom would have been cheaper, I suppose. He wasn't doing much, with his dad missing and Turner Construction mostly out of business."

"You're right," I said thoughtfully. "Thank you, Hannah. You've given me a lot to think of."

"I may find out more tomorrow!" she said.

"Hannah, now listen to me; you be careful. I don't want

you asking too many questions." In every detective book I've ever read, the one who gets snoopy gets in trouble. I couldn't bear the thought of little Hannah being targeted. This was serious. I heard someone yelling in the background.

"I'm coming, Mom. Yes, I'm getting off the phone now. I'll talk to you tomorrow, Merry," she said, and hung up.

I hope she had heeded my warning. I headed to bed, making sure Becket was comfortable first. He seemed to be okay, though he was still standoffish with me. He watched me, and it was unnerving, especially as I undressed and did my nightly ritual of shower, face cream, and hair. It seemed as if he was not used to being in the presence of a woman.

Sleep came fairly quickly, and I was happy about that. I thought about Shilo as I nodded off. I hoped she had found love. Would I ever? "Miguel," I whispered, "will I ever find anyone like you?"

Chapter Twenty-four

※ ※ ※

I HAD A strange dream. I saw Miguel, but he was just leaving for work. I clung to him at the door, like I often did, but he told me he had to go, and I was upset. Then something woke me up—something sharp and painful— before I had a chance to ask him why he had to leave in such a hurry.

The "something sharp and painful" was a full set of cat claws. Becket's method of waking me up was by smacking my face. He looked better, a lot better. Even his coat had regained some gloss. Being a naturally bright person, I figured that he was hungry. Yawning, I wandered downstairs, with him following me, and opened a can of tuna. I plopped it into the saucer of one of the cups that came in the box of mugs I had bought from Janice Grover. I then remembered I had a case of cat food, but it was too late. He ignored the tuna anyway, prowling back and forth near the door. Light-bulb moment—my brain is slow to work before my first coffee of the morning—he had to go to the bathroom, and didn't like the litter box I had bought. After almost a year of living in the wild, he had developed certain habits, I supposed.

I looked down at him as he paced back and forth, scratching at the door in the butler's pantry. "You won't go far, right? You'll just go out, do your business, and come right back?"

He looked up at me and meowed loudly. Sounded like a "Sure, just let me ooooout!" to me. "Okay, all right. I'm losing my mind, talking to a cat. I'm trusting you here, so go out, do your business, and come back in. You're still on the mend, fella." I opened the door, expecting Becket to saunter out, but he suddenly became an orange streak and headed directly for the woods. I hopped outside, my slippers hitting the cold stone, but he was already gone.

"Darn cat!" I said, only it wasn't "darn." I had a million things to do, but how was I going to do any of it when I was worried about the cat? The vet had cautioned me that he might seem fine, but was still recuperating; she wanted to see him again in two days. That would be hard to do if he was roaming the woods. I futzed around for a few minutes, but there was nothing to do but go looking for him. I hopped from foot to foot in the cold morning air, considering dashing after him then and there, slippers and all, but then the castle phone rang. I ran back into the kitchen.

"Hello?" I gasped.

"Merry, darling, are you okay? Did I catch you at a bad time?"

It was Pish, of all people! This early? I looked at the clock. "Why are you calling me at six a.m.? I didn't think you even knew the early hours existed."

"Sweetie, I was a financial planner and investment counselor for *how* many years? I used to get up at the crack of dawn to read the financial news before hauling myself downtown. I don't look at dawn's crack anymore, but I still *do* know it exists. Enough of that; I have *news*!"

"What kind of news?"

"The kind of news I can *only* deliver in person."

I stood there, phone in hand, perplexed. I held the receiver away from me and glared at it for a moment. Was he kidding? "In person? I can't come back to the city right now."

"That's why I thought I'd come to *you*!"

"You would come all the way here, to Autumn Vale, the backwater of upstate New York? To tell me what?" My stomach twisted. "Pish, is it dreadful news?"

"No, darling, it's *not* dreadful," he reassured me. "Not for you, anyway. But it *is* fascinating!"

"Hint! Please, Pish, a hint! I have to go search for a cat—long story—but I'll die without a hint."

"It has to do with Autumn Vale Community Bank. And that's *all* I'm saying! I'm heading out this minute to catch a flight, but I *need* you to meet me at the airport in Rochester. You're only an hour away from Rochester, right?"

"If that. More like forty-five minutes, depending on the driver."

"Well, my flight leaves in an hour, and it's *only* an hour long, so best get moving."

"Darling, I can't . . . but maybe . . . okay, all right." I sat down in a chair and thought quickly. "Look, some way or another I will make sure that someone meets you at the airport." I took down the flight details, then hung up, since his cab was waiting at the door and his ancient mother was yammering at him in the background.

I raced upstairs, woke Shilo up—she had gotten in very late the previous night—and told her about Becket and Pish and the whole shemozzle. She drowsily agreed that she could go fetch Pish at the airport in Rochester.

I stood over her watching her drift back to sleep. "Maybe I ought to go," I fussed, glancing at my watch. "I'll just run out, see if I can get the cat, then . . . if Becket won't come to me, to heck with him," I said. "I have too much to do to be ruled by that feline conniver."

Shilo chuckled sleepily. "Don't you worry about it. I'll

go and fetch darling Pish. If I can't figure out how to get to the Rochester airport, I'll rope McGill in to help."

I sat down on the side of her bed. "What's going on between you and McGill, Shi? I've never seen you spend this much time with a guy." I knew his secret, but supposed that he hadn't actually proposed to her yet.

She sat up and hugged her knees, yawning and rubbing her eyes. Her dark hair tumbled over her shoulders in waves. "Do you remember way back, when Julia Roberts married Lyle Lovett and everyone thought it was so weird?"

I nodded.

"I always thought her biggest mistake was divorcing him," Shilo said dreamily, and yawned again. "That guy had character, you know? I mean, they got married real quick, and that was because the connection was immediate, intense . . . but she let it get away from her. Dumb girl. You find that kind of guy, you hold onto him."

I didn't say another word. She was an adult, and it wasn't up to me to caution her against moving too fast. Shilo had been beaten up by the world when she was young, I figured, and deserved to find happiness however she could. She didn't have contact with her family, as I had told McGill—*that* I knew—so her friends were the only family she had. I remembered how serious McGill seemed about my darling friend. I kissed her forehead, and said, "I'm going to get dressed, see you on your way, then go out to find that little monster."

A half hour later, after running Shilo through what she had to do, calling McGill, and telling him she'd pick him up in my rental car—I just could not subject Pish to both Shilo's driving *and* her car; it would be inhumane—and making sure she knew what flight he was arriving on, I was out the door to look for the cat. Okay, so I had stalled, not really *wanting* to go search for the wee beastie in the woods alone, hoping he'd come back on his own, but knowing I didn't have a choice since he hadn't.

He was probably all the way to Canada by now, I figured, but armed with sliced chicken breast from my dinner the night before in a plastic baggie, I waded through the weeds across the field toward the forest. I paused at the edge, peering into the shadowy depths, as a crow cawed raucously, and a wind came up, tossing the tops of the trees. "Here, kitty, kitty, kitty," I called, hopeful that I could tempt him out with just the magical sound of my voice.

No kitty.

"Becket, come on, boy! I have chicken!" That would have worked with a dog, but not Becket. I had been seeing his orangey hide on and off for weeks, but now that I wanted him, he had melted into the woods like an Iroquois hunter.

A breeze rustled the long grass behind me; I shivered as I mumbled a stream of invective against Gordy and Zeke, my nonexistent grounds crew. Then I took a deep breath, thinking of how pathetic Becket had looked when I found him near death, and started down the path into the woods.

"Becket! Here kitty, kitty, kitty!" I said, rattling the plastic bag. "I have chicken!"

I peered into the green, shadowy depths every few steps, looking for a streak of orange. Where had that cat gone? And why? I didn't get it; he had a home, a litter box, food and water and a comfortable bed, with a shirt of my uncle's draped over it, so the smell would be familiar. He had the run of the castle, his home, even if my uncle was gone. Why had he taken off first chance he got?

As I walked, I couldn't help but let my mind drift to the troubling mystery of Tom Turner's murder. I hoped that the mystery was like a sweater I once had, one that had a loose thread. I picked at that thread so much, it eventually unraveled and the whole sweater fell apart. Maybe if I picked at the threads of this mystery it would all fall apart and I'd see the pattern, as I had that knitted sweater.

The threads that I kept coming back to were:

1. There was no evidence that Rusty Turner was dead.
2. And the body in the woods had been there a little while, at least.
3. Tom Turner was following some female for Andrew Silvio.
4. Isadore Openshaw hated Dinah Hooper, who had taken away her job at Turner Construction.
5. But now, Isadore virtually ran the Autumn Vale Community Bank on her own; Simon Grover seemed to be a figurehead roaring for his coffee and reading the funny papers.

When I thought of the bank, I wondered what Pish had to tell me. It was seriously distracting that he was coming to the castle. What would he think? What would he say? I knew that he must have something very interesting to tell me or he would not come in person, but I suspected that half the reason for the trip was his curiosity about Wynter Castle and the town of Autumn Vale.

Then my mind Ping-Ponged back to the murder. It all kept coming back to Isadore Openshaw. Was she the woman Tom Turner had been hired to follow?

Every now and then, as I walked and thought, I remembered that I was supposed to be looking for Becket, and I'd call him. There was no cat to be seen. There was rustling in the bushes, and an occasional noise, there was birdsong, and the wind tossing the treetops. I could hear a loud motor somewhere, like a dirt bike. A screeching blue jay followed me, and a group of crows—that was called a "murder," right? A murder of crows?—chattered and cawed. No Becket.

I stopped. Did I even know where I was? It should just be a simple matter of following the path back to the castle, right? I turned around, and realized there were a couple of paths I could have come from. I'm not terrible with maps, but we've already established that my internal GPS is not flawless. It had seemed so easy while Lizzie was leading the way. But the forest was pretty big. Even the lousy plat I had seen in the Turner Construction office had placed the size at about three hundred acres. That's huge. But I wasn't going to panic.

I heard a noise in the bushes. "Becket? Here, kitty, kitty, kitty! Come on, you darn cat. I have chicken!" I waited. Nada. "Fine! Be like that."

I sat down on a stump and opened the baggie, took a piece of chicken breast out and ate it. Weird breakfast. I hadn't had my quota of coffee, just one cup gulped as I raced around getting Shilo out the door, and I was seriously grumpy. Somewhere, that dang engine sound, like a buzzing mosquito, echoed again through the woods, reminding me of my determination to post No Trespassing signs at the perimeter, by the highway past Wynter Castle. Just one more of a gazillion tasks to do.

Something else came back to me, while I sat on that stump in the forest pondering all of the events of the last couple of weeks.

- A dirt bike parked on a side street.
- Someone on a dirt bike coming out of the woods onto the highway.
- The sound of a dirt bike in the woods when Lizzie and I were looking for the encampment.

Why hadn't I mentioned any of that to Virgil Grace? I hadn't thought it important at the time, but it sure did seem like a lot of run-ins with what could be the same dirt bike. It was that cumulative effect of several sightings, not the dirt bike itself, that made me wonder. I couldn't hear it anymore. Maybe the rider had gotten bored and left. I hoped so. I didn't want to be run down on the trail.

But none of this was helping me find Becket. I got up and looked around. Wait . . . was that a patch of orange? I hared off after it, and damned if it wasn't Becket, just ahead of me! He paused, looked back, and then headed off again, loping with a staggering gait.

"What is wrong with you, cat?" I muttered. I should have just let him come back on his own, but it felt like it was my duty to look after him now. Becket had been important to my uncle, and now he was my responsibility. I checked my watch. Another fifteen minutes and Pish would be landing at the airport in Rochester, some time in baggage claim, then another forty-five minutes or so for McGill, Shilo, and Pish to make the return trip. So I could look for the cat for another few minutes, but then I wanted to get back to the castle and make sure it was presentable for Pish's first view.

Reenergized, I stuffed the chicken baggie in my pocket and charged off in the direction Becket had disappeared. I caught sight of him again, on the path and followed. I was just opening my mouth to call out to him when I heard a shot. I ducked and huddled in the shadows, cowering as another shot rang out.

What the hell was going on?

And how did I get out of it?

Was there some kind of hunting season I didn't know about? Even so, it was my property and no one had permission to hunt. Again, I needed to post signs, *copious* signs: No Hunting! Private Property! No Trespassing! Lots of exclamation marks. The dirt-bike driver . . . were he and the hunter one and the same?

And then, at long last, the penny dropped.

Where had I seen the dirt bike? Outside of Dinah Hooper's apartment.

Who did I know who was an acknowledged hunter? Dinah Hooper.

Who had access to all of the Turner Construction, and probably the Turner Wynter accounts? Dinah-freaking-Hooper.

I remembered in that moment the letter I had found among

my uncle's stuff, the one that was addressed to Turner Wynter Global Enterprises. I had never heard their business called that before, and that struck me as odd. Something teased at the edge of my brain, but someone was coming, striding through the forest with a great deal of confidence. Hunkering down in a shallow depression, behind a bushy undergrowth, I watched through a leafy branch. A figure in camouflage loosely cradling a rifle, strode past me, then paused. Blonde hair piled high, glittery earrings, rounded form: when the figure turned I was not surprised to see Dinah Hooper. But her expression! I'd never seen her like this, furious and determined.

Practically holding my breath, terrified that she would see me, I heard a noise in the distance, and then a streak of orange crossed the path. She raised the gun, and I was sure she'd aim for Becket, but no, that wasn't her quarry. Who was, then? Me? But she had no cause to come after me, and couldn't have even known I was there.

I heard more noise, and staggering out of the brush came another figure. It was an old man with a long, tattered beard; ragged, filthy clothes; and a battered hat pulled down over his head. He was running—or rather, staggering—and stumbled and fell. I heard a grunt of surprise from Dinah, then a hiss of satisfaction. She raised the gun, sighted along the barrel, and pointed it at the old man, who finally saw her as he lumbered to his feet.

"Dinah, please, don't shoot!" he wailed, arms raised in surrender.

I gasped in surprise, then clapped a hand over my mouth. It had to be Rusty Turner! Dinah whirled at my gasp, and the old man took his chance while she was distracted, diving into the bushes with a loud grunt and cry of pain. He was old, but quick and crafty.

Dinah swiveled the gun back to the pathway. "You come out now!" she yelled, sighting along the barrel. "I see you moving around, Rusty. You want to die in the bushes? Like you left my boy to die alone?"

"He tried to kill me, Dinah! I'm sorry, but what was I gonna do?" The poor old guy's voice, barely heard from his hiding spot, quavered with fear. He sounded hoarse and weak. "He tried to *kill* me."

Her boy? Who the heck . . . oh! Dinty Hooper. My eyes widened as I figured it out; so *that's* who the body in the woods was.

"Dinty was a good boy," she sobbed, the barrel of the rifle drooping. "He was only doing what was best for me. Now come on out and face—"

She was cut off by Becket, the feline ninja, leaping at her from behind and knocking her off balance. She screamed, the rifle went off—a wild shot that clipped some leaves, which fell in a fluttering flurry of green and sent a crow cawing raucously out of the tree—and she staggered sideways. I broke from cover, darting down the path to where I could see Rusty Turner emerging. I grabbed hold of him. "Run, now, while you can!" I said.

He gabbled and clucked as I dragged him back off the path, staggering and stumbling along over downed trees and through thick underbrush. I could hear her shouting behind us, and what I feared most: the sound of Dinah, much more athletic than me, crashing through the bush, following our far-too-obvious trail of leafy destruction.

My mind was whirling through all the details, trying to make sense of the shifting tides of my uncle's life, death and business affairs. Rusty's disappearance. Tom Turner's murder. A thousand questions to which I had no answers hopped though my mind like Magic on a wayward path. But one came to the forefront; had my uncle indeed been murdered, run off the road, as Gogi suspected? I feared the answer was yes.

Rusty was a dead weight, dragging at me, and when I turned I was alarmed. His filthy face was ashen. He was an older man, and I needed to stop. Besides, I could no long hear Dinah crashing along behind us, so maybe we had evaded her.

If that was the case, then we should be quiet so we wouldn't alert her to our whereabouts through carelessness.

He plunked down on the ground, and I watched him, worried. His breath was coming in heaving gasps, but that calmed quickly enough, and ruddy color came back to his cheeks, above the straggly beard.

"Are you going to be okay?" I whispered, wishing I had thought to bring a bottle of water.

He nodded. I let him catch his breath while I listened for Dinah coming after us. I couldn't believe she would give up. If what I suspected was true, it was much to her advantage to kill us both, and leave our bodies in the woods while she made her getaway. It might be days before anyone found us.

My mind raced with conjecture. I eyed Rusty, and felt my heart wobble. Poor old man! He must have been . . . my eyes widened in shock. Had he been living out on the land for ten *months*? Through a long, upstate New York winter? I set that aside to marvel at later; I couldn't get distracted. We needed to both get out of this fix, and fast.

I could hear the tentative sounds of something: bushes rustling, footsteps . . . Dinah, now cagey enough to be careful in her search?

"Merry Wynter, I know you're here," she said in a conversational tone, so close I almost jumped out of my skin. "I have nothing against you. We could be allies. I know for a fact that you've inherited that big, old castle and that you don't have money to fix it up or live in it. I have a hundred ways for you to make money."

Her tone was honeyed, persuasive. I glanced down at Rusty, and his watery blue eyes had a pleading look in them. I shook my head. There was nothing she could say that would convince me to give him up.

I couldn't see her, I could only hear her, and it was terrifying. I was squatting in a muddy ditch, hidden (I hoped) by greenery, with a fast hold on the arm of an old man who was in very poor health, listening to a madwoman try to tempt me to give up the old guy to her not-so-tender mercies. She intended to kill Rusty. But she didn't yet know that I was not on her side. I could either stay where I was and wait for her to find us—given that she was holding a high-powered rifle I figured I knew the outcome of that scenario—or I could do something about it.

I let go of Rusty, fixed my gaze and pointed my finger at him then at the ground, hoping he'd get that I was telling him to stay put. I crept away from him as quietly as I could until I was behind where I thought Dinah was standing. I sighted Becket crouching nearby, his tail slashing back and forth, his gold eyes fixed on a spot. That had to be where Dinah was. Good cat.

Doing my best to hide, I said, "We can talk, Dinah. But you have to let Rusty go."

There was a pause; as she tried to figure out where I was? Probably.

Then she said, "I will. I don't *really* mean to kill him, you know, just scare him some. I love the old coot."

And I was a dainty ballerina. "Did you say something about him killing your son?"

She was silent, but after a minute, she said, "Yeah. But . . . but Dinty tackled him, I guess. Poor old Rusty couldn't help it. Dinty never did like him, so I guess he . . . I don't know."

Weak. I would have bet that Dinah sent her son into the bush to kill trusting Rusty, and it went sour somehow. I'd best leave it alone if I wanted her to think I was willing to make a deal. "I *am* interested in how to make money," I said, moving slightly to try to see her. I caught sight of her; her back was to me, and she still had that damned rifle up, finger on the trigger, but as I watched, she was honing in on my voice, and turning, scanning the forest with her rifle sight.

I crouched and moved out of range. She had no intention of making a deal with me; she still wanted to shoot me.

"What about Tom Turner?" I asked.

She whirled, her eyes scanning the woods near me. I was wearing a green sweater. Maybe I melted into the background.

And then it came to me, two things at once: Dinah was likely the one Silvio had Tom following, and she had killed him because of it.

Chapter Twenty-five

❋ ❋ ❋

WHAT HAD HE discovered about her that made him so dangerous? Was it about her enterprises, or Rusty still being alive, or something else?

"What *about* Tom?" Dinah asked as she turned, looking for a target.

I was not going to oblige by answering. I heard rustling in the bushes, and figured it was likely Becket, up to his stealthy panther moves—"Moves Like Jaguar"—I almost giggled. Old Maroon 5 song references rarely make me laugh, so this was hysteria; not good at that moment. Stifling my laughter, one hand over my mouth, I tried to figure out what to do. Where was Rusty now? Had he managed to gather his courage and get away? How could I handle a sharpshooter with a high-powered rifle using only the strength of my muffin-baking hands?

So many questions, and not a single answer. There was only one chance, I figured, and that was to move back toward the castle, *if* I could figure how to do that. I *knew* I should have gone to Girl Scouts, like Grandma wanted me to. Mom

opposed it; said they were just a breeding ground for conform-
ist fembots. I squinted and looked up through the glowing-
green canopy above. It seemed to me that when I was at the
castle watching the sunrise, it was over the arboretum. Since
it was still early and still rising, I needed to walk away from
the direction of the sunlight to get back there, right?

Made sense to me.

But as I had been pondering, Dinah had not been quies-
cent. She was gone from her spot, and I didn't know where.
Damn! I could run right into her while trying to escape.
How was I going to lead her away from poor old Rusty, and
yet stay safe myself?

I had to get moving. I took a deep breath, scanned the
forest around me for any revealing blonde, piled-up hair, and
began to steal through the forest like a jungle cat. Okay,
maybe not like a jungle cat, but I sure hoped not like a charg-
ing rhino. It wasn't going to be easy, because I couldn't use
the path, even if I could have found it. I spotted Becket. He
looked tired and cranky, distinctly in a bad mood, and I didn't
blame him. For the first time, it occurred to me that all those
times I had caught sight of him, he was trying to get me to
follow him. Had he been trying to lead me to Rusty, to get
him help? Stranger things had happened.

I was hearing rustling from everywhere, now, and didn't
quite know what to make of the sounds. In the forest with
me were Dinah, Rusty, and Becket. The cat I could see, but
the two humans eluded me. I hoped that Rusty had either
gotten away, or was hunkered down somewhere safe. This
was exhausting. I stopped, trying to catch my breath, wishing I had worn yoga pants or anything more forgiving than
form-fitting DKNY jeans.

Needing to get the heck out of there so I could call Virgil
and tell him about the nutbar in the woods, I put some speed
on, and began to climb over fallen branches and crash
through foliage at a faster pace. I looked over my shoulder,
as I went, fearing the worst, that Dinah, rifle cocked, was

following me or drawing a bead, or whatever expert marks-women did.

And that's probably why I almost ran right into her.

"Stop!" she yelled.

I whirled to find her on the path toward which I was headed, rifle up, aimed right at me. Damn. "Hi, Dinah." I caught my breath and considered my options. Groveling while begging for my life seemed about the only one.

"You should have taken my deal."

"I didn't actually hear a deal," I said evenly, trying not to let my eye flick behind her, where I saw a figure creeping up on her with all the stealth a seventy-or-so-year-old man can muster. Inside, I was screaming No, Rusty, don't do it! But I tried not to show it. "Uh, so, I guess it's silly to even think that you will just leave and let me go?"

Regret in her pale eyes, she shook her head. "No. Can't do it."

"The body in the tent is your son, Dinty?"

She nodded, her eyes blurring. "Idiot. I told him to go take care of Rusty, but he must have underestimated the old coot. I've been looking for him for months; figured he'd taken off. He's disappeared on me before."

She hadn't known Dinty was dead—or at least hadn't been sure—until Lizzie and I stumbled over the body. So . . . "Why try to kill Rusty in the first place?"

"I wasn't ready to leave town yet. I thought there was more I could squeeze out of this operation. It took so much to set it up!" She sighed. "I should have left town a month ago, I guess. Look, Merry, I don't want to kill you, but you haven't left me much choice."

"You have a choice; don't kill me. Leave town."

"Not an option," she said, shaking her head. "I don't want to do this," she repeated. "I'm not a killer."

Rusty was getting closer, a rock in his hand. Damn. What were the chances this would come off okay? Not great. "You keep saying you're not a killer, but you did kill Tom Turner, and on my property!"

"I *had* to. He was trying to blackmail me. Once he figured out what I was doing—and that took a while, fortunately, because he was one dumb jerk—he wanted a cut just for keeping his mouth shut. That effing lawyer was figuring things out, and set Tom on my trail."

Stupid Tom! Why didn't he just take what he'd learned back to his employer? "So he wanted money?"

She nodded. "Like I'd pay for him to keep his mouth shut. He said he needed cash for something important."

"What about my uncle? Did you kill him, too?"

"Your uncle was an interfering old fool and deserved what he got," she said, raising the gun and sighting. "This is not personal, I just—"

Rusty leaped, stumbled, and the rock he had intended to bring down on her head instead bounced harmlessly to the ground and rolled away as the old guy fell to his knees. But she was momentarily distracted. I charged and using all my weight, bulldozed her, knocking her to the ground where she lay, stunned. Sometimes there are benefits to being bigger than your average ballerina. I snatched up the gun as Rusty, his hermit face twisted into a grimace of hatred, scrabbled over, picked up the rock, and brought it down on her head.

"Stop!" I yelped, but he had knocked her out.

"That's for Tom," he hollered, and dissolved into weeping into his filthy hands.

Autumn Vale . . . the only spot in upstate, surely, where a Shakespearean drama, with lovers killing each other's sons, played out in the woods surrounding a castle. Weirdness compounded weirdness. I leaned over Dinah; she was breathing but was unconscious. I had the rifle, so I didn't think she'd be any more danger even if she managed to get up and follow us. I grabbed the old man by the arm, hauled him to his feet, and said, "Come on, Rusty, we need to get out of here. If I'm right, we're only a little ways away from the castle grounds."

It took longer than I thought, but we finally emerged from the woods and started across the weedy expanse. The heavy sound of a motor vibrating the ground startled me as we broke through the last line of trees; lo and behold, there was Gordy atop a tractor, hauling a piece of machinery that was mowing and piling the dry grass into neat rows. His buddy, Zeke, was standing to one side, watching, gesticulating, and yelling critiques. I stood stock-still at the awesome sight, just as, sweeping up the drive, came my rental car and behind it, Virgil Grace's sheriff's car. I almost dissolved into tears of gratitude.

Sometimes your prayers are heard, I guess. It wasn't until later that I found out the serendipitous arrival of the sheriff was owing to Shilo's gypsy instincts. She just felt something was wrong—bad vibrations, she called it—so they stopped in Autumn Vale and, miracle of miracles, convinced Virgil to follow them to Wynter Castle. At that moment, though, I was just grateful for the "coincidence."

I dropped the damned rifle and helped Rusty over to the cop car. Virgil made him get in and sit while he called for medical backup. I babbled about Dinah in the woods unconscious, telling the sheriff about all she had confessed to, and Virgil assured me, as he called for his deputy, that they would be able to find our path, given that we had crashed through the brush with all the delicacy of a bull elephant.

Finally I turned, looking toward my friends. Pish, darling man, held out his arms and I staggered wearily over to him; he folded me into a hug. I was about to exclaim that I needed to find poor Becket when the ginger cat strolled nonchalantly out of the woods and picked his way through the long grass, eyeing the giant tractor and mower. It was silent right then, while Gordy and Zeke gawked at all the action. It would be all over Autumn Vale by noon. McGill was on his way over to the fellows, and I hoped he cautioned them to keep their mouths shut until we figured out the whole mess.

A half hour later, Rusty Turner had been taken to the hospital in Ridley Ridge, accompanied by his tearful daughter, Binny, who had screamed up to the castle in her van after hearing the news. She babbled to us that she had actually known/hoped/prayed he was alive for a few days, because he'd managed to get a note to her, asking her to meet him. That was the day she tootled off, leaving me in charge of the bakery. Unfortunately, terrified and stalked by a half-crazed Dinah, Rusty did not make the meeting. She was left frightened for her father, but not sure who to trust. In retrospect, if she had told Virgil about the note he could have taken care of everything, but Binny didn't know what her father had done, at that point, and was afraid of setting the law on him.

She had him back now, and I hoped everything would turn out all right.

Shortly after the ambulance had taken Rusty and his daughter away, Virgil learned that his backup, on the way down the highway toward the castle, had found Dinah wandering along the road, blood streaming from a head wound. When they arrested her, she began to babble, despite Miranda warnings. She claimed that Rusty was the mastermind of a huge money-scam ring, using his company and Turner Wynter as giant sham companies with hundreds of offshoots. I got it then; Turner Wynter Global Enterprises, the name on the envelope I had found in my uncle's desk, was one of the fake companies she was using.

I had a feeling Isadore Openshaw would be involved somehow, but I didn't know how yet. Pish, eyeing Virgil Grace with some interest, told him not to listen to Dinah, or at least, not to believe what she was saying. He had a lot of information that the sheriff was going to want to hear.

We—Pish, McGill, Shilo and I—headed inside. To avoid repetition, Pish commanded that we wait for Virgil to join us. The sheriff had a lot to do before that, though, so—after giving me time to clean up, change, and have a cup of coffee—Pish wanted a tour. He was mesmerized by Wynter Castle. Finishing up in the grand entrance he slowly turned around, his fancy wingtips making no sound on the gorgeous, flagstone floor, as he stared up at the rose window, the gothic arched doorway and the magnificent, crystal chandelier, glittering dully in the morning light.

"Who would *ever* guess that such . . . such Gothic *splendor* would be found in the backwoods of upstate?" he asked, his trembling voice echoing off the ceiling. He turned and clasped my hands in his. "Darling, you *must* keep this magnificent absurdity!"

"I can't afford to, Pish, dear. I really can't!"

He looked thoughtful. "All right. I'll accept that . . . for *now*. But we'll talk some more."

We finally returned to the kitchen, and Virgil Grace joined us ten minutes later, with a deputy accompanying him.

"Merry, Shilo, McGill, Mr. Lincoln," Virgil said, gathering us all in his gaze. "I understand you have information to give us concerning Ms. Hooper's criminal financial activities in Autumn Vale."

"I do Sheriff, but I'm going to let my dear friend start," Pish said, deferring to me.

The deputy sat down behind Virgil to take notes.

"I was suspicious of the dealings of Turner Construction and my uncle's venture with the Turners, known as Turner Wynter," I said, to preface Pish's information. "None of it made sense. Binny Turner let me in to the Turner Construction offices and we looked around. I have some knowledge of development planning, and it was all wrong, everything I saw. Binny and Shilo found stuff in the accounts that didn't add up. I can now tell you that Dinah Hooper was clearly using Turner *and* Turner Wynter to spin off shell companies, and using those shell companies to run some kind of financial scam. I told Pish, who is not only a financial adviser, but also has been used as an expert witness in court cases involving financial malfeasance, and he snooped around for me. He came here to tell me what he found out, but he wanted to wait for you, Sheriff, before he spoke, so I'm hearing this for the first time, too."

Pish gathered us all in his gaze, and said, "I didn't realize when I set out this morning that I would be giving this information to the police. Let me work my way through it from the start. Merry called me with troubling questions about Turner Wynter Construction, Dinah Hooper, the Turners, and all of their dealings with Autumn Vale Community Bank. Here is what I think has been happening, and what we ought to do about it."

While dramatic in his day-to-day life, Pish eschews the use of italics in his speech while giving evidence or talking about his profession. He can be succinct, and gets to the point rapidly and clearly. The tale he told was riveting, and introduced me to the new word *smurfing* as it pertained to financial crimes.

His take had a lot of facts, but involved some conjecture, too, relating to people other than Dinah Hooper. It took some convincing, but Virgil finally agreed to let Pish and me run a scam of our own on the bank employees, namely Isadore Openshaw and Simon Grover. We set it up to happen the very next morning, getting the confirmation late that night that federal investigators would be involved as well, since it looked like this was going to be part of a federal investigation of a con group that extended farther afield than just Autumn Vale.

None of it would be possible without Pish's help, but after a few phone calls, the feds knew that Pish was a reliable and competent aide who had done this kind of thing before.

Virgil took me aside before he left. "I think I owe you an explanation about your uncle's death."

"Dinah Hooper did it."

"Yes, but not with her own car," he said. "I've known for

some time that Isadore Openshaw's car was the one that ran
Mel off the road, but I knew she wasn't the one who did it.
I had a reliable eyewitness account that placed her at home
that morning. Ms. Openshaw swore up and down that she
didn't know who could have stolen her car and brought it
back."

"It was Dinah who had the car, then," I filled in. "And
Isadore was . . . maybe scared to tell the truth?"

"That's what we think. Tomorrow we'll know more. I'm
glad you're okay, but I'm mad as hell at the chances you
took," he said gruffly, his hand on my shoulder. "Anyway,
I'll see you tomorrow morning."

IT WAS ABOUT A HALF HOUR AFTER THE BANK OPENED
the next morning. Pish, Shilo, and I drove into town and
parked on Abenaki. Dinah's apartment door had a crime
seal on it. I had heard (during a second, late-night call from
a gruff and very sexy-sounding Virgil Grace, thanking me
for our information and giving me confidential updates) that
she had several impressive computer systems set up, ones
that had been confiscated by the federal agents who were
now swarming the town. What was on the computers would
likely give forensic accountants many months of work to
untangle. Dinah Hooper was a grifter extraordinaire, I had
a feeling, and she had not been working alone.

As we walked down Abenaki, I gave Pish the official tour
of the town, such as it was. He noted all the empty storefronts
and clucked his tongue. "This place has potential," was all he
said.

Shilo took off to meet up with McGill, (who had indeed
warned Zeke and Gordy, on pain of legal punishment, to
keep their mouths shut until everything was sorted out) so
Pish and I strolled into the Autumn Vale Community Bank
together. I allowed Pish to take the lead. Isadore looked nervous at the sight of me and my briefcase-carrying, Brooks

Brothers–wearing companion, but Simon Grover, in his glass office, appeared oblivious, drinking coffee and reading the only local paper, the *Ridley Ridge Record*. We approached the teller window, just as Gogi Grace entered through the curved, glass doors.

Isadore tried a smile, but it looked ghastly, a rictus grin. "Ah, there is Mrs. Grace. You know, I had better look after her. Such a busy woman! How are you, Gogi?" she called out, straining to look over our shoulders. "How are you doing with that shocking book we're reading in club?"

Gogi ignored Isadore as she examined Pish and met my gaze, eyebrows raised. I had a sense that she might already know what was happening from her son. "I'll wait, Isadore. You look after Merry and her companion, first."

Pish set his briefcase on the teller window ledge, opened it, and took out several bank records, and laid on top the envelope—now open—addressed to Turner Wynter Global Enterprises.

Through the barred teller's window I said, "Miss Openshaw, this is Pish Lincoln, my financial adviser. He has questions regarding my uncle's accounts. As Melvyn Wynter's heir, I give you permission to tell him anything and to fully answer any questions he may have about accounts involving my uncle's company."

"I . . . I believe I already told you . . . I'm not sure—"

"It's quite all right, Miss Openshaw," he said comfortably, with much the manner of a genial doctor. "I'm a trained professional. Now, looking through Merry's uncle's records, we came upon odd references to all kinds of bank accounts opened under different names, some variations of Turner Construction and Turner Wynter Construction and even Wynter Estates."

That was not quite true, beyond the one envelope with "Turner Wynter Global Enterprises" on it. We had done some guesswork, and Pish was an excellent bluffer. You do not want to play five-card stud with him, as many have discovered to their poverty. He may look like an effete art dealer, but he has a sharp and pliable mind, and a great poker face.

Miss Openshaw stoically held her tongue. Hoping the wire I was wearing was not visible, I said, "I just want to know what is going on, Miss Openshaw." I watched her face, over which an array of expressions, from fear to indecision, played. "I'm sure you're aware that Dinah Hooper was arrested yesterday for murder and attempted murder. She's been talking. A *lot*. Of course, being the kind of woman she is, she's been trying to shift the blame onto others for things she has done."

That was all true. She was now trying to blame Isadore for everything, including my uncle's murder. Isadore had been desperate to point me in the direction of Dinah, but didn't have the guts to come right out and accuse her. I wanted to know why. "I keep thinking there is more to her staying in Autumn Vale, and her dealings with this bank and Turner Construction, than meets the eye. Do you have anything to say, or do we need to call in the feds and have them go over the bank records account by account, starting with anything labeled Turner or Wynter?" They were going to do that anyway, but she didn't need to know that yet.

She folded. I mean that literally; she actually *crumbled*, as in, sank beneath the counter, wailing incoherently.

"Goodness. What's this all about?" Gogi said with a glance at me. "I think it would be permissible for us to go behind the counter to help the poor woman," she said.

By the time Simon Grover clued in that his teller was distressed, and had bumbled out, loudly asking what was going on, we were all behind the desk, helping Isadore to her feet and over to a chair by a desk.

"Why don't you tell us what's up, Miss Openshaw?" I asked, giving Gogi a look to keep her quiet.

Gogi satisfied her need to do something by getting a glass of water and offering it to Isadore, who gulped greedily, then waved it away.

"What's going on here?" Grover blustered. "I'll call the police. You people should not be behind . . . why, it's trespassing!" He wailed on in the background, but no one paid any attention.

"I want a lawyer," Isadore said.

Pish straightened. "All right. I was hoping there was a rational explanation exonerating you and the bank, but I guess I have no further business here."

"No, wait!" Isadore clutched at his sleeve, her gooseberry-green eyes wide with fear. "Are you really a financial adviser?"

He nodded. I spoke up, as gently as I could, "Miss Openshaw, we aren't trying to pin anything on you. But there is going to be an investigation into Dinah Hooper's involvement with this bank, and what we suspect are a number of accounts opened to launder money, using Turner Construction and Turner Wynter, among many, many other shell companies, as vehicles. Dinah Hooper has admitted to me that she killed my uncle and Tom Turner. I believe she masterminded a lot more. Now, if you were to cooperate, I'm pretty sure you can help us find the truth." I was careful not to promise anything legally, because that was not up to me.

Isadore wept a bit, and again called Dinah names, including what I had thought she said was the "devil's pawn," but was apparently "devil's spawn," or child of Lucifer. She was convinced of that. She finally calmed enough to tell her story. She came to Autumn Vale about eight years before to live with a cousin (not a brother; she had only claimed the fellow was her brother so no one would think it scandalous that she lived with him) but when he died, leaving her his bungalow and car, she decided to stay. It sounded to me as if she had escaped a hardscrabble life, and finally had what she had always wanted: a home and a couple of jobs, one part-time at the bank, and one part-time doing bookkeeping and secretarial work for Turner Construction. Everything was good for a few years.

But then her past, in the person of Dinah Hooper (not her real name, by the way) showed up. Dinah was a grifter, and had used Isadore before in an illegal enterprise. She was sent to torment her, Isadore said, spawn of Satan that she was. Isadore had escaped her clutches, determined to *go* straight and *stay* straight, but Dinah had finally tracked her down and threatened her with exposure if she didn't go along with a scam. Autumn Vale was the perfect town for what she had in mind, Dinah told Isadore, and her job at the bank made it even *more* perfect.

All Isadore had to do was first, quit her job at Turner so Dinah could have it. Coincidentally, the former bank teller was retiring about then, so Isadore was promoted to a full-time employee. Then she had to deposit the money Dinah gave her into Rusty's bank accounts. Isadore did that, but of course the demands escalated until she was opening accounts for Dinah, using a dozen or so different shell company names, and making cash deposits to each account, small enough that the FDA would not be alerted to any impropriety. There is a threshold below which banks are not required to inform government agencies about deposits, and Dinah was careful to keep well below limits. That is called, in the banking industry, "smurfing," as Pish had explained the night before.

Isadore babbled about a lot of stuff. Dinah had created a ghostly workforce to go along with these different shell companies, which allowed even more accounts to be opened. She was running another kind of scam, too, a version of the so-called 419 or Nigerian swindle, which was why she had the multitude of computers and the knowledge of high-speed Internet in Autumn Vale. I had a feeling we were going to find out a lot more over the next few days.

As sometimes happens, I was right.

Chapter Twenty-six

❋ ❋ ❋

T HE NEXT DAY, observed by Becket, who sat like a statue
on the flagstone terrace, I supervised Zeke and Gordy's
continued cleanup of the castle grounds. Binny's white van
roared up into my now-weed-free (thanks to Zeke!) parking
area. The baker got out, carrying a box, and striding toward
me. Had she come bearing cannoli?

"How are you? How is your dad?"

"He's going to be awesome, thanks to you. I don't think
I really . . . in the craziness yesterday, I didn't get what you
did for him, you know, and how much I have to thank you
for." Her face, now adorned with a more open, natural
expression, was very pretty. Her dark hair tied back, she
looked relaxed and almost happy. I hoped she would accept
all the changes that were about to come her way.

"Don't mention it. I'm relieved it all turned out okay. So
he was hiding out since he disappeared last year because
Dinah told him someone was out to kill him, right?"

"Yeah. That note I got . . . it said to meet him at the hunting cabin on the Turner Construction land—it's an old cabin

back in the woods where he used to take me when I was a kid—but like I said, he never showed."

"You really didn't see him until yesterday."

She shook her head. "I wasn't even a hundred percent sure the note was from him. I just didn't know!"

"Look, do you want to come in for a cup of tea, or coffee?" I said, waving my hand toward the castle.

"No, I'm on my way to the hospital to pick up my dad. They say he can go home now."

"He is one tough bird," I said in admiration. "Did he really live out in the woods all that time?"

"Sometimes in the woods, sometimes he broke into sheds to sleep, sometimes he even went back to the house, but he didn't dare stay there." She shook her head. "Can you believe it? Dinah had him convinced Russian gangsters were after him."

"Russian gangsters?" I wanted to laugh, but that would have been inappropriate.

"I know, right?" she said, shaking her head with a smile on her pink-cheeked face. "It was a couple of guys she worked with. I remember them . . . they came into town with fake accents and black suits." She laughed out loud, a great honk of sound.

I could see Lizzie in her; the Turner gene pool was strong in both of them. "Dinah had him reeled in."

"Still, who believes that kind of crap? I guess I shouldn't be so hard on him, but he should have talked to me." She shifted the bakery box from one arm to the other.

"He probably didn't want you to be involved." Or he didn't want his beloved daughter to know about the mess he had made of things. "If you don't mind me asking, did he know about what she was doing, at any point?" I had been wondered about that; was Rusty aware of the illegal nature of what Dinah was doing from the start, or was he totally oblivious?

"Not really." She grimaced and shrugged. "He kind of knew about some of it, but she told him there was a legal way to make money by setting up some corporations. He and poor old Melvyn had been working on a plan to develop this place to be Wynter Acres." She shuffled in place, kicking at the flagstones that edged the drive. "Tom drew up a plan, and got his buddy Junior to give it the green light, and it got bundled into the whole scam operation. My dad found out, but he didn't want Tom to get in trouble. Then Melvyn got wind of it, got POed, filed a lawsuit to stop them using his name, and threatened to expose the whole thing." She shook her head.

That explained the shoddy plat. "It's a mess," I said, "and it's going to take time to sort out." Junior Bradley was going to be in some trouble, too, it sounded like.

"You better believe it," she said fervently.

"But the good thing is, it looks like we'll be able to get rid of any outstanding lawsuits between us. We'll talk about it another day."

She nodded. "Anyway, when Dad got scared by her fake Russian mobsters, Dinah told him he should use his hunting cabin in the woods, just disappear for a while. She'd help him out. He took money out of the bank and gave it to her to help him. She supposedly used it for food. He lived in there for a long time, and she kept upping the ante, telling him the thugs were back, and if he came out of hiding they might kidnap *me* to try to pressure him."

"She is some piece of work!"

With a glowering look that reminded me of Lizzie, Binny said, "I can't *wait* to see her in court for murdering Tom!" She hung her head for a moment. "Anyway, poor Melvyn must have been suspicious, and I guess he told Dinah that he was going to the cops to tell them what he knew."

"He got a bank statement in the name of Turner Wynter Global Enterprise, one of Dinah's shell companies," I explained. "He was suspicious, all right. All that time he had thought Rusty was in on it, but I think he finally figured out it was Dinah at the heart of it. Especially after Rusty disappeared."

"Melvyn's death scared Dad. He heard about it, and I think that's when he began to wonder if Dinah was scamming him. He left the hunting cabin in the late spring, from what he told me last night, and Dinah has been looking for him ever since."

"That's why she kept showing up on her dirt bike in my woods! If I'd known it was her . . . but everyone looks alike, on a dirt bike in a helmet."

"Anyway, that's why I want to give this to you," she said, shoving the box at me.

I stared at the box, which clunked when it moved. Okay, so not cannoli. Darn!

"It's the Italian teapot you admired in my shop. It's something Dinah gave to me, and I don't want it. She said it was valuable . . . *real* valuable. Told me to keep it on a shelf in the shop for good luck. But *you* like it and have no connection with it so . . . would you take it? Partly as thanks for . . . for everything?"

And partly just so she didn't have to look at such a vivid reminder of Dinah Hooper and all she represented, I thought. "I'd love it," I said sincerely. "I'll look after it well."

"I'd better go," she said, looking off to where Zeke and Gordy were taking a break in the shade. "It's looking better out here. Not so much like an abandoned graveyard."

Which reminded me . . . "Binny, there's one thing I still can't figure out . . . why was Tom digging holes on my property? Did he or did he *not* know that Rusty was still alive?"

"I just don't know," she said on a sigh. "I can't believe he knew Dad was alive, or he'd have told me. Maybe Dinah will spill her guts."

"If Dinty was alive you'd have him to contend with, too."

"I know, but Dad still feels bad about that. Dinty was a lug, but I don't think he knew what his mom was up to. My dad has a feeling Dinah told Dinty that he—Dad—was trying to kill her, and that's why Dinty went after him."

"Hey, it was him or Dinty. I just don't understand why

Dinah stayed around Autumn Vale for so long. It would have made sense for her to tie up loose ends and take off, start fresh somewhere else."

Binny shrugged, then snuck a look at my face, and looked away, shuffling awkwardly. "I gotta get going. I'm going to pick up my dad, and we have a lot to talk about. Uh . . . Gogi Grace said . . . she told me something in confidence, something she says you already know."

I waited.

She eyed me again, but then broke eye contact and looked up at the sky. "I guess . . . that girl who has been hanging around, that Lizzie Proctor . . . she's Tom's daughter, Gogi says. Now I get why Emerald kept coming into the bakery. She always looked like she wanted to talk. Maybe she was trying to get the guts to tell Tom the truth. I only knew her as an old high school girlfriend of Tom's, but I guess they were more."

I believed that Tom already knew the truth, or suspected, and that's why he wanted to make money, to help his daughter, but I didn't say anything. "Have you told your dad yet?"

She shook her head, tears welling up in her eyes. "I want to be sure, first."

"Gogi is sure and Hannah is sure; I think they both have good instincts about it all. By the way, Lizzie took some pictures out here of the castle and promised to take them in to the library to show Hannah. Can you—"

"I'll make sure she does it," said Binny, already in stern-aunt mode.

They were all going to be okay.

TWO DAYS OF HECTIC ACTIVITY FOLLOWED. I BAKED muffins at the bakeshop, fielded a few irate phone calls from Janice Grover (she thought I was behind the tub of boiling-hot water Simon Grover and his bank were now in; I set her straight, then went there to buy some stuff), orchestrated,

along with Gogi Grace, an emotional meeting among Lizzie
Proctor, her grandmother, and mother, and Binny and Rusty
Turner. Among all the bustle, I chauffeured Pish back and
forth to the police station. My dear friend was "helping" federal officers as they tried to figure out, with the assistance of
Isadore Openshaw and a sniveling, frightened Simon Grover,
all the financial monkey business Dinah Hooper had created.
The woman had been busy with several different scams,
among them, ones using the US Postal Service, which, ironically, could wind up costing her as much jail time as the
murder charges would net.

I finally had a day to myself, and was out on the front
step, drinking a cup of coffee, accompanied by my ginger
cat, Becket. Gordy and Zeke struggled manfully along the
arboretum forest, clearing brush from the edge; they were
almost halfway along. Those guys were proving to be worth
every penny I paid them, and the goodwill I was getting in
town from hiring locals was astounding. I was making
friends. Befriending Gogi Grace, capturing the murderer of
Uncle Melvyn and Tom Turner, and restoring Rusty Turner
to his daughter and the community didn't hurt, either.

Shilo was gone somewhere with McGill, who had finished all of the hole filling, even the one poor Tom Turner
died in, and she had offered to ferry Pish into town this time,
where he was yet again consorting with the federal forensic
accountant. This was like a grand holiday for my wise and
wonderful pal; financial scams were a hobby of his, and he
knew a lot about them, enough so that he was writing a book
on the topic, of which this would be a chapter, I was sure.
It said a lot about his reputation that he was actually being
utilized rather than shut out of the process.

I heard before I saw the giant truck lumbering up my
long and winding drive. It finally came into sight, and pulled
up in front of the castle. A burly, sweaty driver jumped
down, grumbled his way over to me, and announced, in a
growl, that he had my stuff.

He had my stuff . . . yay! It was here, out of storage, at long last! I gave a little hop of happiness, overjoyed at the prospect of unwrapping treasures that I hadn't seen in years. Zeke and Gordy helped him offload, which only took an hour or so; I directed and Becket oversaw the whole affair from a place of honor, the round table in the center of the great hall. Everything labeled "Teacups" or "Teapots" was to go into the dining room, where the box with the Italian teapot still sat, unopened, on the huge dining room table. Everything labeled "Kitchen" went into the kitchen. Every other box should be piled in the great hall, I told them, so I could unpack and disseminate the contents.

I then declared I was serving a big meal in the kitchen for Zeke, Gordy, and the sweaty driver, who proved to be more human once he was given a towel and washcloth and offered a place to cool off. They all accepted my invitation. We were having a spurt of indecently hot weather in upstate; it was enough to make anyone a little tetchy, as locals called it.

But I still had made soup and sandwiches, as well as a batch of corn muffins. After a long lunch, the truck driver gave the two fellows a ride back into town—neither had a car, but that hadn't been a big problem while they used Gordy's uncle's tractor, which had now been returned—and I was left alone in my beautiful castle.

My insanely beautiful, despicably impractical, infinitely precious, huge castle.

I wandered through, admiring the furniture. Once Shilo and I had taken all the Holland covers off, we found there was a theme to the furnishings, in the largest part of the castle. Eastlake was the most common style, but Pish told me that it was all part of a Gothic neo-medievalist–style revolution of the late Victoria, era. I'm glad he knew that, because I didn't have a clue. It was all big, garish, and yet strangely magnificent, scaled to fit thirty-foot ceilings and forty-foot rooms.

I made my way into the dining room, where the boxes

labeled "Teacups" and "Teapots" had been piled. I hadn't
opened the box Binny had brought yet, but I pulled it toward
me across the oak table and used my fingernail to cut through
the tape, which held down the lid. I opened the flap and took
out the gorgeous Italian teapot, a Capodimonte piece with a
raised relief pattern of a girl and donkey. It was in beautiful
condition. I took the lid off and examined it carefully, but
there were absolutely no chips.

But there was something inside. A piece of paper. Maybe
Dinah had left a little note for Binny. I plucked it out and
opened it, smoothing it on the tabletop. No, it was a snatch
of poetry.

> *For some are sane and some are mad*
> *And some are good and some are bad*
> *And some are better, some are worse—*
> *But all may be described in verse.*

What the . . . ? I recognized the piece; who was it by? It
was . . . I searched my brain, sure I had heard those same
words before. Aha! T. S. Eliot. From "Old Possum."

Becket leaped up on the table and nosed the box, causing
it to fall on the floor.

"Stop it, Becks!" I hollered, pushing him away. He came
right back and nosed at the teapot, then at the note in my
hand. "Becks, don't . . ." I paused as my hand brushed
against his collar, which I had put back on him. The tag on
it that gave his name and that was all, was plastic, and had
survived the almost-year he had spent in the wild since his
master was killed. But the tag was oddly thick.

Why hadn't I noticed that before?

My attention was pulled back to the note. The quote was
in different handwriting, a nice, cursive script, than some
of the other scribbles on it. And there were underlined words
in the verse. It all seemed gibberish, and there was a string
of exclamation marks, and a faint penciled phrase. I held

the paper up to the light. "What the hell does this mean?" was scribbled in a slanting hand different from the poem.

I wished I knew.

I couldn't shake the sense that there was some significance to it all, something I was missing. I retired to the kitchen, made a pot of tea, and sat in the chair by the empty fireplace, where, for the first time, Becket leaped up onto my lap. I toyed with his collar, and the tag. The plastic disc covering his name fell out, and out of the opening came a thin packet of paper, which folded out like a paper doll, maybe twenty discs long.

Just then Shilo came into the kitchen with Pish, both of them overheated but excited from their day. I couldn't attend to what they were saying, though, because I was still puzzling over the paper disks. On each disc was a Latin word or phrase, beginning with *Quercus macrocarpa*, and on through *Acer pseudoplatanus, Tilia Americana*, and so on. On the back of the last disk was the name "Kilmer."

Well, of course when I shared all of this with my friends, Shilo said, popping the lid on a can of cola, "Val Kilmer? Why would old Mel write down Val Kilmer's name on his cat's tag?

Pish frowned over at her. "Are popular references the only ones you know? Perhaps it refers to Joyce Kilmer . . . you know, 'I think that I shall never see a poem so lovely as a tree?'"

"So she liked trees and poetry, huh?"

"It's not a 'she,'" I said absently. "It's a he . . . I mean, Joyce Kilmer is a 'he.' They're actually distant cousins, I've heard, Joyce and Val. Pish, do these Latin words mean anything to you?"

He leaned over the chair arm. "Hmm. Well, animals and plants are often called by their Latin names. Does that help?"

My eyes widened. I had actually seen some of these same words, on plaques in the arboretum! I shared my discovery with my friends, and said, "I wonder . . . okay, is this crazy?

My mind is making connections. Could this be associated with the woods, and, perhaps a treasure hunt, or something? There are rumors that my uncle left a stash of money somewhere. Maybe that's why Tom was digging holes on the property. Maybe Dinah thought it was true, that there was money here somewhere, and set Tom onto the task?"

"Could be," Pish said.

Shilo hopped up and down. "A treasure, a treasure! Let's go look for it."

"How?" I said. Wait . . . tree names. Slowly, I came to a conclusion and spoke up. "I think that there is something to this, and I think it has to do with the arboretum. If these are tree names, then the woods is the place to look."

Pish plunked down on the chair next to me as Shilo danced around the kitchen. "You know what, my dear, I think you just may have something. And I want to be in on the fun. I have a proposal to make. I would like to rent a room from you for the foreseeable future, and move some of my things here. This fraud investigation has got my juices going, and I'd like to make it the central story of my book-to-be."

"Is it going to be that big a story?" I asked, startled.

"Sadly, my dear, I think so. I'm pretty sure it's going to go national, if the financial papers get ahold of it. I am trying to do *all* I can to help the Autumn Vale Community Bank stay alive, because it is in grave danger of folding. *That* is the more important story here. Those federal investigators don't really care, but I do. I hate to see small, local banks fail. Diversity in the banking industry is unfortunately becoming quite rare."

"Yikes. I care, too. These folks have been through enough tough times."

His tone honeyed and persuasive, he said, "If I stay and rent a room, Merry, it would help you with the utility bills, which are *not* going to be pretty this winter. And I can help, then, with the treasure hunt!"

"Deal," I said, not adding that he had not needed to sweeten the pot, so to speak. Having him around was a treat.

"Deal, deal, deal," Shilo sang, spinning around.

I took a deep breath. An adventure had begun. In fact, I was in the middle of an adventure, but hadn't stopped to realize it. I grinned over at Pish, who smiled back, then we both turned to watch Shilo spinning around the kitchen, out of control with love and joy and happiness, followed by Becket, who lunged and batted at her fluttering scarf.

I couldn't wait to get started.

Recipes

Golden Acres Banana Bran Muffins

Yield: 12 Muffins

1 ½ cups bran flake cereal
1 cup mashed ripe banana (2–3 large)
½ cup milk
1 egg
3 tbsp. vegetable or canola oil
1 cup all-purpose flour
¼ cup sugar
2 tsp. baking powder
½ tsp. baking soda
⅛ tsp. ground nutmeg
¼ tsp. cinnamon
¼ cup chopped pecans (optional)

Preheat oven to 400 F. Grease or paper line muffin cups. If greasing, use cooking spray.

Combine cereal, bananas, milk, egg, and oil in a bowl, mix well and let stand. Stir occasionally to break up cereal. Let stand at least 10–15 minutes or however long it takes for the cereal to break down completely.

Combine flour, sugar, baking powder, baking soda, spices, and nuts (if using) in a separate bowl.

Add flour mixture all at once to cereal mixture, stirring until just moistened.

Divide evenly among prepared muffin cups.

Bake 20–25 minutes until toothpick poked in center comes out clean, or until muffin springs back when top is pushed down.

Bacon Cheddar Muffins

Yield: 12 muffins

½ pound bacon
⅓ cup bacon drippings
1 egg
¾ cup milk
1 ¾ cups all-purpose flour (use half all purpose and half whole wheat, if desired)
¼ cup brown sugar
1 tbsp. baking powder
2 cups cheddar cheese, shredded

Cook bacon in a skillet over medium high heat until crisp. Remove the bacon from the pan, drain on paper towels. Reserve the drippings and measure out ⅓ cup. Once the bacon is cool, crumble it. In a medium mixing bowl, combine the egg, milk, flour, sugar, baking powder, and bacon drippings. Stir until combined. There will still be some lumps. Stir in the bacon and cheese until evenly distributed. Divide the batter among the cups of a lightly greased muffin tin.

Bake at 400 degrees for about 15 minutes, until golden brown. Remove from the pan and cool or eat warm.

Gouda and Harvest Vegetable Chowder

2 tbsp. butter
1 medium onion, diced
2 cups cauliflower finely chopped
2 cups broccoli finely chopped
1 cup grated carrot
3 cups good quality or homemade chicken stock
2 cups milk
¼ cup all-purpose flour
1 ½ cup shredded Gouda; you can substitute a different
    cheese if you like. Cheddar works well!
salt and pepper to taste

Melt butter in large saucepan. Cook and stir onion over medium heat until soft.

Add cauliflower, broccoli, carrot, and chicken stock. Bring to a boil. Reduce heat, cover and simmer for 10 minutes or until vegetables are soft.

Whisk milk into flour until smooth, add to vegetables. Cook and stir over medium heat until mixture boils and thickens. Remove pan from heat, add 1 ½ cups Gouda and stir until melted. Season with salt and pepper.

Optional, to serve, sprinkle with ½ cup cheese and buttered croutons.

Enjoy the Bacon Cheddar muffins with the soup! Mmmm!

> "[McKinlay] continues to deliver well-crafted
> mysteries full of fun and plot twists."
> —*Booklist*

FROM *NEW YORK TIMES* BESTSELLING AUTHOR

Jenn McKinlay

Going, Going, Ganache

A Cupcake Bakery Mystery

After a cupcake-flinging fiasco at a photo shoot for a local magazine, Melanie Cooper and Angie DeLaura agree to make amends by hosting a weeklong corporate boot camp at Fairy Tale Cupcakes. The idea is the brainchild of Ian Hannigan, new owner of *Southwest Style*, a lifestyle magazine that chronicles the lives of Scottsdale's rich and famous. He's assigned his staff to a team-building week of making cupcakes for charity.

It's clear that the staff would rather be doing just about anything other than frosting baked goods. But when the magazine's features director is found murdered outside the bakery, Mel and Angie have a new team-building exercise—find the killer before their business goes AWOL.

INCLUDES SCRUMPTIOUS RECIPES

jennmckinlay.com
facebook.com/jennmckinlay
facebook.com/TheCrimeSceneBooks
penguin.com

M1287T0313